Mrs Meg
Pie Shop.

a fantasy by Nik Gehenna © 2018
Other books by the same author:-

Mirror of Illusion
The Orrery of Power
Choose Your Mask
Myrrorball (with Major Roxbrough)
Dead Broads Don't Squeal

Contact the author at:
jarquix@yahoo.com

One.   **It was the** appearance of the extraterrestrial ship that had caused Sellers to plummet to a painful death. After that, he knew nothing. All was sable, ebon, a period of non-being. Until consciousness suddenly returned! That was the most surprising thing. He had always thought death the end, the grim finale, from which one would never awaken. Examining his condition, he could neither see nor hear. Lacked the senses of taste, smell, hearing. The only sensation open to him was feeling. He was aware of a deep coldness. Despite the frigidity, he did not shiver; it became apparent why he had not have a body. Simple existence was his lot, waiting for something to happen. When nothing did, the only avenue open to him was memory. Sellers thought, the first naturally those regarding the last few moments of his life. He had been on a clifftop, halfway between Bridlington and Flamborough, leaning out into the drop to get exactly the shot he desired with his digital (Single Lens Reflex) SLR. That was when the unidentified flying object had appeared in the sky. One minute it had not been there. The next instant, with an imploding suction sound, it was overhead. Sellers, naturally surprised, looked upward, lost his precious purchase on the edge of the crumbling cliff... He did not choose to recall the instant of his demise. Before he could begin examining other interesting incidents in his life, a voice suddenly issued from inside his brain.

'*Hello. Do not feel alarmed, I am going to help you. I am an engimedic, who intends to put you back into a body*'.

'*A body*', Sellers thought, he could not feel a mouth with which to speak. '*What's wrong with mine? Where am I? Who are you*'?

'*I apologise, our vessel was the inadvertent cause of your body's destruction. Do not worry, I can create a replacement. I am the engimedic aboard the craft*'.

'*Destruction*'? Sellers thought wildly, '*Can't you mend my body? The two were attached. My body - me*'?

'*It was beyond our powers to replicate. Do not worry, the replacement will be superior. It will function admirably for you, with a minor addition*'.

'*What do you mean, addition*'?

'*I will tell you more about that later. Your body will have a duridium skeleton. The original was quite brittle in that respect. The muscles will be nyloplanyon. Other than that, we will cover it with pseudo-flesh, you'll pass among the human species undetectable. You will be stronger, faster, more durable, is that acceptable*'?

'*I'm going to be a robot*'!

'Not at all, you will be a biotron, most of your parts will be of actual flesh, blood, as before you will look from the outside, as you did '.

Sellers thought about that, *'Erm... can you affect some improvements'*?

'Improvements'?

'Yes, you know, aesthetic in nature. Like making me taller, more muscular, handsome, so forth. How well do you know humans? Who are you voice? You never told me'?

'We are your neighbours', the engimedic told him in perfect English. *'From Mizar A, a spectroscopic binary, a visual double star with Mizar B, naked eye binary with Alcor in the constellation you called Ursa Major'*.

'So your planet orbits Mizar A, what do you call your world'?

'We call it world, home, planet, just like you. The improvements you require"?

'Oh yes, I want to be a hundred and ninety-six centimetres, with eighty-five kilos of muscle, an actual warrior's body, if you understand what I mean by that. I want emerald eyes, thick blonde hair, a full blonde beard. I want to be handsome, very handsome. Are you able to do this? Do you understand what I want'?

'You wish to be as an Adonis'?

'You know what one is? How long have you been watching our planet'?

'Quite a long time'.

'You will not invade it, are you'?

'It would prove impossible for us. You see, we are from the principal taxonomic category that ranks above species, below family, that you would refer to as Odonata, infra-order Anisoptera'.

'I assure you I wouldn't', Sellers informed, *'Could you describe yourself to me'*?

'I have large, blue, multifaceted eyes, two pairs of strong transparent wings, sometimes with coloured patches, an elongated body, divided into thorax, abdomen. I have six legs. Weigh not even a gram, am eight hundred of your millimetres long. Bright orange of hue'.

'An insect, kinda like a dragonfly'?

'If you wish to ascribe an appellation to me, I would prefer Mizaroa. For though I resemble the creature you named from your world, I am seven times more intelligent than you Hominina'.

'All right, don't get precious on me, Doc. So, can I see an image in my mind's eye of the guy I'm going to be, can you project it into my brain'?

'I am Mizaroa, it is easily within my capabilities. There, is that the sort of creature you desire to become'?

'Whoa, yes. Only there is one other little improvement I desire', Sellers noted, hesitantly told the engimedic what it was.

'You Hominina spend a great deal of time considering, pursuing what is only a biological function. We shall do it for you. Now as to the other matter I mentioned previously, you will, in return for all we have done for you - also have a Cerquibrum sharing your thoughts, experiences, actions'.

'A what Doc, a Cerqui.....'?

'A Cerquibrum a brain companion or mind-rider if you will. It will help with our studies of your kind. Our observations will be so much closer, the Cerquibrum will also share your emotions, drives, the...'.

'Just a second Doc, you want to put an insect into my brain! You can't do that my brain's my second favourite organ. I'm not having a voyeur in it, no deal'!

'That is a shame', the Mizaroa responded genuine sadness somehow in his tone, 'We will have to look for another subject then. A pity - you showed very interesting characteristics. Oh well, technician, turn off the machines, let this one go'!

'Half a minute', Sellers made his thought sound like a scream if such were possible. 'Let this one go, does that mean - what I think it means'.

'It means you do not wish to assist us, therefore, termination is the only course open to us'.

'Termination, that's another word for death, Doc. You mean to say that if I don't play ball you're going to exterminate me'?

'If by "playing ball", you figuratively mean cooperating in our brief experiment, then you seem to grasp the condition of your reanimation Hominina', the engimedic from Mizar A informed, 'Now...'.

'Hang on Doc, I've not refused. After all, I just need a bit more information, if you understand. I mean to say I've never had so much as a gnat in my head to date'.

'The process is quite simple for us. We only ask that besides your own recorded engrams now living in our computer, we also add the engrams of one of our race. It will be painless, I assure you".

'That's not what I'm worried about, Doc, I mean to say, won't it make me schizo or something, like with two personalities in my head at the same time'?

'Is the horse schizophrenic, when the jockey rides it home during the race when they team up to create a winning unit'?

'Hardly the same thing, Doc, the rider isn't in the horse's head is he'?

'*The analogy is still apposite. The process will be much the same, but the partnership will be an internal one. Your body will have all the refinements you desired, you will live for three times the length you are expecting unless you are unfortunate enough to contract a fatal illness. However, our recovery scheme should pick something like that up before it is too late.*'

'*Recovery scheme*'?

'*The fortnightly reports you'll allow the cerquibrum to return to us, here on the east coast of your homeland*'.

'*You mean to say I have to come back here, let you bugs natter to one another every other week*'?

'*There will be a fortnightly report made, as I have already said. Unless you would prefer that besides the cerquibrum in your engrams, you also allow us to plant a transmitting device that...*'?

'*All right, all right, I agree with the two-week trips. Is that it Doc? Or do you have any more surprises for me*'?

"*I have none. Do you wish to proceed with our mutually beneficial arrangement*'?

'*Yeah, bang my engrams into an Adonis made of super-steel, that nylon material, slap a bug in there too. Let's go on the adventure of all time. One small step for man, one giant buzzing spring forward for the bugs of Ursa Major*'.

Sellers began winking out of conscious thought. There was an indeterminate period of total non-being, blackness, void. He felt some sort of sensation return, pain. Terrible white-hot lancing agony that gripped his entire body. He convulsed, jerked, feeling cold metal beneath his shoulder blades, buttocks, heels. There were pinpricks of light, brilliant yet either far away, or very diminutive, overhead. Daring to open his eyes, heard a basso rumble he did not recognise, then gasped,

"For goodness' sake Doc, if you can hear me? Hit me with the morphine or something, I'm in agony".

No response. The pain continued. Red-hot needles twisting in every organ, sinew, the expanse of flesh. The darkness, was it an operating table, even one made for bugs, why was it so poorly lit? In the same instant, two things occurred simultaneously. One - the pain began to slowly but surely recede. The second was Seller's sudden realisation of scale. Of course, he was not in an operating theatre for bugs! He would never have fitted. He was many, many times larger than an Ursafly (as he currently thought of the insectivore of Ursa Major). So they must have put him in the hanger bay, or whatever they had for one. He rose to a sitting position, promptly banged his head on the craft's hull. Smashing one light to tiny pieces at the same instant. Sellers was roughly the internal height of the craft. He burst into an uncontrollable giggle at the thought of hundreds, no thousands, of tiny dragonfly creatures trying to load him into the vessel initially. Abruptly, his laughter stopped. They had done no such thing, had they? The little devils had cut his brain from his skull - if it had been in one piece, just recovered that. Or maybe they had used laser beams, tractor beams, all the paraphernalia available to Captain Kirk. Yet they had built him to a scale that he had demanded? Was he one of their fleet? Was the super steel of his bones the same stuff as the hull of their ship? Had they used the nyloplanyon for bulkheads or some other heavy-duty bug construction? He quit that line of enquiry, turned his attention to a more immediate problem. How was he going to get out? Sellers called out that he was ready! Not sure exactly what it was he was ready for. Had the mind of an alien fly implanted itself in his brain at that point? Was the vessel landed? It would be ironic if he kicked open the hangar door, eased himself out of the bay, only to plummet to a painful death - again! Thankfully, the Mizaroa had put something in place for this very eventuality. In response to his keening wail, a tiny screen set into the roof of the hangar blinked on. As Sellers noticed it, Arabic lettering floated across its 30mm display. The information contained thereon read,

All is well, Hominina, the procedure was a success we have constructed your body exactly as promised. Once you have read this, the hangar doors will open. You can ease yourself out onto the beach at Flamborough. We have exhausted many of our elements to create you, so it will be one month before we require you to report back to us for your initial communication. Fortnightly thereafter. Alas, we could not construct elaborate clothes, but your modesty is intact. Get back to your internal combustion vehicle without too much trouble. Balurzuura is in place but will be dormant for a while. Now you can go.

The door to the hangar eased down onto the sand as Sellers reflected,

'What sort of name is Balurzuura'? On the other hand, he could hardly expect an Ursafly to be called Dennis or Sheldon? The draft from the beach felt ridiculously cold on his new skin. He realised he was naked. Fortunate then that he always kept a change of clothing in the boot of his car when visiting the east coast. How far from the vehicle he was, how many individuals would he encounter along the way? Neither of which he could be certain. It was an inconvenience. Glancing around the hangar bay, he spotted a huge tarpaulin. The sort used to cover a flight vehicle when inside the parent craft. It would be voluminous by Ursafly standards, as he snatched it up, tried to make a loincloth out of it, it only just encircled his waist once. Skimpily knotted at the front, Sellers twisted it around so that most of the cloth hung over his groin. Even so, an unfortuitous gust of wind would reveal his impressive credentials displayed for anyone's examination. Ironic if he survived death, only to be arrested for flashing, indecent exposure. There was no help for it. He was desperate to leave the space vessel, reach his car. The only item of acquirement was the utilised tarpaulin. He could see between his feet that the day was grey, the breeze frigidity itself. It was going to be a chilly jog to the car. With an ungainly series of shrugs, he extricated himself from what could well have proved to be a steel coffin, wriggled onto the sand. His flesh crawled with lack of warmth but forcing himself to ignore the discomfort, he finally regained his feet. There was only one sensible course of action open to him. Get to the car as quickly as possible. Take no notice of anyone else at all. He ran, noticing at once that the ground did not hurt his bare feet as he had expected it would. The coldness of being naked did not prove a problem either, for he found he could run faster than he ever had in his life. He didn't labour for breath, estimated he was possibly running at something close to fifteen miles an hour! Thank goodness he always took a change of warm clothing to the east coast in case it caught him out in the rain. Even more fortuitous were his keys attached to his wrist by a looping retainer, placed there by his benefactors though painfully tight around his Adonis' wrist. The button released the boot, he snatched up the garments, dived into the hatchback turning the engine and heater on instantly. He had never experienced getting dressed in the cramped confines of a 1399cc hatchback. It was a skill he decided he would never have to learn. The previously very baggy XL garments were then fitting, something he never liked. He felt much more comfortable if his clothes had plenty of room inside them. The Mizaroa had kept his hands and feet the same size, his spare trainers, gloves, still fit perfectly, he began to warm through. Lowering the passenger-side sun shield he looked at himself in the mirror on the back of it. Chiselled features gazed back at him, delightful. Long blonde hair that fell onto his shoulders in ringlets, the thick blonde beard, the emerald-clear eyes. It was the face of a very handsome man, that of a Greek god or classic Viking. He suddenly felt a stab of pain in his midriff, hastily raised the now tight sweatshirt. Whilst looking for the cause of the discomfort admired the six-pack that rippled beneath the skin of his gut. Suddenly laughed, realising what the source of the somesthesia was - hunger! The new engine that was his body would need more fuel in the form of food, he had not eaten since...what time was it? The dashboard informed him it was close to 17:22. He had practically lost a day on the vessel from Ursa Major. Time to do something about it then, gunning the motor, he set off on the B1255 south-west toward Bridlington, Rissoles-R-Us. Decided he was going to have not one Cheese-Riss-muffin, chips, full-fat pop, two of everything. Felt he could have had a very good attempt to eat an impressive quantity of horse. Despite the hour, there were lights on, as a small flurry of snow suddenly filled the air. Sellers turned the switch on the end of his side blinker rod, activated his own. At least the snow had been predicted in what he called the *weatherscope*, named by him due to the number of times it was inaccurate. Its fanciful nature which, he viewed both with equal amounts for scepticism, but on this occasion, the meteorological boys had gotten it *right on the button*. By the time he reached Rissoles-R-Us, a light dusting of snow was beginning to settle rather than melt on contact with the tarmac. He was still struggling to keep warm, running his new engine on an empty tank, so pulling his collar up around his cheeks, he hurried inside. At that time of day, it was quite busy. Waited patiently enough, queuing, came second nature to him, as he was English. Finally, he reached the counter, ordered, Fortunately, his wallet had been locked in the boot when he had gone in search of the elusive photograph. Pity about his camera, on balance, the day could not have been described as a loss. Seated at a table, he waited patiently for the number to be called out (he was 23!) when he spotted something on the television, the one provided for customers, bolted to the ceiling of his booth. It made his blood run cold!

Two. **Sellers had voted** in the referendum to determine whether England should stay in the Common Market, then called the European Union, or leave. Fiercely super-patriotic, he believed in the sovereignty of England, voted to depart. He had also done his best to persuade as many people as possible to agree. So he had been very pleased when the majority had done the same as him. As he gazed at the television in disbelief, however, the report was making no sense.

Charles Yves Jean Ghislaine Michel visits Her Majesty as she abdicates the throne of the new Republic of Angleterre - European Union. The subtitle recorded.

It was a nightmare. How had the change taken place? He suspected who was behind it. The Mizaroa had done more than change his body. They had wreaked havoc with reality, but why? In a flash of inspiration, he opened his wallet to find it full of euros in place of the previously placed Sterling. He pulled out his driving licence disgusted to find it a Permis de Conducere, but at least his name was the same Tod Sellers (nickname Salt; for obvious reasons). How could the Mizaroa have fashioned such a bizarre change to the entire country? Or...? Had they only damaged his brain? He could not trust his senses any more? As luck would have it, the girl came with his order just as that possibility occurred to him. It afforded him the chance to test at least one of his theories.

"I'll miss the old gal, won't you"? He asked her, nodding toward the screen. She glanced over, upward, remarked,

"I voted to come out, but the majority wanted this. Next thing you know, we'll all have to learn Flemish. Anyway, enjoy your lunch if you want anything, just call out".

She awarded him with the most dazzling of smiles, the first in his lifetime. He knew it was because of his new, alien-created appearance. Was the trade-off worth it? His new, superbly attuned body for the sake of his sovereignty. More to the point, why did one have to be balanced off against the other? What sort of alien scheme did the creatures from Mizar A have in store for him? Was it really necessary to change the entire country's fate just because Tod Sellers differed from that which he had been? While he ate quickly, almost feverishly, he closed his eyes, tried to contact the Cerquibrum - Balurzuura. He amused even himself with the tentative nature of his first thoughts,

'Er... hello. Can you hear me? Or do I mean, can you think to me, is "hear" the right word when I'm not speaking aloud? Are you aware of where you are, do you know who I am, I have some questions? Are you dormant, in some sort of informative stage, think something, please?'

A response was there nought. Two Cheese-Riss-muffins, with chips, full-fat pops later, he was still hungry, much to the girl's amusement ordered his third full menu. Probably even the most rotund of customers in the history of Rissoles-R-Us had never seen one patron down three of the gut-busting beauties in a single sitting. In between bites, Sellers attempted once again to solicit some sort of response from his cerquibrum. His mind rider had fallen off the figurative mount. The line was ringing, but the Mizaroa was not picking up the encephalographic receiver. Perhaps the process had been bizarrely botched? After all, how could such tiny brains as the dragonfly-like creatures have, possibly harbour vast intellect? Had they ruined the recording, were the engrams of Balurzuura only partially complete in the transfer into his brain? After all, from the Mizaroa point of view, his - Sellers' brain was the alien one. Such conjecture accompanied caliginous worry, for if the operation had been a failure, what in what other way were the alien scientists remissive? Would bits fail in his new semi-organic structure? Worst still would small indefinite quantities of his anatomy fall off! As he was finishing the then adequate meal, at least in terms of quantity anyway, he noticed a commotion louder by degree than the already ambient sound pressure levels of the eatery. It was coming from the far end of the place, concerning his position. Curiosity brought him to his feet. He wandered toward it. Three youths with fashionable baggy clothes, low crotches, Nazi haircuts, were guilty of being party to the disturbance. It involved them in a heated debate with a middle-aged woman, the girl who had served Sellers. It was easy to deduce that the middle-aged woman was the manageress, summoned hastily to the scene because the youths had created an unnecessary ruction of some type. Sellers approached the waitress, asked,

"What's wrong, is there a problem here"? The girl looked close to tears as she blurted,

"They're saying the food was poor, they want another meal, without paying again".

"I see, did they eat the first meal"? As she was hastily nodding, the tallest of the youths, though much lighter in weight than Sellers with his improved physique, noticed his appearance on the scene - snarled,

"Oy, it's nought to koofing do with you, leave it".

"Was that outburst directed at me, Young man"? the confident Sellers enquired, "Because if it was, I'm only standing a metre from you, or are you labouring beneath the erroneous perception that I have hearing difficulty"?

"What"? the tall youth demanded.

"The polite response when one lacks comprehension - is pardon", Sellers corrected enjoying the exchange. One did not need to be a mental giant to get the better of the youth.

"Oy, frenge-face", one of the other youth's suddenly blurted, "Koof-off, like my mate said, this hasn't' got nought to do with you".

"By the use of a double negative, you obliquely suggest that it has. If it hasn't nothing to do with me. Then it *has* something to do with me".

The focus of the trio's animosity switched from the manageress at that point, transferred to Sellers. Who also heard the older woman whisper to the waitress,

"Go ring nine hundred and ninety-nine".

That he heard it caused the newly improved homo-superior to marvel at the selective nature of his improved auditory canal.

"My mate's just told you to frenge off milfung, so frenge off".

"Does anyone of you speak English without resorting to profanity"? Sellers wished to know, "Because I'm finding it offensive in extremis".

"Look milfung", began the tallest then, "Why don't you get out of here, before something koofing nasty happens to you"?

Something rather obnoxious already has", Sellers replied, amazed at how calm he felt, "You"!

The tallest promptly pulled a knife and one other, his acolyte, it was patently clear, encouraged,

"Stick him, Tyrone, let's see some blood"?

Tyrone, emboldened by the boost to his ego, made to feint a lunge. At that very moment, it was as if he were moving in slow motion from Sellers' perspective. The injection of adrenaline into his super-tuned body, strength, reflexes, had moved into a higher conscious - physical state. A slap of the back of his left hand sent the knife clattering from Tyrone's grip. With his free right fist, he tapped (or thought he had) the boy on the bridge of the nose, to demonstrate how quickly he could move. Tyrone's nose immediately caved into a bloody pulp of mashed cartilage. Blood spattered onto his grubby tea-shirt, splashed all over the floor.

"What the koof"! One other gasped as Tyrone crashed backwards over two tables. He did not get back up.

"May I proffer a piece of advice, gentlemen"? Sellers then asked the other two. Mouths open, they nodded mutely. "Get out of here, before I render pain unto you, the like of which, you have never experienced before. Furthermore, I eat in here regularly; so return here - never".

The duo exited the Rissoles-R-Us with nearly as much prestissimo as Sellers had used in dispensing with Tyrone's offensive. Suddenly the girl was at his elbow,

"Thank you, Sir, but you had better go now before the rozzers arrive. You know how it is nowadays. Instead of seeing you as a hero, they're just as likely to arrest you for assault. When they get here, my description of you will be the worst in history".

Whilst she had been talking, she had pressed a slip of paper into his hand, folded his fingers over it. Tod smiled, thanked her, took the sound advice. Only when he had gotten back into his car did he open the paper expecting a money-off voucher. It was a note instead. He read what was there:- 07709 555321. He was still smiling about that as his Jazz reached the A19 on his way back into Selby.

Three. **By the time** his Honda pulled into the parking space at the side of his studio, the light was failing. The abode resided over a solicitor's office in Hall Gate at the Centre of Doncaster. On the outward journey, he had gone with some reasonably expensive photographic equipment, two sets of clothes. Returned minus the change, the pictorial representation instrumentality, but the trip had been a huge gain in some respects. The new Tod was stronger, swifter, brighter, with a greater life expectancy. Something the very,

very wealthy would have given almost all their financial abundance for. One negative was the fact that he would have to make the trip back to Flamborough regularly, but was that still a given with no space bug in his mind? Where was the Mizaroa? How could Sellers even remember that name, or that the nomen of the creature, in particular, was Balurzuura? Even as he strode beneath the grey sky, his steady tread over the shining streets of the wet town, he found he could remember every item on the Rissoles-R-Us menu, how much they cost to the cent. A sixth sense caused him to gaze above the window of the doorway he was just unlocking. Sure enough, he received the expected shock. The name of the solicitors was different. The studio that had been his; if indeed it was still there, was now over Delano Girard - Procureurs Juridiques. He did not need to speak French to know that it was still a solicitor's office, but did not know who Girard was. Yet the key fit. When he keyed in the alarm's number, it still turned it off. Like someone on a mysterious expedition; which he was. Climbed the stairs to his apartment, tried the second of his keys. This one worked as well. Turned on the light, relieved to see his apartment. Sofa, audio gear, flat-screen plasma. It made him rush from one room to another. Nothing seemed changed. All as before, kitchen, bathroom, office, darkroom, thank goodness. Sellers priority was to let Mrs Meggins from the Pie Shop in. She had been out all day, would proclaim her dissatisfaction most vociferously, once finally allowed entry. Meggins was Seller's black and white cat, a tiny moggy, who weighed only 2.6 kilos. Never seemed to put on any weight - no matter how often he fed her Sheba. He had owned her three years from being a kitten, loved her like no human. She was ill-tempered, only happy when she got her way, but that did not diminish his affection in the slightest. Her name had originally been Miggins, but on her first visit to *We-R-petZ*, ready to see if she was old enough to be neutered, the particularly pretty, shapely receptionist was Irish. When the vet had asked who was next, the girl had announced her with her Gaeilge brogue. Miggins had become Meggins. Sellers had not argued, having found the entire episode amusing, not to mention the receptionist. Thus the one-time Blackadder character had given most of her name to the cat, but with a twist. Sellers turned the two heavy keys to the steel door at his apartment rear, the one that led to the iron steps of the fire escape, whistled the cat. Bounding up the metal run, bleating on every step she rushed in. Looked up at her loving owner, yowled a long, disgruntled protest at his unexpected tardiness.

"Don't you worry baby, I've some lovely biccies for you", he informed in the sort of language one uses to a baby in a pram.

Poured out some Purina into her dish, she began to crunch her way through them, the soft oscillating vibration of her purring issuing from her throat at the same time. It sounded like a small machine chewing up grit, never ceased to make him smile. That was the *family* sorted. The next step in the operation was a good hot soak in the bath. He had no plans after that. Slipping into the bathroom, divesting himself of his former emergency clothes, tossing them in the laundry basket. Quickly ran a bubble bath, eased himself into it. From the sill on the far side, above the tiles, picked up a wonderfully curled, pattered paperback, opening it where his bookmark was carefully positioned the night before. *'Lady Don't Fall Backwards by Darcy Sarto',* was an unintentionally very amusing crime drama. Sellers favourite place to read was in the bath. He topped the water up several times until his new golden tanned skin had turned quite red. Reluctantly put the book down, reached for his favourite teal-coloured bath-sheet. England was back in the Common Market, big deal. He could handle that change to reality. As long as he still had his favourite teal bath-sheet, as long as he had Meggins, everything was alright by him. Slipping on a long flannelette nightshirt, he cleaned the bathroom, not leaving until he had polished to perfection - looking like he had not used it. Sellers strolled into his lounge. Some negatives were still to process, old sepia-tone photographs to work on for a customer. His mood was wrong to be looking at anything like that for a while. Seating himself on one of his recliners, he ran through the events of the last 24 hours in his mind. It was incredible as if written in a Science Fiction novel read by him, he would doubtless have left it unfinished, as too far-fetched to make it possible to suspend his disbelief. The settee made certain he had almost fallen into a troubled doze when the telephone rang. Not waiting for the answering machine to engage, he rose smoothly on his nyloplanyon muscles, picked up the handset. It was his mother, just as he had suspected it would be. She rang most evenings approximately at that time,

"Everything all right"? the photographer inquired, "What's Pop doing"?

"One of his watercolours at the table. I'm just listening to Classic FM. I rang you earlier but that horrible answering machine started so I rang off".

"I went to Flamborough for the day".

That was just about his only contribution to the conversation. His mother liked to talk - mostly about her day. Suddenly she astonished him,

"And have you seen anything of Zander this week"?

Sellers had no idea to whom his mother was referring. In his pre-accident body, he knew none by that name. Also realised he could not currently meet his parents, for if he did, how would he explain his incredible transformation? He told her he hadn't. She continued talking about the mystery man. Telling him strange family details about someone whom Sellers did not know. A vital clue came in her conversation.

"... of course he was always very like me, while you take after your father..."!

Sellers had a brother he had never met! Firstly, the vote going the wrong way, then the influx of French, now the latest bombshell! What had the Mizaroa done besides a few alterations to his physiognomy? More importantly, why? It troubled him that at that moment that he had far more questions than answers. Sellers was a man who liked order, careful planning. It appeared the aliens from Mizar A had thrown that systematised existence out of the proverbial window. Perhaps the alterations were an experiment to see how he would cope? If that was the case, they should have warned him. The more comfortable of two thoughts occurred, the other seemed on the face of it, to have more sinister implications. What if the changes were some an accident one even the Mizaroa could not control? If that proved to be so, how could simply changing Tod Sellers result in so many alterations to the country? He was not even a tiny wheel in the great machine that was his world. Curiously, such constant fretting would have normally given him a headache. On that occasion, he did not even feel a tightening of the eye muscles. His super-body was coping with all his self-induced stress. Still, no sign of the cerquibrum. Was it because of some strange assessment of his cognitive powers? He leaned back in the recliner. Mrs Meggins from the Pie Shop suddenly jumped into his lap. She purred loudly, her tail quivering standing straight up. As an experiment, he stroked her fiercely. A procedure that usually had him reaching for the cetirizine shortly thereafter. On that occasion, there was no smarting of the nostrils, no stinging of the eyes. He was no longer allergic to the fur of the creature he loved. Meggins washed her paws fastidiously, sweeping them over her bony little head. At some point that day, she must have gotten wet. She was black and white, her body black, paws, face, albescent, but amusingly under her little wine glass nose was a black Hitler moustache of sable fur. It gave her a wicked look even when, as now, she was in virtual ecstasy. Sellers forced himself to stay in the chair for an hour before concluding Meggins had enjoyed her love, lifted her into her doughnut-bed, looked for something to amuse. He was wide awake, knew if he tried retiring, he would not sleep. He went to his book pile, picking up Wilbur Smith's - Golden Fox. It amazed him when he had read the entire thing in thirty minutes! So he turned on his Black Rox amplifier to allow the PSVane KT88 High Fidelity Series Vacuum Valve-Tubes to warm up. Selecting Brahms, he placed the LP onto his rega RP6 turntable fitted with a Nagaoka MP110 cartridge, lovingly lowered the needle into the groove. The Monitor Audio RS8's sounded sweet as a nut, as the mellifluous melodies drifted out of the tall mahogany cabinets. Taking some Vampire Toes, squeezing it into his diffuser, he connected it to his e-cig, with a glass of Q.C. Rich Ruby sherry in the glass at his left hand settled down for the first side. Followed by side B. By the end of the performance, relaxation, achieved enough to get ready for bed. Mrs Meggins already curled up on the far corner of the double duvet. After thoroughly cleaning his pearly white teeth, he slipped beneath it himself, allowed his breathing to slow, his relaxation technique to commence. Imagined a pink tube 15cms long, from its pink tranquillity in the form of a mist, he breathed it in. Then he allowed the fuchsia tinged vapour to relax his feet. The effect was running up his calves, into his thighs. The process continued until his chest, every muscle in his arms was as at rest as they possibly could be. The torpor crept into his neck, his jaw, the muscles of his face. Finally, his ears became so relaxed by the salmon mist, he could no longer hear. He had never needed to relax the muscles of his scalp, sleep had always been achieved by that time. That night was different. He reached the top of his head, still had not achieved slumber. One thing was certain - he had no intention of just laying there, unable to drop off. Sellers arose, threw the nightshirt over his head, quickly changed into running shorts, singlet. He tugged on his best silver-grey Silver-Shadows, attaching the front door key to a special thin belt that ran around his waist, tripped down the steps, ran out of the front office door of the solicitors. It was when he discovered he could run. Truly run. Not like the poor trotting he had conducted before his enhancements, but like a gazelle. Settling into a comfortable pace he felt he could maintain for quite a few miles. Began to let his feet take him through the wet streets that shone with the ambient amber glow of the lights. He found himself on the A638 allowed the endorphins to begin to soothe his brain as the run relaxed him. At Bawtry, he turned sharply left, ran off to Austerfield, Mission. The next village he was aware of examining he was in Misterton. Had run twenty miles, the return would double. The surprising thing was the length of time it had taken him. Forty minutes! An average speed of thirty miles per hour! Humanly impossible. *Was* he human any more? Retracing the route, he pushed himself! Was back in the heart of Doncaster in thirty-seven minutes! He touched the bottom of his trainers, which were decidedly warm with friction. Without even breaking a sweat. Not especially cold, but he usually arrived home lathered after a run had never been for a forty-mile round trip that had only taken him seventy-seven minutes! A cool bath anyway, a further ten minutes cleaning, polishing. Mrs Meggins looked up, yowled in frustration at him.

"All right, I'll turn off the light, stumble around for a bit, Megwinda", came the promise, discovered as he hit the switch with his eyes open he could see in the dark. Controlling his breathing, concentrated on listening, could hear the conversations of passers-by down on the street. It was a good job the abilities were selective by his will or they would have driven him to distraction. It would have been like being in a noisy discotheque - indefinitely! Could his acute hearing turn off? Yes. Sublime. To enjoy the peace - of total silence. Going through his relaxation technique once more, he was asleep before he reached his torso.

Four. Swamp lay beneath him as he hovered over the swirling blue mud. He was as light as the soupy atmosphere he could swoop, glide, hover. His wings were so adaptable, so elongated, so powerful. The images that flooded into his brain were myriad, confusing. Departmentalised into hundreds of tiny tiles that reminded him of televisions stacked upon one another, each showing a slightly different angle of the same view. It looked like some bizarre stained-glass window that did not quite make sense. That was what it was like to see with multi-faceted eyes. He knew that his optic organs had no less than twenty-four thousand ommatidia each. Sellers was a predator, able to stay on the wing for few days, weeks. He was a fast, agile, flier, sometimes migrating across oceans, often found near water. He possessed a uniquely complex mode of reproduction involving indirect insemination, delayed fertilization, and sperm competition. During mating, he would grasp his female at the back of the head or on the prothorax, and she curled her abdomen under her body to pick up sperm from his secondary genitalia at the front of his abdomen, forming the *heart* or *wheel* posture. Loss of his natural wetland was threatening his existence around the world that orbited Mizar A. He desperately feared being caught for food by the huge and dreadful Stolysørdordere. Yet those terrible hunters used images of their bodies as symbols of courage, strength, and happiness and their bright colours and agile flight admired in the poetry of the same awful race. Ironically, the Mizaroa were three-hundred and twenty-five million years old in racial age, whereas the infant Stolysørdordere had walked upon the surface of the fourth planet that orbited Mizar A for a paltry ten thousand. Sellers suddenly realised two pieces of information. One was that he was hungry, the other that he was carnivorous. This grim discernmentation told him he ate a wide variety of insectivorous creatures in the world. Ranging from beings that closely resembled small midges, mosquitoes to some butterflies, moths, damselflies, even smaller Mizaroan! He selected a large prey-creature subdued it by biting on the head and carrying it by the legs to a perch. There, he stripped, discarded the wings ingesting the head first. It was disgusting. He savoured the warm ichor that flooded into his mouth-parts. He awoke bathed in sweat and slightly repulsed by the incubus. It was easily the most vivid delusive-mare he had ever experienced. The sounds. Smells and vibrant colours had been like those existing within a giant virtual reality programme, or maybe even more. Like living the situation for real. Throwing back the duvet, Sellers went to the bathroom, ending his ablutions with a strip wash. Then he threw on a pair of bohos over his trollies and a cheesecloth blouse over his now impressive chest. On his feet, a pair of well worn, comfortable Gandhi sandals. Ate an apple, two plums, three slices of wholegrain toast covered in butter and honey, washing it all down with a mug of hot strong tea.

"Hello" a voice seemed to issue from the apartment. Sellers whorled around. Apart from Mrs Meggins, who was still eating her morning biscuits, he was alone, demanded, "Where are you, I can't see anyone"? He would have recognized the metallic tones of the intercom connected to the street below, the voice had not come from there.

"It is I, Balurzuura".

Balurzuura, the Mizaroa! The insectivorous alien had finally made contact. Thoughts were as though a voice was sounding in his ears. Sellers had expected such not an actual voice, one that seemed to speak accent-less English.

"How is it I hear a voice, one with a cultured English pronunciation"?

"I thought such a touch would please you when we are alone? The creature eating cannot speak nor understand us - can it"?

"Meggins, she understands me, but you're right, she's mute. What about when we're in the company of others? I don't want to appear schizophrenic"?

'I will send mental communication as I am doing now', came the thought, 'Is such a system acceptable to you'?

"Until I decide otherwise, I guess I can live with it", Sellers returned aloud. "Why has it taken you so long to break your silence"?

"They anaesthetised me for the transfer", Balurzuura informed, "I guess the anodyne was more soporific than expected by the surgeon. I am pleased with the effect. Are you happy to have me as your Cerquibrum"?

"Not really, but it was preferable to death".

"Ah, but you were only dead in one layer of the multiverse", Balurzuura noted.

"Multiverse"? Sellers seated himself on the sofa, demanded, "What is the multiverse"?

"We live in the multiverse, lay-lines of cosmos, each existing on a separate plane".

"Do you mean the universe"?

"There is not a single version but many, the multiverse. Multivariate cosmos, all existing like lanes of a highway. Once one decides on a layer, it often involves leaving the lane at a junction, following a route to the next highway. In your lane, you fell, were killed, so we took your quiddity from an adjacent lay-line, used it to revive you". Realisation dawned on Sellers,

"So that's why this world has a certain difference from what I was used to! The French solicitors in place of the English, the vote to stay in the Common Market. This is not my Universe"!

"It was the closest one we could re-animate you into, with the minimum cosmic flux. In essence, it is not the lay-line that is erroneous, but your memories. You possess the memories of layer опсгош 55572893, but you now exist in layer опсгош 65572893. It was the best we could do. We easily suited you to adapt to the minimum of changes".

"Minimum of changes"! Sellers smiled ironically, "I seem to have acquired a brother, you call that a minimum change"?

"I do", the voice told him, "For example, in опсгош 68572893 you have two brothers, four sisters, whilst in епсгош 78572893 you are female...".

"Aycee"! Sellers cut off the alien thought, "I think you've made your point. With my improved mind, I understand the concept of the multiverse. Balurzuura, I'd appreciate you going offline so to speak, so I can do some work"?

"I do not go offline, but can remain silent if that is your desire"?

"It is".

To Seller's surprise, he felt his head clear slightly. Alien engrams subsided to a point where he could not detect them at all. It was almost as though his apartment was quieter. As though the silence was deeper, more nigrescent than it had ever been before. Subconsciously, as if to fill a void that did not exist, he turned on the radio it was just giving the local news... the disappearance of the local Gulf hero Major Alston mysteriously missing for three days. South Yorkshire Police are conducting enquiries, expect to have some success within the next few days. The news item came to a halt to be replaced by a rather annoying advertisement... Have you had your Scrunchies today? I don't feel the day has started quite right if I don't begin it with a nice bowl of Scrunchies. Covered in cold milk, the wheat just tastes so good. I feel fitter, keener, more able to meet the rigours of the day. Why is it that Scrunchies are so good? It's because here at Cabisco we make your Scrunchie sized cereal with so much wheat, one whole grain to every single Scrunch. If you can't taste the goodness, feel the benefit of the vitamins the minerals, we'll give you your money back. Yes, that's right, with Scrunchies you get a money-back guarantee. How many other breakfast cereals will offer you that? The answer is none. Here at Cabisco, we're so confident you'll love the scrummy taste of new Scrunchies that we'll give you your money back if they disappoint you with their yummy flavour, their energising properties. That's new Scrunchies, from Cabisco... Sellers promptly hit the off button perhaps silence was not so bad after all! He had some work to do on negatives, a painstaking restoration that few other photographers entertained any more. He could not afford to turn work down, no matter how labour intensive. Not that he was doing badly, but he would have been much happier if more work was available. All that came his way since the explosion of digital, were the specialised jobs - a rare portfolio. Requested by some young woman hoping to make her mark in the areas of glamour or high fashion. He could throw up a backdrop, a few umbrellas in seconds, illuminated by the slave-driven flash. The lounge became a temporary studio that somehow seemed to relax the girls more than if the place was purpose built. Come to think of it, it had been quite a while since he had shot a series of glossies for a girl's portfolio, which was a shame because, for the work output, they were the most lucrative. Restoration, reproduction of old pictures paid the bills, but they were more painstaking to work on, paid less. As was usually the case when he went into the darkroom to work on something intricate, no sooner had he settled to his task than the buzzer went. Annoyed he threw the switch, requested tersely,

"Yes"?

"Sellers Photographica"? A female voice enquired.

"That's right, mister Sellers speaking, how can I help you, do you wish to come up"?

"Please, I wanna ask you if you're interested in doing some work for me"?

"I've released the door. I'm above the solicitors, just go up the stairs, I'll meet you at the top, please"? he requested, covering his current project, turning off his safe-light. Opening the door, blinking in the momentary brightness of day, he went to the front exit of the apartment to wait for her. They arrived at the same instant. Sellers took a deep breath, for as the young woman reached him, it startled him to see she was one of the most attractive girls he had ever set eyes on. Having seen photographic models for all his working life, that was a great compliment, but the young woman before him easily deserved the accolade. She stood a modest 160 centimetres tall. Sellers judged her weight to be around 54 kilogrammes. He took a quiet glance at her vital statistics, estimated them to be 88-66-86. Her long chestnut hair cascaded over her slim shoulders, teased out with hairspray. She had brown eyes beneath impressively arched eyebrows. Her nose was straight, narrow, her lips fine rather than full, accentuated by scarlet lipstick. Around her neck was costume jewellery in faux jade, gold, both fake, from her ears, hung matching pendant earrings in the same design. Only with admirable presence of mind did he stop ogling the beauty to concentrate on what she was saying.

"... modelling, so I need a portfolio of about ten shots, some in fashion-wear, some glamour, are you bookable"?

"Miss..."?

"Elv, Nicole Elv. Nicole's fine".

She offered him a slim hand, a radiant smile. He took it; it was fine, graceful as the rest of her but quite cool.

"Please come inside? Do you have pressing engagements in the next couple of hours, Nicole"? He savoured her name on his tongue, thinking it a good fit.

"No, I was hoping you might ask that I have some outfits in this holdall, for the glamour I thought just black stockings"?

Sellers felt himself swallow, realised he was nervous at the prospect of seeing Nicole Elv au naturel. Ridiculous, as a photographer, he had seen many young lady's goodies, always concentrated on such matters as lighting, poses, shadows, rather than entertaining any notions of liaisons. If one did not remain professional in his line of work, word soon went out. That was the end of one's career.

"We'll see", he replied, "For wardrobe, makeup, poses, Nicole, that's where my expertise will be of paramount importance. Maybe you have nothing suitable in your bag, don't worry, I have some outfits, all freshly laundered that I keep for this sort of work. Just take a seat on the sofa? I'll set up the lights, backdrop, we can see what you've brought. Before I start, would you like something to drink"?

"Coffee please, black two sugars".

She followed him into the kitchen, all swishing fabric, expensive fragrance,

"That's Gaulie Anura's *Seduction* isn't it"? He asked her, switching on the peculator.

She smiled genuinely pleased, "You know your fragrances, mister Sellers. Yes, I work in the Anura concession at Maison de De La Fontaine, in Baxtergate.

"You must call me Tod if I am to call you Nicole", he returned as he put sugar into a white porcelain mug. At the same instant, he was thinking, *'Maison de De La Fontaine, Jeeziss, what has happened to Doncaster'!*

"Of course I wouldn't be able to afford anything by Anura if I didn't get free testers from time to time. Have you seen the prices"?

He had, only too well when a former girlfriend had asked for some at Xmas. That had been the end of Mandy. She was just too high maintenance.

"If your model's career takes off, maybe you can buy some for yourself", he smiled, handing her the mug. "Give me a few moments to set up the backdrop, lights, we'll have a look in your bag of tricks".

He was halfway through the job when Balurzuura suddenly observed, *'Have you detected the female's pheromones Sellers? She is receptive to mating'?*

'I thought you'd agreed to doze or remain silent'? Sellers protested while fixing an umbrella.

'Will you mate with her once you have taken the images? It will be useful for my research'? Balurzuura requested in what seemed a reasonable thought pattern.

'Human beings don't mate so readily as female Mizaroa it would seem', Sellers countered, *'There is a complicated, often lengthy courtship ritual involved before coitus ever takes place. Now, will you please go back to sleep or shut up'?*

'Please begin this ritual for my studies then'? Balurzuura asked.

'Balurzuura, the young woman might already have a partner. It's highly likely that one so attractive as she, does. In addition, she might not find me to her liking, she might go for dark-haired men as she is brunette, so I'm afraid that...'.

'Wait one moment while I check, please', the Mizaroa cut him off.

'Check? Check, what the devil is he thinking'? Sellers wondered, he had almost set up the gear by then.

'The female is currently unattached, finds you very attractive, she used the term "yummy" in her thoughts, I think she would let you inseminate her'.

'How could you possibly know'?

'I read her mind. It's less complicated than yours. It was quite easy, she remains unaware that I could perceive her Cerveaun Valuriass'.

'You read her what? What the hell is Cerveaun Valuriass'?

'Thought emanations, brain broadcasts, mental waves, whatever you like to call them. The female is broadcasting vigorously, you could easily...'.

'Stop Balurzuura! What you did was unforgivable, you mustn't do it again, it's an immoral violation of a person's privacy, do you understand'?

'So you will not take advantage of her receptivity'?

Sellers sighed, *'Receptivity, as you refer to it and permission, are two very different things. I'm making a professional union with this girl. One that requires intimate trust, so you must fall asleep or stop thinking for a while so that I can do my job'.*

"All ready", he told the brunette beauty, "What do you have to show me"?

She rose lithely to her feet. Even her movements were graceful. Unzipping the bag, she showed him her outfits, it impressed him. They were of tasteful, high-quality design, obviously bought with staff-discount from her place of employment.

"I like the crimson pants, the black leather top, the white blouse with crimson stripes, the royal blue beret. I think we should try some combinations of them, then you can gradually disrobe if you feel comfortable doing so"?

"I'm sure I'll be fine", Nicole returned chirpily, "I want to do some topless pictures, even some nude if you're alright with that"?

"I'm a professional Nicole, we can disrobe as far as you wish. It will not affect my experienced approach to the job in any way", Sellers soothed. His heart missed a beat at the prospect of producing something tasteful with the girl nude. They began. His eye glued to the SLR (single-lens-reflex) eyepiece loaded with 35 mm transparency film. Using Fuji as he preferred the colour bias to than over its rivals. Commenced with the 100 mm lens, swapped to a 135 mm when he wanted something more suited to a closer portrait. It was a little slower, so he adjusted the flashguns accordingly. Sellers used Zuiko lenses fitted to two Olympus OM-1 purely manual cameras, giving him all the creative control. He also used Hoya UV (ultra-violet) filters, plus hoods. The entire procedure required maximum concentration to get optimum results, but he kept a dialogue of encouraging comments. Remarks, designed to keep the girl at her ease. Some of his *patter* humorous, to make the session not too serious, keep the girl at her ease,

"Lick your lips"? he requested at one point. When she did, he responded, "Now lick mine"!

She laughed and immediately told him, "I would if you wanted me to"!

She did an evocative pose soon after, he cried out, "My god, the camera's on fire"!

With a disarming drop of the blouse, she displayed a perfect upper body. By the way she twisted, turned, pouted, posed, she was entirely comfortable with her nudity. Confident with her well-proportioned form, lovely overall. He thought he had himself under control until she shrugged off the g string to stand naked before him.

"Do a half turn, Nicole. We're not doing pornography, just acceptable glamour"? he asked her shakily clearing his throat of the frog that had appeared in it. After three rolls of 36 exposure film, she tired, it bathed him in perspiration.

"All right, we're done, get dressed, we're not operating at optimum any more. You can use the bathroom to get into your clothes".

"You've been the perfect gentleman, Tod", she smiled. "I felt at ease with you, thank you".

She strode into the bathroom, comfortable with the fact that she was not wearing a stitch. Sellers packed his equipment away. Shaking with a combination of fatigue, stimulation, who should then reappear in his thoughts but Balurzuura?

"When she went into your ablution room, harboured a faint regret that you did not, here I quote her exactly, 'make his move and try it on'. You seem very attracted to her in your turn. Why not act upon your emotions, Earthopian'?

'Earthopian, where in the world did you get that appellation'? Sellers attempted to deflect the Mizaroa.

Not that easy, *'It is as good as any other, for a strain of mammals who call their planet after the soil. Why did you not engage in coitus with the female, she is fertile, I have ...'.*

Once again Sellers cut him off, *'You shouldn't be checking for such things, Balurzuura, it's impolite. You've no idea how a woman's mind works. Just because she'd like me to attempt a seduction, it doesn't mean that she'd respond positively. Women don't always do what they'd like to do. I'm prepared to discuss this with you later once we are alone together. Right now I need to talk business with the girl, so belt up, stay quiet, please'?*

The door opened, Nicole Elv strode into the room, "How much is this going to cost me, please, Tod"?

"That depends how many shots you intend to include in your folder, the quality you'd like, the quality of the inlay on the front of it. Let me show you some mock-ups before we discuss your budget".

In the end, she selected faux brown leather with gold leaf inlay, simply stating her name. Inside, in plastic sheaths for protection, she would have six 25.4 x 30.48 cm and four 20.32 x

25.4 cm shots with the best of each pose clothed or otherwise. Sellers would select those based on his experience, training at University, he was a member of the Royal Photographic Society, had a degree with honours in the subject. The cost to her would be 287.55 EUR. Delighted with the price, thinking it most reasonable, she agreed.

"All right, I'll probably develop the films this afternoon. Be in the darkroom tomorrow sometime, I'll send an order for the folder from London Graphic Centre by email, they charge me **74.45** EUR for that but engrave it free as I am a regular customer, but I've incorporated it into your price, so don't worry it's agreed, there'll be no extra charges. The folder will be here in a couple of days, delivered by UPS. Can you give me a 15% deposit, please"?

"Yes, cash", she counted out 50 euros, told him, "Don't give me any change just take it off my bill please, Tod".

"Thank you. Here's your receipt, when I've finished the portfolio, do you want me to fetch it to the store, or do you intend to call in for it"?

"What about my giving you my mobile number, then you can ring me when it's ready"?

"Fine".

"07709 555230, are you going to write it down"?

"I'll remember it. That's it for now".

"It's been fun, thanks for being so punctilious, professional. Call me"?

"Of course, the moment the folder's ready".

Her expression was one of hope, candid optimism. She added, whilst he opened the door for her, "Maybe sooner, Tod, call me whenever you want".

He smiled sheepishly, closed the door, "Whew, what a babe"! Stomach grumbling, time for lunch, he was famished.

Five. *'An interesting female',* Balurzuura suddenly commented in his mind. He was busy fixing himself two doorsteps sandwiches, one cheese, one corned beef. A visit to the supermarket would be necessary soon at the rate he was going through groceries. For the second time that day, he heard someone at his front door rather than the solicitors. To his astonishment, it opened. Someone else had a key! He never gave his key to anyone! Who was casually letting himself into his apartment? At the same instant, the two men asked,

"Who are you"? The other added, "And what are you doing in my brother's apartment"?

So this was Zander Sellers. In double-quick time, Sellers looked him up and down. Average height, average looks, brown hair medium build, very ordinary-looking indeed.

"I'm renting this apartment from mister Sellers". Quick-thinking was becoming something he was getting quite used to, "He never mentioned to me that anyone else had a key".

"He never mentioned to me he was going to rent this place out, where's he gone"?

"I've no idea", Sellers did not want to send the man on a wild goose chase, "Told me he would be in Europe for a while, why I could rent the place fully furnished".

"Curious", Zander mused, "He lets no one touch his High Fidelity Kit".

Sellers smiled, "That's right, he asked me not to touch it either. As I'm not into music, it doesn't matter to me".

"I would have thought you'd enjoy a bit of noise while you work out"?

Sellers suppressed a smile, "I put earplugs in, it's surprising what your mind gets up to if you just give it the chance to think".

'Indeed', the Mizaroa mused with insectivorous irony.

"Now if you don't mind, unless there's something you wish to collect I'd like to get on with my day. I'll trouble you for the spare key, I want some privacy you know. I might not have been alone".

"There's nothing it was just a social visit. Here, take it. I wouldn't want to barge in if you were together with some of your *gym buddies*". He thought the new Sellers a queer! That amused him. There was no need to correct Zander. It had been quite obvious to Nicole that he was a regular, healthy guy. Zander dropped the key into Sellers' palm, being careful not to touch him,

'He does not want to risk contamination. Is homosexuality contagious in this world'? Balurzuura desired to know.

Once the door had closed behind the never-known brother, Sellers replied aloud,

"I suggest you cease probing the thoughts of others, you'll only end up with more questions than answers. That is ceasing unless I ask you to find something out for me. Maybe I can get on with the rest of my work for today with no more surprising revelations".

'Ah yes, well there might just be the one thing you need to know', Balurzuura sounded almost apologetic. It worried Sellers more than almost anything else previously that day,

"It had better not be an additional condition, Balurzuura, because we already have our agreed deal. Don't try to mess about with the contract".

"It is nothing conditional. Not conditional, contractually anyway'.

"You'd better just come out with it then. Or should that be in with it"? He laughed at his sarcastic observation.

'On the planet you regard as Mizar, the Mizaroa are not the only sentient species. There are different nationalities of Mizaroa, other creatures with the abilities the equal of ours'

"And you're telling me this because..."?

'Because we have a mortal enemy Sellers, a sworn foe who seeks to undermine anything the Mizaroa seek to achieve or accomplish. What would you like me to refer to this foe as, the real name would not be within your powers to pronounce, even in thought'?

"Call this enemy of yours the Zaromi. Why're you suddenly revealing this to me, I'm not in some sort of danger, am I"?

'It is doubtful, but not impossible'.

"How"?

'The Zaromi can also create cerquibrum. My captain has informed me that they already have some on your world, one or two even in this area'. "Tell me about this enemy? Give a mental picture of what they look like so I can envisage an Earth equivalent. Are they from the same mould as yourselves? Do they fly? Are they small? Do they have multi-faceted eyes? More legs than humans"?

'The closest creature compared to those on Earth would be the Acrididae'.

"I don't know the term"?

'They are are typically ground-dwelling creatures with powerful hind legs which enable them to escape from threats by leaping vigorously. They are hemimetabolous in that they do not undergo complete metamorphosis rather they hatch from an egg into a nymph or what you would describe as a "hopper" which undergoes five moults, becoming more similar to the adult at each developmental stage. At high population densities, under certain environmental conditions, some species can change colour. Our foe has the typical insect body plan you describe of a head, thorax, abdomen. They hold vertically the head at an angle to the body, with the mouth at the bottom. It bears a large pair of compound eyes that give all-around vision, three simple eyes which can detect light, dark, a pair of thread-like antennae that are sensitive to touch, smell. Downward-directed mouthparts modified for chewing, two sensory palps in front of the jaws. The thorax and abdomen segmented with a rigid cuticle made up of overlapping plates composed of a material you would think of as chitin. The three fused thoracic segments bear three pairs of legs, two pairs of wings. Their forewings, you would think of as tegmina, narrow, leathery. While the hind wings are large, membranous, the veins providing strength. Legs are

26

terminated by claws for gripping. Each hind leg, particularly powerful; the posterior edge of the tibia bears a double row of spines, a pair of articulated spurs near its lower end. The interior of the thorax houses the muscles that control the wings and legs. If we meet in flight, we emerge victorious, for we are the better fliers. On the ground, their extra size, powerful weaponry mean we are vanquished. Does that provide you with a mental image of them'?

"Sure, thank you for the lecture! On Earth, they'd be Grasshoppers. What I want to know is how this affects me? You're telling me because it might affect me, aren't you"?

'I am merely warning you that there is at least one Zaromi cerquibrum out there. Form a new liaison with caution'.

"Can't you tell if I meet one, with that *tapping-in thingy* that you do"?

'Yes, only after I have "tapped-in" as you phrase it. Be careful that is all, the female was uncompromised if that is about which you worry'.

"It wasn't. You don't have permission to read *my* private thoughts. Only to receive the ones I direct at you specifically, is that understood"?

'Indubitably'.

"I'm not very pleased about the fact that I wasn't told about this until it's too late to decide - regarding it. There isn't anything else you want to confess to me, is there"?

'Nothing. It would not have adversely affected your decision to avoid death, would it'?

"Don't get smart with me, Balurzuura".

'I shall try not to Tod, but compared to you I "am" very smart'.

"It's an expression, not a comparison".

'You seem to have a lot of them. Perhaps I will understand them better with passaging time'.

Sellers had eaten his sandwiches, followed with a thick slice of fruit cake, a chocolate biscuit, drank a tin of energy before deciding to go down to the supermarket for more foodstuffs. Mrs Meggins from the Pie Shop came in. Accepted a saucer of milk, he had left the fire escape door slightly cracked so she could enter the place while he was in. She got in her doughnut bed, washed fastidiously. Purring furiously, Sellers shut, then locked the door, knowing she would be in for the afternoon. He exited by the front, past the solicitors, out onto a brightly shining day. The sun lifted his spirits as he dragged in a lungful of less than totally clean air. A figure suddenly seemed to approach him at inhuman speed. His own highly tuned senses detected the motion. He whirled toward the other. It was Major Alston! The image was suddenly available to his super-tuned mind. The Major had gone missing. Sought by South Yorkshire Constabulary. Sellers went to say hello, at the same instant that Balurzuura screamed into his mind,

'Throw yourself down...'.

The Mizaroa's warning was too late, for Alston promptly drew a service revolver, fired. The first bullet tore into Sellers' leg, a second missed. It was the third that hit him in the head, the third fateful projectile which shattered his brain - killed him stone dead!

Six. *'Sellers, are you responsive yet'?*

'Hello, engimedic. Here we are again. Who am I this time? How on Earth did you rescue my body'?

'One of our other "experiments" brought you to us in an automobile. Inefficient devices but none the less effective'

'I suppose you sent him some sort of mind signal? You could have done that before the Major shot me. Why did he shoot me, anyway? I've never met the fella'?

'He is the host of one of our enemies'.

'A Zaromi cerquibrum? You've retrieved my thoughts once more. Does this mean when you reanimate me, I'll be free of Balurzuura? Will I find myself on another branch of the multiverse highway? Experience yet more changes to my world'?

'You have learned a lot from Balurzuura. We shall keep the two of you together. Clothes are on the beach, left there by our other host, but you will have to make your way back to your hometown'.

'I'll still have my new body'?

'Replicated inexactitude. You may have some difficulty with the local constabulary when you surface once more. I feel certain you will think of something suitable to say to them'

'Money'?

'In the clothes, along with your keys. Once you get used to this new arrangement with us, you might elevate yourself to Agent'.

'I'm not sure I'll ever get used to these bizarre changes. Or that I'm even me any more. Aycee, I'm ready to wake up starkers in your hanger yet again'.

No sooner had he thought about his last instruction to the Mizaroa, than he was once more cast into a pit. A fuliginous black chasm. He did not wait, for it was a period of non-being, simply devoid of everything, including time. The return of consciousness heralded with it - actuality. He shivered. It was a brisk afternoon. The hangar lay on the cove beneath Flamborough lighthouse. Sellers crawled out of it, hurried into some clothes. Thankfully, they were in keeping with his usual fit, style, comfort. Checked the money in his pocket. Low and behold, it was sterling! With some luck, this layer of the multiverse was closer to his own than the last one he had been in. Hopefully, he would find the money useful. The keys looked unchanged. Thank goodness for the agent, whoever he was. He had given him a great start, even if it stranded him on the east coast. Ascending the rough pathway onto the road above, he trotted toward Bridlington. In his super-efficient form, he could get there in less time than waiting for the very infrequent bus service. Rissoles-R-Us provided his best chance of getting home. Borrow more money for a train ticket, from 07709 555345. Did he know her name? What he knew was that she liked him, might well risk the loan. Confidently, he strode into the place. His luck was in, 07709 555345 saw him at once, smiled. She hastily delivered the tray she was carrying to approach him,

"Hello again, I thought you had either decided not to ring me or lost the number, I don't even know your name"?

"It's Tod, and you're"?

"Louise, pleased you came back Tod, what can I get you"?

She embraced him with a light kiss on the cheek.

"I need a big favour? I was hoping you might help me"?

"What sort of favour"? It was sensible of her to be naturally cautious. He understood that.

"I've rowed with a mate whom I came with. He's driven off in a huff, left me stranded with only the cash I've in my pocket. It's not enough to get me home on the train. You don't know me from Adam, so if you say no, I'll understand. I'll get the money back to you soonest, what do you say"?

"The ticket will be"?

"Around £15 I think, I've only £7 on me, some coppers, I'm hungry too"!

She leaned in close, promised, " I'll fetch you something to eat. On the house - for getting rid of those louts. I'll loan you a tenner, all right"?

So he had thrown the youths out in this reality too, useful to know. Thanking her, she went to get him a Cheese-Riss-muffin, chips, full-fat pop. He took a seat watched the silent TV that had the text running beneath it. Thankfully, at lunchtime the *muzak* was low, so he did not feel as oppressed as usual when in such places. Once more England had pulled out of the Common Market with what the polimedians (politicians that are just a joke) had described as a hard-exit. In the current layer of reality, Scotland had remained. Declared themselves no longer part of the United Kingdom. It had led to Wales declaring independence. The constituent countries of the Kingdom had all become separate. Sellers found the changes fascinating, but he had always been proudly English, preferred where he then was, as to the reality that had let the Belgians run his country. Louise returned with his food, a ten-pound note,

"Here handsome, do you think you'll ring me this time"?

"I will 07709 555345", he gave her a winning smile, "I'll have to get this money back to you once I'm reunited with my car.

"So you might be Bridlington way on, where I live perhaps"?

"I'm going to make a point of it. Expect me to call to thank you for helping me out".

Bridlington was one hundred and four kilometres from Doncaster, a car journey of one hour forty-five minutes. It would make a pleasant trip for him. The girl was kind, not bad on the eye, so he would have a night out to repay her.

Whilst on the train, he connected with Balurzuura,

'What do you know about this reality, Balu? Is my business still going to be there when we get home? My cat, my towel, I love that teal coloured towel'?

'I do not know Sellers, only what you saw on the monitor in the eatery, that England is once more sovereign in its own right. I could try tapping-in to some of the other passengers on this train? See what else I could glean'?

'Do that for me, please. Although I don't suppose any of them'll know if Alder and Goofy are still there, or if my studio is above it'?

Sellers smiled at the remembrance of his meeting with the solicitors when he had bought the premises above them. Upon being introduced to Goofy, he had observed,

"So you're a Goofy solicitor are you"?

The other had looked at him with glazed eyes, noted with a voice filled with ennui, "Oh, that's hilarious. None have ever said that to me before".

It had amused Sellers anyway. The other's lack of amusement made it funny concerning his twisted humour. Sarcasm only worked, if one understood it, he pretended he didn't,

"None, I would have thought you'd get it all the time", he had grinned. Further amused when the solicitor had replied with dead-pan features,

"I do, Sellers, I do".

Though he had found the pair of them aloof, pompous, he now wished they would exist once more in Hall Gate, for it meant by inference that his studio would be there too. Although life with the Mizaroa contained no guarantees.

'You are in luck Sellers', Balurzuura suddenly intruded on his thoughts, *'One passenger is thinking about a visit to his solicitors and it is Alder of Hall Gate'*

'My studio'?

'Why would he be thinking about that? The other passengers are of no help'.

'No, it'd appear neither are you, Balu. Thanks for trying, here we are, Doncaster, it'll not be long before I find out for myself'.

Skipping off the train, onto the platform, he discovered it to be several degrees warmer inland, sunny too. Cheering, even if homeless, he did not have a reserve strategy. He rushed to find out, moving so swiftly that others gazed at him in some astonishment as he flashed past them. In a ridiculously brief period, he was in Hall Gate. The front door onto the street was unlocked, so he passed through that, rushed up the stairs beyond. His key fit! He keyed in the numbers to the alarm 57936258416. There was a sound of the electronics accepting the code - in he went. There had been some annoying changes! The décor remained the same, so too the furniture. Gone was his plasma screen television. Not replaced by anything, simply where it had been, lay empty space, an entertainment void. Glancing over to the computer he saw the reason, the monitor there was a solid-state cathode ray tube. It seemed plasma screens had either not developed in that reality, or they were so exorbitantly expensive that Sellers could not afford one. At least his precious high fidelity gear remained unaltered. Next stop the bathroom, finding his teal coloured bath sheet. Went to throw open the fire escape. Even before he whistled her, Mrs Meggins from the Pie Shop came bleating up the iron steps, complaining most vociferously at his absence. He poured her some - One by Purina went to his safe to get his credit, debit cards, some notes. Time to shop he would take the Honda, do so out of town, hoping to avoid Alston. Before closing the safe, he changed the combination. In the past, for ease of memory, he had used the same code as for the door. Now he possessed eidetic recall he could hold two different strings of numerals in his mind with no difficulty whatsoever. He changed the safe to 85248736848. Closed it, keyed in the new number once to test it. It opened just as it should. Finally, after the unscheduled delay, he was ready to go shopping. The time had crept around to 18:15. Mrs Meggins from the Pie Shop was getting washed in her doughnut bed. Looked to be in for the evening so he left her, but as he left the apartment he called,

"Be good, Megwinda. I'm leaving you in charge while I go get some snap. He had given her the Christian name Megwinda shortly after the fateful trip to the vets. It was much simpler than using her full title. It was a lovely evening as he walked around to his Jazz, but he almost passed it by, for the make had not altered but the colour had. The change delighted him. Instead of *Fire Red,* the Honda was *Everton Blue.* Not that

Sellers would get to see his favourite team much if he did not replace the plasma with something. He needed to shop firstly, then work on Nicole's negatives, or she would chase him to do so. A pleasant thought, but he desired more - to remain professional in his work. It meant determining his evening. Sellers detested shopping with a vengeance. In order of agitation, he hated the piped muzak that the store manager insisted upon subjecting the customers to. It was not his choice, no matter whose it was, it was not the choice of the majority. Silence would have been a preferable alternative. He also hated how ignorant, inconsiderate, impatient, the other shoppers were to one another, to him. *Trolley Power* seemed to rule the day. The worst exponents of this were the old women. Closely followed by the ancient men. In his more cynical moments, Sellers referred to these as *coffin dodgers*. The older they became, the more they thought they had a right to push in, barge freeze certain isles of traffic while they told each other how old they were. As if simply not dying was some sort of achievement. Finally, he hated to see the greed, the gluttony of fellow shoppers as they waddled in their obesity, trolleys filled to overflowing, buying enough food to feed central Africa for three months because the weekend was coming up. They were the same with lager, wines, spirits, a total lack of self-control, making problems for themselves in terms of a catalogue of ailments one could avoid by simply not doing anything to excess. Before his new body, Sellers had sipped the odd glass of sherry in the evening, but it had never progressed to two glasses. Smoked an e-cig but never to the point of dizziness. Ate some red meat but not every week, ate salad in hot weather, happy to eat carbs in the winter, but his dinner could always go on a side plate rather than the one with the largest diameter in the set. Then, of course, the furnace needed more fuel, but he still only ate when hunger gnawed at him and he would watch his sugar intake. He hoped he would see many years, by being moderate in all that he did. So it was bitterly ironic to him that Alston or some other agent was bent on his destruction, but he intended to do something about that. He drove toward Mexborough before the trauma that was the supermarket - went into Shooters World. After handing his firearms licence over for inspection, he bought an EAA Windicator .357 Mag Revolver with 2-inch Barrel. The revolver had existed over twenty years, still held true to the original mould. Windicator was the German word for Vindicator. It sported classic features like the nickel-plated steel frame, 2-inch barrel, 6-shot cylinder, hammer block safety, full rubber grip. It was a proven performer, not the sleekest, lightest, or prettiest, but dependable - worked. In the end, that was what mattered to

Sellers. It would fit in the leather shoulder holster he already had from his days in the gun club, so that the next time Alston appeared, he might not be the victim. He was still expecting a police visit to ask him why he, the prior victim in the crime was still alive... or... maybe in this reality the assault had never taken place, it was all very confusing, but he was developing a type of *go-with-the-flow* attitude to the entire situation. The Vindicator fit into his jacket pocket, he put a box of shells in the boot, then went to Lidl buying – ironically – a trolley full of food, since becoming a huge man who needed plenty to keep him going. *One*, for Mrs Meggins from the Pie Shop, including some litter tray crystals. Only too aware of the time, he drove back to his apartment, unpacked the shopping hurried into the darkroom. Who had time for a plasma television anyway?

Seven. **The results from** the shoot he had undertaken for Nicole were some of the very best work he had ever done. Admittedly, it was with an exquisite young woman, but his posing of her, the exact moment of opening and closing the shutter were his part of the product, added to which was the way he had lit his subject. Knew she could not fail to be delighted by the result. He selected several frames to enlarge, spent longer than he realised exposing larger papers, processing them. Just as he was hanging the last one up to air dry, Balurzuura suddenly leapt into his consciousness.

'Are you enjoying good health, vitality this morning, Sellers'?

'This morning, what do you mean'? He glanced at his LED watch. 'I see what you mean. I have to get some sleep, didn't realise the time'

It was 05:03. He had been awake for almost twenty-four hours. Leaving the darkroom, he hurriedly cleaned his teeth, throwing off his clothes, threw on a nightshirt before tumbling into bed. Mrs Meggins from the Pie Shop gave him one of her looks of disapproval for disturbing her. She had been curled up at the diagonal corner from his head. His entry had disrupted her slumber. On that occasion, it did not take long for Sellers to fall asleep. Even he tired after a long day that had included violent death, rebirth, incident. Mizar stank. One enormous swamp. Sellers hovered over a juicy-looking gnat, with incredible skill, plummeted downward, caught the squirming creature in his mandibles. Crunched down, the delicious yellow ichor burst from the gnat's body, running through the taste receptors of his mouthparts. A secondary delight of chomping through its crunchy bits. Only the wings were of no use to him. Allowed to flutter down into the mire. One gnat was not enough, still hungry, time to go hunting afresh. Suddenly a voice in his head declared,

'You are enjoying the sensation of flying, are you not? Sellers? Thrilled by the chase of the hunt, do you mind if I make a suggestion'?

'Not at all'.

'Why don't we swap for a while? You can stay here in the subconscious part of our shared posterior cortical hot-zone, while I will take over as the mentality that runs the physical body. Look upon it as a holiday for yourself, a mind-vacation in which you can effectively be me, live on Mizar A for as long as you desire'?

'I'm not sure why you've suggested such a thing, Balurzuura, but I like the arrangement just the way it is. Thank you. With each of us in exactly the positions we are now. The only person who is going to control my body is me'.

'Very well, I just thought to mention it as an opportunity'.

'Don't bother mentioning it again. I'm not interested. If you could move my body around, what sort of position would that leave me in? Would I be conscious'?

'You would in effect be the cerquibrum, able to see, hear, feel just like normal, but an observer. Who knows, you may also inherit the ability to perceive the epigrammatic transmissions of other humanoids'?

'You mean mind-read as you can'?

Sellers hovered over what looked like a crusty, delicious beetle crawling down the branch of some unknown tree.

'That is what I propound, although I remain uncertain if you could master the technique'.

'I don't need to while-ever you're lurking in the background, that's the arrangement that suits me very well thank-you-very-much'

The cerquibrum fell silent as Sellers woke up in a sweat. Was that a dream, or had the conversation taken place? If it had, it represented a certain aspiration by Balurzuura. To take control of his body, such a scenario had sinister ramifications as far as Sellers was concerned. He sent a mental question to his mind-legatee, but Balurzuura was *out* at the present moment. His bedside clock told him it was 10:12, five hours' sleep. He felt as refreshed as his old body had after eight. That was a useful improvement. To spend long hours awake to explore new avenues, acquire greater knowledge, filled with positive possibilities. Time for a bath. Putting baby bubble-bath into the water, he cleansed himself with Camay, a favourite soap. Towelled himself dry with his beloved teal bath-sheet, dressed in black/bronze boho top, yellow/brown striped boho pants. Choice of fragrance was simply a dab of patchouli oil. Tying back his long golden locks with a hair elastic, set about cleaning the bathroom. Sellers had something of an OCD for cleanliness, the upkeep of his apartment. By the time the job was finished, W5 spray liberally employed, the place looked like a show bathroom. For breakfast, half a grapefruit, cereal, two slices of toast spread with thick-cut marmalade. Pots washed, he was ready to go once again onto the streets of Doncaster – a dangerous place. Putting the gun into a Moroccan jacket, as it was too warm to wear the shoulder holster, he was ready to see if House of Fraser was once more English. More importantly, a stroll down Baxtergate hoping to see the beautiful Nicole Elv. Or would the Mizaroa have changed her in this junction of the cosmic highway? As long as she remained physically the same, he felt he could handle any other changes. A second meeting, something he eagerly anticipated. More so than taking Louise out to dinner.

'Balurzuura', he thought, *'Can you mind-tap ahead? Tell if any Zaromi agents are in the vicinity. Particularly Major Alston'?*

'I will do my very best Sellers. You can defend yourself, can you not'?

'I have no desire to conduct a gunfight on the street. The South Yorkshire Constabulary tend to take a dim view of such behaviour'.

'I detect no wandering encephalographic transmissions in the immediate surroundings. You are safe. If you would let me animate your body for a while until ...'.

'No deal Balu. I wouldn't ask again if I were you. The answer will always be the same - in the negatory'.

Cautiously, despite the assurance of his cerquibrum, Sellers strode out into Hall Gate, ambled leisurely down its length until it became the High Street. At Clock Corner, he turned into Baxtergate, drifted in the market's direction. Sure enough, House of Fraser was once more in the place where he remembered it had been for some years. It was a glorious day. There was the constant chatter of birds filling the air, the odd buzz of flies, wasps, as it heated up. A rare occasion in England, a bright day filled with sunshine. Sellers glanced at his wristwatch, a favourite Russian tank commander's analogue model. It told him it was swiftly approaching noon. Wandering through the cooling curtain of the store, found himself among the concessionary islands. It took him but a few moments to locate Anura. The instant he did, he had found her. Nicole Elv looked unchanged. He must have photographed her. Otherwise, how did he still possess the negatives? The moment she saw him, all his doubts evaporated as her beautiful features creased into a pleasing expression of pleasure.

"Yes, Sir", she quipped, "What can I help you with today, we have a range of fragrances for the discerning man, also beauty skin products, hair applications, hair removal items. Or; are you buying for the little lady"?

Sellers falling in with the charade, stuck out a lower lip, said in a melancholic tone, "Alas - I have no little lady, I am all alone, there is no one to look after me".

"That's because you don't wear the right odour-toilette, Sir", the ravishing girl chuckled as she continued, "With *Allurement* for men by Anura, women will suddenly find you irresistible, you will push them away".

"I only want to attract one young woman - take her to lunch? A business lunch", Sellers laughed, "Do you think she'll be free".

"I'm on lunch hour 12:30 to 13:30. Do you want to wait at the side entrance consigned to staff, or shall I meet you somewhere"?

"What about the Blue Donkey in Market Place, I can have a drink ready for you"?

"I'd better not at lunchtime if anyone smells it on my breath...".

"One before the meal won't hurt, but I can have something hot instead or a soft drink, whichever you prefer"?

"I'll risk one Pina colada then, thank you. I'll be there around 12:40 it takes ten minutes to get out aycee"?

"That's fine".

Balurzuura said to him, *'You still entrance her. Will you have sexual intercourse with her this afternoon? My studies ...'.*

'No. Broadcast when I first ask for you, otherwise, you might ruin the delicate mating ritual, then we'll never do it', Sellers exaggerated for the sake of mental peace. That proved effective. The cerquibrum went silent as Sellers walked around to the public house/eatery. He ordered a cider for himself, the girl's drink, glanced at the menu. There was much that might satisfy his ravenous hunger. He had not eaten for over two hours. Nicole soon wafted in, heads immediately turned. She was easily the most attractive girl in the place, but when the young admirers saw Sellers, their interest evaporated. For in his company, it made them the most glamorous couple in the place.

"Am I on time"? She asked breathlessly, "Wouldn't you know it I got a customer just before I was due to come on a break".

"Don't worry about it, but I'm conscious of how the time is dissolving for you, so let's order? We can talk while we dine".

She ordered a hot roast meat sandwich, even though he urged her to choose anything she wanted. He ordered the Homemade Soup of the Day with a warm buttered Roll for his starter. For his main course, a 28 Day Aged Sirloin Steak, with Roast Potatoes, Side Salad. Then he finished with the cheeseboard.

While he was busy loading the calories into his mouth, he passed over the portfolio he had prepared for the girl. The faux brown leather with gold leaf inlay simply stating her name had been a wily choice. Inside, in plastic sheaths for protection, she examined her six 25.4 x 30.48 cm, four 20.32 x 25.4 cm shots, the best of each pose clothed or otherwise, that Sellers had selected from the transparencies.

She told him, "You do good work Tod, the results are prime quality, but do you think my posing is as good as your skill with the camera".

After but a moment's debate, he replied in total honesty, "I could tell you had done little glamour work before Nicole, but you certainly have the looks to make it in the industry. You can only get better with practice".

"It was the first time I had ever done nude work in front of the camera", she admitted.

He adjusted his approach. "*The* very first time"!

"Yes".

"Then you did extremely well indeed. I would not have guessed. Like I say, with a bit of work, I think you can carve out a career for yourself in modelling".

"Could you recommend me to any agencies"?

"I have some phone numbers, Nicole, but I wouldn't send them that set of stills. Except maybe that one - possibly that one".

"One bikini, one topless, but no nude"?

"That's right, your nervousness shows through the lens you see. The lens misses nothing, forgets nothing, forgives nothing".

"So how do I get over that, I didn't feel *that* nervous"!

"Only by working with me some more, getting used to being nude in front of me".

She grinned, "Getting used to being naked in front of you, eh, Tod, is that the most subtle move, or do you mean it professionally"?

"We can take it either way", he tried to keep his tone level, even. "If you wish to keep our relationship on a professional level, Nicole, I can be professional, respecting boundaries you decide upon".

She smiled, her expression slightly evocative, "And would there be any alternative to that"?

"We're both single. I find you incredibly attractive. If you'd like to go out on a date, see where we take it, it would delight me to get to know you better".

He had never been so confident in the company of *any* young woman, Nicole was the most beautiful girl he had ever been in proximity to. She seemed pleasant, possessed a knockout figure, liked him. He wondered if she would tell him she preferred to keep it professional.

"Are you free Saturday night, we could go clubbing"? She was confident in her appearance, the effect it had on men.

"I'm free, but I'd rather have a root canal than attend one of those dreadfully noisy hell-holes. I'd much prefer drinks at my place, maybe a movie"?

"Or perhaps you could rent a DVD or stream"?

"I've no television, didn't you notice"?

"No", she echoed thoughtfully, "I thought I saw one of those *old-deep-things*, but now I think on it, it was in a girlfriend's. No television how bohemian. Well, drinks then the Vault".

"The Vault"?

"The cinema on Bawtry Road. May we see 'A Wrinkle in Time' it had a budget of $100 million"?

"Science Fiction, I know nothing about the film but I love the genre. Do you want picking up, or can you get to my place at say 18:00"?

"I don't finish work until then".

"I'll meet you. We can walk up to my apartment. Bring an overnight case. You can bathe, change, while I make tea. We'll get a taxi at 21:45 go see the evening showing of the film".

"You want me naked in your apartment again, do you, mister Sellers"? She murmured. He was a little taken aback by her forwardness, despite himself. He said to her most properly,

"Just for bathing Miss Elv, I assure you".

"*Are* you sure"? she breathed provocatively. It was plain she was the proverbial putty in his hands.

"Of course", he declared. "I'm first a foremost a gentleman, Nicole. As such, will treat you like the lady you are at all times".

He saw the tiniest flicker of disappointment in her eyes at that declaration, but she smiled to cover it, kissed him gently on the lips, before declaring,

"I must go. See you Saturday, bye".

She left in an afterglow of perfume and promise.

Eight.   Sellers seated himself on his sofa. Sweet sherry in one hand, e-cig in the other, while the strangely compelling vibes of 'Tales from Topographic Oceans' emanated from the speakers, filling the room with melody, his mind with various mental images.

'The vibrations you indulge in prove very stimulating to both your conscious and subconscious, Sellers', Balurzuura noted without an invitation to participate in the overall experience.

'Wait until it ends, this passage is one of my favourites', the Adonis responded as harshly as he could with thoughts alone.

It seemed effective enough, for Balurzuura waited for the end of side two, aloud Sellers reported,

"That was wonderful what a talented set of composers, musicians. I doubt we'll ever see the like again"!

'You call the vibrations in the air music. How is music different from the vibrations a train makes roaring down the track'? The cerquibrum desired to clarify.

"Music is a combination of vocal, together with instrumental sounds combined in such a way as to; produce beauty of form, harmony, expression of emotion. In my case, I find it both stimulating whilst at other times relaxing. It always conjures mental images, as I attempt to follow one thread of it or another. Noise is not music. Noise is simply a sound, especially one that is loud or unpleasant, that causes a disturbance of jolted senses. In the wrong hands, we can use it as a very effective weapon".

'Having no flaps of unsightly skin on either side of my head, like you humanoid, I detect both by use of my antenna, but I discern no difference between the two'?

"Poor you Balurzuura. Before you even ask, no you can't listen to some by taking total command of my body, I'll keep my ugly pink skin flaps to myself thank you very much".

'You do little in the evenings do you not, Sellers'?

"I have listened to music. Soon I will read in the bath. I'll probably have an early night. Your constant pestering fatigues me. What do you mean by questioning me, anyway"?

'You never hunt. I think the furred carnivorous mammalian quadrupoid of the Felis silvestris catus or Felis catus has much more fun than you'.

"Fun from your relative position may not be something I would regard in the same way, it's a matter of perspective, preference. Not only that, there is a distinct lack of game in Doncaster, Balurzuura".

'Game is also a matter of perspective, Sellers'.

"What's that supposed to mean"?

'Does everyone in Doncaster deserve life, are they all worthy to continue in existence'?

Sellers considered that at some length before replying, he had to remind himself he was talking to an alien, with very different social, moral, ethical codes to his own.

"I'm not qualified to make such a decision regarding those who only deserve to be extinguished. Further, the Constabulary of this area would not agree with my assessment even if I made an arbitrary appraisal, they'd remove my liberty. Thusly your experiment'd yield less significant results"

'I am a hunter by creation, Sellers. I miss the thrill of the kill. Your existence seems dreadfully dull compared to mine'.

"I'm sorry to be such a disappointment. Perhaps you'll report such to your commander, then we can end the association"?

'I would were it not for...'!

Sellers felt a momentary alarm at the observation that Balurzuura had almost revealed something he did not want him to know.

"Were it not for what, Balurzuura"?

'Were it not for my assignment, I am, after all, a scientist'.

"I don't think that's what you almost let slip, Balu. I want to know what you almost told me".

'That is all, I have told you the truth'.

Sellers tried a lie, to see if the cerquibrum could tell when he was using falsehood,

"You haven't, I can tell by the *tone* of your thought patterns you're hiding something from me, what is it"?

'Sellers, I have told you the truth, there is no need to ...'.

"Tell me 'what *were it not for*' means, were it not for something, or were it not for someone, *tell me* Balu"?

The alien en-grams in his brain broadcast nothing. The lack of reply was more indicative of any falsehood than the Mizaroa could have committed than thought-antiphon.

"If you don't tell me what you nearly blurted into my mind Balurzuura, I'll turn you off"!

'You do not possess such power', but the thoughts were slightly ill-at-ease. It would seem that whether he could, the Mizaroa believed Sellers still possessed such control. It was time to experiment, to flex his mental-muscles. Closing his eyes, regulating his breathing, relaxed his body as much as he could, he imagined his thoughts as a finite being of real dimension, a certain faux-physicality. Sellers thoughts were a brain-monkey. The monkey was Sellers' cerebration. All that his mind produced was in that creature. The 'monkey' had eyes the size of saucers, bright blue fur, yet recognisable as a non-<u>hominoid</u> simian. Sellers thoughts were the platyrrhine, a marmoset with an azure pelt. Mind control created purely a box. Thought alone conceived the box of steel. It had solid sides, a huge hinged top. One that could seal shut, bolted with a magnificent padlock of immense size. A padlock cast from duridium that only a huge duridium key could fasten or make it spring free on its immense flexible duridium coil. Next came the tricky part. His search for Balurzuura.

'Sellers, what are you doing'? The thought suddenly issued.

The *cognition-monkey* scampered toward the emanation.

'Sellers? ... humanoid, I know you are not slumbering. Why do you not answer'?

The cognition-monkey refused to do so. In that instant, Sellers realised he could keep his thoughts from Balurzuura if he so desired. The brain was his, his thoughts had pervaded it for years. How could the tiny engrams of an insectivore hope to compete with that?

'Sellers, I do not believe you have lost the ability to answer, must, therefore, conclude that your lack of reply is deliberate. That violates your contract with Engimedic Eahuura'.

Sellers was slowly wading through vast swathes of tall grey strands that were neither leaves nor curtains yet both at the same time. In the brain, all disordered, it seemed. He knew he was getting closer to finding the dragonflied-type thought animation that he had imagined Balurzuura to be. As for the other, he fell silent again, perhaps realising that to broadcast risked detection. Could he catch glimpses of what Sellers created in his imagination? Was this some private Glimpserama? Or one they both inhabited. Such had the sort of logic that one learned from trying to remember next week. In his mind, Sellers was the creator, reducing the Mizaroa as a harmless spectator. Cognimonk (as Sellers had designated the pseudo-creature) continued to wade through the strands of vestains (as Sellers had designated the strands of his mind). Down the length of the thick slate-filament pulses of electrical energy crackled, descended, they were brilliantly albescent with cornflower edges of the shadow. Sellers knew on an instinctive level that this was the inner-representation of the energy inside his brain. He tried to listen for the Mizaroa. Cognimonk had very sensitive ears behind tufts of white fur on either side of his sapphire coloured head. In a moment of unexpected success, Cognimonk heard a tiny pattering of insectivorous feet on the vestains. Balurzuura was close, agitated, uncertain. Had expected nothing like this bizarre scenario from his human host. It was like nothing experienced by a cerquibrum before. Or if they had, they had not reported it to Engimedic Eahuura. The Mizaroa's nerve failed. He scurried up the height of a particular strand of vestain. Quicker than any actual monkey could have moved, the Cognimonk sprang forward at the speed of thought. In one front paw snatched up Balurzuura. Or at least the mental projection of the Mizaroa that Sellers had created in his imagination. It worked, Balurzuura mewed,

'What are you doing Sellers, release me, or you might inadvertently damage my physique? How are you doing this? Why'?

"I'll answer all your questions when you answer mine", Sellers was obdurate, "Were it not for what, Balu? If you don't answer, I'll place your mind in my duridium box, lock you down, incarcerate you in the total absence of any form of stimuli".

'You have not the power'?

"Let's see, shall we? I think it's time for a demonstration - who is boss around here, Balurzuura".

Cognimonk trotted over to the casket, dropped the quite numbed, tiny form of Balurzuura, threw the lid down. Not needing to lock it, the weight of the imaginary lid was so great that a form the size of a dragonfly had not the strength to lift it - fly free.

'Sellers, let me out"! Balurzuura demanded.

The response was silence.

Sellers, let me free"!

Nothing.

'Sellers, I cannot move. Sellers, I cannot move, I can feel restraints, Sell ...'.

Suddenly Sellers opened his eyes at a mewling noise behind the fire escape door. Rose carefully to his feet, heightened physicality kicked in just as it always did since his death. Threw the massive bolts, let *her* in. Mrs Meggins from the Pie Shop was not in an excellent mood.

"Now then Megwinda, what seems to be the trouble"? The Adonis asked the feline, as though she could understand every word. "You seem to be agitated. Why don't I pour you some nice Purina? You can get them down you - to ease your fractured nerves. Then you can sit on Daddy's lap, get some lurv while Daddy plays with the alien. Jeezis, you couldn't make dialogue like this up - could you"?

The little crunching machine that was the cat eating, purring simultaneously, never ceased to amuse Sellers. He was feeling a little smug to start with. Never in his wildest imaginings could he have envisaged overpowering Balurzuura with so little effort. For the first time since the experiment had begun, he felt in control of his destiny. Poured himself a glass of gin, added some tonic, a slice of lemon, re-seated himself on the sofa. It was about time to see how things were going in the back alleys of his mind. Closed his eyes, conjured the Cognimonk, there it was waiting for him. He went over to the box as the Cognimonk himself. Raised the lid, thought to Balurzuura,

'See who's superior? You'll answer my question. Otherwise, you go back in the box'.

'All right' the tiny adversary suddenly resigned himself to the situation, *'Only promise me I never go back in there. It was like a tiny slice of death. Dark, no stimuli, almost non-being. I did not think humanoids possessed such mental powers'.*

Sellers resisted the temptation to claim he might be the only one, a reassembled super-being with incredible mental dexterity - aptitude.

"You've my word that if you behave, acknowledge me as master of this body, your instructor, then you'll not go back into the casket. Tell me this terrible secret you sought to keep"?

'It is the Zaromi', the Mizaroa began, *'They do more than cerquibrume, they take over the mind of their host, do a very similar thing to what you just did to me. Essentially, once a Zaromi goes into the mind of a humanoid, the body loses its humanity, becomes a walking, talking, totally controlled creature'.*

"A Zaromoid", Sellers decided on the nomenclature. "An insidious invasion. How far have they gotten with this? What are the Mizaroa doing about it"?

'To start a war with weapons of the type you have, would cause countless arrests for murder, it would incarcerate many cerquibrum', Balurzuura explained, *'We are working on a Disinter-gun. Once completed, it will leave no trace on any level of the Zaromoid that we fire at. You will get one the instant we complete one'.*

"A gun that disintegrates the target"?

'Yes'.

"You're trying to make of me a trooper in some preternatural war held on Earth but being conducted by insectivore. I'm not interested Balu. You never told me how many of these Zaromoid there are"?

'I do not know the exact number, but it is the early stages of the invasion. You could be the commander of the forces of Mizaroa".

"Look Balu, I'm happy with my life here the way it is, what I'm happy doing. I will accept a Disinter-gun once you've developed them. If I carry one for my protection, does that mean the Zaromoid can disintegrate me"?

'They are a goodly way behind us in physical technology. Seeking to develop by taking over humanoid bodies. I doubt they could produce such a weapon for hundreds of years'.

"Then mine shall be for self-defence. I'm going to do some reading. With my new mental acuity, I can read stuff that was intelligible to me before. Tonight I'm going to try Ulysses by James Joyce".

He read the book, dismissed it as naïve, affected, went to bed. His dreams - filled with images of dragonflies, crickets locked in mortal combat. Mostly the crickets won, slowly, hideously, devoured their vanquished foes. Not a pleasant series of dreams. He awoke at 06:13, not in a favourable frame of mind. The mobile telephone rang the alarm to inform him he had an appointment. Dental, with everything happening he had forgotten to cancel it. None attendance on the day would cause a fine. It might prove amusing to attend, but what would they make of him? Probably busy as they were, they had forgotten what he looked like, his dentistry had changed too. Still, it would be an amusing distraction from the Mizaroa – Zaromoid conflict. So he made the appointment to see what would happen. The other positive, he remembered the assistant to his dentist being young, very attractive. He wondered if he had the wherewithal to get a date with her. Would juggle his women if he had to, not that he had ever been in that position before. Play the field a bit, make up for the scarsity of romance in his past. Firstly though, the morning ritual, which he raced through. Get up; ablution-ate, feed Mrs Meggins from the Pie Shop, dive in the bath, clean the bathroom. A drive to Ackworth, which was where the Mount Dental Practice was situated. The Jazz responded to his need for speed that day. He was early to arrive for his appointment. The receptionist was new (were they not always?), accepted his appearance without a qualm. He could smell disinfectant, hear the soft whir of a dental drill. They covered the walls with extremely uninteresting notices about teeth, dental hygiene. He read them all at a glance, dismissed them as boring, unworthy of future reference. Sooner than expected, they called his name over the intercom system, allowing him to stroll into Surgery One. The diminutive, studious Spanish dentist looked at him. A faintly quizzical expression crossed her swarthily handsome features. Sellers glanced away, smiled at the very young, equally pretty Annie, who blushed under his attention. Did anyone do that any more? How coyly sweet?

"Mr Sellers"? The dentist asked, curiously, "Ah, what's your date of birth, please"?

Without hesitation, he told her. She almost shook her head, glancing at his dental records on the screen before asking,

"Please take the seat, any problems since last time"?

"None, you said that my teeth were in superb condition, remember"?

Again she glanced at the screen, which showed evidence of fillings, two crowns, several missing teeth on the right lower jaw.

"Aycee, open up? Let's do an inspection, shall we"?

Sellers could feel a lascivious double entendre well up in his mind regarding the sweet young Annie, *'Yes Annie, open up, let's do an inspection'*!

No sooner had the dentist looked into his mouth than she gasped in shocked disbelief,

"This isn't possible unless we've got the wrong records on our system. You are Tod Sellers of 8U Hall Gate, Doncaster"?

"I am. What seems to be the problem, Dear"?

"The strange thing is I don't remember you, Mister Sellers. Your records aren't accurate, but that's not the most significant fact here".

"Oh! What is then, please"?

"Mister Sellers, you have the most perfect set of teeth I have ever seen in all my years of dentistry. None missing, zero cavities, no previous dental work done on them, not even a filling, no sign of wear nor decay in the slightest, congratulations you have perfect dentistry. May I take x-rays of your teeth for our records so that we can correct them"?

"Go ahead".

With admirable swiftness, the Spanish dentist did just that, was soon looking at the images on the computer.

"You don't even need a polish, Mister Sellers. I guess we'll see you in six months. No, make it nine, I can't imagine you'll need anything then either".

"Fine", Sellers rose from the low long seat, gave Annie another winning smile. She simpered. There was no opportunity to speak to her alone. If he wanted to, he certainly knew the number of the practice. Satisfied with his flirtations, he was driving happily back to his apartment when the articulated lorry suddenly swerved directly into the path of the Jazz. The impact was at sixty miles an hour. The car crumpled into a mass of twisted, crushed metal. Inside it, it turned his body into agonised mush, pangs, throes of terrible pain - before blackness enveloped him for the third time in his existence. The super man tumbled into the atramentous chasm of death.

Nine. *'Oh pudenda, not again'*, Sellers cursed as the awareness of existence returned to his mind. He could still receive no stimuli like sight, smell, taste, or physical feeling, but he could detect alien thoughts being broadcast directly into what remained of his mind.

'Hello again Sellers', familiar Mizaroa thoughts were suddenly in Sellers quiddity, 'It is I, your engimedic'.

'How's it fluttering' Sellers cracked. Becoming somewhat blasé about the whole phenomenon of loss of life, which was no longer the end. It was not even the beginning of the end for him, not even the end of the beginning. Could go on for a long tedious time, a whole series of reality changes, temporary interruptions that everyone else would consider cessation.

'I do not understand that greeting, humanoid, but I do not suppose it is important that I do. They involved you in a murder attempt. Fortunately, you were under the supervision of Balurzuura ...'.

'Now hang on one second', Sellers thought abruptly, 'Balurzuura does not supervise me. He's a mind-jockey, that's

all. A mentality-strap-hanger who most of the time does as I instruct'.

'He <u>did</u> broadcast the distress-emanation that we picked up, took what remained of your brain into our ship'.

'My brain'! Sellers would have gasped if he possessed a larynx, *'What about the rest of me'?*

'In the collision with the much larger, heavier vehicle, which incidentally the Zaromoid was driving ...'.

'No kidding'.

'I assure you we do not deceive you. As I was thinking; in the collision, it separated your body from your head'.

'Decapitated'?

'Precisely, but we took your brain aboard our vessel. Able to produce an exact duplicate of your former carcass'.

'Comforting', Sellers returned sarcastically.

'We knew it would relieve you', the engimedic did not quite understand the dark humour of his humanoid subject.

'I want to tell you this', Sellers then informed. *'I'm sure these constant reports from my cerquibrum are pleasing you, but my untimely demises are becoming tedious. I want better protection? How are you coming along with the Disinter-gun'?*

'Progress is being made with the weapon, although I am forced to point out that in neither case would it have been much use to you, Sellers. You seem to have treated the threat of the enemy with casual indifference to date'.

'That's not true, I just don't want to become embroiled in the conflict, to where it changes my entire life'.

'Yet we would observe that it has already done so'.

'That's why I want protection. A hot babe who is also good at fighting - self-defence, I'd let her share my apartment'.

'We will take your request under advisement'.

Sellers was becoming agitated, *'How long will it be before you make some sort of decision'?*

'In the fullness of time. As to your current position, you will find yourself once more on the beach. Clothes will be in the boot of your new car, taken out in your name - paid for.

'So this time I get a vehicle, that's more like it. Why the coast every time though, can't you find a landing site a little nearer to my home'?

'No'.

'What about the changes? Will this junction in the ley-lines of the multiverse be much the same'?

There seemed to be some amusement (insectivorous - in nature) in the thoughts of the engimedic as he replied, *'Sellers, that is all part of your next discovery, I believe you call it fun'?*

Blackness followed. He awoke just as before. Naked, a set of keys, including those to his apartment, in his hand. This time, the sprint to the car resulted in startling two walkers. The man merely turned to his partner, noted,

"It takes all sorts, but he must be cold"!

She replied appreciatively, "He didn't *look* cold"!

Sellers threw on the boho cheese-cloth blouse, cotton pants, tied his hair back with the thoughtfully supplied band. The remit must have been, 'leave hippy clothes'. The vehicle was a silver Polo GTI 2.0 TSI 200PS 6-speed gearbox, which could certainly *shift a bit*. How did he merit such expenditure? That caused him to ruminate somewhat. Just how long had the Mizaroa been on Earth? With access to such resources? Could it be that besides Zaromoid there were also Mizaroid? Were Balurzuura, Eahuura as benign as they purported to be? Sellers felt that his former ignorance was something he might gladly have returned to. Death was not something he had previously thought it to be! It was too ... complex. As he drove, certain changes became apparent. The most striking - all the road signs were in German. He had not immediately digested that for the simple expedient that he could read in the language without even thinking about it. Further, when trying to speak out loud such expletives as, fool, be careful, dozy cow, came to his lips as, täuschen, sei vorsichtig and dösige Kuh! He knew Balurzuura would be unavailable for a while. Presumed it part of his borrowed quiddity, or the Mizaroa had done it during the rebuild, knowing it would prove useful to him. The common tongue in England was then the same as in Germany. What strange occurrences had taken place that led to such weird circumstance? The conjecture was beyond the scope of Seller's imagination to answer. Was his home country now actually part of Europe? In the Common Market once more, or something even stranger? Finally, he pulled into Hallentor, Doncaster automatically glancing up to the sign above the solicitors. It read Fass und Hering Rechtsanwälte (Fass and Hering Solicitors at Law). Thankfully, the key worked. The code for the door was unchanged. Let him into the apartment. It was barely recognisable! Everything was in monochrome. White walls, black leather suite. Albescent cupboard doors set into ebon cupboards all created by Schreiber. The television set was back, but it was no longer Japanese rather Loewe LED flat screen. His precious high fidelity equipment had changed beyond recognition. It altered the turntable to a Thorens TD 203, fitted with TP 82 arm and TAS 257 cartridge, the combined cost a cool $1100 in his known reality. He checked his pocket to see what the currency was in England; it was the Reichsmark. The valve amplifier had transformed into an AudioValve Assistant 100 Mark II driving the bizarre-looking Telefunken 1938 Field Coil Speakers. Despite the loss of his prized gear, Sellers could not wait to hear the new rig. Firstly, he had to explore the rest of his apartment. The bathroom was in black tiles a white suite. The once favourite teal bath-sheet - black! A thought occurred to him. Where was Frau Meggins vom Kuchenladen!? Sellers cracked the fire escape door, in she came mewing her usual displeasure, he gave her a saucer of evaporated milk from the Bosch fridge freezer, his washing machine an Allgemeine Elektricitäts-Gesellschaft or AEG. Germany ruled England in all matters product-wise, how much else did they control? Time to sit at the Nixdorf Computer, discover exactly what world he was living in. What he read in Bösepädie surprised him in no small amount:

Operation Sea-lion (*Unternehmen Seelöwe*), was Nazi Germany's code name for the plan for an invasion of England during the Battle of Britain in the Glorious War of our leaders' glorious plan for the Third Reich. Following the Fall of France, the German Führer and **Supreme Commander of the Armed Forces** hoped the British government would seek a peace agreement. Our Führer reluctantly considered invasion only as a last resort if all other options failed. As a precondition, he specified the achievement of both air and naval superiority over the English Channel, plus the proposed landing sites. It took our glorious forces longer to achieve that than expected previously. Thusly, the threat of an invasion remained unrealised until the Autumn of 1944. Once the German High Command and Hitler himself had serious hopes for the prospects for success. Numerous barges gathered on the Channel coast. Enough to convince the English cabinet that seeking, signing a peace agreement was the best option for them. Thusly Hitler's issued statement on 16 July 1940 - Führer Directive number 16, setting in motion preparations for a landing in Britain, had achieved the aim he had envisaged. He had prefaced the order by stating: "As England, despite her hopeless military situation, still shows no signs of willingness to come to terms, I have prepared the necessary to carry out, a landing operation against her. This operation aims to eliminate the English Motherland as a base from which they can continue the war against Germany. We shall occupy the country completely." The code name for the invasion was *Seelöwe*, "Sea Lion". In that junction of the multiverse, Germany had won the war, created the Reich that would last a millennium, made Europe one vast superpower. Sellers did a bit more reading on the resultant conclusion to WWII. Russia had still turned the Germans back, reclaimed most of the eastern zones of Poland, Bulgaria, Romania. There a combined Anglogermanic Army had stopped them, thrusting up from Greece. The new German state of Großbritannien forced the Russians to agree with the iron curtain but never had entered the Fatherland. America had never entered the war having no intention of aiding the Soviet Union. Had avoided war with Japan by the timely intervention of Großbritannien in the east who had negotiated a successful oil deal between the two conflicting nations. They had paid reparation for Pearl Harbour in electronic, motor, plus other goods. The dream of a united Europe achieved by 1948, but not by the grouping of so many nations. Rather under the Nazi jackboot. No one had ever created Israel, which benefited the middle east as a result, which in Sellers current reality of residence was much more stable. The only Jews who had survived were those living in the DRA (Democratic Republic of America). Seventy years after the war (1939-48) the world comprised three great superpowers, DRA, Great Germany, the Japanese Empire, who had invaded most of the far east, including Australia, whom Great Germany had allowed them if they kept Ozeanland and Antarktis. The USSR had descended into poverty without aid carved up by the great triad. In the nineteen fifties to sixties, DRA had undertaken a series of military actions into what had once been South America, became the 101st to 122nd states. They had formed a United Nations in the late seventies, with far fewer constituent parts. The German and Großbritannien cabinets had carved Africa up, which no longer existed in its own right. Scandinavia eventually agreed to Germanic rule, most of the middle east remained under Großbritannien control. The only nation that was truly independent of the big three, Canada. The atomic bomb had dropped much later, in the nineteen-eighties, by the DRA with permission from Great Germany. Deployed on Baghdad bringing peace to the middle east by the iron fist of technology.

Sellers turned thoughtfully away from the computer. Found himself part of what was far from perfect, but in some ways, it seemed more stable than the one from which he had originated. The Japanese Empire had stabilised Korea, Vietnam, before they had even happened by subjugating China. The iron curtain was no longer any sort of credible border, the Poles, Bulgars and Romanians had achieved independence from the crumbling Soviet Union that had never united. Each had received the aid they had so desperately needed, once agreeing to various annexations by Germany, DRA, Japan. The axis had won the war, but it had not been such a disaster for Großbritannien as one might have feared. The Commonwealth still existed under German/English joint ownership. Once Hitler had executed Churchill he had been very fair with the English, suitably harsh with Scotland which no longer existed as a separate country. Großbritannien had enjoyed a separate parliament since the fifties. The English Fascist Party seemed far more efficient than any Sellers could remember in *his* history. A world without the existence of Scotland and France had to be an improvement. He smiled. The World Football Cup could still start with 24 countries. England having a much better team. The single threat to that layer of reality was from the Zaromoid. Would the German/Großbritannien Reich finally fall at the hands of invaders smaller than the length of their hands? He went into the fridge, taking out a Kölsch (beer) from the Bosch. Settled in front of the Loewe. What he saw immediately caused him pleasant wonder. The fifth manned mission to Mars had just landed near Isidis Planitia with a crew of six commanded by Flug-Pilot Astronaut Kapitän Hans Muller. It had been a joint enterprise by the tripartite union of Greater Germany, the Japanese Empire, the DRA. Without the space race, that world had done much better in the exploration of the solar system. Sellers watched with fascination, but his eyelids drooped. One thing about death was that it was a shade taxing on the vitality. Not only that, the Kölsch hit his system venomously, despite him loading up with snacks. Turning off the television set, he went into the bedroom, stripping as he proceeded. Frau Meggins vom Kuchenladen was already on the end, mewed a complaint as he pushed under the sheets. He was asleep before his head hit the pillow. Incubus invaded his brain from the very first instant. In his past, Sellers had endured nights the like of which he was now experiencing. None so violent, so disturbing. He had usually attributed past incubus to an act of folly, miscalculation too. This time, a reason was there none. There was no tasty piece of *supper-cheese* stuck firmly in one of his *corners*! No rather heavy toke on his hash-filled bong (an indiscretion of his wild adolescence). No unsuitable reading of Bloch just before slumber, nor the viewing of a vivid video-nasty. It was unfair. He had done nothing to deserve it! Once again he was Mizaroan (surprise surprise) but this time rather than the hunter, he knew instinctively, as only one can in dreams, that he was the prey. The hunters were the Zaromi, one of those dreams that men frequently have, where one is fighting – fighting, winning every violent altercation, but with no gain at the end. For no matter how many times one vanquished one's foe, another sprung into existence to challenge. The violence was unending. He crunched through chitin, tore legs from their sockets, felt the delicious ichor of the enemy run through his mouthparts, all to no avail. Finally, horror of horrors, the leader of the cricket-resembling alien faced him with the face of Louise! Sellers tried to scream, but dragonfly-type mouth-parts are ill-designed for that particular function. What issued forth in its place was a sort of insectivorous crackling sound. The queen of the Zaromi was on him with her humanoid mouth she whispered in his ear,

"I'm going to flutter you, then when we're done I'm going to eat you alive"!

Sellers woke to scream hoarsely, the bedsheets sodden with the perspiration of his Foul-Fantasmic-Torment.

Ten.   When Inigo Felton finally died he thought, as one would expect, that was decidedly that! Born of a fierce fan of Priestley, hence his ironic name, Felton senior had taken him into the fishing trade almost before he had left school. Inigo had known nothing else his entire life, which he spent in Bridlington. He had married a local girl, fathered three children, provided for all of them until they left home. At sixty retired, while his wife, having converted two bedrooms, one room downstairs to suitable accommodation, *took in* during the height of the season for a bit of extra money for the bingo. That was pretty much Felton's existence from birth to death, at seventy-four. With his death, events took a much more exciting turn! Closing his eyes, he let out a last gasp. The pain vanished along with eyesight, hearing. All other sorts of sensory stimuli save one – thought.

'Inigo Felton'?

'Yes! I'm he, that god'?

The answering thought seemed slightly amused at the notion, *'I assure you I am no false deity not a being with anything other than quiet scientific powers, but I feel I have a rather tempting offer for you, Felton'.*

'An offer for me, but I'm dead! I am dead, aren't I? If I am, who're you'?

'Your body expired, correct. Your engrams, quiddity are still intact, I, the engimedic of the Mizaroa, can do something about that'.

'What on Earth is an engimedic? Who're the Mizaroa, when they're all at home'?

Eahuura carefully explained at length. Once done, he offered the same deal to Felton, as he had to Sellers, ending by informing,

'You only have a finite amount of time to make your decision. Your engrams will soon decay, even if we have them in our memory banks. Indeed, the collective storage from a recently deceased corpse is a technique I have only recently been able to master. I'm rather proud of my achievement'.

'And so you should be, Eehu', Felton always felt there no harm in paying a compliment when the opportunity presented itself, *'You're a master of techniques way beyond any scope of my species. So, to be clear, I currently don't have a body,*

you're offering to create one for me if I agree to share my new mind with one of your kind'?

'Precisely, though you must expect certain changes to reality as I have already informed you, for I will not deposit you in the same lane of the multiverse in which you expired'.

'Something of a relief. The family would never understand if I whisked back up from my deathbed, asked what was for lunch. Am I to be an android then'?

'You will be human. Admittedly, I will make your skeleton of duridium instead of fragile bone. Your muscles will be nyloplanyon but pseudo-flesh that would pass an examination by your medical humanoids will cover these'.

'What about money, what will I do for a living'?

'We will provide a financial start for you. We have an occupation for you to pursue'.

'What am I going to look like? I mean, I don't want to reawaken only to discover I'm an old man again'?

Eahuura assured, *'You can decide your age, appearance. You must do so with some alacrity, for the reason previously mentioned'.*

Decision made, Felton then asked, *'I'd like to be twenty-five again. Taller, say six feet. Could I be better looking as well, leaner, but with a bit of muscle - you know'?*

Eahuura assured, *'I will create a man it will please you to be. You will awaken on a secluded cove in Flamborough. A vehicle provided for you will contain clothes, effects, money. You are to drive to the town of Doncaster, find accommodation, wait for your cerquibrum to issue you with further instruction – clear'?*

'I've got all that, gosh this is ...'.

Felton fell into a fuliginous shaft of nothingness before he even had the chance to thank his benefactor. During the period he was told much of interest by the engimedic, whilst in *learning-sleep*. An indeterminate period without corporeal term elapsed. Like the death, he had expected when he had originally died. It ended when he woke! The north-easterly breeze that buffeted his uncovered skin was not something that bothered an old salty sea-dog like Felton. Climbing carefully to his feet, discovered that he could do so with no protesting joints. No aches, pains of any kind. Felton looked down at his hands and feet, was young, vital, fit again. It caused him to laugh in delighted glee, his voice that of a young man, too. Realizing his nakedness, he sneaked toward the promised Suzuki Sport turbocharged 1.4 with 138bhp at 5500rpm, an improved torque of 170lb-ft, the engimedic had promised it would be more fun to drive than his old Citroën. When he first saw it though, he burst into laughter. The model was a shockingly bright lime-green. With the keys he had awoken with clutched in his hand, he popped the boot, dragged out the clothes. They were not something Felton would have possessed or worn in his previous life. Trolleys replaced y-fronts. His socks were fawn, he had always worn black. Over them, he pulled a blue and white hooped hoodie, navy cargo pants. Felton had previously dressed as an old man. Had always worn a traditional shirt, cant-elope trousers. For his feet, in the place of stout boots, were a pair of what he called plimsolls - Reebok trainers. Thusly garbed, undetected by any who might have cited him for indecent exposure, he climbed into the driving seat, pressed the starter. The resultant purr that answered him was much quieter than his old Citroën 2CV. He pedalled the gas, nearly shot out of the back window. It would take a few moments to adjust to the power the new vehicle possessed. Engaging the clutch to adjust the mirrors, he set off toward Bridlington, of all places, a logical stop on the way to Doncaster. Rather than take the longer, faster route to York - down the A64 - A1, he thought he would drive through; Beeford, Brandesburton, Skirlaugh down the A165 to Hull. From which, it was a pleasant journey through South Cave, Gilberdyke, Goole on the M62. What he was going to do for the Mizaroa, where he was going to stay, he was still in the dark about, but he had a thousand Reichsmark in his pocket a great deal to learn about the world he then found himself in. Turning on the radio, Felton could not understand a word being said. That did not surprise him as much as the money had. Germany controlled the world they had deposited him into in part (a significant part). Felton did not speak any language other than English, even that only in Humbersider-English. Perhaps the cerquibrum would be of some assistance, once he made himself felt in his mind. The sounds of Kraftwerk suddenly issued from the radio, he hummed along to it. In his world, he had been a fan in the seventies to eighties, at twenty-five again, his taste in music had not changed. The tune ended, followed swiftly by Tangerine Dream, their fabulous Rubicon album. It was still playing when hungry; he stopped for something to eat. There was a place immediately before him, called *Frikadellen-sind-uns*. The aroma from it promised much to his salivating mouth, so he pulled in. Perhaps he could get by with sign language? He took a seat at a double table. A shapely young waitress came over to him almost at once, smiled in a friendly fashion. Her name badge said simply, *Louise*.

"Hallo, kann ich bitte Ihre Bestellung entgegennehmen, was möchten Sie"? She seemed to be asking a question.

"You wouldn't happen to speak English, would you, by any chance"? Felton asked in half-hope.

"But of course", she smiled charmingly, "We all learn it at school, ja"?

"Yes, but you're German aren't you"?

"No Sir, I'm local, a Humbersider, from Bridlington".

Felton decided not to show his ignorance. *Something very different must have occurred to this England for the first language to be Kraut'*, he thought, asked,

"What would an average sort of order be here, I don't want any pickled red cabbage or anything like that".

"Aycee, what about; Frikadellen, Käse' Bratkartoffeln und Salat. That's minced beef, onion held together with an egg, shaped into a rissole, in a bun with cheese on top, at the side fried sliced potatoes, salad DRA style".

"Yes, that sounds good, I'll have that".

"And to drink"?

"Do you have tea"?

"Es tut uns leid, nein, wir haben Pepsi Cola, Kaffee, Bier, Wein, und Limonade", she said under her breath, he got the gist of it, even though she seemed to have lapsed into her first language.

"Pepsi Cola bitte", he managed, his German limited to that which he had exposed himself to over the years as war films, documentaries about WWI, WWII.

"Natürlich, Sir, normal oder Diät"?

"Diät bitte".

"Danke für Ihre Bestellung, es wird in Kürze bei Ihnen sein", she seemed to promise it would come, when also, he nodded, smiled. He was going to struggle if Doncaster was as German as Bridlington. A very curious sensation seized him. it felt like his brain 'wriggled'!

'Hello', he thought.

'Yes, I am just coming out of the anaesthesia, you are Felton are you not'?

'Felton, yes, Inigo Felton. Your name's'?

'Long, ungainly for the humanoid palate, tongue, so for convenience, I am happy to answer to the nomenclature of your choosing. I suggest you select something of a single syllable'.

'Are you a girl dragonfly, or a boy'?

'My persuasion is currently female'.

That was a surprise, Felton had expected a Mizaroa of the same sex as himself, still, according to what he had learned from Eahuura this female may be a fella in the future, that meant a suitable name should not indicate gender, so he thought,

'I'll call you Kim then'.

'Alright, so what are we about, humanoid'?

'We are about to eat', Felton smiled at the speech pattern of the Mizaroa, then he asked, *'This England we find ourselves in speaks a language called German, this is going to hinder me unless you can help'?*

'Of course, I shall access my superb memory in linguistics. Learn the tongue you inform, then download it into your subconscious at a reasonable speed'.

'Reasonable speed, what'd that be for a twenty-five-year-old man'?

'Parts of your brain tissue are no longer organic, rather filled with the ability to access, store data at approximately four kilobits-a-second', Kim informed him, *'You should be able to speak German in a couple of minutes'.*

Louise returned with the order, "There you are, Sir, enjoy your meal", she said in German, thinking his reply would be in monosyllables. Instead, he smiled, returned,

"I'm sure I will. Thank you for your earlier patience".

She looked at him a trifle uncertainly before sashaying away. He noticed what a nice rump she had, then smiled, reflected, *'And I'm young enough to do something about it once more'.*

Kim realised it was a private reflection, for she did not comment. Just as Felton was *tucking in,* he realised a woman was standing opposite his table. Glanced up - what an outstanding example of femininity she was. Tall for a woman around five-eleven, divine figure, with lovely cascading honey-blonde hair, very attractive facially, on the back of her head was a beret. She wore a fawn windcheater brown slacks, sensible flat shoes, natural, he supposed, for someone her height.

"Do you mind if I join you"? She asked in a rich contralto, which only heightened her allure. Surprise was Felton's initial reaction. There were plenty of empty tables. Surely the woman was neither single nor making some sort of pass at him? That sort of thing had never happened to Felton in his previous lifetime.

"Not at all", he smiled, "Do we know one another"? He knew they did not. Such would have been impossible.

"No", she replied, as she glided down onto the seat opposite him, "I'm Alice". She held out a short but thin hand, her shake typically slack.

"Inigo", he responded, she said - as most did,

"How unusual, is there a story behind that, or did your parents just have a great sense of the memorable"?

"A bit of each, I guess. Have you ordered anything to eat, Alice"?

"Yes, I didn't want to wait, so I went up to the counter".

"You're in a hurry then"? He wondered.

She grinned, "Just impatient, no hurry. I'm hoping to get to South Yorkshire later on, but the buses are dreadfully infrequent so I thought I'd have something to eat while I waited".

"Where in South Yorkshire exactly? Sheffield perhaps"?

"Doncaster, I'm on my way to visit a sick aunt in the Hospital there".

"Have you booked a seat on the bus or bought a ticket of some sort"?

"No, I might even take the train instead, so I've nothing yet".

The food arrived. Louise looked at the couple curiously but said nothing. When she had gone, Felton asked,

"Did anyone tell you I was about to drive to Doncaster"?

Alice looked surprised, pleasantly so, smiled, explaining, "I see how this could look to you now, Inigo. I didn't know. I can get there on my own, don't feel obligated to say another word. Just don't enjoy eating alone".

Felton could not decide whether to believe that, he returned, "Well I'm not much for travelling alone, so you're welcome to a lift if you'd like one"?

Alice seemed to mull that over before answering, "Only if I can split the cost of the fuel with you. Oh, I can trust you can I, what I mean to say is, this is just a lift, that's all I'm accepting if you understand what I'm getting at".

"Just a lift, but being as I'm going the right way, you don't need to pay me for fuel".

Alice ate in silence for several seconds before deciding, "I pay half for petrol, or I'll get the train".

"I wouldn't even know how to work it out, Alice".

"I would. You hit *Trip* when we get in your car, petrol's 1.417 Dm per litre. I can work out the cost once you tell me how many kilometres your car does to the litre".

Felton laughed, "Good luck with that, Luv, I haven't the foggiest, the car's a Suzuki Sport".

Alice promptly pulled out a mobile phone from her Aigner Olivia handbag, looked it up, she asked, "What size engine"?

"1400 turbocharged", Felton was grinning. All that trouble - he was going to Doncaster, anyway.

"6.1 litres will go 100 kilometres", she told him, "So that's 0.06 litres per kilometre. How far is it to Doncaster"?

"About 110 kilometres, give or take, making the cost of fuel 9.5 Dm or 4.75 Dm apiece".

Alice was still using the calculator on her Gigaset mobile telephone before raising her eyes to Felton. "That's right! Had you worked it out previously"?

"No. I'm just reasonable at mental arithmetic".

"Reasonable is not the word, that's impressive. What do you do Inigo, for a living I mean obviously"?

"I have a fishing business", he returned, staying within his comfort zone, "I'm on my way to negotiate a price for some of my catch to be sold on Doncaster Fish Market".

"Impressive for someone your age".

"Not really. The boats were my father's, his father's before him. I'm more of an accountant than a hands-on trawler, hence my swiftness with the petrol calculation".

"What's the name of your company"?

"Felton's Fish, not very imaginative, but effective after all this time. What about you Alice, what do you work at when you're not visiting ailing relatives".

"I'm a sales representative for GlaxoSmithKline it has a market capitalisation of Dm 91.8259 billion".

"Ah! There's not as much money in fish".

She laughed and laid one of her hands on his, "I don't imagine there is Inigo, but I'm only salaried, you're the CEO".

"The lads just call me the pen-pusher, there's nothing executive about my office, I can assure you".

The hand stayed in place. "You're modest. I like that Inigo, it's a rare quality in young men nowadays".

He almost told her he was not young, but seventy-four years of life had taught him the value of when to keep his own counsel.

"I'm just going to the Gentleman's Rest Room to wash my hands. Then we can set off if you're ready"? He asked her.

"I'll do the same and then meet you back at this table".

"Alice", he quipped, "You can't go into the Herren".

She laughed her delightful contralto once more playfully punched his arm whilst tilting her head to one side, about 45 degrees, exposing the opposite side of her neck,

"You know what I meant, silly". She was using well known flirting techniques with him he could not understand why.

Once he had extricated himself from her going to the toilets, he had his answer when he was washing his hands afterwards. Glancing upward into the mirror over the sink, the man who stared back at him, whilst still being essentially recognizable as Inigo Felton, had changed in very subtle ways. Hair decidedly thicker than it had been in his twenties, in the past. Thicker, shiny with good health, vigour. Eyes, whilst still brown, sparkled with the same sort of dynamism, the whites devoid of any veins, the pupils as inky as the darkest raven's wing. Nose a trifle shorter, narrower, mouth and lips slightly finer. He was handsome whilst in his past; he had only been average looking.

"Well hello", he *smarmed* at the reflection, "Little wonder the lay-dee thinks you are more than just a fishing catch"!

Was the lady also single, or was she just after an amusing tumble with a bit of rough - he wondered? There was also the distinct possibility that she had just accepted the lift, feeding his ego with a bit of frivolous flirtation. She had already told him all she wanted was the journey. It was a tremendous risk getting into a car with a strange man. Was she incredibly naïve? Or did she have an agenda in which he was ignorant?

"Well me'old cocker, there's only one way to find out, isn't there"? Felton asked the reflection, before strolling out of the place, resuming his seat at the table to wait for her.

As was the usual case with a woman, she took a considerably longer time in the bathroom. When she finally joined him, her extra preparation had reaped the benefit. Hair rearranged, make-up refreshed, she looked lovely, although it did not particularly enamour him of the beret.

"Ready"? He desired to know monosyllabically.

She nodded. He led the way to his motor, placing her tiny wheeled bag in the boot before they proceeded out of the car park.

"I'm going through Hull rather than York", he told her, but she did not have a preference - why would she? The journey by road would be much quicker than that by rail or public transport in the shape of a bone-crunching bus.

"Would you prefer silence or some music"?

"Silence definitely, you don't look like you'd enjoy the same type of music as me".

"Oh, really, what'd that be"? It intrigued him.

"Light classical, nothing with guitars, nor drums".

"Silence it is then, anyway we can always fill the void with witty repartee".

She chuckled at that, "And what sort of amusing conversation did you have in mind, Mister Felton"?

"A surname, perhaps, your marital status. Do you have siblings, you know, the usual stuff".

"My full name is Alice Mawson, divorced, free as a bird right now. I've got a brother in South Africa, he's an engineer, another in Azerbaijan, he's a schoolteacher. You"?

"Single, no siblings".

"Wow, that didn't take long, any children"?

That caused him to pause for thought. He was now younger, physiologically than his four children. So once again he described the new Felton, not the one who had died,

"No, you"?

"Thankfully not, my marriage only lasted two years".

"Irreconcilable differences"?

"Sort of. I wanted to work, keep my money, he wanted to spend it all on beer and whores".

Felton did not feel that set right with the image of the young woman beside him. She was young, attractive. Why did her husband wander in such a brief time? It would not be good manners to pursue it, so he said nothing for a while. It seemed alright to convey his sadness at her betrayal, even if he doubted its validity.

"This car doesn't smell of fish", she objected suddenly.

He was surprised by the observation, "Should it? Why should it"?

"You said you were the owner of Felton's Fish. Surely your car would have picked up the aroma, the fabric of the upholstery, for example, fish has an all-pervading smell, doesn't it"?

"I never use my car for work. When I go onto the dock, I use the van".

"Sensible".

"Don't you drive, Alice"?

"Yes, of course, I do, but my car's in the garage at the moment. I took it in for a simple service. They found something that required parts they didn't have".

"Did they not offer you a loaner"?

"It's not that sort of garage, just a local chap who does it in his spare time. I thought about hiring but they're so expensive".

"You don't get a company car from GlaxoSmithKline"?

She laughed at that, "Those days are over Inigo, cutbacks, the world recession you know, why we even had to fight for the continuation of the petrol allowance a couple of years ago".

"We"?

"I'm in the union T&G actually, most English employees are, otherwise the Germans would walk all over us. Right, this has been nice but I'm going to have to ask you to pull up just here, close as you can to that man on the roadside".

"What"?! Felton began stupidly, "What do you mean pull up? Who the hell is he, your husband? I'm not stopping Mrs Mawson, I only agreed to give *you* a lift".

"I'm afraid I must insist", she returned calmly. As he glanced at her, he was astonished to see she had withdrawn a small calibre pistol from her handbag. "If you don't do exactly as instructed, I'll shoot you. Do you believe that, Inigo"?

He pulled up.

The man opened the back door driver's side, slipped inside. "Everything go to plan"? He asked simply.

"It was too easy", Alice confirmed, with satisfaction. The two knew one another. What was their relationship? What was going on?

Eleven.   Nicole was unchanged. She spoke perfect German, but other than that, Sellers could detect no other alterations to her. As they had previously arranged (but in English) they visited the Gewölbe, watched 'Eine Falte in der Zeit'. Sellers had found it very thought-provoking, the various paradox that could result in being able to traverse the fourth dimension had always fascinated him. They were driving back to his apartment. She had asked if they could return for drinks.

"After all", she had said, "Why endure the noise, clamour of a public house in the middle of Doncaster on a Saturday night, when you have an *intimate* bar for two in your place"?

The way she emphasized the word intimate had been enough to convince him it was a splendid idea. He wondered at young women of the age. They seemed to have less moral fibre than granny. Or was that simply a fallacy? Granny had been a *right little raver* in her heyday?

The car parked; the duo walked around the buildings up into the apartment. Sellers put a CD of Mozart piano concertos on the audio equipment, on low volume, turned on a couple of lamps rather than the light in the ceiling. It set the scene for seduction - Nicole Elv seduced. They kissed on the sofa, but before long, both breathless with unsatiated passion, she climbed to her feet led him to his bedroom, by her dainty hand. Undressed one another, half-naked, laughing, they fell on the bed, their mutual foreplay continued.

"I want you, all of you, completely", she murmured in his ear in soft Germanic tones, while the concerto continued in the room. It was already pretty obvious, he reflected, as he unclipped her brassiere. Her body was feminine perfection. He nibbled at it hungrily. Took one of her rubbery nipples into his mouth, felt it harden in excitement. Trailed down from the delightful mound to the flatness of her stomach, then lower still until he had run an eager tongue from her valley, into the delights of her forested chasm.

"Oh god, that feels *so* good", she murmured as his tongue did its work. After a while, she grasped his head, pulled it back to her mouth, promising,

"Kiss me, now it's your turn".

When it *was* his turn, he had to control himself not to explode into her mouth. Finally, she came back up to him, demanded huskily,

"I want you in me".

Afterwards, when both of them had erupted in almost unison, they lay together, their sweat mingling, both satiated.

"I don't normally behave like this, so soon. I don't want you to think I'm easy", she told him, "But there's just something about you, Tod, some quality. You're not like any other man I've ever met".

Balurzuura was suddenly in his mind for the first time since Sellers had requested some privacy for the evening.

'She could not know. She must talk figuratively. It was a very interesting process. The pair of you certainly shared mutual pleasure. Would you do it once more for my study log, this time be certain of impregnation. It would make everything complete'.

"Are you alright"? Nicole asked, "You seem to be miles away, you're not unhappy with me, are you"?

'Of course not. I've listened to what you said. I feel something special for you too, babe". *'Get out of my thoughts until tomorrow morning, Balu'!*

"Will the insemination lead to an egg Sellers, just tell me that before I do as bidden'?

'I'll tell you tomorrow, now go'.

"Thank goodness", she sighed, "How horrible it would've been if only one of us thought something incredible was going on".

'You don't know the half of it' he thought, as he kissed her, felt certain parts of him responding readily for a repeat performance.

Twelve. Felton glanced at the man through his rear-view mirror. Who barked,

"Just drive, we're going to Doncaster".

Only then did he observe the intruder was also wearing a beret sloped onto the back of his head.

"So this is a strategy", he thought aloud to both of them, "You planned this from the very beginning. You'd better introduce yourself, Mister".

"Let's get one thing straight from the very beginning", the man growled in response, "You're not giving orders, making suggestions or doing anything - other than what I koofing tell you, got it"?

"You get this", Felton retorted feeling unnaturally calm given the situation. "*I'm* at the wheel. *Frinsle me off*, I can drive this car into a ditch, river or turn it over. So let's have a bit of mutual respect for one another? Even if we are adversarial. Now, what's your name? Why want my car for a free ride"?

"You'd better tell him", Alice decided.

"Shut it", the man barked at her.

"That's the last time you talk to the lady like that", Felton snapped. "Get this into your head. I can kill all three of us in this machine, or you can start being civil, a little more cooperative. So, for the last time, who the koof are you? Why Doncaster"?

The man seemed to struggle with inner turmoil. His features twisted, contorted bizarrely. It was as though he might be bipolar. Finally, he replied, calmer in tone,

"I'm Einuur".

"Einuur Mawson? The lady's husband"?

This seemed to amuse the man who chuckled, with a sort of ironic tinge to the mirth.

"Just Einuur, no other name. You can call me Einuur, don't bother with a title. No, I'm not married to Ailuura".

"Ailuura"? Felton echoed, "You told me your name was Alice", this to the woman.

Mysteriously, she looked saddened, noted in leaden tones, "It *was* Alice".

"Was, what do you mean by that, you can't change your first name, only your last". Wondered then, '*Or at least you couldn't in the England, I knew before*'.

"How much do we tell him if we want his help"? Alice/Ailuura asked Einuur.

"He's a Mizaroid! What do *you* think"?

Felton gasped, "You know! You know what I am, so you must be ...".

"Zaromoid", Alice/Ailuura agreed instantly, while Einuur glowered at the back of her head. "The berets have a special lining, blocking your Mizaroa from detecting our tappings".

"I was told by my engimedic, whilst in learning sleep, that you're my enemy".

"It does not have to be that way", Alice put a delicate hand on his upper arm and squeezed it slightly. "You can come over to us".

"Come over to you, whilst I have a Mizaroa cerquibrum, how on the two planets could that possibly work"?

His question seemed to soften Einuur somewhat, for he said in a reasonable tone, "We could take you to our ship? Have our engimedic take out the Mizaroa, replace it with a Zaromi cerquibrum".

"Until I know which would be the least inconvenient to me, I prefer to wait-see, if it's all the same to you. Anyway, I believe we're currently going the wrong way, so I ask you again, what's your business in Doncaster? You could've gotten there in much simpler fashion. What use am I to you if I'm a man with a Mizaroa in my thoughts"?

"It's the Mizaroa that *makes* you useful", the woman told him, "We need you to get close to a man who also has one, isn't that why you're already going to that town"?

"I don't know, I haven't been told", Felton replied honestly enough. It was getting warm in the car. He switched on the air conditioning.

"Did you switch that on because lying makes you sweat"? Einuur wished to know, suspiciously.

"I'm not lying. All I've been told so far is to go there, wait for further instruction. What do you want with the man? Why can't you approach him yourself"?

"He may know about the berets", Ailuura told him, "Choose to attack us for being Zaromoid".

"I'm new to all this, so I don't know why he'd do so", Felton reasoned. "It seems the man you're talking about is your enemy. It'd also seem that you consider me one"?

"Aren't you"? Ailuura asked at once.

"Not at all", Felton returned earnestly, "The conflict is not between us, it's between them, I'm not interested enough to get involved in it".

"He's not yet subjugated"! Einuur said to the woman. There was the faint tinge of awe in his resonance. She looked impressed by the revelation.

"Subjugated"! Felton repeated, "What're you talking about? Who's gonna enslave me? No one will subjugate me".

"You know nothing of Balurzuura"?

"I don't know the names of any Zaromi, nor any Mizaroa".

"If he's not subjugated, he could be telling the truth", Ailuura offered, "He may not even know of Balurzuura or Moluura".

"I've heard of neither", Felton freely admitted, hoping his candour might go some way toward placating the unusual pair. "Who are they"?

"Moluura's our leader, supreme commander, fuhrer. Inhabits the body that used to be Michael Cowie, he's Zaromi". Einuur told him. Ailuura continued,

"Balurzuura is his mortal enemy, the leader of the Mizaroa. By now he'll have subjugated the body of one Tod Sellers, the man you're supposed to be on your way to protect".

"Protect? Protect from you two, by any chance? Are you assassins"? It was falling into place for Felton. "Why on Earth are you letting the aliens play out a war in your bodies, why are you letting them use you like that"?

Einuur sighed, "You don't get it yet, do you Felton's Fish? I 'm Einuur, I control the limbs, the actions of this humanoid body. Just as eventually, your cerquibrum will take over in yours, soon".

"No"! Felton declared, horrified, "That's not the deal I've with the engimedic, not the deal at all. I remain in charge, my cerquibrum is nothing more than a polite observer"

'A polite observer', Kim echoed in assurance.

"And she's just confirmed it". Felton added in triumph.

"She"! Ailuura sounded distracted momentarily, "You've an egg-layer in your mind"?

"Yes, a female. I call her Kim".

"Ridiculous name", Ailuura chuckled, "For a ridiculous situation, when she takes over I wonder what she'll make of her penis".

Einuur observed impatiently, "She might be male herself by then. I told you the Mizaroa were Sequentially Hermaphroditic".

"Let's hope this Mizaroa becomes a protogynic before she, he, or it takes over then" Ailuura grinned, "Otherwise Felton's Fish is going to be one very confused girl".

"Neither of you understands, do you"? Felton asked them then, "The very fact that I have a female cerquibrum proves the Mizaroa have no intention of turning me into some sort of alien zombie. Otherwise, why risk the confusion of sexual orientation? You two may be slaves, but I'll never be".

Einuur reminded, "You're not talking to slaves, Felton's Fish, you're talking to future *slave masters*".

"What've you done to Alice Mawson, Ailuura"? Felton suddenly asked the girl.

"She's in a figurative cell. I created a phrenic container of considerable strength, placed the humanoid cognition inside it, locked it with an acumen-padlock. She's not suffering, can get out when I desire it.

"Why lock her up in the discernitation-oubliette, anyway? Do you intend to commit crimes she wouldn't agree to"?

Einuur cut into the duologue, "This is all academic Felton's Fish. The point is you're going to protect Balurzuura. We've instructions to ... terminate his arrangement with Sellers".

"Firstly, stop calling me Felton's Fish, the name's Felton. Secondly, when you say terminate, you mean; cease, conclude, discontinue, eliminate, put an end to, don't you"?

"He means to do what we must, to end the war swiftly before more humanoid hosts are fatally damaged", Ailuura tried to convince him of their altruistic intent.

"Fatally damaged", Felton echoed. "Fatal as in an inconvenient, messy interval, or destroyed as in truly, dreadfully fatal"?

"Even with our technology we can't always bring some creatures back to their former levels of vitality", Einuur explained, "It depends what's left, the extent of the disintegration".

"Creatures"? Felton practically murmured, "Creatures, Kim, is that how you view us human beings? As just another animal living in this world"?

'No. We do not, but the Zaromi is not like the Mizaroa. Their thoughts are sometimes as alien to us as they seem to you'.

"What're y'doing"? Einuur demanded harshly, "Are you in the state of rapportation"?

"Rapportation"! Ailuura virtually spat, "It's a myth, Einuur, a piece of Mizaroa propaganda to weaken our resolve".

'Tell them we are', Kim thought to Felton, *'We are simpatico, empathic toward one another'*.

Felton repeated the message.

"Nonsense", Einuur forced a laugh.

'If it is, ask them to remove the tapping-shields. Let me see if I can reach their humanoid captive ratiocination'.

"If it's nonsense, take off the tapping-shields? Let my cerquibrum reach your humanoid captive ratiocination"? Felton requested.

"And have them polluted by Mizaroa coherencentive? Do'ya think we Zaromi are stupid, humanoid"? Einuur sneered.

"Humanoid", Felton repeated. "Humanoid, so you no longer consider yourself a member of humanity, Einuur? No! Of course, you don't. You've never been a human being, have you? You might have the body of a member of humanity, but you're devoid of it. I, for one, aren't. That means, due to our opposing natures, I must do all in my power to oppose you".

With that, Felton swung the wheel so violently the car swerved before it rolled over several times, coming to rest on the side verge, steam hissing from the fractured radiator.

Thirteen. Fortunately, when the explosion took place after Nicole left, Mrs Meggins from the Pie Shop was out for the day. The resultant crashing down of the roof caused only one fatality. One fabulous body torn, mashed to a gory mess of ruined flesh. It was that of the target, Tod Sellers.

'This is getting highly inconvenient, very tedious' was the first thought that entered Sellers' mind when his ruined brain reactivated eventually by the engimedic. The alien ministration to his physiological state, mental imperative, returned smoothly,

'We are taking steps to protect you better from the Zaromoid Sellers. Before plans could realize fruition, Major Alston struck again'.

'What's his problem? This extremely violent nemesis needs sorting out. Where's my distintegun or whatever you choose to call the ruddy thing'?

'Actually, we call the weapon a disinter-gun Sellers, it should be easy on your tongue'.

'I prefer it easy in my pocket', Sellers complained, *'Crack on with the koofing thing'!*

'It is proving an inappreciable amount perplexing due to the intricacy of miniaturization'.

'I should have thought that right up your alley'? Sellers was sarcastic, *'After all, you're pretty miniaturized yourself'.*

'I can assure you we are doing our very best. In most industrious fashion. Don't worry about your dwelling. We will transfer you to another branch in the lay-lines of the multiverse. We restored it'.

'That's all very well. I'm not used to these constant changes'. The human host of the alien was becoming embittered. *'One minute I have a brother, we're back in the Common Market, the next he disappears, then I find I have to learn German ...'*

'I know', Eahuura interrupted, *'I have received a full report from Királálynővonazóreginăcondător Balurzuura'.*

'Királálynővonazóreginăcondător'? Sellers echoed, his mind eidetic, *'What the devil does that very lengthy title convey if you please'?*

'I will answer that', Balurzuura's mind suddenly intruded upon the duologue, he must have been detecting the tappings all along, *'There is no direct corresponding translation into English Sellers, but the closest I can come to something you would recognize is authoritarian'.*

'You mean to say you're the Mizaroa Big Cheese, the Big Enchilada, the High Muckamuck around here. Why wasn't I told? It seems I've got the plum job while you lot have kept me in the dark'.

'For your peace of mind, your safety', Eahuura interjected.

'Oh yeah, we can see how that turned out'!

The other two minds in the trilogue were silent for a reflective moment before the engimedic informed,

'Now you know why you have been a constant target of the Zaromoid. It is not you whom they wish to eliminate permanently. Rather, Királálynővonazóreginăcondător Balurzuura is their primary target'.

'That's not a comfort, not at all. How come it never puts us out for the permanent count'?

'To date, I have sent a tappings transmission back to the ship in time for our remains to be recovered before putrefaction had become too advanced for your brain to be revitalized. It was close this time. Our closest agents only just extracted your crushed skull from the wreckage of the building. Your brains were running out through ...'.

'Yes, yes spare me the gory details thank you', Sellers cut the Királálynővonazóreginăcondător short. His stomach churned at the thought of it. Or at least the nerve messages his brain generated to do so were deigning to convince him of the sensation. *'So, is it back to square one, do you have to build me yet another Adonis? Do I have to journey to Doncaster again? See what my apartment looks like in Reality Zeta'?*

'Reality Zeta'?

'The sixth letter in the Greek alphabet. The sixth version of the multiverse that I'll have inhabited. By the by there are only twenty-four letters in total'!

'The multiverse is infinite', Eahuura pointed out.

'Yes, but my patience isn't. I don't intend to be killed an infinite number of times, thank you very much'

.

'To that end, we may have something approaching a solution', the Királálynővonazóreginăcondător of the Mizaroa informed him, *'This time we have another reanimated humanoid to accompany you, to guard us at all times'.*

'A bodyguard, what's the guy's name, do I meet him right away'?

'Please let me reanimate the humanoid shell for your mind? Transport your quiddity into it from Reality Zeta. You can then meet a fellow humanoid recently reanimated following a fatal accident', the engimedic requested.

Sellers obligingly fell mentally silent, thinking in a chasm of nothingness was not his idea of a good time. The state he proceeded into even less filled with sensation. It was not disquieting, for it was nothing. Oblivion, like every person who had ever walked the Earth, he had experienced oblivion before, antecedently of birth.

Fourteen. The pain in Lady Oxenford of Heartbridge's limbs was the worst she had ever experienced. She had known pain! It had been her bleak companion for the entirety of her adult life. She remembered grimly the time the family doctor had been to see her. During her very difficult adolescence, she simply put all the discomfort down to the state of becoming a woman. Her mother, the lady of Heartbridge, had not accepted all the aches, discomforts, pains her daughter had complained of. They summoned doctor Ottershaw to the house.

The good doctor had been the family physician for two generations was growing into the autumn of his years. He had dispensed with his surgery some years before but accepted the odd private consultation; it being one such that he never turned down. He enjoyed the house itself, for one. A grand mansion place that, in an earlier time, had belonged to the mill owner of Heartbridge. Nestled on the edge of the Calder River in West Yorkshire, Heartbridge had been a milling community, the surrounding blackened chimneys still grappled their way into the sky like the claws of some stone, mortar, brick beast.

They built Heartbridge House from good Yorkshire stone, not some baked block that would moulder away after the second century. Its roof was good welsh slate, held in place by verdigrised copper. The inside was vast swathes of decorated plaster of Paris, alabaster, mainly painted pure white. Family photographs broke the constant visages of albescence up in the more modern room's canvases by <u>Ruscha</u>, <u>Yayoi Kusama</u>, <u>Muniz, Serra</u>, <u>Gerhard Richter</u>, <u>Takashi Murakam</u>i, Major Roxbrough. There were also very large sculptures standing on the oak wood floors. No matter how modern the pieces, the general impression was always of a bygone age when the British Empire ruled the world (or most of what counted).

Having observed the pieces, they forced Ottershaw to admit that the leather furnishings looked contemporary. The huge flat cathode-ray television in the lounge proclaimed the house to belong firmly in the twentieth century. The butler had shown the good doctor into the opulent splendour of the property. It delighted him to meet Lady Oxenford once more, her female heir to the Heartbridge title. Lord Oxenford had passed away, a victim of consumption, shortly after the female baby had blessed their union.

Doctor Ottershaw", Lady Oxenford cried at his entrance, "So long since we've seen you, which is a good thing yet a pity, you really must come to the house socially, you'll always be welcome. What would you like by refreshment before you give your consultation"?

"Have you some lemonade by any chance"? The medical man desired to know.

"I'm certain we have, if not Cook, will make some freshly for you, Doctor. Now come, sit down while the butler fetches your beverage. I've no idea of the latest local news. You must bring the two of us up to date"?

Ottershaw glanced at the pubescent young woman at Lady Oxenford's side, reasoned privately that the sick looking individual probably could not have cared less about the local gossip. The poor thing had dark smudges beneath watery eyes. Eyes that regarded him rather like the orbs of a cow being led to the slaughter. He knew then that it was she, rather than her mother, that they had summoned him to see.

True to the respectful manner (and the fact he was being paid by the hour) he chatted away with Lady Oxenford until she was ready to get around to matters medical. Finally, after two glasses of lemonade (freshly made, he noted) fine stem-ginger biscuits, the good lady came to the point of his calling.

"It's Kyla, Doctor", she began.

'No wonder I was struggling to remember the child's name' Ottershaw wondered, *'It's one of those fashionable created, also rather silly'*.

"She's torpid, lacking energy says she's in pain".

Ottershaw transferred his full attention to the girl, asking in a kindly tone, "When does it hurt, Lady Kyla and where"?

"Most of the time", Kyla had told him, "In my joints, my back, mostly at night when I lie down. It keeps me awake. I can't get a good night's sleep for it. It makes me miserable".

Ottershaw nodded sympathetically, pulled out a stethoscope from his bag, "Is it worse during your monthlies"?

The question caused Kyla to blush fiercely, "I've only really had three! One when I was fifteen, then two last year, none this".

"And you are how old"?

"Seventeen".

Ottershaw frowned, asked, "Please disrobe to the waist so I can examine you. I expect you'll be most comfortable doing this in your bedroom. Call me when you're ready"?

Kyla blushed a deep scarlet, asked, "How much am I to take off"?

"Everything, I wish to listen to your heart, check your blood pressure, examine your bust, eliminate lymphadenitis while I am about it, you can throw on your dressing gown until I do so, your mother can be a chaperone to make certain you are comfortable being examined by me".

"I'm not comfortable being examined by you", Kyla confessed, her misery increasing by the very second.

"You'll need to be examined if you want an accurate diagnosis", Lady Oxenford stated firmly. "Go do as the doctor instructed".

The girl left looking distressed at thought of the entire procedure, plainly finding it highly embarrassing, although it was the doctor who had helped her into the world.

The two remaining chatted for a few minutes more. Ottershaw rose to get on with the examination, Lady Oxenford accompanying him up the staircase, toward where both knew Kyla to be. Seated on the bed looking very forlorn, in her dressing gown as advised. The doctor took out a sphygmomanometer, from his bag, took her blood pressure firstly, with the stethoscope from around his neck he listened to her heart from the front before requesting the girl drop the robe, to allow him to do the same from the back. Finally, horror of horrors, he went back to the front, examined her breasts, lymph nodes.

After what seemed like an age, he instructed,

"You can get dressed now, Lady Kyla. Your mother, her Ladyship and I will be back in the lounge. They had only reached the stairs when Lady Oxenford asked,

"What did that tell you then Doctor"?

"It's too early to say Lady Oxenford, but I've found enough to cause me some concern. I'd like your daughter admitted to Heartbridge Infirmary for a week. For a battery of tests, at the end of which I should be able to give you an informed prognosis".

"Do you know anything now? Do you suspect a fatal condition"?

"I expect nothing immediately fatal, but more than that, I don't wish to say just yet. Will you be wanting a private room at H.I."?

"Of course, give her the best viable treatment Doctor, she is the last of the Oxenford line".

Two weeks later, the three of them found themselves in Kyla's private room in H.I. Ottershaw had just arrived, his features giving nothing away.

"Well, Doctor? You've conducted all your tests. What's wrong with my daughter"?

Clipboard in hand, glasses flashing in the sunlight, Ottershaw came directly to the point. "Lady Kyla is suffering from acute oxalate poisoning".

"I beg your pardon Doctor Ottershaw"! Lady Oxenford was most irate, "But that's impossible, no one is trying to kill Kyla, what on Earth are you suggesting"?

The good doctor took a seat, began a somewhat lengthy explanation. "Lady Kyla has been suffering from joint pain, inflammation. She has been slow to heal when accidentally injured, I believe? She currently complains of fatigue, insomnia, her cycle is erratic. My diagnosis has only been possible after extensive (expensive too) tests conducted exhaustively this last week. The reason it took so long for me to conclude was that every reported case of oxalate poisoning is unique. The signs, symptoms are widely dissimilar from person to person. Thusly, no recognized symptom pattern is the telltale sign of oxalate trouble".

"But you said poison, Doctor? You said Kyla has been poisoned"?

"If you allow me to continue Lady Oxenford"? Ottershaw requested did so prompted by the resultant silence, "Medical tests for oxalates are rare. We've conducted them in this case because of funds provided, the standard of care I've undertaken. They could have been extremely invasive, or inconclusive, or both. Here, I have some small knowledge of the subject, thusly performed the tests with a minimum of intrusion - when dealing with Lady Kyla. Urinary oxalate, for example, is rarely measured at all. When done, it's tested badly, more often than not. Due to inadequate preparation, handling of urine samples before the chemical analysis. The same holds true for testing other tissues—blood, skin, bone. Basic health care providers don't order these tests because they aren't aware that oxalates can irritate the nerves, harm connective tissues, irritate the digestive tract, trigger inflammation. Many other, better-known causes can create similar symptoms, so they assume the problems result from something else".

"I am not creating an issue with any of your techniques, Doctor, but you said poisoned"?

"I examined your daughter's joints most thoroughly, Lady Oxenford", Ottershaw went on as though no interruption had occurred. "The sharp, tiny oxalate crystals so often *physically* similar that they're easy to confuse with other crystals in tissue samples were present. My tests didn't tell me much regarding severity, however, even then. The severity of oxalate build-up in Lady Kyla's body does not correlate with the measured amounts of oxalate in her blood or urine. Though she undoubtedly exhibits all the symptoms of oxalate problems, she may have frequent usually brief spikes in oxalate in her urine, perhaps in the blood as well. But it is impractical to measure frequently enough to detect these patterns under normal circumstances. So this pattern cannot accurately be predicted or even considered.

During severe periods, the kidneys can be so full of oxalate, that it will get trapped there. Not show up in the urine. Oddly enough, the timing of symptoms will not coincide with the consumption of high-oxalate foods. That is because *symptoms may flare up* when Kyla's body releases stored oxalates, which happens *when she will not be eating them*. Oxalate poisoning, like many other forms of poisoning, starts as a silent - gradually progressive disease. It affects each person differently. When the symptoms finally surface, thusly interfere with one's life, some people may seem to tolerate high-oxalate foods, while others - clearly don't".

"So what foods are we talking about"? Kyla found her voice at last.

"Potatoes, lettuce, watercress, rhubarb, beetroot, spinach, chilli, pizza, soy, almonds, all nuts, in fact. Carrots, celery, beets, alas - chocolate. Although, I must add that even among health experts, there is no consensus about which foods contain how much oxalate, which other foods to replace them with. For example, data from before 1980 - even data published by the USDA - contain measurement errors that make them unreliable. Then there is your mother's hothouse ..."?

"What about my hothouse, Doctor"? Lady Oxenford snapped, it was her pride and joy,

"It contains several genera of flowering plants in the Araceae - family, namely Philodendron and Dieffenbachia, merely

71

touching those plants without gloves can lead to oxalate poisoning in one susceptible to such".

"Just tell me this", Lady Oxenford demanded finally. "Can you cure Kyla? If she never goes in the hothouse, never eats the foodstuffs you've mentioned, what then, will this poisoning reduce, or hopefully even vanish"?

"I'm sorry Lady Oxenford, but I can offer no medical guarantee", Ottershaw admitted. "Now we know what Kyla is suffering from, we can attempt to reduce the effects. As I said earlier, even among health experts, there is no consensus about which foods contain how much oxalate, which other foods to replace them with. We can only continue to monitor Kyla's health closely do the best for her".

"How"? Kyla suddenly cried, "How can you tell me what not to eat, what to eat instead when you don't even have a definite list? What will happen to me? What will happen if I get worse, how bad will it become"?

Ottershaw had the grace to shrug, "If we can't manage the symptoms, they progress. You could suffer such joint pain that movement would become extremely painful, possibly even loss of mobility. We can help you sleep with the help of medication, but I would have grave concern for your kidneys. It hasn't come to that yet though, not by a long way".

At first, the careful diet seemed to reap fantastic improvement. It was in these successful days of management that Kyla's mother, Lady Oxenford, had an announcement to make that would shape part of her daughter's future.

"Now you're feeling so much better I've decided to have a party for you", came the revelation. "You must invite your friends. I'll invite mine too to make a nice number of guests".

"I don't want a party", Kyla informed her lone parent simply. Then added, "And I don't have any friends".

"Oh nonsense", came the response, "It will cheer you greatly. Of course you have friends, friends from school".

Kyla had attended the Balcourt School for Young Ladies as a girl. A boarding school from which she had emerged in her teens with no successful academia to her name. She had not lacked intelligence, merely industry. Lessons had bored her, she had taken no interest in them, feeling her future set, anyway. She was the product of *old money*, where a decent education was by the by, sometimes even a hindrance.

"I hated school", Kyla reasoned aloud, "And I hated most of the spoiled little madams that went there. Most of them will be impregnated, married off by now, with a brat hanging around their necks.".

Lady Oxenford pursed her lips in disapproval of her daughter's crude observations. She had been wanting to do that quite a good deal throughout the past couple of months. Her mind made up. When Lady Oxenford decided something, there was little in the world that could shake her resolution.

In the end, Kyla agreed to invite two of her friends from school, the two she had hated least of all. Lady Oxenford invited the rest of the guest list. This included other Middle England, relatives, some so distant that they had rarely ever met. She sent out invitations over the social network. The ratio of acceptance to rejection was about equal. Ironically of the duo, Kyla had agreed to include on the list, both accepted. Even Madison Reed of Illinois, whom Kyla would have thought to be in America, could promote attendance, due to her stay in the Lake District at the time. The other young woman was Lady Jennifer Cove of Kentmere, who, according to the younger Lady Oxenford, was - *a real stuck-up bitch!* When she read on twitter that both would indeed attend the social gathering, it dismayed Kyla in no small amount. She went through her wardrobe in complete dismay, had nothing suitable for the occasion.

Upon demanding a new frock for the grand accession, her mother took it mistakenly as a show of enthusiasm, promptly whisked her off to Leeds. There she bought a lovely garment from *Dress2Party, a Jovani Platinum* in cornflower-blue, that went right to the floor. A delicate mass of *strapless jersey dress with a chiffon train,* an absolute steal at $807.96. Of course, she also had to have some ball slippers to wear under it. At Schuh, she selected some powder-blue Majorca High Heels that were reduced to a handsome $60.59. Finally, the handbag, a Ted Baker (but of course) in pale-sky, a bow detail satin clutch bargain at only $114.47. Thusly, she was ready to face the rigours of the ordeal. It had only cost her mother the paltry sum of $983.02. Kyla had agreed to use her make-up, wear her underwear to save the Lady's purse. She bet those bitches Madison and Jennifer had cost their parents more if they intended to turn up!

The promises to attend increased. The guest list was finally roughly finalised at sixty-five. Kyla had never realised she was so popular, possibly because she was not! Strangely, she was rather curious to see how Lady Jennifer of Kentmere and Madison Reed of Illinois had turned out. She remembered Madison as a high cheek-boned almond-eyed girl who had mercilessly given young lads a tough time with her sudden mood swings, capricious nature. While Jennifer, her dark good looks, had drawn plenty of admiring glances, she had considered none good enough to be her school sweetheart. Kyla herself had neither high cheekbones nor dark good looks. The only reason either of the two had suffered her - she was competition for neither in popularity nor brightness.

The trio were now nearly eighteen, had not seen one another for over twelve months. Kyla little doubted the other two had gone on to further education, while she had barely waited to escape Balcourt School for Young Ladies, never to sit in a classroom ever after. The time of the event drew nearer, several lorries arrived at Heartbridge House. Conveyed a variety of consumables, drinks, plus extra linen, towels, for several of the revellers would stay at Lady Oxenford's the day of the party, the following day until they were once more vital enough to travel. It would not be a debauched excuse for drunkenness, excess, such was not Lady Oxenford's style. Some guests would be certain to overdo things, yet others would have a great distance to travel to and from Yorkshire. So Oxenford arranged for some twenty-three to stay until the afternoon following the revelries.

On the morning of the party, the first of the guests who would stay the weekend arrived. Kyla was in her bedroom, having arisen late, knowing the night would be a late one. It rudely interrupted her from some quiet reverie in her bath when the loudest, most booming voice that anyone could give rent to, *landed* in the hall. Having met the American in question before, she knew her mother's long time friend, Prentiss J. Hackentyre, had arrived. Hackentyre was from Dearborn, Michigan, *big in steel*. He was the CEO of A.K. Steelholding, the largest producer of steel in the world. After meeting Hackentyre for a few minutes, one knew all one ever wanted to know about the production of steel. After several longer, one knew all one did not wish to know! If one stayed in the company of Prentiss J. Hackentyre longer than that, then one knew everything about steel in America that one would hope to forget!

Kyla dried herself carefully, her limbs feeling a little eased by the hot water, despite having taken her naproxen sodium (Aleve) just after eating her morning tray. She never breakfasted with Lady Oxenford, preferring to greet the day with some contemplative silence, the company of her cat, Lucy Fir, a small ginger moggy with a temper to match her name. Sighing, she slipped on brassiere, pants, threw a white boho shirt on which boasted pretty lace down the chest, slit sleeves held up by only two inches of material on the shoulders. It was her favourite shirt for the nice weather. To this, she added a pair of boho pants in large black and white houndstooth.

Thusly prepared she went down to meet the human whirlwind that was the American CEO of the *gordamn biggest steel company in the world*. It would prove a momentous day for Kyla, the most significant detail of which being that it was the day she first met Tab. Prentiss J. Hackentyre had yet to progress from the hall as Kyla descended the staircase which ended in the same area. He was busily shouting to Lady Oxenford, he had no concept at all of what constituted an *indoor voice*. Already her mother was looking severely fatigued, probably wondering why she had invited the friend of her youth. Kyla then noticed the young man just behind the magnate's shoulder a thunderbolt smote her! Her heart immediately began to hammer in her chest, her pupils dilated, she began to glow (ladies never perspire). She could not take her eyes off the object of her immediate obsession. Few men can be described as gorgeous, it is usually a description used for the fairer sex, the most notable exceptions being Ed Harris, George Clooney, Errol Flynn. The young man who Kyla was then transfixed by was decidedly in that bracket too. He had film-star looks, the faint slant about him of a young very blonde Brad Pitt. Although in Kyla's somewhat biased opinion, if the two had been standing side by side, then Pitt would have looked comparatively plain. Finally, her feet began to obey her brain she descended the rest of the way into the hall. Her temporary paralysis had been nothing to do with her condition either, she had been struck by cupid's arrow, instantly, hopelessly in love for the first time in her young life. For his part, Tab noticed the pale, rather timid young lady only when she had fully descended into the hall to remain standing behind Lady Oxenford. He mused it was rather strange clothing for a maid to wear until he heard the mousy little creature use the term 'mother' thusly surprised to learn that this was the young Lady Oxenford. His appreciation of her immediately became realigned; this young woman was *worth* getting to know, this young woman was from *old money*! In his some-would-say elegant drawl, he demanded, when Prentiss J. Hackentyre breathed in,

"And who is this delightful young creature at your elbow, Lady Oxenford"?

Her Ladyship spun around, detected the fruit of her loins for the first time. She gasped in relief. It might well be an opportunity to escape, escape from the verbal clutches of the CEO of the *gordamn biggest steel company in the world*.

"There you are Kyla", she smiled in a combination of affection, alleviation, "Prentiss, Tab, allow me to introduce you to my daughter, the next Lady of Oxenford and Heartbridge House, Kyla. Kyla, this is Prentiss J. Hackentyre, as you might remember? This young man is his sister's son, nephew Tab. Mister T. Mahula".

Tab eased past his uncle, taking Kyla's hand, pressed it to his beautiful lips. She was so dizzy she almost swooned away at the very British show of decorum, gentility. He looked up into the timid little thing's eyes, felt compelled to explain,

"My mother and Uncle Prentiss' sister married a Hawaiian Prince, hence my somewhat unusual surname, my Lady".

"My lady"! Prentiss howled with laughter. Prentiss J. Hackentyre had an immense chest. His laughter was as the boom of a medieval cannon, "This ain't the eighteenth century Tab. I'm certain Kyla will not mind you calling her by her Christian name, ain't that right Cornelia"?

Lady Oxenford winced at his crudity, but admitted, "Since we are now an American state, Prentiss, I suppose what the Americans say, goes, is that not correct"?

"Thar ya go, only a satellite state at that, Cornelia", Prentiss J. Hackentyre was quick to point out. "Now then, ar don't mind admitting I'm fair parched, so when is Jeeves going to get me one of those poofy lager-beers you have ovah here"?

Jeeves, whose real name was Mellers, stepped forward, suggested grimly, "Morning tea is to be served in the morning room directly, mister Hackentyre".

"Ar don't want any of that Paki rubbish" Prentiss J. Hackentyre bellowed, totally ignorant of the fact of any possibility of the existence of etiquette, blatantly racist to boot, "Get me a man's drink Jeeves, one of those stupid Schol things they have in Scaninaviaa".

Lady Oxenford came to Meller's rescue, "Get Prentiss a pint of Weihenstephan Hefe Weissbier, Mellers".

"Ruddy Krauts, you wouldn't think we whopped their sorry asses back in 42-45 would ya Tab, they sell their stuff all ova the world? Still, forgive and forget, eh".

"While you are refreshing yourself, Uncle", the gorgeous nephew began, "I was wondering if Lady Oxenford would allow me the honour of taking a walk in this lovely British morning air, showing me the gardens".

"The gardens are truly lovely this time of year", Lady Oxenford enthused, "But perhaps Kyla would do the honours for me? I have so much else to supervise"?

Tab smiled. He had meant the junior of the two ladies all along. Gallantly he held out an arm, Prentiss J. Hackentyre (big in steel) hollered an objection,

"But you ain't even unpacked yet, yer rascal"?

"I would hope that one of the staff would be so kind as to do that for me", Tab returned smoothly, whilst at the same instant Lady Oxenford was instructing one maid to do just that.

In a daze, Kyla looped her arm through his. Together they escaped the clutches of the CEO of the *gordamn biggest steel company in the world.*

Outside, the birds were proclaiming their joy at the beautiful sunny weather. The soft sound of flying insects accompanied them. Kyla led Tab to the prettiest of the gardens, a lawned area surrounded by borders of flowers, their scent thick in the air. It was a heady mixture for a girl who had spent months in her rooms in the House. She felt intoxicated by the entire experience.

"Oh look hybacinths, I've never seen them outdoors before", the beautiful youth told her.

"Hy-a-cinths", Kyla corrected almost absently, emphasizing the syllables, "They're called hyacinths".

"Yea, they're nice", he did not sound as though he had noticed the correction.

"And them there they're white Ani-mones, I like them too".

The second time Kyla did not bother to correct his mispronunciation of anemones, maybe it was his accent that was fooling her ears.

Later, he admired the Cam-Poola Meteor (campanula Meteora), the Ace-toors (asters) and the Deloss-Sperma (delosperma). On seeing the latter, Kyla did not know how she kept a straight face. She coughed, asked him,

"Would you like to see the pond"?

"Would y'all wowee a real pond, like how big darlin'"?

Basking in the nomenclature of affection, she said meekly, "Probably not as big as the ones in America, but we have swans, ducks, of course".

"Let's go see the ducks then darlin'". It seemed Tab had settled on the title as the one he was going to address her in from that moment onward. Kyla certainly did not mind.

He seemed delighted with the pond, the swans especially. Tab had the almost innocent wonder of a child, but Kyla found it appealing, for at the school she had attended, the exact opposite had been the reaction of the girls to most things.

"Oh really, how very exciting", had been Madison's sarcastic rejoinder at almost every end and turn. Jennifer, equally without wonder.

"Yawn yawn, yawn, got a cigarette"? Had been her usual reaction to new experiences.

By the time they got back to the house, Kyla had decided she was going to fall in love with the half exotic Tab Mahula. They reached the hall, breathless, glowing from the sun, breathless because the house was at the top of a steep rise. Their return coincided with Lady Jennifer Cove of Kentmere's arrival. She of the dark good looks, impressive bust. She looked at the returning couple with mild disinterest, before a quick double-take afforded Tab a radiant smile. It caused Kyla's heart to sink. Her bust was modest when compared to Jennifer's, but then most girls were - comparatively.

'Jennifer's probably cost about $4 thousand', Kyla thought bitterly, as she watched Tab for his reaction to it, the girl

attached to it. Strangely, he gave a polite nod, returned his attention to she – Kyla.

"I know we don' have no traditional dancin' no more darlin', but will you save some dances' fo me too-night"? He asked her in his rather fatiguing drawl.

Her heart leapt fairly out of her chest at that moment of super-sweet triumph over one of her chief adversaries. Tab had preferred her to the rather pneumatic Jennifer.

"I will, Tab. Now we must freshen up for luncheon, served in the day-room".

He kissed her hand again and then took his leave. Both she and Jennifer watched his divine butt go up the staircase to his room.

"Kyla, you dark horse", the Lady of Kentmere observed, "I gave that gorgeous hunk one of my best smiles, he returned his attention to you. Are you doing him by any chance"?

Kyla told the most incredible lie, "Oh, as often as his stamina can manage it. You can have him when I'm finished if you want".

"Kyla Coleman (though Lady Oxenford had been married twice, Kyla had never changed her name from her father's - to her step-father's) you saucy mare you, when we were at school you never showed the slightest interest in boys, indeed you never showed the slightest interest in anything".

"That changed with my first climax", Kyla tried to say that without laughing, "After one, you always want more, don't you"?

"Well yes, I suppose, but you know ladies don't do that sort of thing too often, don't you"?

"With Tab, if I don't have a multiple, he has to try again with more effort".

"You divine slut", the Lady of Oxenford was in awe of Kyla, "I am soo jealous, wait till Madison hears about this".

"Oh, it's just between the two of us. You must promise not to tell her"? Kyla requested, knowing that Jennifer would do so, no matter what she swore.

"I promise, of course", the two of them were both lying.

Kyla asked a maid to show Jennifer to her room, went to freshen up herself. It was the happiest she had been since her diagnosis. The oxalate poisoning was not uppermost in her mind. A further delight awaited her at luncheon. Tab had waited outside the Morning-room, then escorted her in, insisting upon sitting next to her. Fortunately, Lady Oxenford was unaware of what was taking place, labouring as she was under the constant barrage of her old friend Prentiss J. Hackentyre. The steel magnate seemed suddenly to notice another in the room, was insistent that Lady Oxenford introduce him to,

'The young Lady Oxenford's raarther interesting looking friend'.

It was Jennifer, naturally, the *randy old goat* (as Kyla then thought of him) spent the rest of lunch having a conversation with her chest. He was old enough to be Jennifer's father, but also rich enough that the Lady of Kentmere did not care!

Kyla spent the afternoon in the company of Tab, who seemed happy to spare no time for any other guest. Those who would stay overnight continued to arrive, mainly Lady Oxenford's friends. During that period, Madison landed on the main front lawn in her father's helicopter. It seemed mister Reed of Illinois was also big in something or other. The two former school chums found one another. Jennifer immediately confided in her best friend in all the world that Kyla and a young, very handsome young man were having regular, satisfactory sex. As Jennifer put it, they were *at it like rabbits.*

Kyla just hoped they would not decide to question Tab on the subject, but he seemed content to be Kyla's exclusively constant companion. Before she had time to think about it, she dinnered before getting ready for the evening carousal. Bathed, dressed with care, once in her new things thought even she was not without some attraction. As she floated down the staircase to the *Ballroom*, the ubiquitous Tab was at the foot of them to greet her.

"Y'all look right purty Miss Kyla darlin' and no mistake", was his philosophical opinion. He was not the sharpest knife in the drawer, but he seemed enamoured of the young Lady of Heartbridge. She returned that feeling magnified several-fold.

The two had cocktails, danced, took the air on the terrace. They were together exclusively. Kyla proceeded through it all as though in a fantastic dream.

"Ar've beena thinkin' when ma Uncle returns to the good ole U.S. Of A. Ar might stay on a wharle", he proclaimed to her delight. "There's ar meetin' at Doncaster on Monday and there's a filly runnin' there as cannot lose".

"Doncaster? Meeting"? Kyla was out of her depth. "Oh! You mean horse racing"?

"Ar surely does darlin', would ya'all like to come with me to see the ponies a-runnin'"?

"I believe I'd love to".

"Ar'll get me a hotel bookin' then and we can go together".

"You don't need a hotel, you could stay at Heartbridge, as *my* guest". Kyla decided, "I've never had a guest before. Mother is always saying that I should. She wants me to mix with people my age".

"That's mighty decent of you", Tab smiled, "Ar accept".

To Kyla's amazed delight, he then took her in his manly arms, kissed her slowly with tender gentleness. At that moment, she knew she, beyond any shred of doubt, was hopelessly in love.

Kyla did not sleep that night for two reasons. The first was her feelings for Tab, but the second was the ache in her joints from all the dancing. She accepted both gladly. Her life had just become worth living for the first time since childhood. She stayed in bed until six arose abluted before drifting painfully down to breakfast. Of course, the servants were up. They all arose at five. She broke her fast alone. Kyla went into the gardens at the back of the house, seating herself in the watery sun, reflected upon the events of the day before. Could it be that Tab was simply the kindest of kind young men who thought to spend time with her to make the party go wonderfully for her? Or did he have some reason to seek her out? Namely, that her gentle nature, mien, was a gem of attractiveness in the fields of mediocrity, through which he had been searching? Was Tab the sort of man who wanted a soul mate rather than a playmate? She could only ardently wish it to be so with every ounce of her fibre. Were it the case, she would be more devoted to him than any woman had been to a man. An hour passed in that sort of private fantasy. Slowly, the other guests filtered down. Those who had a long journey to make were the ones who were rising early to begin their travels. Lady Jennifer Cove of Kentmere was one of them. The instant she spied Kyla through the French windows, she gesticulated that the young Lady of Heartbridge join her. Reluctantly, Kyla did so. Pleasantly surprised when she did.

"You looked very glamorous at the party last night, Darling. That gown was simply divine. With the blond hunk on your arm, you made the rest of us quite jealous", Jennifer told her through a mouthful of cornflakes.

"Really"? Kyla was so pleased to take the compliment, "Thanks Jen, that's nice of you to say".

"Don't mention it. It's the truth", came the sincere response, "I don't think it overjoyed Madison that you were the centre of attention, but it was your turn darling you took it well. Do you think you and the American will start seeing one another seriously"?

"I'm not sure if I want that sort of thing just yet", Kyla lied. "I thought next year I might travel. You know, see something of Europe before the Americans carve it up into newly formed states".

"That sounds intriguing. You must let me know if you decide to do that because I would be pleased to join you in Italy, or Germany".

"If I decide not to get tied down then, I'll text you on Twitface".

"I hope you do darling, now I'm going to rush off, catch the train home, I enjoyed the party, thank your mother for me - will you"?

"Of course".

Jennifer leaned over, made the kissing noise next to Kyla's cheek. She had never shown such friendliness before.

Two hours later, Madison Reed of Illinois dragged herself out of bed, sought Kyla, "Come, talk to me while I have some *brekkie*, will you, Honey"?

Kyla was pleased, so to do, for Tab had still not surfaced. She felt lost without him.

"I have to say you and the guy from the U.S. Were 'the' couple of the ball last night, Kyla babe. I loved the frock. Tab is some catch if you want to keep him".

"That's decent of you to admit, Madison. After all, you've not been so complimentary toward me in the past, have you"?

"You know how it is in school and all, but you certainly were the star last night for sure. I think, just between you and me, that Jennifer was seething, she likes to be the centre of attention. So when will you guys tie the knot"?

"It's too soon for me to define myself by getting married. I was thinking of doing some travelling this summer giving myself chance to think about my options".

"Sounds good too", the American admitted, "Say I'd love to meet you in Austria and Luxembourg for a few days. They're to become American states in the next few years. Will you let me know if you decide to tour"?

"Surely", Kyla grit her teeth at the Americanese, "If I take a tour I'll text you on Twitface".

"Daddy will have sent the chopper by now, so I really must go pack. If I don't see you again, keep in touch, Honey"?

The two of them made the kissing noise on each other's cheeks. Tab appeared at eleven fifteen, looking bleary-eyed, dehydrated,

"Ooh babe I think I overdid it on the sauce last night. My head is ringing like a drum". (Ouch)

"Come and have some black coffee, burnt toast"? Kyla offered ministration to him. He shook his head at the suggestion.

"Coffee's fine, but I'll have some ham and eggs, the eggs done-over-easy, then a pineapple juice for the sucrose. That's the way to cure a headache. Do you have aspirin"?

Kyla felt gratified that Tab had made Heartbridge House feel like home to himself, even in the short time he had been there. She wondered if he would consider living there permanently, as the next Lord of Heartbridge, though she did not relish the idea of changing her name from Coleman to Mahula, then again she did not need to if she did not want, it was the modern way. She led Tab into the morning room, gave Elsie his order while she poured him some coffee. Elsie, who had a retroussé nose at the best of times, held it even higher, sniffed her disapproval at a breakfast order at practically noon. She also informed her young ladyship no aspirin was in the House, only Paracetamol or Brufen.

"Parraa ceetamol"! Tab echoed, "Poison, dear me, the most poisonous drug you can have in this fine place. But I'll take a couple of Brufen if you rightly purlease".

"There's a Fayre at Bingdon Moor this afternoon, Tab", Kyla said as he eagerly demolished the bacon and eggs. "Would you like to go"?

"I would surely luurv to go darlin' only my allowance for the month has run out. Uncle Prentiss is strict about such things. It is a pain in the butt. Anyway, I don't have transport of ma own as I came to Heartbridge with him".

"I have my allowance. You'd be my guest, don't worry about money", Kyla offered. "As for transport, I have my little 124 Spider".

"What in tarnation is a Spider"?

"Come see".

She led him to the garage showed him the 138 bhp Fiat 2-seater sport in racing red that had cost her mother $36,328.64.

"Go get your purse, then what are we a-waitin' fur"? he enthused, jumping lithely over the passenger door straight into the seat beyond.

It caused Kyla, not the slightest hint of disquiet that he so readily accepted that she would fund the entire trip. If Prentiss J. Hackentyre was mean to him, then she would gladly pay on that occasion to have his fabulous company. As they sped down Otley Road, doing an easy fifty, Tab enthused,

"Say this lil-ole car is fabumazing. I'll bet it can do a ton on the highway. Have you opened the baby up yet Kyles"?

Kyle's. Kyle's. He had a nickname for her already. How she loved him, she asked,

"You mean 100 mph on the motorway? That's illegal Tab, I'd lose my license if I got caught".

"It's around the same in the you ess". He admitted, "But I'll wager there's a few as don't take no never-mind to that".

"While I do. Take a never mind. I want to keep my license".

He laughed uproariously at that, "Hell Kyle's we'll have you speaking Yankee afore the end of the day or I'm a limey, so help me".

Bingdon Moor Fayre was a mish-mash of a gipsy caravan fairground, a huge flea-market stuck on the side of it. As expected, well attended, Tab was far more amazed by the stalls of junk than a fair he had probably seen the like of several times in America. Like a delighted infant, he kept picking up items from various stalls, exclaiming,

"What in tarnation is this, Kyles"? Or at other times he would exclaim, "This is truly fabumazing", or "This is incredublous".

He had a diction all of his own did Tab Mahula. In the end, Kyla bought him a few items that she thought total junk but which delighted him. A set of horse brasses, a copper hunting horn, a huge copper funnel. They weighed him down with their bulk, forcing them to return to the car before then proceeding to the fair-ground. There they shot at clay pipes, tried to hoop prizes placed on coloured blocks of wood. Kyla insisted upon having her fortune told. Madame ZaZa, whom the facade promised was a genuine Romany - third generation, dressed in dark silks, some of which partially concealed her features, for she wore half over her white hair. She smelled of patchouli and cigarette smoke in equal amounts. Her bright red varnished nails were a little cracked in places. Kyla and Tab entered, Kyla took the seat opposite Madame ZaZa's circular table. At the centre of the table was a rather sad looking, nicotine-stained Crystal ball that looked as though it were plastic - manufactured in China.

"Now then my lovely", the grimalkin cackled, "Do you want the ball, the leaves, the palm or the cards"?

"I think my palm is the most personal. Please read my palm, Madame ZaZa", the delighted Kyla requested.

Madame ZaZa (real name Edith Ackroyd from the static caravan site at Bradwell) requested, "Cross my palm with silver then, My Dearie, or as the coins have gone for many a year now, slip a fiver in my hand".

Kyla dutifully gave the gipsy a $5 bill. Eyeing Tab from beneath her cowl, Madame ZaZa began,

"I see romance in the very near future, My Dearie, a romance that will grow and grow and lead to marriage. From this union will come hale, hearty issue - two girls, one boy. It will be the beginning of a long, happy life for you, your blonde suitor, that will end with five grandchildren. Certainly, there will be some tribulation along the road, times when some, as would despair, but you will be strong. You will overcome such difficulties from those periods, you will be more robustly resolute as a result of triumphing over them. Your son will be the main achiever who will go into the army ... no wait ... not the army, a service, but wait until it grows clearer. He will become a surgeon, that's it, a famous heart surgeon. Once again, hearts will figure in your future, Dearie, for someone already connected you to some sort of heart...".

"I live in Heartbridge House", Kyla blurted.

"And hearts will always be a part of your destiny. You have a good heart, a loving heart, which you will give to this blonde suitor if you give it to him unreservedly without condition. You will both be happy for your long, eventful lives. Sorry, My Dearie, times up, make way for the next punt ... customer who wishes to hear their future from Madame ZaZa".

Kyla exited the tent in a sort of dream. If she had been told the events of the past few days a week ago, she would not have credited them with any sort of credence. She turned to Tab asked,

"Do you want to have yours told"?

Amazingly, he took her in his arms said gently, "Arm a thinkin' ar just heard mine Darlin'. Seems to me our future is together".

He kissed her she thought she would swoon with happiness. Her heart was full of joyful promise.

When they attended the race meeting at Doncaster, he looked suddenly saddened. In tune with his every facial expression, mien, she asked at once,

"I sense a change of mood in you Tab, what is it, Sweetie"? She had always hated the *Madisonism* of the expression that showed affection, but in her case, when she called him by it, there was a new meaning. Her use of the appellation was entirely sincere.

"Nothing, Darlin', it's just that if I had my allowance for this month ar would surely have enjoyed a brief flutter on one or two of the ponies", he informed her. There was the hint of hopefulness in that, albeit reluctant revelation.

"Would it make you happy, Sweetie", she began, "if I furthered you a loan out of my allowance so you can do exactly that"?

His face lit with joy at the suggestion, then noted, "But of course ar would pay ya back once my allowance came through, Darlin'. Are ya sure you don't mind"?

"Of course I don't. How much did you think to risk".

"Risk, Darlin', risk", he chuckled, "Why it would be no never mind, if there is one thing ar knows, it's ma ponies. Ar can refund ya'll as soon as they ran the last race".

To her amazement, his disappointment, the horses simply refused to run to his carefully anticipated stratagem. One after another, they determined not to deliver the result he had predicted. By the end of the meet, the entire $555 had gone.

"Ar just don't understand it, Sugar", he almost wailed, "Some of my bets could not miss". Miss, they had. Her hastily produced bankroll was no more.

"Only now has it occurred to me", he suddenly brightened, the old Tab back, "Ar become unlucky to compensate for ma new luck in love".

"Love", she simpered, "You have feelings for me Tab"?

"Ar spoke too soon", he looked worried. "Ifin I could but hope...".

"You didn't speak too soon, because I feel it too. I think I loved you the moment I set eyes on you, Tab".

They kissed passionately; the money forgotten.

That night, whilst Lady Oxenford slept, Tab crept into Kyla's room. After whispering apologies, furtive fumbling, she lost her virginity.

"I want to get married, Mother", Kyla told the lady of Heartbridge House at breakfast the following morning. A piece of scrambled egg fell from her mother's fork on its way to her mouth. It made a soft, splatting sound that conveniently filled the shocked silence.

"Heavens, who too"?

"What on Earth do you mean by that question"? Kyle demanded, irked by her mother's obtuse response - lack of perception.

"Under the circumstances dear, I don't think it an absurd inquiry", Lady Oxenford bristled.

"Why to Tab, of course. Who else could it be"?

Her mother paled, noted wryly, "Tab Mahula, our current house-guest, whom you have known precisely three days. The young man who lost your allowance yesterday in a fit of gambling".

"Yes, Tab. He didn't lose the money in a fit but a carefully planned permutation".

"Obviously not planned with enough care", Lady Oxenford observed with some bitterness. "If I may proffer you a bit of carefully considered advice, Kyla ...".

"If it's to ask me to delay Mother, then forget it. I have no intention of waiting weeks while you decide what's-what".

"Weeks"! Lady Oxenford looked down in despair at her rapidly cooling eggs, thinking that she could only return her attention to them once they had become quite inedible. "I was going to suggest an engagement of, say, eighteen months".

To that piece of information, Kyla then reacted in an unexpectedly bizarre fashion - as far as her mother was concerned. Bursting into gales of ill-controlled laughter. Whilst it was nice to hear her daughter displaying merriment, finally, Lady Oxenford ardently desired it to be under very different circumstances.

"I'm sorry, Kyla, but I can't agree to this union. Anyway, what about your *condition"*?

Kyla's illness was oft-referred to as *'the condition'*. As though the mere mention of oxalate poisoning by name would allow it to flare up in resurgent vigour.

"My condition, Mother", the younger lady informed, "Has become far less of a hindrance to me since I've been in love. Last night I surrendered my virginity to Tab".

"You did what?! Vile harlot"! Lady Oxenford exploded in a fit of pique worthy of a Medieval Parson, "Under this my very roof! He goes, he goes this morning. No! Let me rephrase that, he goes when he gets his Yankee backside out of bed this afternoon".

Noted by one and all at Heartbridge House was the fact that Tad Mahula, while fit and vital, found rising seemingly insurmountable before noon.

"If Tad's thrown out of his home, Mother, I'll go with him".

Lady Oxenford considered this for a few moments. Regarded the steely glint in her daughter's eyes, the rebellious resolve looked unadulterated.

"If you do that, I'll be alone", she almost whimpered.

"Don't be ridiculous, the place is full of staff".

"Staff? Oh! The servants you mean, they're not real *people*, Kyla ... are they"?

"Mother", her daughter began, "You're an anachronism from a bygone age, but so help me, I love you too. The servants are the real people. It's you who's incongruous. When we're married, living here looking after you, we'll bring you into the twenty-first century. We'll have balls, gay doings, the place will become known as a thriving estate full of love, the patter of tiny ...".

"Dear gods"! Lady Oxenford interjected, "You can't be pregnant! I mean to say, how could you know, it's too soon to tell Kyla, doesn't work like that I mean to say ...".

"I'm not claiming to be pregnant yet, Mother", Kyla's tone was suddenly one of a weary disposition, "but I'm planning to be, Madame ZaZa has foretold it you see".

Lady Oxenford gripped the edge of the table with such wildness, her knuckles went immediately white with the pressure of the constraint. It was as though she were attempting to maintain her clutch on reality.

"Madame ZaZa"?!

"Yes, at the Fayre, Tab took me too. I have my fortune told, it's preordained that we're together, married, with heirs to the title here".

"I see", Lady Oxenford suddenly felt quite sorry for herself, "I apologize for being in the way of your *plans* then Kyla, perhaps it would be better for you together with your Lothario, your despoiler of sweet, naïve maidenhood if I were simply to slope away, perish somewhere".

"Now you're being pathetic", Kyla observed, annoyed. At the same moment, it occurred to her there had been a subtle power-shift in the House. The mention of marriage had moved that potential in her direction. "We'll have a quiet civil ceremony with the minimum of fuss, few guests. I can't think of many - I like enough to spoil my day. Then, when the time is right, we will let people know about our alliance. He will stay here in the main bedroom. You'll move into the one he now occupies. I'll join him naturally. He'll assume the title of Lord Heartbridge, whilst I'll take the name of Oxenford. We'll look after you, Mother, you can stay here for the rest of your life".

"I am not in my dotage, Kyla. I'm fifty-five. Do I have any say in this heinous scheme of yours at all"?

"Of course. You can agree to it continue as family, or live here in the company of 'unreal people' while Tab and I go to live with Uncle Prentiss".

That Prentiss J. Hackentyre (big in steel) had not then been consulted about such an arrangement, was ignorance that both he and Lady Oxenford shared.

The latter felt her resolve collapse.

"If that Yankee is going to despoil you nightly, I guess he had better do it with the blessing of a license". She conceded, "But mark my words Kyla, this folly will end in tears".

Never was a truer word spoken.

It had been five years in the past. Lady Oxenford - gone; Tab - gone, the money too, only the pain remained.

The instant Tab had informed his uncle of the union, his allowance had abruptly ceased.

"Don't worry, Sweetie", Kyla had assured when the piece of news was announced, "I've my allowance, more than enough to keep us both. If we need more, I'll ask mother for some of my inheritance".

"Inheri(cough)tence", Tab had brightened, despite the arrival of a suddenly mysterious cough, "How much is the *Old-bird* worth, Darlin' Wifey"?

"I thought I asked you not to refer to her in quite that derogatory fashion, Sweetie"? Kyla had responded. It was still in the days when she needed to do so before Tab had ripped all the spirit out of her.

"Sorry Darlin' Wifey, so you mentioned inheri(cough)tence", again the word seemed to stick in his throat, "Do you know the value of it -perchance"?

"Not the exact figure, our solicitors possess all the shares ...".

"Shares"?

"Yes, father invested in stocks, bonds, what have you, before the unfortunate ...".

"Have you say a ballpark figure"? Tab tried his best to sound nonchalant, failed miserably in the attempt.

"I guess roughly a couple of million, not a vast fortune".

"Two million bucks"?

"Roughly I suppose, but in today's day and age it's not a stunning amount really, is it? What it is though is enough to raise our family here at Heartbridge ...".

He did not appear to pay attention after that. It was the beginning of a series of disastrous misfortunes for the occupants of Heartbridge House. The first - Lady Oxenford's stroke. An unforeseen disaster left her mute, paralysed down the left side. Kyla took to nursing her while she waited patiently to become pregnant. Unfortunately, Lady Oxenford failed to recuperate, neither did the pregnancy materialise. Finally, one evening Kyla suggested to her loving husband, the then Lord of Heartbridge, that they might go for fertility tests, viable treatment if needed.

"Darlin Wifey", he had begun with a grin, "There's nothin' wrong with ma baby-gravy, them thar little swimmers are champions one'n'all. You go fur the tests ar'll go make us some investments. I'll need another ten thou".

"Another ten thousand, that will wipe out my account Tab, what do we do then, how do we live"?

"That ten thou will soon double, don't ya'll worry that pretty little head about that darlin'. No siree-bob pretty soon Tab'll be bringing home the bacon just from the interest in the investments".

He failed to mention that the *investments* were in Heartbridge's local casino, to be specific - in the predictions of the behaviour of its roulette wheel. So it left Kyla to take the tests, receive the devastating results alone.

"I'm sorry, Your Ladyship", Ottershaw had told her seriously, "But your chances of firstly conceiving, secondly carrying a child to term are very slim indeed. They'd result in a severe risk to any fetus. No, your best option is adoption".

When she had tearfully relayed this information to the Lord of the House, he had said calmly, "Not to worry, Darlin' you fill out the forms we'll adopt. I'll love him like he was ma very own".

He seemed ignorant of the difference, the way Kyla felt about having her baby.

"Say, Wifey", he began then as though it settled the matter satisfactorily, "do'ya think you could sub me a couple of thou, only there's a ...".

"I couldn't if I wanted to", she heard herself snap. "You've had all my savings. You'll have to wait until my allowance is due again. Mother also needs constant attention. You help me not one jot, so that's that *Lord* Heartbridge"!

The following morning Maisie found the senior Lady Oxenford quite dead!

The resultant inquest revealed nothing untoward. It seemed because of the stroke, the findings proclaimed, Lady Oxenford Snr's brain had failed to instruct her lungs to continue functioning. In short, she had suffocated. The determination was ultimately death by natural causes. Kyla was dreadfully unconvinced. That night, she had slept badly. Tab had gone for a *drink of water,* had been absent from their bed for a suspiciously long time.

The next few days he was meekly tacit. Finally, when he mentioned the inheri(cough)tence, his wife, the Lady of Heartbridge, had turned upon him, announced savagely,

"That money is for the raising of our children, Lord Heartbridge. You'll not be using it for any of your thus-far unsuccessful investments. In future, you will receive a monthly allowance from me in the form of a direct bank transfer. Don't come to me for any further cheques".

"Monthly allowance", he had echoed feebly, "What level of support am I to expect for being the Lord of this House, Darlin' Wifey"?

"One thousand per month", came the terse report.

"*One!* One thousand, why my expenses alone won't ...".

"Then curb them, Sweetie, because that is how much you are going to receive forthwith"!

The following day, Lord Tab of Heartbridge left. Kyla never saw him again.

Eight years later, the condition had gradually worsened. Not only that, they denied her the adoption for the very reason of her illness. She retreated into a shell of pain, regret, bitterness, her only company being the unreal people, the servants. The pain in her limbs was the worst she had experienced, grim for one who had known it so well! It had been her bleak companion for the entirety of her adult life. She remembered the time the family doctor had been to see her. It had been during her very difficult adolescence. Longed for a return to those days, how differently she would have conducted her next few years. It was not possible to turn back the clock. What she did had passed could neither alter nor erase. All she had to look forward to was a life of terrible pain, loneliness, unfulfillment. She would never trust another man. The experience with Mahula soured her as to the prospect of any future romance. None of it seemed worth the risk or effort.

Nothing did!

With difficulty, she climbed into the Spider, resolve absolute. Her will on the study desk, written only hours previously, she had left the estate to Cat's Protection. Kyla's foot remained on the accelerator even though it caused terrible throbbing pain in her right knee. Calmly driving at the stout, trusty, giant oak at ninety miles per hour. Death - blissfully instantaneous.

Fifteen, *'Do you sense my presence in your mind'*, came the thought.

'Yes', Kyla thought back. *'How on Earth did I survive the crash? Who are you? A doctor'?*

'You did not survive, the impact resulted in multiple fatal injuries, which killed you, Kyla Coleman'.

'Killed? Then are you Saint Peter, or have I gone down'!

'One of your servants was one of our agents', came the mysterious reply. *'They got your brain out of the wreckage, placed it in the appropriate container so we could receive it at the ship'*

'This is the worst joke anyone's ever played on anyone else' Kyla noted, *'How can I supposedly hear what you're thinking'?*

'I am transmitting thoughts directly into your mind'. Eahuura thought to her. *'Please cease with the questions? Allow me to explain what has happened to you? The future you might decide to pursue'?*

'Future'! Kyla could not resist. *'What possible future could there be for me? The crash killed, didn't it'?*

Patiently, after several interruptions, the engimedic informed the former Lady of Heartbridge who he was. What the Mizaroa wanted from her ended by thinking,

'We can place your mind into a device we will call a humadroid. A construction comprising; duridium skeleton, nyloplanyon musculature, biologically regenerated, cloned organs, flesh moulded to your specification. In return, you will become a companion of Sellers - protect him'.

'So you want me to be a type of Terminator'?

'One moment please while I access the reference in our databanks'? After a brief pause, Eahuura confirmed, *'In broad terms, the reference is appropriate'.*

'I won't look like Arnie though, will I'?

'You can tailor your appearance once. Before we manufacture you, do you wish to convey some parameters'?

'Do I'! Kyla could hardly believe her good fortune, a second chance at life on Earth. She imagined how she would like to appear, asked Eahuura, *'Can you observe the projection in my mind? Make me look like that'?*

The engimedic confirmed, *'We possess that ability'?*

'Right, then make me like that, please? I'll have one of your race in my brain too, helping me'?

'Observing, the cerquibrum may offer advice at certain times'.

'What about knowledge'?

'Explain, please'?

'Can you download weapon knowledge into my memory? If you want me to protect this photographer, I need to use various weapons. Oh, I also would like to do kung-fu, can my new super-memory have that to access - when needed'?

Eahuura confirmed, *'We will furnish your eidetic memory with those skills. User requests, do you have any more'?*

'Can't think of anything else. I just want to thank you for making life possible for me again, without pain. Be assured of my best efforts to protect the photo-snapper. I'm going to imagine what I want you to make me look like now. Here goes'.

'This is what you want. Accomplished as requested, good luck Kyla of Heartbridge, your past life is over. You will now live as a guest in Tod Sellers apartment'

Total oblivion possessed Kyla for an imperceptible period.

Sixteen.   Sellers had obligingly fallen mentally silent. Existing in a chasm of nothingness, not his idea of a good time. The state he proceeded into was even less filled with sensation. It was not disquieting, for it was nothing, oblivion. Following the indeterminate period of non-being came rebirth. He found himself once more naked on the beach at Flamborough, this time under the cover of darkness. His eyes immediately switched to infra-red. He had not thought it any longer possible for him to be astonished. After all, his recent *death* had taken several fantastic turns over the past few existences. What regarded him on the beach caused him to gasp in stupefaction, delectation, in the same instant.

The bodyguard was also on the beach. Naked, as expected. Sellers had never naively even stopped to consider the possibility that the bodyguard would be female. Not just muliebrous, beautiful, with the most divine figure that ever graced the feminine form. In a rich contralto that under the circumstances was no surprise at all, the nude, no doubt fecund figure asked,

"Have you never seen a girl with no clothes on before"?

"Like you, no", he blurted without thinking, "If you're reanimated then, besides scientists, the Mizaroa are also artists".

She smiled, twirled around, oblivious to the effect that such an action was having on Seller's already racing heart.

"I feel no pain! None, for the first time in many, many years". She was speaking mainly to herself. Her body was perfection, tall, tanned, with tight musculature, perfectly rounded buttocks, broad full, yet firm breasts. Chestnut tresses fell in ringlets down her back. The bodyguard suddenly stopped to regard him with china-blue eyes. Her lips were glossy, pink - finely bowed at the front. When she addressed him, she revealed a perfectly white set of teeth.

"They didn't do such an awful job with you either, did they"?

"Erm no, thank you, I'm Tod Sellers, are you supposed to be my bodyguard"?

"Not supposed to be, I am. Lady Kyla Coleman of Heartbridge".

"Lady Coleman"! Sellers repeated amused, "Well I think we'd best get out of here, Your Ladyship, back to Doncaster".

"All right", she picked up her underwear. Asked him, "Are you humadroid too Mister Sellers"?

"Humadroid? Oh, I see what you mean, I've human organs, flesh, but they made my skeleton of duridium, muscles - nyloplanyon, does that answer your question"?

"It does. Do you also have a cerquibrum in your brain"?

"In my mind, rather than my brain, I refer to him as a mind-jockey".

"What's the name of your mind-jockey"?

That amused Sellers, as he pulled on a pair of blue boho pants decorated with peacocks, "My mind-jockey is Királálynővonazóreginăcondător Balurzuura".

"Right, the Mizaroa leader, I'm briefed, was just checking I got the right naked humadroid".

"That's funny".

"Is it"? She hesitated, hooking up her brassiere. Not a winning moment as far as Sellers was concerned. "I've never been funny before".

Sellers chuckled, "I'm sure that's not true. Then again - if you were in constant physical torment, I don't expect you desired the odd chuckle".

"Checkerooni".

"So your cerquibrum, who's he"?

"I've woţialideruliavezetőelesége-királálynővonazóreginăcondător Vezetőéţia in my mind".

"Balu's wife"! Sellers was flabbergasted, "The sly-dog never told me he had a chick on the side, I thought 'he' could be his wife - when he became a she".

"You speak Mizaroa"? It surprised Her Ladyship.

"Balu taught it me one night when things were slack".

"The Királálynővonazóreginăcondător does not mind you abbreviating his name"?

"He's expressed no displeasure at the compression. Try thinking to woţialideruliavezetőelesége-királálynővonazóreginăcondător Vezetőéţia, try Tőéţia".

As she pulled on a wind-cheater, Lady Kyla said aloud, "Tőéţia - ma-am, have you any objection to my using a contraction of your rather lengthy title"? She smiled and told Sellers, "She hasn't, that will save time".

"You don't need to speak out loud to your cerquibrum", Sellers smiled at the stunning beauty, "Just think to the Woţialideruliavezetőelesége-királálynővonazóreginăcondător she'll think back. Otherwise, you're going to get some weird glances in public".

"I'm not sure that I care what sort of glances I get from common people, Mister Sellers".

"Oh! Then, in that case, I do beg your pardon, Your Ladyship".

"Are you ready? my Spider's repaired up near the lighthouse".

"Your Spider"?

"My Fiat 124 Spider, curiously I'm reborn to be wild".

"It's a car"!

"No, we're going to return to your apartment on the back of a tiny arachnid".

"That's your second wise-crack, Your Ladyship. Lead on then to the sports car, if you would be so kind". He followed her perfect rump as it moved in her joggers, like two soft-boiled eggs jostling for position in a bowl of jelly. So transfixed, he nearly lost his footing on two separate occasions. Only superb reactions, balance, stopped him from stumbling.

"Stop looking at my posterior", Lady Kyla suddenly chided.

"How did you know I was? Have wing mirrors fitted to that divine chassis of yours, Your Ladyship"?

"No, I just know how the mind of a young man works. You were young, weren't you, when you died I mean"?

"Mid-twenties. You"?

"I'm a contemporary. Oh! My, they've done a good job since I crashed it, successfully killed myself".

"This is your hara-kiri wagon"?!

"The very one, don't worry. I'm normally a very safe driver. How d'you die"?

"A fall", Sellers kept it simple, "Are you hungry by the way? I'm starved".

She cast a critical eye over him as he slid into the passenger seat, observed sarcastically, "Yes, you look like you're falling from together. Where will be open? It's gone midnight according to my internal chronometer".

"Motorway Services, we can take a minor detour so I can get sarnies, snacks, a drink. Surely you wouldn't say no to something warm inside you"?

"I understood that innuendo, Mister Sellers, behave, or I'll be testing the strength of your duridium ulna".

"Please get me food, Your Ladyship, or let me drive. In fact ...".

"Forget it clubby, none drive my car but me".

"Oh yeah, right, that turned out fine last time out, didn't it"?

"If you want food, the best thing is to stop talking", she advised with mock solemnity. He took the hint.

They made a stop, Sellers re-fueled, then filled the tank of the Spider. Kyla discovered several hundred dollars in one of her pockets, those with the head of the Queen. Sellers was curious wondered what his apartment would look like in Americas 52nd state. The 51st being Canada. As they drew closer toward Doncaster, it intrigued Sellers to see skyscrapers dotting the skyline at various junctions close enough to towns. The reality possessed an Americanese England. They finally reached the town, their destination barely recognisable to him. He wondered if recognise should therefore be spelt with a zed (or zee). All the Frenchgate Centre contained tall skyscrapers. The name had changed to the Eisenhower Towers. Similarly, High Street was Roosevelt Boulevard, Hall Gate – Watergate. Kyla parked the Spider around the back of the correct block, which clawed its way twenty stories into the South Yorkshire night air. The strange duo walked around to the front. An enormous plate at the base of the correct location contained a list of names of the occupants of the tower block.

"Hard to believe", Sellers finally muttered.

"What is, Mister Sellers"?

"I live on the 15th-floor look, here's my name, not only that but on the 16th floor is a photographic studio, which also seems to belong to me, or should I say the quiddity that was me, before the Mizaroa supplanted it into my current form".

"Current form? You speak as though it were only temporary. Is there something I've not been told? Something that I should know"?

"I've been dead more than once. That's why I need your protection. It doesn't mean you're going to wear out or anything like that".

"I see. Are we going to stand out on the pavement all night, or go in"?

"Sure". He pushed open the doors that were unlocked. A guard behind a reception desk was waiting to stop all intruders. He smiled at their appearance,

"Good evening, Mister Sellers". Glanced at Kyla, grinned back at the photographer, "I hope you had an enjoyable time, Sir? Are you both going up"?

It was plain he thought Sellers had picked up Kyla, taking her back for a night of horizontal shenanigans.

"Yes, have a pleasant evening", Sellers managed, not knowing the guard's name, unable to address him by it. They walked over to the lift. Sellers pressed for the 15th floor. Whilst they waited for it to descend, Kyla suddenly slipped her arm through his, then kissed him on the cheek, for the benefit of the still watching guard. Finally, the doors opened they stepped inside. Kyla chuckled,

"I've never been a one-night stand before".

"It's hardly a position to aspire to".

"Just a novel experience for me, Mister Sellers. Please excuse my temporary lack of decorum".

"Understandable, given your potted life history". He was referring to the ones they had exchanged during their drive back from Flamborough. It had whiled away the time usefully to them both, as they were going to spend some time together.

The doors opened onto a corridor lit by bright LED's. Traversing a tessellated cushion floor of blues, greys they went to the door with Sellers name plaque beside it. Apartment 23 on the 15th. Sellers fumbled in a pocket looking for keys, Kyla pointed out,

"There's a plate next to the opening side of the door. It looks like a finger or thumb jobbie".

Sellers tried his thumb. Nothing happened. The index finger of his right then produced the desired result. There was an electric clunk, the door yawed about an inch. He pushed it the rest of the way and fumbled for a light switch. Once again, he was unsuccessful in his attempt to decipher his place. The Lady of Heartbridge suddenly spoke loudly, succinctly,

"Lights, full up".

The place burst into bright LED illumination. Sellers whistled.

"Whoa, is this a futuristic pad, opulent, isn't it"?

The lounge into which they had entered was huge fully 30ft square in an open-plan format that had the kitchen in one corner. There, in her basket was Mrs Meggins from the Pie Shop, a litter box beside her, two empty dishes beside the basket.

"Megwinda"! Sellers cried, rushing to fill one dish with water, searching the plain white overhead cupboards for some Purina. When he had located it, he turned to fill the second bowl, only to see Mrs Meggins from the Pie Shop purring furiously in Kyla's arms as the girl tickled her chin.

"She never goes to strangers, you're truly blessed", he exclaimed, delighted that Her Ladyship shared a love of cats. Kyla let her down. The cat crunched the food, still purring, sounding like a tiny, delightful grinding machine. He glanced once more around the apartment – *his* apartment.

A place of all whites, royal blues, "Looks like I'm still an Everton fan even in this reality", he said to no one in particular.

An enormous leather suite with a three-cushion four-seater sofa, two vast recliner chairs. The audio rig was all American tube-technology. A massive plasma - attached to one wall. It must have been an 85-inch model, at the very least. Beneath it was a humongous 6.1 Onkyo surround sound receiver. He had dotted the excellent KEF eggs in the corners.

"How many bedrooms are there"? Lady Kyla suddenly inquired.

'There will be no need to make up the bed in the guest bedroom Sellers', Balurzuura suddenly informed his host, *'My wife and I would like the vicarious pleasure of sexual intercourse this evening'.*

While Sellers processed this shocking information, he saw the girl cock her head on one side, obviously hearing Vezetőéţia tapping her. Then she blushed a shade of deep pink, asked Sellers in hesitant tones,

"Has your cerquibrum suddenly requested of you"?

"Yes. It appears he wants to use my body in a remote connection to his wife through coitus with you. Shall I explain the notion isn't particularly acceptable to you"?

The Lady of Heartbridge considered it, before noting carefully, "I owe them re-animation, the chance to exist without pain, feel under a certain obligation, yet my mores shrink from what is being requested".

"I understand. I don't feel differently, even though you're very desirable, beautiful. However, you know the nature of men, so you're once more in the driving seat, Lady Heartbridge".

She returned hesitantly, "I wonder if I could daydream my way through it? Attempt to divorce my thoughts from the activities of my body. I understand where Tőéţia is coming from.

Balurzuura suddenly urged, *'There is just such a state if the girl ...'.*

"No"! Sellers warned the woman, "I don't advise that Lady Heartbridge, you may find it very difficult to reaffirm control, if at all".

"You mean ..."?

"That the Mizaroa would try total take over, subjugate you to a sort of zombie, the Zaromi do it to their hosts. That's part of the reason you're here to protect me".

"You have more experience of this mind-riding than me. What do you think we should do? After all, we owe our lives to the Mizaroa even if they're not human".

"I can only advise that you decide what you are comfortable with".

"I'll try an experiment then", she decided aloud, crossing the room swiftly threw her arms around Sellers muscular frame, "Kiss me, Mister Sellers, gently if you please, no tongue".

Sellers grinned at the latter condition, dipped his head, gently kissed the girl's fabulous lips, without asking, descended still further, gently kissed her neck, moving gradually upward until he was nuzzling the lobe of a perfect ear. He heard her take a sudden gasp of air, declare,

"That will do, thank you, your demonstration was most instructive".

Sellers waited, she asked him,

"May I have a bath? You take one too"?

"Of course, Your Ladyship, I don't know myself where that door leads but ...".

"That's all right. I'll find everything. If I can't, I'll shout for help. You've seen me already in a state of undress".

"Just to be clear, what are we doing once we've both bathed"? He was almost certain what her declaration was going to be, but wondered how she, a lady, would phrase it.

"You're going to get lucky, Mister Sellers. I don't wish to disappoint our alien benefactors".

Sellers kept his features carefully neutral. In the presence of a lady, he must be the perfect gentleman. When she had left him, suddenly felt a pang of guilt when he remembered the lovely Nicole.

'Just put your mind into a state of ...', Balurzuura began.

"Forget it", Sellers cut him short, vocally as well. "You're not having the chance to take over. I'll just have to live with the guilt. You can enjoy your wife somewhat vicariously".

Meanwhile, Kyla was running her bath, inspecting the various fragrances available in the bathroom. She felt thrilled at the prospect of sleeping with Sellers. Tab had always proved to be a disappointment in bed, added to which was the fact that she, Kyla, had always been in some level of pain or another. Their union had not proved either fruitful or satisfactory to her, but this, she felt certain, was going to be a completely different level of sexual encounter. Firstly, he was even more handsome than Tab, in addition, he was a virtual superman when it came to endurance. Just as importantly, she could match him in vitality, secretly she felt desire. This time, she, a Lady of Heartbridge, was going to have sex for the physical pleasure of it. She scrubbed herself, marvelling at the toned smoothness of her tanned limbs, then towelled herself dry on the whiter than white bathroom linen before slipping on a blue robe that was several sizes too large for her. It was his - or intended to be his, which was which? It was slightly confusing. She used the only toothbrush, walked down the narrow passage between the bathroom, the bedroom, into the lounge once more.

"The bathroom is ready when you want it, Mister Sellers. Sorry, but I used the only toothbrush I could find. Don't know if there's a spare lurking anywhere. Didn't do too much searching".

"Don't worry about it Your ... say, am I to continue calling you Your Ladyship after we've ... after this evening"?

"It sounds rather nice to me. Call me Kyla if you like, it pleases me to hear you call me Your Ladyship. It's nice. If you find Mister Sellers too stuffy, I will gladly use a forename, anything other than Tod, for a private reason I might tell you about someday".

"I don't have a middle name".

"How would it be for you could pick your own? What would you be happy to answer too"?

He smiled, "Anything"?

"Within reason, anything sensible".

"Salt".

"Sol! Jewish isn't it. Oh! Silly of me, I just got it, Salt, Salt Sellers, very amusing. All right, I'll try it, Mister ... Salt".

"Right then, I'll go bathe. What colours are the towels"?

"White, why, what possible reason could you have for asking me that when you're about to find out for yourself in a few seconds"?

"To get over the disappointment, I used to love my teal coloured towel, best bath-sheet I ever had, now I suspect it's lost in the earlier lay-lines of the multiverse motorway".

"Has anyone ever told you, you have a rather strange sense of humour, Mister Sellers"?

"Not since I was killed, no. Death makes you dreadfully busy, you know".

She smiled, "It's white, your bath-sheet, it'll be the dry one".

"I'll be as quick as I can".

"Rush nothing this evening. I want a towel colour to be your only disappointment before we go to sleep".

"Now that was quite witty, a little risqué too. You're not all seriousness yourself, Lady Heartbridge".

"Really? I used to be, death must become me".

She turned into the only door she had not been through previously, commanded the lights to come on. What greeted her caused her to gasp in surprise. Its walls were dark navy, the ceiling black, but through them gleamed tiny LED's, the effect was of a night sky. A dark-green carpet just possible to discern under the *starlight* added to the illusion of being under a moonless sky outdoors. The bedding was cotton, also all black, all furniture in the room was in black-stained walnut. It was the perfect setting for a night of horizontal pleasure. Kyla reflected that the previous Sellers must have been a player. The current occupier of his quiddity did not seem quite like that, thank goodness. He had dealt with a tough situation with admirable tact, another factor in her surrender. Despite that, she lay trembling in the bed while she waited for him to join her. Must have dozed off, for when she awoke, his lips were on hers, tenderly, patiently. For a while, she stopped thinking altogether. His paced care aroused her far more than urgency she was soon *ready* for him. Instead of doing what she thought he would, he promptly jumped out of bed, pulled drawers open, a futile gesture in the dark, unless he had x-ray vision (she was ignorant of his infra-red at that point).

"What on Earth are you doing"? she gasped, her voice hoarse with the desire evident in her ears.

"Looking for them, you know ... the protection. Your arrangements are interrupted. I don't want to act irresponsibly".

"There's no need", she laughed, "I don't have the structure. I asked it left out, for reasons of my own".

"Oh", he chuckled climbed back into the bed. The two held one another, laughing.

"I bet I looked pretty silly just then, eh"?

"It was very thoughtful of you, Sellers, very thoughtful. I'll call you Sellers if you don't mind. Now stop laughing, where were we"?

He stopped. They kissed for a while longer before she gave herself to him. It was very, very good for both of them. Two hours later, almost dawn, she gasped,

"We'll have to stop. There's only so much fluid, in even our bodies, there's always another day".

"Another day, you mean you want to do this with me more than once"? He sounded naturally delighted considering the events of the past 120 minutes.

She chuckled throatily, noted, "We've already done it more than once. In fact, we've ...".

"Who's counting"? he gently rolled off her, before observing wryly, "But perhaps Mizaroa only mates once every ...".

"Next time, we'll be doing it for neither Tőéţia nor Balurzuura", she told him candidly, "But for me. With your cooperation, if you agree to it, of course. It's up to you, Sellers"!

Seventeen.   Michael Cowie had never been a regular, run-of-the-mill sort of person. His tastes had always been rather extreme, never reflected by his peers. He had plenty of friends, yet they always considered that, though dependably solid, Michael owned a certain quality that was difficult, if not impossible, to discern. Some girls considered this unique something to have sinister connotations. He was little interested in academia, even though he was far from unintelligent. It impeded his specifically special talent. Though neither artist nor musician, Michael Cowie had wonderful hands. The medium that he worked in was wood. If it were possible to build something out of the fruit of trees, he could create it. He left school, uncaring for qualifications. The first thing he decided was to create a workshop in his mother's backyard. That no such structure existed deterred him, not in the slightest. On a single weekend, he had the wood delivered - constructed a solid structure. He had drawn no plans other than a hasty sketch that existed on the back of one of his cigarette packets. The tiny diagram - neither conforming to scale nor perspective. It was all he needed, for he could see the building in his mind's eye.

One sunny weekend, it was up. By the end of Sunday, he was waterproofing the roof with Everbuild AQLIQRFBK7 Aquaseal Liquid Roof Sealant. He had constructed; floor walls, two workbenches, roof, in the time it would have taken anyone else to do the floor. By the third day, he had stained the entire exterior, added electrics taken from a spur in the house. Hastily painted a sign, which he put under the bay window of the front of his mother's property. It proudly proclaimed him as Carpenter Cowie, informed the rest of the village that no job was too small. At first minor jobs came in at a trickle, but then the word regarding the quality of his designs, the selections of various timbers, got around. Soon he was having to turn some offers away. The good thing, as far as business concerns were that the jobs were getting bigger in scale. Larger and larger companies were hearing about the Carpenter from Lincoln, who could build anything out of wood. The other attraction, apart from quality, he was not greedy. Never charged vast sums for labour, merely satisfied to be doing the work, giving himself a reasonable living. That was before Americanese firms infiltrated their 52nd State. The skyscrapers mushroomed into the sky everywhere. Interiors needed constructions that were sound, unique, aesthetically pleasing. Cowie's Carpentry Ent could not find enough hours in the day. Different firms tried to entice him away from competitors by offering ever-increasing bonuses if he could meet their deadlines. Cowie had been doing some timber interiors for Skanska, who were building some vertical apartments when a suited business-looking type approached him one afternoon. Cowie looked up from the wood he had been planing, a beautiful piece of bird's-eye maple stipulated by the customer rather than him. To see an opulently corpulent man in his late fifties gazing at his work with an eagle eye,

"Mistaa Cowie", he asked in Americanese. When Cowie nodded, he went on, "Arma Prentiss J. Hackentyre, arm sure you've heard of me"?

"Afraid not". The carpenter rubbed the dust from his sweaty hands onto the sides of his boiler-suit legs to accept the pudgy outstretched hand of the American. Impressively, Prentiss J. Hackentyre had a firm grip, an assured handshake that declared him a shrewdly determined operator.

"Well now, arm big in steel, Sir. Ma company has just secured a deal with the Bechtel Corporation to build some li'l ole scrapers here in Leen-carn. Now arm gonna supply the structure, but arm a-wantin' you to do some of the interior timber-work".

"That's very flattering that you should think of me, Mister Hackentyre, but I already have a full diary for the rest of this year - halfway into next".

"Cancel it, Sir"! Hackentyre suggested in all seriousness, "You have the chance to sign a lucrative deal with the biggest damn Corporation in the world".

"I've never cancelled commission to work in my brief business life, Sir. I want a reputation for dependability, integrity".

"Commendable Mistaa Cowie but don't go makin' no li'l ole decision till you've seen the bottom line, Sir".

"Money has never really been my chief concern, Mister Hackentyre", Michael replied with all candour, "I just love working with wood".

"Not even lots of money"?

Despite himself, Cowie was curious. "What sort of figure are you offering"?

"The twenty-story Leen-carn Estoria has a budget of $115 million, Sir. The costed budget for the timber interiors is $15 million. We can get the wood for a million so you do the math".

Fourteen million dollars. For that he could move out of his mother's, build his own home, design, make the interior himself. It was the last part that attracted him the most, to live in a house that he had designed himself. Hackentyre had not finished,

"And aar have a sweetener. The top apartment in the entire set-up is yours ifin you want it, the twentieth floor will have but two massive apartments you can have the aspect you wish - gratis. You will have built the interior yourself will be-ah sittin' on top of the world".

Cowie did not need to hesitate any further. He held out a hand once more. As they shook, told the steel magnate, "Get all that down on paper Mister Hackentyre, I'll clear my diary for Bechtel".

At first, the new contract gave him untold satisfactual pleasure, but he realised, as he worked his way gradually from one floor to another, that it could well be the last time he would do constructive work with his hands. He would finish the building, be wealthy beyond his wildest imaginings. Equally, wealth would effectively render him redundant, for who had ever heard of a multi-millionaire carpenter? Certainly, he could do some hobby work, maybe even construct the interior of the upper apartment. Would take the greatest of pains over if he was going to be in the Estoria. The drive, creativity, would atrophy. Or would others consider him completely insane to give the money away? Carry on working? Neither option seemed sensible. Depression claimed him, even as he was designing, creating the last few rooms, the very last two, one of which would be his, if he wanted it. Moving from the workshop to the plushest tower in the town was the desirable thing to do, but then what? On the last day, when no more architrave was required, he lay down his saw, feeling it to be an ultimate act, one he certainly did not relish. As though from nowhere, Prentiss J. Hackentyre suddenly strolled through the doorway, gazed around him in appreciation.

"Y'all have done a quality job", he enthused. "This sure is work to be marty proud arv".

"I'm proud of everything I've ever created in wood", came the sad response.

"Y'all sound down fella", the magnate noted, "Don't Y'all worry none though pardner, when you see your bank balance it'll be the start of a comfortable life for y'all. Now then, which of the two summit suites are y'all gonna select"?

"I guess the east-facing", he responded leadenly, "So that the rising sun will light my bedroom to arise to, shade, blessing it in the evening".

"This one then", Prentiss J. Hackentyre looked even more closely at the superbly jointed panelling that adorned most of the walls, "Sure is a purty fine dig to hang out in pardner".

"Don't expect a house-warming party", Cowie cautioned. "I won't be having one. I'm not in the mood to party right now".

"Once you've handed in the tools, spruced yourself up, y'all might change your mind", Prentiss J. Hackentyre chuckled. "Anyhoos pardner, I'm gonna shoot, y'all move in as soon as you want, once the decoratin' boys have done their stuff, so long".

The decorating boys were admirably swift. They painted the places where Cowie instructed them so to do, varnished in others where the wood was the thing. The electrics, all other utilities, had preceded him, the newly appointed security officer for the building, gave him his keys a week later. At first, he amused himself by furnishing the place to his tasteful requirements. Buying a huge Lincoln Four Poster Antique French Style Bed, a snip at $1731.52. For the lounge, his tastes ran to a Harley Contemporary White Leather 3 Seater Electric Recliner Sofa, two electric recliner armchairs at a cool $3463.29. Selected mainly because the frame was solid oak. Turned his attention to entertainment, spent $539000 on a C Seed 262 television that promised 262 inches of 4K heaven. It was a tiny dent in the fortune he had amassed, which grew with interest every day. The stereo system then accounted for another $31979.88, a McIntosh MC275 - 2-Channel Vacuum-Tube Amplifier, fed by a Luxman D-380 Valve CD Player, all coming out of Monitor Audio PL 500 II monitors created in piano gloss black. Adding further accessories, utensils amounted to very little, so he started shopping for designer clothing.

It suited Cowie to seek Steam Punk style clothes, kitted out an entire wardrobe for a poultry $1200. The total bill he had run up came to $577,374.69. Just over half a million dollars of his now gradually growing fortune that increased at a rate of $1.4 million per annum, or $604,297.77 per week. He listened to some music, watched a few feature films, after a month, he turned to reading. That consumed another two. He had everything he wanted, not especially desirous of travel, could access the world on his massive television without the discomfort of flight delays transfers, the need to meet others. The latter was becoming an increasing problem. Never a great mixer, he became reclusive. Had built himself an opulent prison. The event that would transform his existence forever took place shortly thereafter!

They made contact! Cowie, seated on one of the recliner chairs reading, his eyes growing heavy with the continual need to focus on the tiny print of paperback. Despite his best effort to keep the fatigue at bay to finish the current chapter, his eyelids betrayed his brain. He dozed.

'Hello Cowie'.

The connection made him instantly alert. Who could have gotten past his security system? The complexity of it was like Fort Knox.

"Who's that? Where are you"? He demanded, going to his antique roll-top bureau (lovingly restored), pulled out his **Colt® Cobra® Double-Action Center-fire revolver**.

'There is no reason to be alarmed. Your search for me will reveal nothing at all. Was I even present in your home, I would be but 5cm in length. I am Gryllidae, not humanoid'.

"A grasshopper, yes. I believe I've fallen into an Enid Blyton book. I must be dreaming".

'Actually, my race is more closely related to crickets than grasshoppers, but you get the idea. I am insectoid, not humanoid, as I already informed you. Searching for me is pointless. I am not physically present. The thoughts you are receiving, transmitted in a process that has become known as tapping'.

"No, I don't believe that. As I'll question my insanity, I'll know I remain sane. The only other feasible explanation is that this is some bizarre prank somewhere in this place is a hidden speaker".

'I assure you that if I were to classify myself in the humanoid fashion, I would be; Clade – Euarthropoda, Class – Insectoid, Order – Orthoptera, Suborder – Ensifera, Superfamily - Grylloidea, Family - Gryllidae'.

"You've gone to some trouble to perform this ruse, whoever you are, but I'm just not buying a talking bug. So the game's up, give it a rest".

'It would seem a demonstration is in order, could a hidden speaker do this ...'!

Cowie suddenly lifted his left hand, took the pistol from his right, placed it on one of the occasional tables he had himself created. He had no control over the action at any stage.

"Then this is a hypnogogic suggestion. Someone is in my mind but I doubt it will be a talking bug".

'You realise hypnogogic is not a proper word in Americanese'.

"Well, as you're not a real bug, it will suffice for my purpose".

'Allow me to explain. To make to you the offer I came so to do? If you remain sceptical or simply uninterested, I will leave, never to return to you'.

"As I cannot banish you myself, other than perhaps letting this hypnogogic sensation run its course, I don't seem to have a workable alternative - do I"?

'Sit down then, relax. I will tell you the story of Mizar A. Of the two sapient races who populate a planet orbiting it, of our war, the invasion plans the Mizaroa have for subjugating humanoids on Earth. We the Zaromi will stop them, with the help of people such as you Cowie'.

"Crikey! Have I got a weirdly twisted imagination"?! Cowie chuckled, "Aycee brain-bug, give me the story".

The Zaromi, one Moluura, told Cowie a Zaromi-slanted version of events, what he wanted the man to know, finally after a few minutes informed,

'I, therefore, wish to remain in your mind? For the link to be anything other than temporary, you must travel to our ship - undergo the cerquibrumoscopy. Or, as promised, I will leave'.

"You're the leader of the cricket-bugs? Want me to be the leader of the human/bugs"?

'We prefer the terms Zaromi and Zaromoid, essentially that is what I am offering you, the position of Colonel, as you would phrase it, like your Colonel Gaddafi'.

"I'll do the trip to Scunlington", Cowie decided, "If only to put an end to the illusion here".

'And if it proves not to be a paramnesia. What then'?

"Then you came along at the right time. I'll be the Colonel of the Zaromoid, though hopefully not ending as Gaddafi did".

'We hope so, too. Intend to win the war over the Mizaroa, before they subjugate your fellow humanoids'.

"I don't much care about that", Cowie confirmed the Zaromi commander's suspicions concerning the humanoids misanthropy, "I just want to be on the winning side"!

Cowie made the journey to the outskirts of Scunlington in an admirably short period. His Mercedes-Benz S-Class Saloon practically drove itself to the location Moluura had given him. There, nestling under carefully arranged foliage, was a model of a spaceship. Or so Cowie thought. As he looked at it in the wasteland field that was not visible from any roads, he marvelled at the detail on it. Finally, bent slightly, peered into the front of what he thought of as a large cockpit, held an eye to the wind-shield. Drew back, gasping in astonishment. Inside the huge model was a nest of crickets. Surely no longer a prank. Who would bother to fool him? It was too elaborate, the detail, effort, would have been tremendous. There remained only two possibilities. That he was going mad. All was paramnesia. Possibly more fantastic, his eyes and ears perceived reality.

He decided if he were insane, then the only sensible thing to do was follow the delusion to its conclusion. This choice seemed to cover both scenarios. Going around to the rear of the huge model, he wriggled under the vegetation, into a vast docking bay. Crawled, writhed, until his entire body was in the metal cowl of the vessel, waited. The resultant interval was not lengthy. Suddenly, expectantly, he fell into total oblivion.

'I observe that you have accepted our veztőőöndər's offer of fusion with his mind', a new tone of thought snapped the eternal darkness.

"A what"? Cowie mouthed the words, heard nothing.

"Veztőöndər Moluura has offered to have his engrams grafted into your brain, humanoid, a great honour, a very great honour indeed".

"And you are? Where is Moluura"?

'I am the engimedic who will perform the procedure. Soon you will converse with our esteemed Veztőöndər at will'.

"Crack on then, let's get this show on the road".

'You are desirous of haste suddenly'?

"And you catch on quickly, doctor-bug. Go for it. Let's see where this phantasm takes me next".

It was instantaneous. Preparations must already have been in place, suddenly Moluura thought to Cowie,

'You will awaken, crawl out of our vessel in a couple of your seconds. Cowie, the cerquibrumoscopy consummated, we share your brain'.

Before Cowie could make a reply, he woke, writhed his way back into the field, "That wasn't as spectacular as I could have imagined, so I guess this must be happening. I thought I'd be in some strange Frankensteinic laboratory with some a band around my head linked to wires that led to constantly crackling equipment, like in the old Universal movies".

'Frankensteinic, another maladoptism Cowie, you seem to enjoy doing that'.

"I like to play with language, yes", Cowie admitted. He made his way back to the car. Firstly, making sure he concealed the spacecraft beneath undergrowth, some bracken.

'You do not need to speak to communicate with me. You can just think your responses. I will detect them just as you distinguish mine'.

'Like this'?

'Exactly, if you are more comfortable vocalising when alone, then that is also acceptable'.

"Good, because otherwise the whole thing still seems like an aberration, even though I'm now convinced otherwise".

'This vehicle is efficient'?

"It's a satisfactory drive, why, do we have some travelling to do"?

'You and I, Colonel Cowie, are going to set up, coordinate, a unit of soldiers to fight the Mizaroa. It will involve driving. The vehicle looks equal to the task'.

"You're looking at it through *my* eyes"?

'The image is very singular in its presentation. I am certain I will adapt to it given time'.

"Oh, right, you're used to seeing everything through bug eyes, aren't you"?

'Our vision is multi-faceted, the scale of all we survey is actual, rather than gigantic'.

"It doesn't look too big to me. There again, I'm bigger. How d'you get so bright with such a tiny brain"?

'On Earth, you have a saying Cowie, size is not everything. This is right, is it not'?

Cowie laughed, "The saying isn't referring to brain size, but I take your point. Here we go, travelling Earth-man style".

Eighteen "**Arma sorry sir** but the radiators plumb busted so the best we can do is offer y'all a new loaner. Good job y'all had so much cover'n'all. The loaner should be here within a litt'ol hour".

"Du scheinst ein amerikanisches Twang entwickelt zu haben und sprichst Englisch (You seem to have developed an American twang, you are talking in English)", Felton observed, then switched to English himself, demanded of Einuur.

"What have you done now"?

"What have I done"? Einuur was angry, but then it seemed to be his usual state of mind. "You turned the car over into another lay-line, not me".

Ailuura explained, "It would seem the crash proved fatal to us, probably crushed to death, but the Zaromi has transferred us into a different layer of the multiverse - so that we can continue with our mission".

"Mission! Impossible", Felton postulated, "It's not possible, is it? I mean, the change was seamless".

"You're not used to the seamless-transference then", Einuur was suddenly gloating, "The Zaromi have for some time, round about the time Moluura took a human form".

"And the Mizaroa don't possess it"?

Ailuura shook her head in Felton's direction, "No doubt they will develop the facility soon".

"Or maybe they won't", Einuur seemed to have developed a southern twang to his own Americanese.

"I'm not sure I can cope with all these changes", Felton mused aloud. "They're just too sudden. I'm not used to it".

"It was you who killed us all", Einuur pointed out. "Stupid of you to still consider death to be the ultimate act in your life".

As a gust of saline tinged drizzle blew into their hair, faces, bodies, Ailuura suddenly shivered, moaned, "Where's that loaner"?

"He seemed very efficient", Felton assured her, "I'm sure it will be here soon". He sought to comfort her, even though she seemed to be his enemy.

"I'm driving this time", Einuur barked fiercely into the moistly chilly night.

The vehicle was with them after a total wait of forty minutes. It was a Chevrolet Impala finished in Blue Velvet Metallic, hardly the stuff of loaners, yet it was the England that then spoke Americanese. Greatly influenced by their longtime allies. As Einuur drove, Felton saw a landscape of lights that beamed up into the sky, obviously huge tower blocks, or as they were probably more aptly called - sky-scrapers. Einuur drove with careful efficiency, sometimes breaking the speed limit. Only on empty roads as the faintly coral tinges of dawn lit the eastern sky, the strange trio entered the outskirts of Doncaster. Einuur seemed to have an exact location in mind, for he drove just as purposefully across the town. Over to its northern side onto a bridge which spanned the River Don. Felton saw a plaque proclaiming it to be Saint Mary's Bridge. He pulled up into an underground car park that must have run parallel to the river. As they climbed out, they could smell the dampness in the air. Not the familiar saline tang of the north sea though, but the dirty aroma of a muddy river.

Entering a lift, Ailuura informed their captive, "This is the Twenty-three Horseshoes tower hotel. Close to our mission, where the one you're to get friendly with, lives".

"What then"? Felton demanded to know. "Do you intend to get him to side with the Zaromi, or are you going to hurt him"?

"You talk too much Ailuura", Einuur grated in his guttural way, "I told Moluura that you should not be on this mission, you're not trustworthy enough since you became female".

"What"! Felton demanded, "You mean I was attracted to... to a...".

"Relax", Einuur smiled for the first time since the two men had met, " You wanted to poke Alice, not Ailuura, she's always been a girl. Don't worry about being on the slide".

Ailuura protested, "Must you be so coarse Einuur, we'd only just met".

"Humanoid males are like that", Einuur informed. As though an expert on humanity. "If they see a pretty, shapely female of their species, their first thought is the possibility of an association leading to copulation".

"Sadly, in most cases, that happens on a subconscious level, but not all men act on such urges. If they do, they do so gallantly, patiently. It remains but their ultimate goal".

"And did you see me in that way"? Ailuura wished to know, a strange tone in her voice. The doors saved Felton, those to the lift swishing open. Leading to a red-carpeted corridor lit by overhead LEDs, painted with plain white walls.

"I already have the swipe card", Einuur explained. "We're all in room twenty-three. Nice and cosy, it'll stop you from getting into mischief, Felton".

"I hope I get a bed", the Mizaroa host of a cerquibrum gasped. "I'm bushed".

"There will be three. Moluura booked an extra one, at his own cost".

"Why is he so good to me"? Felton quipped as Einuur swiped the device that released the lock on the door. It yawned open with a metallic crunch. Inside was a spacious room that could have hosted over three with ease. In one bedroom, a double bed, in a smaller - a single. The general area had a suite in its centre, a table for eating at, three high-back chairs pushed under it. The staff had attempted to see that three people would find their rooms satisfactory.

"Anyone mind if I get a bath firstly"? Felton asked. "At least you have luggage Einuur, you'll have to loan me some clothing".

"Relax", the Zaromoid retorted in reply, pulling open a drawer in one unit to reveal brand new underwear. Tugging the sliding door to a fitted wardrobe to reveal suits, trousers, jackets. "Moluura thinks of everything, get clean - Mizaroid".

"You know I'm not one of those - if such exists at all", Felton felt his blood rushing to his neck, face, "I'm still human with a Mizaroa cerquibrum in my brain".

"Relax Mister Fish", Einuur seemed to enjoy himself, "I was just foolin' with you. Go get your bath. You'll want to be nice and clean ready for the double bed".

"Just a second", Felton demanded then, his hand on the bathroom door handle. "Do you think you're climbing in with me, because...".

"Ha ha ha ha", Einuur saw the humour in Felton's dilemma. He did not want to share with either of the other two. "I've got the single - humanoid. My mating ritual has failed to attract Ailuura in the past, maybe you; a Mizaroa will have more luck. Just think, if you impregnate her, the resultant humanoid would have both Mizaroa and Zaromi DNA in its molecular make-up. It would be a Zaromizoa, ha ha ha ha".

Felton felt the need to punch the Zaromoid. Instead, he observed calmly, "Failed eh, you showed shrewd sensibility there, Alice. Einuur's badly adjusted".

It rewarded him with a look of instant cold fury on his enemy's dark features. "Get bathed, humanoid! Mind your head doesn't slip under the water".

"I'm sure you'll be a gentleman won't you, Inigo"? Ailuura suddenly asked. "I have no desire to mate with a humanoid".

"While I don't want to florinate with a cricket". Felton answered before leaving the two Zaromoid. He had just invented a word that meant having sex with an insect!

He did his best to languish over the ablution, but inevitably, it concluded. Dressing in the pyjamas they had supplied him with, went back into the lounge/reception room of the apartments. Ailuura was already in the double bed, her back turned to the opposite, in which she resided. With as little movement as he could make possible, Felton climbed into the other, turned his back to her own.

'We can converse now. Think your thoughts back to me so that the others cannot tap'. Kim tapped to Felton.

'How do I do that? I don't know the difference'?

'Imagine your thoughts under blankets of subfuscation, guarded by a bright mesh of interference that the Zaromoid cannot penetrate'.

'Those are just words Kim, I've no concept of how to actuate them'.

Kim seemed angry when her thoughts came back harshly glittering, 'Use your imagination'.

'Like you did then to convey irritation'?

'Exactly. Try for Balurzuura's sake'.

Felton, former fisherman of Bridlington, did his best to imagine a blanket surrounding his thoughts. In that imaginary blanket was a mesh of phostiron, an alien metal that blocked all thoughts.

'How'm I doing'? He asked Kim. Responding the Mizaroa admitted,

'That is truly excellent. You are a natural. I think the invention of phostiron should be a priority of our manufacturing machines'

'Thanks, I try. Now, what's this secret communication you wish to give me"?

'I know the intention of the Zaromoid. They want you to get close enough to Sellers to allow them to assassinate him. They will try some sort of coercion, agree to it, but you can then warn him of the impending attack'.

'Why would they think I would defect to their side'?

'They don't – yet'. You must appear to resist initially, then reluctantly submit to their demands. I will help to keep your resolve for us, but it will not be easy. I suspect they will employ some sort of device. It is the only thing that will convince them they can wash your engrams with a new perspective'.

'You mean brain-wash me'.

'I believe I said that. That is all for now. Try to get some rest'.

Kim fell silent. The girl at Felton's side had fallen asleep. He could tell by her deep, rhythmic breathing. She suddenly turned over. An arm came around his chest. Whatever or whomever she was dreaming about, were making her involuntary movements amorous. Felton reminded himself if he responded to them, she would doubtless awaken horrified. Even if she didn't, he also reminded himself she was an enemy. Controlled by a race of insectoid creatures bent on the subjugation of humanity. His task was to help destroy the Zaromoid through this contact - Sellers. How far had it spread? Was every city in the world in the grip of invasion, or ludicrously had the attempt started in England Yorkshire? Surely a full-scale planetary invasion of Earth would not start in Yorkshire? The thought was farcical. It had to start somewhere. The aliens would not know in advance how Yorkshire appeared in the overall dynamic of the world. Mulling these things over in his mind, Felton finally drifted off to sleep.

Nineteen.   **Scunlington was not** the sort of town the name implied, it was quite affluent by local standards. Cowie, under the guidance of the Veztőöndər Moluura, set up a centre of communication there. He directed his humanoid host to the electrical supplier - Tandy. Bought a stack of components that would create a humanly sized tapping amplifier. In the recently hired flat, Cowie spent several hours over a soldering iron while Veztőöndər Moluura added a new skill to his repertoire, that of an electrical engineer. It looked Heath-Robinson when completed, a mass of PCB's two motherboards, many transistors, capacitors, one resistor. Veztőöndər Moluura directed Cowie to plug the handheld mic into one part of the conglomerate, where the man had soldered a quarter-inch female socket. Throwing a toggle, he instructed the following,

"Female Ailuura of the twenty-third hive, you will report to our new base at 23 Christie Gardens, Scunlington, DN15 6TX, where you together with agent Einuur, will receive a special task from your Veztőöndər, Moluura. Set off immediately, come by car".

Cowie then turned the set - off. "Am I to learn the nature of the mission before they get here"? He wished to know.

'Unnecessary. It concerns none you know. Tell me something, Cowie, do you have a dark side. A facet of your psyche that you have always kept quelled'.

"How do you mean"?

'I mean, have you ever fought the compulsion to harm, simply for the dark-joy of it? To give in to your inner demons, do something bad, just to see how it feels'?

"Of course, every man has those moments, but only criminals give into them. Then the consequences are usually inconvenient".

*'What if there were **no** consequences? What if you were certain you could get away with it'?*

"It would be a temptation certainly, ultimately humanity would not miss my – for want of a better word, let us call the individual the target. The target's absence would only improve the world".

'Tell me more'?

"Oh, it's an old grudge. Unimportant in the greater scheme of things. I doubt it would interest you".

'On the contrary Cowie, it does interest me. It interests me a great deal, tell me more'?

"They bullied me at school, that's all. You know what school is"?

'An institution where instruction is undertaken, especially to humanoids under college age'.

"When I was at such, one male humanoid sought to make my life a living misery".

'Why'?

"Simply because he could, I guess. He was bigger, more popular, stronger in every way. So he beat down on me mentally, physically, the whole works. There are one or two of his sort in every school".

'Did you resent his treatment of you'?

"Of course, it wasn't principled. He had no legitimate reason to make me unhappy, just because I wasn't like him".

'Did you hate him'?

"In a childlike way, I suppose yes. Until you asked about this, I don't think about him any more, never".

'The reminisces are too painful. You have buried them deeply in your id'.

"You've got it, Mol. I can call you Mol, can I"?

'Only you Cowie. To all others, I am Veztőöndər, Moluura. So, Cowie, you have a double opportunity. You can see what it feels like to excise your inner demons. Rid the world of Target'.

"What do you mean"?

'I mean', Veztőöndər, Moluura's thoughts were lancing into Cowie's brain like shafts of burning icicles, *'That with a weapon of Zaromi construction, you are going to kill Target'!*

Strangely, Cowie did not object to the directive, rather asked, "What sort of weapon"? Then he realised what he had just done. The question was not whether he would or would not kill the one who had bullied him, but if he could do it with impunity. He went on,

"You see Mol, even though we humanoid are in some ways primitive when compared to the Zaromi, we have quite sophisticated detection techniques for a murderous crime. I would be of no further use to you languishing in a penitentiary would I"?

'You would not' The Zaromi Veztőöndər agreed readily, *'The problem is something my engineers have worked on. Now have a suitable solution'.*

"Really, what sort of solution"? Then as an afterthought, "Something that leaves no DNA evidence behind? Is it a gun of such alien construction that we could never trace the ammunition"?

'You are on the right lines, Cowie, but it is not a gun in the sense you would use the term. Rather, it is more accurately a stabbing weapon'.

"Surely not a knife? You would work on nothing so ordinarily established. That rules out; sword, lance, pike, so I give in. What have you insectoid genius' come up with"?

'I think you would call it a thermal lance'.

"Some sort of torch, like an acetylene"?

'It does not fire any sort of flame, Cowie. Rather it gets white-hot. Except for the handle, of course. It is a stabbing weapon that also cauterizes the wound at the instant of penetration'.

"That sounds painful. Sounds like one could inflict several wounds with it before actually delivering the coup-de-grâce"?

'Exactly. You can experience the joy of murder, the pleasure of torture, both if that is your desire'?

Cowie gave it a couple of seconds' thought. His dark side raging against his saner reason. Finally, he smiled, noting,

"He made my life a misery. There's no need to ask me his name, for it serves our purpose to regard him as *Target*"!

When Cowie thought about it, he had always envied those who acted with no constraints bound by morality. The world considered them malign or deranged, but that was perspective. Sometimes, when so-called tyrannical men had acted for pure motives, to achieve a certain goal. One they considered would benefit the majority. Cowie thought about Target, realised that the world could only improve by his absence. He would kill him. Or rather, he would execute him coolly clinically for the betterment of mankind.

"How will we find this man whom I must extinguish"? He wanted to know. The reply was one of an amusing thought.

'Cowie - really? This is the age of the web, social media. It has never been easier to find anyone, no matter how circumspect their activities. I am going to allow the location of your target to be secured by you. It will be part of the pleasure of your realised intention'.

"I'm not sure if pleasure is quite the right word", Cowie railed against it, "Perhaps satisfaction in a mission of necessity, accomplished with as little fuss as possible".

'Semantics, my dear humanoid. No matter, you will still feel the fulfilment of the kill. I can promise you that'.

Cowie realised the Zaromi was right. No matter how he regarded the notion, it ultimately caused him a detached intrigue. It was the ultimate power trip. Even with all his money, others could not have committed the act knowing that they would avoid detection, ultimately punishment. It lifted him above the rest of the struggling masses that were his fellow man. He, Cowie, had become elevated to a different plane. He was higher than all others; superior. Hom-superior had finally graced the world of Earth, it was he!

Veztőöndər Moluura, leader of the Zaromi, had been quite right. Locating the target was simple. The poor fool was on face-twit. Not only had he joined the rather inferior social vehicle to record his turgidly lame daily activities, but the dope had included his contact details for all to see. Cowie sent him an invitation to associate, although the bully had treated him so badly, he seemed to remember him, whilst conveniently forgetting the systematic abuse.

Target: If it isn't my old school chum Cowie. How'z u buddy?

Cowie: Keeping busy. Know what would be cooler than messaging on here?

Target: What?

Cowie: We could meet one evening in a bar, go over old times. See if we can remember all the guys from back then.

Target: Cool. When? Where?

Cowie: I see you're in Rowle. I could drive over one evening soon. Do you know of a nice place to meet?

Target: Yup Spaghetti Sid's it's banging LOL

Cowie: Next Tuesday 20:00 would suit, you?

Target: L8R mi old. I'll be there grate to ear from you.

Grate?! He had misspelt the word great? Used the acronym for laughing out loud. *Deserved* to die! As Cowie had expected, Spaghetti Sid's was what someone could only generously describe as *a dump*. There again, the town of Rowle, dilapidated, old-fashioned, was yet to receive the benefit of Americanaidosity. Cowie made certain all the locks, security measures, were in place in his car. It was worth over three-quarters the value of the town! He slipped through the dull smog of the city, the thermal lance banging assuredly against his leg inside his voluminous bohos. Collected it just in time to avoid cancellation. The lance had been in the ship's hangar, just as the alien commander had assured him it would. Instruction on its use had been farcically simple. The answer to how it operated had suitably chagrined Cowie. Depress the stud, the lance heats. Up to the optimum temperature in two seconds. Do with it as you will, remembering not to touch any part of the unit - other than the guarded handle. The lance would melt flesh when charged, it would also cauterize any subsequent wound delivered. Once the *deed* was over, a second depression of the violet button would be cool-assisted in two further seconds. Allowing concealment once more without injury. As Cowie walked down the dingy alley that led to the bar's side, its only entrance, an enormous figure who had been subfusc in the shadow suddenly lurched out. Pointed a rusty, filthy pistol at his head.

"Awright bud, this is an impeditation. Get your wallet out, any other valuables, delverate but expediotuslike percepto"?

"I think I do", Cowie felt a strange calmness. He was being robbed in the street, mugged by a firearm. Yet his heart rate had not changed from that of the exertion of a gentle stroll.

"I take it you intend robbery of anything I have upon my person which may be of resale value, is that the gist of it, Sir"?

"Hey bud, Arma not interested ifin you're some sort of fag, just hand over the graft percepto-like".

Veztőöndər Moluura was keeping strangely silent as Cowie asked the perpetrator, "I need to reach into my bohos to extract my money-belt".

"Get reachin' then"? Porcine eyes lighting up with sudden avarice.

As Cowie pulled out the thermal-lance, he also depressed the activation stud. Knowing that its appearance would momentarily confuse the perpetrator. He was not in error,

"What the doame is that"?!

With eager curiosity, Cowie swept forward, bringing the lance into an arc. It sliced through the villain's arm like a hot knife through butter. Several things happened at once; the would-be robber screamed in surprise rather than pain. His arm fell to the ground. Nerves in it jerked his trigger finger. The decrepit weapon exploded. The bullet hit a wheelie-bin of refuse at the side of the alley.

"You fassyú". The villain explained, "You've cut off my arm"!

"Apart from pointing out the painfully obvious", Cowie began, "I'd like to draw your attention to the fact that you're not bleeding. You will survive the injury if you comply with certain conditions I am about to issue".

"I'm not bending over for no fag", came the alarmed response, more reasonably, "we can sow it back on"?

"Amazingly yes. By the right organization. Of which, I happen to be a high-ranking member. So, I'm going to present you with a choice. Do I have your undivided attention"?

The villain suddenly crumpled to a sitting position shaking from head to toe, "I think I'm dying".

"Nonsense, you're just in shock. It will pass. Stop talking, listen. I'm going to present you with the biggest decision of your life. Such as it's been so far".

A face wreathed in confused perspiration regarded Cowie. Yet as directed, the man held his tongue,

"Good, now you can do one of two things; one is that you can live, have your arm restored to you. Two is that I can now end your life quickly, painlessly. It's up to you. Questions"?

"Who are you? How can you do these things"?

"Cowie, your new Veztőöndər. Which means leader in Americanese. Choose life, become one of my men, a bodyguard. I will also furnish you with money, drink, women if you agree to serve me faithfully. Or, I can end it now - swiftly"?

"And you'll have my arm put back on"?

Cowie nodded solemnly. The real Veztőöndər surfaced in his mind, *'Recruitment Cowie, excellent. You exceed the faith I initially had in you - to become host to my mentality. We will restore the arm at the same time cerquiotomize the recruit if he concedes'.*

"I'll have your arm put back on".

"Pay, booze, tarts"?

"A constant supply furnished. If you excel in your duties, what is your name? No! Don't tell me, after all? Soon you will get a new one. What's your decision"?

After he had repeatedly given the former mugger directions to the ship, Cowie proceeded into the drinking establishment. He recognised Target at once. He had changed little in the few years since full-time education. Going over to the waving figure, took the seat next to him, endured a slap on the back,

"Cowie, you bugger. You don't look a day older. Must be the clean living, aye? No women to worry about".

"What're you drinking"? Cowie responded. Ordered two Bourbon and Branch paid with dollars, not trusting to wait till the end, produce a card in a place like Spaghetti Sid's.

"So what are you doing with yourself these days"? He asked after they had sipped the drink. "Are you doing well? I always thought you would"?

"Oh, I'm just doing a bit of this and that at the minute", came the vague reply. "Sort of between executive posts, what about you"?

"I have a little place over in the old town where we used to go to school, keep myself occupied".

"Doing what exactly"? Was Target seeking a job offer?

"Carpentry, my first love - if you remember"?

Cowie could see an image of the coffee table he had lovingly poured his energies into. The one Target had driven a circular saw through. Cut it in half. "You're thinking about the coffee table".

"I was, but we were just kids fooling around, weren't we, Mike? I mean, it's all water under the bridge now, isn't it? Let me buy you another drink"?

"No, I'll get them if you're currently out of work, don't worry about it. I've got them".

"Cool, you're a white man. Always was Mike. I always say that to the boys. Remember Trodga and Brownstain, I still see them from time to time".

Brownstain had once had an unfortunate, very embarrassing accident in his trolleys. Target had found out about it. The unfortunate young lad had then had to live with the nickname for the rest of his school life.

"How are the two of them? I'm surprised Brownstain wanted to keep in touch with you Gripper".

Target laughed, half in chagrin. His nickname had come from the practice of insisting the other boys shake his hand. Subsequently, with superior strength, crushing their fingers until they yowled with pain.

"He's cool now, owns a nightclub in Frissle. Who'd have thought he'd become a businessman, aye"?

Cowie nodded, "Trodga"?

Gripper lowered his voice beneath the din of the bar, "Doing a bit of a stretch on a bum-rap, but he'll be out April, I think".

"A bum-rap"?

"Yeah, some filthy stooly ratted him out, but when he gets out, Trodga is going to fix him".

"With your help perhaps"?

Target, known formerly as Gripper, laughed again, "Us pals have to stick together, right"?

"Abso-effing-lutely I might have a position for Trodga myself, where's he banged up"?

"Armoor", Gripper dutifully informed, "Say my glass is empty".

Inside an hour, Target was drunk, while Cowie had carefully sipped at the same drink. He offered, "Let's get you home now Gripper, can you remember where your flop is"?

The drunken target gave Cowie directions. Leaning on his newfound friend. Supportively conducted to his car. When they reached it, Gripper whistled at the automobile.

"Say, Mike, carpentry pays don't it"?

"You could say that, Gripper. Now climb in the back? I'll have you home in no time".

"You're solid man", came the mumbled reply as he stumbled into the rear seats of the vehicle.

It turned out that Cowie had yet to see the worst of Rowle. He drove through dilapidated rows of tenements, the streets of which were littered with detritus. Finally, at a particular scruffy, filthy block Gripper cried,

"Here we are, home sweet home. I'm in 23, it's on the second floor. We'll have to take the stairs. The lift's busted since the November riots".

"I wonder why none block it", Cowie observed sarcastically, but it seemed it lost the irony on Gripper.

"Probably 'cos this place is going to khaak", was his considered input.

The two of them went up the stairs two at a time, pausing only to navigate past a pool of vomit. Squeeze past a sleeping homeless person of indeterminate age, means - sex. It seemed besides all the benefits the Americans had brought to England; they had also contributed - the ghetto. Gripper spent several moments jiggling a key in the lock of apartment 23 before finally gaining entry. The lock as dilapidated as the rest of the building. Beyond was the typical idea of what a man lives like when a bachelor.

"Excuse the mess", Cowie's new friend began, "My old lady portsided me a couple of months ago. Really bummed me out for a while. I never got around to dusting".

Nor any aspect of domestic cleansing it appeared. Cowie looked around, shocked, revolted at the pile of dirty crockery in the filthy sink. The layers of greasy grime on the bent battered cooker. Rat droppings on the floor. To give his eyes a rest, he looked up at the ceiling only to be confronted by nicotine brown that might have once been magnolia, cream, or stretching the imagination - white. Qualifying the latter, Gripper suddenly produced a reefer,

"Hey man, let's vape some bhang? Being as you bought all the drinks".

"Sure, spark that roach up? We'll mellow out", Cowie responded, referring to the vernacular of certain movie entertainment he had experienced in the past.

"Once a dude gets to know you, you're not so straight-laced as you portrayed earlier, aye"?

"I quite agree", Cowie responded on more than one level, "I have character traits that you would not even credit, considering how I used to be".

"Like you used to be, say what was your nickname at school Mike? I can't bring it to mind"?

"Mollusc", Cowie responded with an icy smile.

"Yeah that's it", Gripper laughed, "Well your mollusc days are over Mike, you can be sure of that".

"I know", Cowie told him. "Ironically, your days are over too, Gripper".

"We all grow up, don't we, Mike? That bag's in the past".

"I wasn't referring to your past Gripper, rather your imminent future".

"I hear you, Mike. I hear you, without a bit of blow now and again life's such a drag if you follow".

"Enjoy the locoweed Gripper, it won't be the end of you. I guarantee it".

"There ain't no guarantees in life Mike, so you have to live for the moment you know".

"No, what I meant to say was - Gripper. That the cannabis won't kill you because *I'm* going to"!

"Ha ha ha ha, kill me with laughter like"?

"No, actually end your life Gripper. You know - make you bereft of life, an ex Gripper, gone to join the choir invisible".

"What"?

"You know, I don't recall you being quite so dense in the past. The weed must have ruined more grey cells than enough. I'm going to end your life, Gripper. The only reason I haven't already started is that you have a smoking roach in your hand. If you drop it on that disgusting sofa of yours, the resultant fire might lead to danger for me personally".

The message finally got through. That which Cowie remembered so well instantly replaced Gripper's former demeanour.

"You're going to kill me, Mollusc. *You*?! You're weaker, slower, so gentle. Threatening me, the cock of Scunny High"!

Cowie pulled the lance free of voluminous bohos, described the second arc for that evening. At first, it fascinated him to see the damage did not register on Gripper's angry features. Slowly, as the shock subsided, the pain registered. He glanced down, cried out in alarm.

"You cut my leg ... *off*"!

"I know", Cowie noted smoothly. Dark satisfaction welled within him, bathed his nigrescent quiddity. "Well, you said you were faster than me. Tell me, are you faster on one leg, do you think? If you are, I'll have to cut the other one off".

"How"? Gripper demanded, his eyes filling with tears, "Why"?

"Oh, I think you know the answer to that second question, Gripper", Cowie returned with satiety. "Because I hate you! As to the first part, I wouldn't bother your peanut of a brain with it. You'll never work out its full potential, you'll be dead long before that would happen".

"You podendor"! Gripper roared, strove to launch himself at Cowie. Loss of such a large limb destroyed his balance, he promptly fell sprawling at Cowie's feet. It was an opportunity to test the device's penetrating ability. With methodical care, Cowie selected the upper lung on the left side, stabbed down into the former bully's body. Apart from the scream of pain, the sickly sweet aroma of roasting Gripper fascinated him.

"Stop, stop, please"? Gripper begged into the carpet far sooner than Cowie would have expected. "I'm sorry Mike. I'm sorry for how things were, don't kill me. I'll make it up to you".

Cowie took a seat in the least soiled of the two chairs, "Exactly how is a no-hoper like you going to do that exactly"?

"I don't know. I don't know how long it will take me. Until you say I have, I will not stop doing all I can to make amends for what I did. Only please get me to a hospital. I'm finding it difficult to breathe".

"That's perfectly understandable with a punctured lung", Cowie felt serenely calm, "However, you had two you know, or were you busy making my life as miserable as possible during biology classes"?

For once Gripper seemed to realise exactly what was happening, maybe even suspecting what was *going* to happen. Not trusting himself to speak. A further apology would not weaken Cowie's resolve in the slightest. Instead, he quietly wept into the carpet. His tormentor suddenly jumped from the chair, turned him over. Propped his back against the sofa seating. Gripper gasped in pain, but looking down at his leg, saw no blood. Eyebrows rose, the next time he spoke it was with a leaden tone acquiescent to his fate.

"A futuristic weapon? One that can remove a limb without blood loss? Who sent you, Cowie? A secret organisation"?

"A secret organisation that wants *you* out of the way, Gripper? Is a dumb schmuck like you so high profile? What you been up to"?

"We both know I'm not. I've amounted to nothing much Mike, so why kill me"?

"Is the fact that you made my life a misery for five years not enough"?

"You're still bitter about it", his head sagged as he asked in quiet tones, "Will you make it quick? That's all I ask now".

"Did five years pass quickly for me"?

Silent tears ran down Gripper's face once he realised there would be no clemency.

Moluura the Veztőöndər suddenly asked, *'Do you feel any sympathy for his position'*?

'He felt none for mine, why should I'? Cowie reasoned logically enough.

'You will cause him more suffering before you end it'?
'I think it harsh but fair'.
'You are the one we have been looking for. The Veztőöndər of the Zaromoid'.

Gripper was gazing at Cowie during the mental conversation, as though he doubted his tormentor's sanity. His puzzlement suddenly turned to terror when Cowie suddenly addressed him,

"Now, where were we"?

When he took off the remaining leg, the screaming was one of pain, fear, desperation. At the removal of the left arm, it turned to hoarse terror. By the time the remaining extremity fell away neatly severed, all he could hear was pathetic gibbering. His ultimate act was to drive the thermal lance into Gripper's eye slowly. The ball punctured, aqueous solution hissed, bubbled as it dribbled onto the dead man's cheek. By that moment, even Cowie was shaking. It was the first time he had tortured a man to death. It would not be the last!

Twenty.   Sellers strolled past the Tandy store, a tall skyscraper. The Woolworth building dwarfed it. Besides that was the smaller yet voluminous Comet, Do It All. House of New New York was between that, American Home Stores. They faced; Maplins, Toys4U,   Stones, Rumbelows, Abraham Lincoln's Cameras. The entire town of Doncaster seemed filled with shops that no longer existed in what he thought of as Reality Alpha. He secretly harboured the faint hope that he would find Nicole in the House of New New York. True, he had slept with Lady Heartbridge, but that was out of consideration for Balurzuura, his Mizaroan wife. He saw no conflict in the two acts. He still found Nicole Elv intriguing on another level. It thrilled him to have two mistresses at the same time. If it were possible, that was, if Nicole Elv still existed in Amercanesean England. So he was ardently desirous of seeing her once more when he passed into the store. Sneaking out while the exhausted lady of Heartbridge slept still had not been easy, but possible. Balurzuura had been most insistent that it was folly. Sellers was still master of his body. All careful arguments fell on stony ground, figuratively thinking. The fragrance Sellers looked for no longer existed, at least not in that layer of reality, yet there may be an alternative that provided the girl with suitable employment. He said to a rather pretty blonde on one concession.

"I'm looking for Miss Elv, Nicole Elv. I understand she works here, I have some glad tidings about her family".

"Nicole", smiled the blonde (not bad herself), "She works on children's wear, on the fifth floor. The elevators are over to your right, Sir".

Thanking her, Sellers strode for the lifts. Elevators indeed! Children's Wear was easy enough to find. So was Nicole, but the girl Sellers saw there was not what he was expecting. Not what he was expecting at all.

For in that current lay-line of the multiverse, Nicole Elv was a Negress!

"Hello Tod, what are you doing in here"? She asked as he hesitated before her, trying desperately not to look too astonished. She offered him the familiar albescent smile, then made even whiter than white by the sharp contrast of her teeth to her skin tone.

"I know it's early", he returned, amazed that his voice was as steady as usual, "But I wondered if you found out which lunch break you were on if I could buy it for you"?

"Let me check with Danni? Then I can tell you. I'd love to see you again, even if only for the better part of an hour".

"As I, would, you", he returned, *'Even though strictly speaking, it's the first time I've seen you'*, he thought.

'Your former lover is now of different **genera** *it would seem'*, Balurzuura observed.

'Not really', Sellers returned, *'Humans come in different classifications, races, sizes, Balu. Their differences are more political than biological'*.

'So you will still desire a liaison with the female, even in her altered state'?

'Brown sugar is just as sweet as white', Sellers replied with a smile.

Nicole returned, told him when her lunch break would be.

"I'll meet you in The Black Bear then", he told her.

"I don't think I know it, where is it"? It puzzled her.

"Well, where do you like"?

"I like the Stars and Stripes. Would you like to meet me there"?

"Sure, see you later".

'I'm not happy about you being abroad unguarded Sellers', Balurzuura complained, *'The whole point of recruiting Her Ladyship was to keep us safe'*.

"I can't meet her in the company of Her Ladyship", Sellers explained as they left the store, "Women rarely tolerate over one sexual relationship at a time. One or both of them would make a fuss about it".

'So you have become what your vernacular refers to as a cad'?

"Possibly, but it's fun, more for you to study".

'There is a distinct possibility that the Zaromoid will try to attack us'.

"I've been dead before. It's not final. Come on, let's look around this bizarre city of mine".

Sellers could not recognise Doncaster. The restructuring of the Americans was evident at every plaza, every corner of his hometown. As he wandered around, he told the Mizaroan cerquibrum,

"I'm running low on funds, Balu, mainly because of all the changes because of your taking over of a part of my mind. It has interrupted my normal business. Can you supply me with funds - please"?

'Some of those we inhabit are very wealthy, more than willing to support us', the cerquibrum conceded, *'I will have some dollars transferred directly into your bank account. It is coming to the point where I would like custody of your body for a ...'.*

"Forget that Balu. We've been over it before. I am the superintendent here. Always going to be".

Without warning, Sellers gasped. With luck managed to find a seat upon which to stumble. The cerquibrum was attacking his mind, trying to force it down into his subconscious. Balurzuura was attempting to take over control of both his mind and body!

Twenty-one. **"Wake up", the** voice was harsh, demanding. Momentarily disorientated, Inigo Felton dragged himself from peaceful slumber to wakefulness. Einuur was bending over him, contempt on his features.

"What's the matter? Where's the fire"?

"Never mind the wisecracks, perform your ablutions. I've a task for you". The revolver in Einuur's hand brooked no argument. Upon his return to the lounge, Felton saw that someone had slightly rearranged the furniture. A cottage-style chair with sturdy wooden arms was now at its centre. Before he could so much as frame a question, Einuur, waving the gun, indicated Felton took a seat in it. The instant he complied, Ailuura strapped his wrists to the arms of the chair with strong tie-wraps. Einuur put the pistol in his shoulder holster, reached for one of his cases.

"You only have to ask me questions if you want information of some sort. I doubt I'll know much of use to you", Felton spoke chiefly to the man.

"Very well", Ailuura responded, "Will you become an agent for the Zaromoid, help us get close enough to Sellers to kill him"?

"Don't be foolish Ailuura"! Einuur snapped, "He'll agree before going back on his word. That's what I'd do if I was in his situation".

"Just exactly what *is* my situation"? Felton wished to know. "If you want to kill this chap called Sellers, what do you need me for, anyway? Why don't you, the girl or another Zaromoid, do it without me"?

"Can't your cerquibrum distinguish Zaromi from Mizaroa"? Ailuura asked, "Now that we had the berets off"?

"Enough of the naïve questions Ailuura", Einuur snapped, help me with this".

He was pulling out what looked like some type of skull cap, attached to which were a series of wires that trailed into the item remaining in the case.

Kim remained silent, so Felton asked reasonably enough, "What's that"?

Einuur smiled grimly, "We call this device a spalvosás. Your cerquibrum can tell you its function".

"My cerquibrum is sort of *out* for the moment. What is it, what does it do"?

Ailuura replied in a concerned tone, "It realigns your sympathies, Inigo".

"What if I don't want them realigning"? Not with a great deal of conviction. Einuur gave a vulpine grin.

"But you're not in charge here, Felton, I am. Now let me advise you, to resist the spalvosás will result in more than a little, shall we say, *discomfort*. So the choice is yours, or that of your Mizaroa. It will smoothly achieve its purpose if you embrace the emanations. Resist, you'll not like what it does to your body or your brain".

Felton struggled, a chiefly useless show of defiance given the circumstances. Einuur suddenly cuffed him upside the head, jammed the cap onto his head, securing it by a strap beneath the chin. Satisfied that the fit was optimum, he bent over the case. Felton heard two toggle switches being thrown. The mechanism filled the room with a soft humming of an alien power. The Zaromoid turned his attention to the captive, began,

"Inigo Felton, which alien race do you have the most sympathy for? Answer or I'll adjust the spalvosás, to give you a little jolt, a *sample* of what might come if you do not cooperate with the Zaromi".

Felton tried reasonably enough, "I have a Mizaroa cerquibrum in my head so my allegiance is to them".

A spear of indescribable agony suddenly racked his entire body from the top of his head to the end of his toes. Felton heard himself grunt, satisfied that it was not a scream. For a nonsensical reason, he wanted to demonstrate as much resistance to the Zaromoid ambition as he could muster.

"That was the physical part of the device", Einuur told him with satisfaction. Enjoying the discomfort he was applying. "Now let me show a level one mental jolt".

Before Felton could respond, a sudden bolt of incredibly destructive energy lanced through his mind. It was worse than the very worst headaches he had ever suffered in his entire life. He sweat profusely even though it was not especially balmy in their room.

"Inigo Felton, which alien race do you have the most sympathy for"? Ailuura asked him this time, before adding, "Please try to realign your allegiances, I beg you? It's the only way to avoid terrible suffering before ultimately giving in to the persuasion, anyway".

"Einuur", Felton promised through gritted teeth, "I don't know how or when I am going to achieve my ambition, but I'm going to kill you".

Einuur laughed, "Really? By the time I've finished with you Felton, you will beg me to let you kiss my feet".

The pain came again, if possible even stronger. That time, Felton gasped, cried out in agony. Kim was suddenly urgently calling to him, but his thoughts sounded faint, subfastigiated by some hither-to unsuspected shield of protection,

'Felton! I want you to use the power of your mind. I will help you. Together we can build a defence against the power of the spalvosás. Listen to what I have to let you know'.

"Inigo Felton, for which alien race of insectivores from Mizar A, do you have the most sympathy"? Einuur demanded to cut in on Felton's mind communication.

"The Zaromi", the sweating, pain-racked man in the chair, gladly lied.

"I believe that was far too easy", the sadist in Einuur said to the other two occupants of the room. A second physical jolt tore through Felton's body. He screamed - blacked out. Unconsciousness was so comforting, the absence of pain. It gave Kim the opportunity for which she had been waiting.

'Listen to me', she urged. *'Build a defence against the Zaromoid device of persuasion or it will catechize you to indoctrination. To become a Zaromoid. My mind destroyed, replaced by the enemy who will take over your body. You will be almost dead, your chances of ever becoming yourself again practically none. Do you understand'?*

'Apperception has never been my problem, has it, Kim? Go on? I'm keen to learn, for obvious reasons'.

'Use the power of your mental resourcefulness. It is time to create, to conceive something by using only your inner chimaera. Imagine in your anamnesis a shield. A mighty folding escutcheon of psychic energy, a huge protective

blanket that will defend your mind. Your skull, neck, body from the metaphysical lances of the spalvosás'.

Felton tried, failed, woke up. Einuur was looking down at him. Felton was wet on his face, hair, shirt. The Zaromoid had dashed a cup of cold water into it to bring him back to consciousness.

"Aah, the sleeper awakens. Good. Do you fancy answering a question or two"?

"Frenge off, koofoid".

Einuur chuckled, "Such language, in the presence of a lady, too. I never realised you were so uncouth, Fishseller".

"I'm going to take time over your death, Einuur".

"Are you indeed, ha ha ha ha? You - strapped currently to the chair, are going to kill your future master"?

"Get on with it Einuur"! Ailuura suddenly snapped, "Your posturing is filling me with ennui. Here let me ask him? Will you serve the Zaromi as your masters? Agree to oppose their hated enemy, the Mizaroa"?

"Why do they hate one another"? Felton suddenly desired to know, "They're both from the same world, why don't they agree to co-exist in peaceful harmony"?

"Who gives a khakk "? Einuur was impatient to use the spalvosás once again. "Maybe the Mizaroa are the niggers of the planet? The point is, they do. The Zaromi will ultimately be victorious".

"How do you know that"? Felton asked him reasonably enough, "How do you know your side will win - Einuur? If you do - what then? Is it your intention to turn all humanity into mindless Zombies, controlled by you"?

"We're asking the questions here", Einuur suddenly raged, "Answer her, or I'll give you another jolt just for avoiding it".

"Just a moment"? Ailuura requested. "Some of his queries need answering. We Zaromi are more purposeful than the Mizaroa. An Empire. Thriving on subjugation. Already we've defeated the Vasishtha, taken them into our ranks. That's why we'll win. We're a bigger swarm, stronger. The outcome can only end in one way".

"The Vasishtha"? It genuinely intrigued Felton. "Why have I heard nothing about them"?

"Because they are all but gone", Einuur was growing impatient. "We conquered them, just as we will crush the Mizaroan Egalitarianism. It is useless to fight against us".

"Can you describe the Vasishtha to me"? Felton persisted, tarried, "What were they like"?

Ailuura told him then, "A conspicuous feature of the order, is that the Vasishtha all have three long caudal filaments. The two lateral filaments are cerci, the medial one - an epiproct or appendix dorsalis. In this, they resemble the Archaeognatha, though, unlike, in the latter order, the cerci of Zygentoma is nearly as long as the epiproct. We Zaromi always regarded the Vasishtha as a suborder of the Thysanura until recognized that the order Thysanura was paraphyletic, thus the two suborders were each raised to the status of an independent monophyletic order, with Archaeognatha sister taxon to the Dicondylia, including the Zygentoma. Did you understand any of that, Fishsalesman"?

"Hardly any except I've just realised that Mizar A is a planet covered in many insectivores rather than just two. You'll not be satisfied until the Zaromi rules over all the others. Just tell me out of idle curiosity, what do the Vasishtha most closely resemble on Earth"?

"You call them Firebrats. I don't believe Einuur will wait any longer, so proclaim your intention please"?

"Unfortunately, I have no sympathy with conquerors", Felton began, "So I must regrettably...".

A spear of heinous pain penetrated his core right down to a molecular level. He promptly blacked out again.

'I want to make that protective box', he thought to Kim instantly.

'A box! Of course, not everyone envisages protection in the same way. How foolish of me'. Kim seemed to gasp in his thought projections, *'Very well, if a box works better than a shield, envisage a box'.*

The thought of future treatments spurred Felton on, the ultimate threat, the spalvosás. He imagined a box. Five sides, made of félmunite (a material impervious to mental or physical attack). It had strength, dimension, mass. Large enough for him to climb inside. Which he did - closing the door behind him. Water on face, shirt soaked, hair plastered to scalp. Back in the room of his torment.

"I've had enough Einuur. I'll do what you want", he offered, "Just tell me what to do. You're my commander all right"?

"Unfortunately, you've not just got to verbalize it", Einuur responded with perverse amusement. "You've got to *believe* it"!

"I do", Felton offered with as much conviction as he could muster, "I'll not betray you, I give my word".

"You *will* do before we're finished. But right now you're just saying what you know I want to hear. I'm afraid the spalvosás hasn't finished with you yet".

Felton's mind jumped into the félmunite protective cell. Heard the crackle of the device - feigned a scream.

"You seem to have grown accustomed to level one", Einuur noted, "Not fainting this time. Perhaps the psychic level will prove more uncomfortable".

Even from inside the cell, Felton felt the emanations nibbling at his mind. He cried out with every ounce of strength, pretended to pass out.

"Good, that's more effective. I do believe he may be on the way to conditioning. The Mizaroa must be pretty weak from that last battering. We can cerquiotomize one of our own soon enough".

"I think you take too much satisfaction from your work, Einuur". Ailuura criticized, "I'll be giving Veztőöndər Moluura a full report to that effect when next we tapp".

"Be my guest", Einuur chuckled, "Moluura did not become our Veztőöndər because of his insectivorian acts for the good of the Zaromi".

"I'm going for breakfast. My host is hungry you carry on alone or take a break too, whichever suits you".

She hesitated at the door, but Einuur made no move to join her. He was a dedicated soldier-Zaromi, in the very worst tradition.

Going to the bathroom, he dashed a cup of cold water on the seemingly insensible Felton. Waited for him to splutter to wakefulness. The Mizaroan host duly pretended to do just that.

"Felton, Felton, Felton", Einuur began savouring the moment with perverse pleasure. "I feel you are on the road to salvation. Alas, you have yet to reach your destination, so we must proceed".

There was the endless repetition of the same, on into the mid-afternoon. Felton tried something new. He confessed,

"Commander Einuur, the creature that was in my mind, it's gone. The Mizaroa's dead".

Einuur nodded to Ailuura, who unpacked another case.

"I wish to serve the Zaromi, my Commander, but I've no cerquibrum to aid me, what...".

"Patience", Einuur halted him, "We Zaromi finally have a portable unit that will aid you. Or perhaps I should call you Zelmuur".

"Zelmuur"?

"Zelmuur is the Zaromi who will soon become your cerquibrum. You'll be re-born. Re-born into the service of Veztőöndər Moluura - the Zaromoid Empire".

Felton feigned a look of acceptance, "Yes, that's what I want to be. In the service of the supreme commander of the Zaromi. Thank you Einuur, for the opportunity. How can I ever repay you"?

"That's easy Zelmuur". Einuur smiled, "You can get close to Sellers, who is the host of Balurzuura - a Mizaroa. You can assassinate your Királálynővonazóreginácondător"!

Twenty-two. Griselda Ebeling had always wanted to be a hairdresser since being a little girl. Had pretended to cut her mother's hair for as long as she could remember. Once she had left school, she went immediately to a hairdressing college passed the top of her class. Her job prospects were excellent, allowing her to choose a resultant position with care. When a post at Billy the Kid's in Gentley became available, she knew that was where she wanted to work. With confidence, that exuded from every pore, breezed through the interview, a short test. The job was hers. She had achieved her ambition. It would have been a dream come true for her, were it not for two clouds on her sunny horizon. The first was her father's fatal heart attack, closely followed by her mother's cerebral haemorrhage that left her paralysed down the right side. What it meant, apart from the terrible upsetment, was that Griselda had suddenly become the only source of income for the household. It would only be at subsistence level for the first few years of her career while she was on a starter-level salary. She hoped one day to open her very own salon, of course, but that did not do her any good at that present climacteric time. Not only was her salary effectively gobbled up when she had looked forward to some socializing - natural in one her age, but the constant care her mother required was a drain on Griselda's energies. The second was the *spasms*. They thankfully did not start when she was mourning her lost father. Nor when her mother needed the most care. Rather, three months later. As a result of what had befallen her, Griselda had lost a few pounds of puppy fat was then a very slim young woman. She had her blonde hair cut into a fashionable page-boy bob which accentuated her long aquiline nose, large reflective eyes. In short, she was attractive, popular with the customers the manager assigned to her. For a while, matters seemed to improve. Until that was, she had the first strange experience that she called a spasm.

"We've got a young man coming in for one of those ridiculous Nazi cuts that they seem to think makes them look good this morning, Grizzly", the manager had said to her. Griselda had asked him not to shorten her name countless times, thus he continued to address her, out of some sort of strange satisfaction. She felt he was constantly saying to her, 'I'm the manager therefore I can call you what I damn-well please'.

The problem was that he was, could. So Griselda had little choice but to act as though she did not hear it.

"So I want you to shave half his head, do a thoroughly good job of an awful job if you know-what-I-mean".

He often asked her if she knew what he meant. It was another of his annoying habits. He had asked her out shortly after recruiting her, at her rather brusque refusal, matters had decayed between them from that point onward.

"But I understand you're married Mister Slater", Griselda had pointed out, "And also that you're in your forties".

"Details, numbers my dear, if you-know-what-I-mean". Had been his reply. (Griselda had been *my dear* up to that point but would become Grizzly the day after).

"I don't", she had told him, "Even if you were younger, single, I'm afraid you're not my type Mister Slater. I go for the slimmer man, who takes care of his physique".

Thoroughly crushed, the rotund, expanding Slater had retired to his office for the rest of the shift. That was how it was then had become ever since. If a customer was smelly, he gave them to Griselda. If they had bad breath, the same. Even if they were interminably dull, the customer became hers. Then she also had to contend with the *touchy-feely* older men. Those whose hands strayed in certain areas, *accidentally*, of course. The stroked rump, the cough that caused them to encircle her waist for support mid-paroxysm. The worst of the lot, those who took the advantage for some *cuppage*, if Griselda were foolish enough to bend over for anything. Then there were the verbal abusers,

"Do you just cut hair for money, Sugar? Or would you be interested in earning four times as much for simply being good to a sensitive mature man"?

"Does this cut come with any *extras* babe, you know, *extras*"?

"After my blow-wave, is that all you blow, Darlin'?

With several dire permutations of the above. All this Griselda took in her particularly overtaxed stride. They had explained it to her in college that they could endure successfully these events if one chose simply to laugh them off. Griselda took the advice and did so. Then came the fateful day, the day she had her first spasm! The customer was a mature lady, one that would normally have caused her no concern at all. Until that was, she entered the salon. Instantly, Griselda knew that something was very wrong about the seemingly innocuous figure. Though she took her seat in a banal way smiled simply at Griselda, the *Lady's Stylist* felt something weird about her. It was difficult to put into words. The feeling. It was a simple extraneous incongruity that trickled up Griselda's spine, lodged at the base of her skull rather like the beginning of a migraine attack. There was something startlingly *alien* about the woman that Griselda and Griselda alone could feel. She tried to begin the lady's cut, but as she drew closer to her, felt a sort of trilling chitinous wave of thought coming from the woman that was not her own! The thoughts were cold, calculating heartless almost like those of worker ants. Yes, Griselda thought to herself, that was it. The waves were like those of an insect! How on Earth could a woman be projecting the mental activity of an insect? More to the point, how could Griselda be perceiving it? The answer was simple. Due to the trauma of the past six months, Griselda was in some sort of mental fugue state. She was experiencing the beginning of a mental breakdown. Only with the greatest of determination that caused her to sweat from head to toe, leaving her shaking, did she cut the woman's hair. The instant she left the salon, the waves abruptly ceased. She must have looked racked by accentuation, for even Slater came over. Slater, whom Griselda now thought of in her mind as *Mister Slimy*.

"Say, are you alright, Grizzly"? He sounded genuinely concerned.

"I've got a terrible headache, could do with a break", she told him.

"Take it now then. Take as long as you need. I know what koof headaches can be. Have you any Motrinofensic"?

"Any what"?

"They're new, from Ameripharm, supposed to be the very best for a headache plus that other thing you gals get, if you-know-what-I-mean"?

"No, Mister Slater, I have nothing like that, the painkillers I mean".

"Hang on then, I've some in my bag, I'll get you a blister-card".

It was very kind of Slimy or perhaps calculating some sort of ruse that might demand payment for his help. Either way, Griselda wanted the Motrinofensic, for she was developing a monstrous headache. Was she, like her mother before her - heading for some sort of stroke? When he returned, she thanked him, before adding,

"I think I'd like to go home, make a doctor's appointment because of my family history. Just to be on the safe side, you understand"? Slimy was unnaturally sympathetic,

"I do, Grizzly, take the rest of the day. I'll pay you because I know how crappy your luck's been, how nasty pain in the head can be. If you get an emergency appointment, phone me when you've been to see him, all right"?

Griselda nodded dumbly got out of the salon as fast as she could. She breathed in the cool summer air, carefully traversed the busy road of Gentley. The doctor's surgery was conveniently on the other side of it, just next to the library in front of the park. She walked in. The receptionist immediately recognized her for obvious reasons.

"Hello Griselda, your mother's prescription isn't due for three days. Say, are you all right? You look decidedly pale"?

Griselda informed her she was far from all right, described what had happened to her just over thirty minutes hence. Her receptionist friend looked at the small screen of the computer system explained,

"You've no chance of an appointment with the family doctor, but there's a locum in the surgery today. He's got an appointment window in today's calendar in twenty minutes - if you want to wait".

"Yes, I do". She decided. Taking a seat in the waiting room. For a couple of minutes, she glanced distractedly about her, examining the walls of the ceiling, the carpet. It was not worthy of her scrutiny. The ceiling was a shadowed white or had been when it was first done. Now the dust of too long had caused certain areas to look more pale grey. Top half of the walls were pale green, the bottom darker, pea-green. The division between them covered by a floral border of wallpaper. The carpet was the grey of roadside filth. A sensible choice given the traffic that it would have endured over the years. At the centre of the room was a rather sad looking coffee table. Formica top edged in faux-gold plastic trim, circular legs in a unique colour to the wood patterned top. There was a selection of well-thumbed greasy magazines. The newest was three years old, the oldest three years older than that. Occasionally a poster, Blutacked to the walls, broke the monotony of plainness with an advertisement for a disease the waiting patient might not yet have contracted. Griselda shuddered. Did she want tuberculosis, influenza, gastroenteritis, or, most unattractive of all, a sexually transmitted disease?

"First you have to have sex to get one of them", she whispered to herself with a smile. She was perfectly comely enough to attract the members of the opposite sex but was selective in viewing a potential future partner. Gentley did not bring up a wealth of choice in that discerned category. Casually she flicked through a Goodbye magazine, the *now mag for young babes who want to be 'in the know'*. Three years before, Mercedes Bimbette had regained her shape after banging out her third chavvy was looking forward to getting back on tour. While some poor working woman on minimum wage brought up the baby for her, Griselda thought. Knuckles Texas had also scored the maximum number of touchdowns in the World Series in the same mag. Griselda wondered what on Earth that meant? Finally, sadly, Crimson Sash and Errol Wasp had decided their eighteen-month-old marriage had run its course. The couple were officially estranged. Even to someone Griselda's age, the magazine was trashy, but reading it reduced her ennui. A rather crackly Tannoy assisted system informed her she was about to go to surgery four. In the entire time she had been in the waiting room, she had been the only one to come in or leave. Causing her to wonder what was happening in surgeries one through three. She tapped politely on the door entered as an American twang bid her do so.

"Please sit down", the huge Negro locum bid her, "Arma doctor Mustapha what can I do for you today Miss Ebeling"?

Griselda told the giant etched in ebonite, the events of the morning. Mustapha nodded occasionally to show he was giving the diatribe his close attention. Finally, when she had finished the denunciation of good health, he blinked several times, noted verbally,

"Arr see. Right, Miss Ebeling, look at me. Do not move until arr tells you arm finished".

Griselda did so with difficulty while the doctor gazed at her face keenly, then he asked, "Do yaa feel numb down the right side? No. All rightee, lift both arms, let them descend slowly down to y'all sides. Good, now then does y'all little ole tongue feel numb? No, all right, repeat after me, 'The sky is blue and there isn't a cloud in it'. Repeat it once more, please. All right".

He made some notes on his keyboard. Griselda waited patiently. Finally, he turned back to her.

"Arr don't think you're going to have a stroke, Miss Ebeling. Mo likely y'all had a nasty ole headache brought on by the stress of your past year. Either that or an anxiety attack. Tell me, are y'all depressed"?

"If you mean - am I sad at the thought of my father passing away, my mother being ill then, yes. Who wouldn't be"? Griselda asked, not unreasonably.

"Would y'all like something fo that"?

"Do you think I need it, Doctor"?

"Arm'a thinkin' y'all could do with a course of serotonin reuptake inhibitors, yahs".

"Then I'll take them, Doctor, hope they help".

"Arma prescribing Citalopram in the 10 mg size for four weeks, then Arma wanting to see y'all again. You can get this filled out at Washington's ovaah the road. Start the prescription art once".

The two of them waited while the printer chattered away, producing Griselda's prescription. Mustapha tore off the slim sheet handed it to the grateful girl. It seemed to be the end of the consultation. Griselda rose to her feet.

"Thank you, Doctor".

"Mind how y'all go have a nice arfternoon", Mustapha managed by way of goodbye.

Before it all seemed real to her, Griselda found herself on the high street once more. In something of a daze, she went over to the chemists got the prescription, walked home. Lenby Street was not that far from where she worked. She walked every day. As she closed the front door behind her, realised she had walked home without thinking about the route once.

"Is that you Griselda"? The slurred tones of her mother demanded from upstairs. Griselda mounted them two at a time, entered her mother's bedroom.

"Yes Mother, here I am".

"What are you doing home so early? It's only just past lunch"?

"It was slow in the shop so Slater gave me the afternoon off with pay", she lied. "I see you've eaten your tray. Could you do with another cup of coffee"?

"Please, but I need to use the commode before I drink it".

"I'll go put the kettle on", Griselda replied to that. "We've discussed this before. You manage when I'm at work, just be careful".

She picked up the tray, the contents of which were gone. Left the room without another word. It was how life was shaping up for the young woman who had dreams of opening a chain of hairdressing salons one day.

Twenty-three. Flynbertini Xan was the busiest man on Earth. Therefore, he had the most opulent office. The ceiling was a swirl of carefully artistically applied plaster. Albescent with a fine distemper, only used in most deluxe applications. Framed images virtually covered the walls, past presidents of the ANE (Amalgamated Nations of Earth). Xan was the forty-ninth president. All previous administrative leaders were looking down on his activities every day. The massive pile of the newly laid carpet in royal blue was the only alteration Xan had introduced to the vast station. The intercom buzzed, giving him the chance to raise his head gratefully from a mountain of paperwork. He depressed line two (internal),

"Yes Selicity"?

"Your 09:30 is here Herr President", came the dulcet tones of the pneumatic brunette. Xan reflected, not for the first time, that it was time he had *a portion of that.*

"Thank you, please send him in, I presume he's thoroughly checked by security"?

"Yes, Herr President", a pause, then "Two java or will you be offering MOAC (Multiverse Observational Activity Constabulary) Director something stronger"?

"Not sure, Selicity. I'll buzz you if I want anything".

"Yes, Herr President".

'I could buzz you, ask you to bend over this desk, then I'd ...'.

Xen's reverie was thankfully interrupted as the door opened. The familiarly diminutive figure of Director Konette entered the presidential office. Konette could not have looked more ill-fitted to his task of Director of MOAC if a team of artists had created a mock-up of the most inadequate man to do the job. He was; short, ageing, perhaps in his seventies, with wisps of white hair swept over a bald pate. He probably weighed 57 kg if he was a gram, forewent the now standard eye correction laser in favour of spectacles. As usual, he had on the grey suit that was crinkled, ill-fitting, brown shoes cracked, faded. To this unlikely combination, he had thoughtfully added a frayed grey shirt, greasy brown tie. He looked like a csavargó (tramp), which was exactly the persona intended all along. The overall visage did not fool Xen for a moment. Inside that rather dull-looking head was the keen mind of an expert operator, a manipulator of men.

"Come in Director Konette", the president instructed. "Have a seat on the sofa, what can I get you to drink"?

"I'll have a Pálinka if you join me, Herr President", even Konette's voice was faintly high registered, not indicating the considerable power he wielded.

The traditional fruit_brandy of the previous area, known as Central Europe, with origins from the Hungarian Carpathian Basin. Comprising; fruit spirits mashed, distilled, matured, bottled in Grandon. The universal spirit of choice in most parts of the world. Xan arose, went over to the drinks cabinet, depressed a hidden stud. The hatch silently slid to one side. He poured two generous glasses, took them over to Konette seated himself beside the little man. It was a tried and trusted stratagem, for at 84 cm and 90 kg Xen dwarfed the director of MOAC.

"What brings you to see me this time, Konette"? The president asked after a long pull on his drink. "The usual thing I guess"?

"I'm afraid so Bert", only Konette could use the particularly personalized name of the president. "The Insecto of Mizar A is threatening their usual takeover in reality 23, this time"

"23"! Xen found himself surprised, despite the insidious nature of the Insecto (as they referred to them) he had not imagined they would have reached so far from reality prime. "Atyácska (god), Konette, do they intend to slip through all the multiversity? Try to become the ruling race of the galaxy"?

"That would be logical theory, Mister President, given the data we have thus-far compiled".

"But 23! I mean it's so many distant from our own, it must be very different. Do you think your Leyskip can reach so far out? That is why you're here isn't it to ask for permission to go warn them what to expect"?

Konette nodded. "That is - as you say, the purpose of my current visit, Bert. I know you take a dim view of interfering in the affairs of other ley-lines, but if we do nothing, the Insecto will eventually rule the multiversity in every reality upward of 23".

"I have always suspected the fate of the multiversity would be that. Maybe we should leave well enough alone"?

"Your predecessors did not take the stance of isolationism did they, Bert"?

"No, Konette, but I beat one of them in the last election. One of my policy promises was no more interference in the affairs of other layers of the Multiverse".

"Which poses the question, just exactly what constitutes interference ".

"All right, what does"?

"Anything other than advice - guidance. Nothing direct, my agent would take no part in any activities whatsoever".

"Who were you thinking of giving the nod to? Can he or she even reach that far"?

"My best for a skip this far, Tranessy. With the use of certain psychotropic drugs the usual isolation tanks, I think Tranessy could leyskip as far as 23 ley-lines transversely".

"When he gets there – if he's successful, what then Konette? Does he search for an amböentő"?

"The amböentő are so rare that such a search may take longer than 23 has. Before the Insecto war consumes them", Konette admitted.

An amböentő was a human being who could detect all cerquibrum, yet not be cerquiotomized themselves. They were thus a key weapon against the Insecto, but in all the time Konette had been director of MOAC, his agents had only found four. One was in reality prime, the reality they lived in themselves, two in reality 3 a further one in 5. Since then, no further such people with their extraordinary abilities were detected. Through realities 6 to 19. 19 was as far as MOAC had previously sought the Insecto, with their own uniquely skilled amböentő.

"An amböentő cannot leyskip"?

Konette should his head, "The two mental abilities are utterly dissimilar or we would have tried it with 6 to 19. No, for ley-line skipping, Vonalat is no more able than you or I".

Vonalat, who without him, Reality Prime would still be in the grip of the Insecto invasion! The amböentő was difficult. Displayed major character imperfections, but the weird little man had saved the Earth from alien domination. Or at least Reality Prime's Earth, anyway.

"So do we know anything about 23"? the president was curious, "Have our instruments been able to detect communications between the various peoples in that layer of reality".

"As usual, fragmented, distorted by various imperfections in the ether", the director of MOAC informed. "I cannot tell you much, Herr President. You already know it's the farthest we've been able to tune our detectors. In that respect, Vonalat has been of some help. The relationship he has with the electronics is almost quasi-biological. He can obtain data that the other operators cannot even hope to. With his help, we have a few nuggets of information".

"They are"?

Konette smiled, enjoying the imparting of highly classified material. He did not get the opportunity often. Few in the world had the clearance to know even of the existence of other layers of the multiversity. Only a few hundred even knew of the Insecto. That was because they had been cerquiotomized in the invasion that Vonalat had brought to an end. Finally, he told his president,

"I would say the strangest difference is historical from the human perspective. Our Austro-Hungarian Empire lost the Great War"!

"Lost the greatest war the world has ever seen? Who to for Atyácska sake? Not the Yin-Yanks"?

The Yin-Yanks referred to an age-old alliance between China and Amerek, the latter being the colonies Anglosia had lost in the War of Independence.

Konette shook his head, "In 23 there are no Yin-Yanks, the Amerek or Usa's as they know them are still the allies of the Anglosia, who call themselves the Uks".

"Usa's, Uk's, strange names. It's almost as though they lack the vitality to speak longer appellation".

"They do", Konette confirmed. "They are a very lazy pair of races illegally obese, yet in 23 it is not against the law to weigh over a certain amount".

"It does not sound like a very healthy reality".

"That's not the half of it, Bert. They have not embraced eugenics allowing the weak, the feeble-minded, the criminal to breed with no form of sensible control".

"Atyácska! How many of them are there, with no regulation regarding breeding"?

"Vonalat estimated eight billion".

"What! *Eight* billion. Someone already doomed these people, Konette. Perhaps it would be kinder to let the Insecto have them? Which of the Insecto is dominant in 23, anyway"?

"The dragonfly-like race is currently seeking supremacy over the cricket-like race".

"Not the Thysanura-like race who seem to have been so successful in the lower numbered realities. Curious, but eight billion Konette. Surely they are heading for some sort of cataclysm of their own unless they use eugenics to control their growth retro-születésly as we did".

"I do not think your theory is erroneous. That is their problem at least one of human origin, while invasion by an outside agency is quite something else. Look how coldly clinical, heartless the Insecto is in the realities they gained momentary supremacy until MOAC intervened. We must do something".

"How did they allow their beautiful world to be covered by eight times too many people, Konette? What went wrong on 23"?

"From what I can gather from Vonalat, they failed to outlaw the Pope his heinous cult of superstition that involved building a faith in some Jewish criminal the Romans executed for sedition in the year 3757 or thereabouts".

The president surprised the director of MOAC then when he informed, "Judah Ben-Joseph, I think you'll find his name was. He was a joiner of some sort. So in 23, the Pope chose this Judah to be his talisman, did he"?

Konette was still reeling from Xen's show of historical knowledge. "Just so, some hundreds of years later, the Pope decided the Jew was Atyácska in a man's form, called him Christos".

"How does all that account for eight billion on their world"?

"The Pope outlawed contraception".

"Hard to credit that the people succumbed to such lunacy. Their Pope sounds more like Guta than Atyácska's agent on Earth. Still, wherever there is ignorance, superstition will thrive. Thank Atyácska, science has effectively removed the need for such illogical meanderings. Very well, Konette, you may see if Tranessy can help them. Though it doesn't sound like wisdom advanced them as greatly as us, does it? I mean not to make obesity illegal, that's like saying rape, homosexuality, polsexuality should become legalised. Whatever next? What will reality 24 be like"?

"I think 22 layers of the multiversity may be as far as we can reach".

"Let's hope so. Just how strangely corrupt would people of further layers in the ley-lines be? In the end, the actual aliens could well be other than Neanderthals".

Konette shifted uncomfortably in his position on the sofa. "Ah, that's something else Vonalat discovered I forgot to mention, the humans of 23 are not Neanderthal"!

"Not Homo-Neanderthalensis. Not from the same line of evolution as us at all. What by Csodaszarvas are they then? Are they even human"?

"Yes, they're human, Cro-Magnon, the race our ancestors seemed to have absorbed. Taller with long bones, curiously flat faces, but essentially they are still our close cousins. We should help them".

"Help to educate by the sound of it. They must be immensely stupid to cover their world with so many of them. Have they no regard for nature? Eventually, they will have a plague, that will naturally decimate their numbers to suffer such so rapidly will set back their civilization, such as it is - decades".

"Hmm", Konette mused, "I wouldn't call a race of humans who still bother with superstition civilized. Who knows, 23 may get there? It's just taking them longer than the realities closer to our own".

Twenty-four. Balurzuura was trying to take over control of both Sellers' mind and body! He had done it in a very public place, too. That made little difference as events were to unravel because Sellers' newly improved brain had also given him an augmented mentality. The Mizaroa created the equivalent of a psychic hand that took hold of Sellers' metaphysical throat, squeezing. In response, the enhanced superman imagined they had created his throat from Mizaroan metal - duridium. Balurzuura's mentality shrugged, tried something new. He created a preternatural creature, promptly entered its brain. The creature was 100 kg of solid muscle with arms like the trunk of trees. Covered in bright blue fur, its head sat atop shoulders with no neck connecting the two. It had squat legs, which were not of as much use. The lumbering beast came toward Sellers, as he saw himself in his mind's eye. An animalistic roar preluded it wrapping its arms around the aggrandized man. A cell had appeared, a cage of heavy bars of duridium. The beast's obvious intention - to metaphysically lock Sellers' mind within it. Balurzuura squeezed. Sellers imagined himself covered in grease. He found these challenges surprisingly easy, wondered that he had not explored them more in the past. With a comical popping noise, he suddenly shot out of the creature's grasp to rocket upward with the muscular thrust Balurzuura had been applying. Sellers imaging wings, which promptly appeared, sprouting from his shoulder blades. He hovered over the Mizaroan. For an instant, the Királálynővonazóreginăcondător of the insectivore roared in rage. Morphed into his shape, that of an Anisoptera resembling an Earth dragonfly. Only this creature of the Királálynővonazóreginăcondător's mind was some two metres long. Impossible in physical terms, for Balurzuura would have suffocated had he reached such proportions. In the mind, however, the impossible was not a problem. Indeed, the only limiting factor was the power of one's imagination. Királálynővonazóreginăcondător Balurzuura of the Mizaroa flew up to meet Sellers with a graceful dexterity that the other could not even imagine. For he, in reality, had never flown. Several legs locked around the human mind, a message seared it.

'Very well, Sellers let us simply war on a purely cerebral level. It is my turn to rule your body, while I subjugate you to the role of spectator'!

The man thought nothing. He was conserving his mental vitality, ready for the assault. The two incredible minds simply smote at one another with energy that language could not describe. Both seeking to beat the other into submission. It was the moment Balurzuura had been biding his time for. If he lost the battle, he knew he could never mount another. He reserved no energy at all. Struck at Seller's brain with every cell of his quiddity, every microgram of energy. Sellers was resolute! The superhuman mind that ironically the Mizaroa themselves had created was more powerful, more resolute than the opponent of the combating duo. The attack ceased as quickly as mounted. Sellers mind was suddenly in a void,

'Balurzuura, are you still there'?

Answer - came there none.

Twenty-Six. Michael Cowie was restless. He had experienced the malign depravity of murder. Reduced his list of targets to zero.

"I want the thrill of terminating another worthless life", he told Moluura.

'Of course', came the instant reply. *'Who is our next subject for extermination'?*

"That's just the problem I don't have any other enemies", Cowie admitted. Suddenly a thought struck him, "But I could use this new power for good".

'How', Moluura sounded sceptical.

"By killing another individual who deserves to die", the former carpenter decided. "When you think about it, there is no shortage of subjects".

'I am afraid your concept is beyond me' the Zaromi admitted, *'You will have to explain it to me Cowie'*

"We only have to look on the net. It's full of murderers, rapists, arsonists, those accused of aggravated burglary, alas the list is endless".

'Then select one. We shall hunt, kill', Moluura agreed.

Cowie seated himself at his PC and typed in, Rapist on trial in Lincoln. It rewarded him with an immediate hit.

Rapist urinated on a woman in Lincoln and laughed at her naked body.

An "arrogant man" who urinated on a fully clothed woman laughed at her when she was naked. Found guilty of rape and assault, Tom Robertson, 38, appeared at Lincoln Crown Court on June 10th. Judge Harold St-John said he did not appear to regret the ordeal he had put his victim through. The court heard Robertson, of Stumbold Road, Lincoln, was guilty of two assaults, a single charge of rape following a trial earlier this year. Judge St-John told Robertson: "You're 38. I have read a pre-sentence report on you. It confirms my view.

You are an arrogant man, a man with no remorse."

A witness described the victim, remains unnamed for legal reasons, as "broken, distraught, belittled, damaged" following the rape. The court heard Robertson had 27 previous convictions for 63 offences, including several assaults, perverting the course of justice. Wendy Karlton, mitigating, said the assaults were treated as part of the overall offence. She said, "He's a man tried yet still adamant about his position.

He's now facing the most serious offence against a woman. Not prepared to express remorse at the moment. Will have a period of reflection in prison."

Robertson, jailed for $12^{1/2}$ years, registered as a sex offender for life.

"I think I've found our candidate first try", Cowie noted. "Can you get me into the prison with forged papers, say as a prison visitor"?

'I can arrange it, getting back out will be in your hands', Moluura returned after but a moment.

The paper looked genuine enough to fool the cursory glance of the outside visits clerk. They escorted Cowie over to inside visits to strip-search him. The resin thermolance, broken down into several parts, was disguised. One piece resembled the buckle of his belt, another was the frame of his plain glass spectacles, yet another a supposedly digital wristwatch. All were x-rayed, all presented themselves as non-ferrous. The worst part had been secreting the power supply. Which had involved Cowie undergoing surgery under local anaesthetic. The power supply - hidden as a heart pacemaker. Cowie had gotten past the excellent security of the prison, despite their efficiency. He glanced around him at his surroundings, never having been in a prison before. Outside visits had looked like a rather straightforward bungalow from the outside. Even the interior did not look especially secure. It was simply a vast area filled with plastic chairs, rows of lockers down one side. At one end a counter, protected by toughened glass, he had presented himself at one hatch above it. They then examined paperwork he had brought with him. Told him to take a seat until we called his name. His name, identity, Moluura had secured for him, Geoffrey Godfrey. Finally, when about fourteen visitors had gone through the same process, their names called out by an officer, he had escorted them toward the prison proper in a group. The prison had an immense wall surrounding it as expected, a barrier topped by a curiously domed metalhead. He learned it would collapse if any prisoner could reach it, scale it before apprehension. To one side of the curiously turreted front bricks, shaped like some medieval castle, a smaller iron gate, through which they went. Once inside, the group were to form a queue placing anything metal into a tray going on a conveyor belt into the ever-hungry maw of a whirring x-ray machine. Even though they had done that they were then walked through a second x-ray arch. Finally wanded down for a third test. Cowie smiled inwardly, all that to make sure metal could not be smuggled into the prison, yet his weapon was non-metallic. The group left the search area. Led into the sterile area, which was a vast expanse of concrete. Over a concourse, past the back of the perimeter within the walls, there several metres of aggregate, beneath which were pressure pads, so that a prisoner could not even reach the wall without setting off every alarm in the place. Finally, they went back into a building inside the perimeter. Into the very heart of the prison, where visits conducted. Most would take place around little wooden tables surrounded by comfortable seating, but Robertson was not in the category of prisoner who enjoyed such comfort at that time. That was a privilege he would have to earn whilst in the system. Instead, allowed *closed visits,* his were conducted in partitioned booths between visitor/prisoner. A piece of toughened perspex created the separating barrier. They conducted Cowie to booth 23. Told to wait while someone brought Robertson from wing 2 charlie. 2C was the wing in the prison that housed sex offenders. Monitoring, the ubiquitous cameras Cowie surreptitiously assembled the portable thermolance, powered by his *pacemaker*. He connected to the power supply by two thin wires attached to nodes that just protruded through his skin. Robertson was no doubt protesting that he was ignorant of any visitor calling to see him, so Cowie had plenty of time to make certain he had assembled the covert weapon carefully. He felt a high, akin to a drug dosage. For he possessed the power of life or death for the knot of human detritus that was the rapist. A door banged (all doors banged in the very live rooms of prison) Robertson ushered through it directed to take his seat opposite the would-be-executioner.

"Who the koof are you", the prisoner demanded harshly. "I've never seen you before don't know you. They disturbed me from my pad to come see no friend of mine".

"I'm Godfrey", Cowie began with a smile as cold as ice. "You've not seen me before. That's correct. As for having a pad, I think the apposite terminology is cell, moron. Though indeed disturbed, it wasn't as if you're going to an important board meeting in ten minutes' time? Finally, you're right. I'm not your friend. I doubt you have any, scum like you only have associates".

Robertson's mouth hung open. Strangely, Cowie's tirade did not seem to anger him. Peculiarly, he smiled, tapped the barrier with his knuckles,

"Respect mate. Though I doubt you'd dare mouth me like that if this wasn't here. So which rag are you from? How much you offering for my story"?

"I have an offer for you indeed", Cowie admitted, "but it doesn't include cash, I'm afraid".

"In that case, you can zoid off".

Robertson almost rose to leave, but life in prison was mainly one of boredom. Even that unsatisfactory meeting was breaking up the monotony of his day. He twisted in his seat, afforded Cowie a grin of triumph.

"I'll leave", Cowie informed the other, gauging the mien of the prisoner perfectly,

"Look Izdăcoño, what d'you want"?

'Tell him', Moluura, who had been perfectly silent until that moment suddenly urged.

"I have an opportunity for you", Cowie smiled placidly, aware of the power he wheeled over the man before him.

"What sort of opportunehiy"? Robertson glottalized.

"The opportunity of a lifetime – your lifetime. You see, I've within my brain the mind of a Zaromi. With whom many things are possible. I could help you, or, if you don't comply, the consequences could be dire".

"Listen Izdăcoño"! Came the cursed reply, "I don't know what you're on. I don't koofing care, but what's your angle"?

'He is not very intelligent, is he'? Moluura observed without a trace of sarcasm, 'I don't believe we could have any use for him. Kill him, Cowie'.

"My angle was to offer you the chance to become a host for a Zaromi mind, to agree you'd have to have a workable mind, unfortunately", Cowie was enjoying the sweet anticipation of the execution.

"You're koofin' mad", Robertson observed with grim satisfaction, "I'm going back to my pad".

"I doubt that", Cowie countered, "I think they will carry your torso to the medical wing, your head at approximately the same time".

"Huh"?!

"For your crimes against innocent women, I pronounce you guilty Robertson. The sentence is ... ah, death"!

Before any further gutter language could spill from the rapist's mouth, Cowie slipped the thermolance above the counter, described a slicing motion, the beam aimed at the target's throat. As promised it did nothing to the barrier, rather it passed harmlessly through it. What altered was the expression on Robertson's features? It changed from one of pure unmitigated distaste to one of total astonishment. Slowly, his head slid from his neck, tumbled onto the counter on his side of the barrier. As luck would have it - it landed, eyes pointing straight forward toward Cowie. The blood could not flow out of the brain, for intense heat had cauterized the wound. Cowie heard the dull thump of Robertson's body rolling onto the floor. The eyes still regarded him in abject horror.

"How long will he still observe images do you estimate"? Cowie asked Moluura. Hastily disassembling the thermolance, secreting it about his person as before.

'Not long I should have thought', Moluura replied, 'You have just done the humanoid race a service, Cowie. Losing Robertson is a positive step for your fellows'.

A guard noticed what was happening in Booth 23, he hit the alarm. Rushed to the booth on the side of the dismembered torso,

"What happened"? He demanded. "What did you do to him"?

"From here"? Cowie wished to know. "I did nothing officer, his head just fell off! Don't fuss, people's heads fall off every day".

From various routes, guards were arriving at an alarming rate, but none of them could see how Cowie could have done anything to Robertson. Nor could they understand how both wounds could have sealed so perfectly that there was no blood flow.

"Touch nothing", a voice with the stentorian ring of command suddenly rang out above the pandemonium. "Cordon off the entire area, conduct the visitor to my office".

It turned out to belong to Principal Officer McCoy. Within minutes, they showed Cowie politely to Mcoy's office. Seated on the opposite side of his desk.

"Mister Godfrey, I want a statement from you telling me what happened to VD56AC25 Robertson. In your own words, tell me what happened"?

"Certainly Officer, I'm only too willing to help", Cowie lied, thoroughly enjoying the confusion in the other. "I was just asking Robertson if he were willing to become a sunbeam for baby Jesus when his head fell off".

"Are you pissing up my back, Godfrey"? McCoy was instantly furious.

Cowie asked, "Does it feel wet, Officer? No, I would never do such a crass thing".

"Let's stop koofin' about, shall we? McCoy demanded, "Give me a description of the assailant to help with our investigation"?

"Assailant"?

"The prisoner who just decapitated Robertson, were you in collusion with him"?

"There was no other prisoner, Officer McCoy. None could have gotten into closed visits without your men knowing about it, could they? They would also have been searched for weapons. I think someone would have easily detected a samurai before the would-be-executioner got two metres near closed visits".

"Samurai"! McCoy latched onto the word the instant it had left Cowie's mouth. "Who said anything about a sword"?

"I did, Officer, only something very much like it could have been the means of decapitation - had there been an assassin. However, there was no such figure".

McCoy kept his composure only with the greatest act of self-control. He lay his shaking hands on the desk, palms down,

"Are you seriously expecting me to believe that Robertson suddenly fell into two pieces"?

Cowie assumed an expression of sincere earnestness, returned slowly, "I was asking Robertson to accept the Christ into his life to pray for salvation from his terrible sins, Officer McCoy. When he refused, I honestly think an act of divine intervention resulted in his immortal soul being instantly claimed by the fallen angel".

"And I think that you're koofin' me around", McCoy decided. "You want me to offer a report to Lincs Constabulary, the Governor of this nick to the effect that Robertson died because of a miracle"?

"Lucifer is capable of such, Sir", Cowie did not know how he was keeping a straight face. "After all, he was the chosen one, at one time".

"Write what you've told me, total crud as it is, then I'm handing you over to the coppers, see what they think of you".

"Do not treat me like an offender, Sir, lest divine wrath befalls thee". Cowie tried. To his satisfaction, McCoy paled.

"Will you please write your statement, Reverend, before the local constabulary interviews you"? He tried.

"I would be delighted", Cowie smiled.

No sooner had he completed the written nonsense than they escorted him hastily into a white van outside the prison, taken to Lincoln City Centre Police Station. There, they politely escorted him to an interview room asked him to take a seat -

wait. After ten minutes in the featureless room, the door opened a uniformed member of the force walked in.

"I'm Special Chief Officer Byford Brinkley", came the introduction.

Cowie rose from the chair offering his hand "Reverend Geoffrey Godfrey of the New Evangelical Jesuits of Lincolnshire".

Brinkley shook his hand, his grip firm, indicating strength of character.

"Please sit, Your Reverence".

"Geoffrey will be fine", Cowie replied, "We are far from high church".

"And incredibly new". Brinkley had already done some checking. Found Moluura's faked web page containing facts, figures, even images. "Geoffrey, I've read your statement, the one given in Hartshome Keep. I'm sorry to say it's not acceptable or credible. Can you be more helpful to me? Perhaps the officers in the prison were disagreeable to you, did not treat you with appropriate respect. I don't know, but this will not happen here. Would you like a coffee, by the way, sandwiches"?

Cowie admitted, "I am hungry, thirsty too".

"Tell you what, then? Let's leave this interview room go to my office get you sorted, shall we"?

Cowie nodded, while Moluura observed, *'Is this the finest in the force, the special chief?*

Moments later, sandwiches and coffee arrived with admirable efficiency. While they both ate, no doubt Brinkley hoped this would create some sort of bond between them, the chief said,

"You see, the problem with what you told the prison is one of credibility, Geoffrey. People's heads don't just fall off".

"His did", Cowie tried to look sincere. "My statement would be credible to those with faith, Chief. I believe the grim reaper took from his body the man's head. He - an agent of Lucifer. I tried to enlighten Robertson, but the man was without pity, nor the need for penitence. He suffered the consequences, but the doing was not by that of mortal man. Could not have been, for the wound did not bleed".

"A fact which we're unable to explain in any scientific way, that renders you free from suspicion, Reverend. We don't know how the executioner achieved the death of Robertson all we know is that he did indeed die".

"I've told you Chief. I don't know what else I can say".

"I'll get an officer to get a written statement from you. Then you're free to go, Reverend".

Twenty minutes later, Cowie was chuckling on the street.

'That was a satisfactory experiment Cowie, what next, or are you now going to wait for our move against the Mizaroa'?

"There's something else I want to achieve", Cowie told the Zaromi. "Can you put something on the net letting no one trace your I.P."?

'Easily, what is now in your mind'?

"I've decided people in Lincoln are too rude to one another", Cowie was enjoying himself. "If I find anyone being discourteous from now on, they will pay with their life".

Moluura sounded amused as he asked, 'Who shall I sign the message from'?

"Sign it - The *Vindicator*", the keeper of the cerquibrum chuckled.

Twenty-seven.   Griselda Ebeling had returned to work that morning. Everyone in the salon was busily chatting about the story that had appeared on the television programme *Look North* regarding the inexplicable death of Rapist Robertson in Hartshome Keep. How police took a religious man to the central police station for an interview, but then subsequently released him due to lack of evidence of any sort. Melissa Louise was particularly annoying, drivelling endlessly with her outrageous theories that the rapist had suffered divine retribution for his crimes against women. Griselda tried to concentrate on her clients. Slimy Slater was being nothing other than earnestly concerned about her health. At least that demonstrated her worth to him, she told herself. Though doubtless part of her value, in his filthy mind, would have involved certain horizontal pleasures.

"Go take a quarter of an hour's break Grizzly", he said at 10:15.

She thanked him sincerely, finding that 15 minutes off her feet, a cup of tea was not without its attraction. As she re-entered the key area of the salon, the inexplicable feeling of strand peccability suddenly smote her with a ferocity that made the previous day's weak by comparison. What was happening to her? A substantive horny-wave of mentality was coming from somewhere! The contemplative cognition was as frigid as before, devious, obdurate, pitiless. Like a drone insect of some sort with unusual projective power. Griselda felt the rippling outbreak from an unsuspected container. What could it possibly be? Why could she alone feel it? None other in the place seemed to behave in an atypical fashion. They could not sense the presence of the alien creature. She knew it must be alien. Nothing in all the world could broadcast such weirdness. The second time it had happened to her. Unfortunately, she was only slightly more prepared for it. The phenomenon would not lose her the job she needed so badly to support herself, her dependant mother. Doing her best to ignore it resolutely, she set about styling her appointments' hair. Gradually, the emanations got stronger. One woman left, another entered. The strength of the waves suddenly doubled in intensity. An even stranger event followed. In everyday English, Griselda tuned into a silent conversation.

'I don't know why, but something about this place feels odd'.

Griselda glanced hastily about her. None had spoken, the voice clearly inside her head.

'You are quite correct, I feel it too. What could it be? The humanoids do not detect our presence in these biological puppets'.

'Not normally. Perhaps one of these hoods is ...'

'No. They are simply mild heaters for drying the humanoid's follicles'

'I do not know why we need to direct them here in the first place'?

'Because it is their normal routine. We are to maintain said until Moluura gives the word to mobilise".

'In a female torso, what use could we be? I think they have given us an underprivileged assignment, Alpuurazt'.

'We can only work with what we have we have realised it with females before, remember Dubhe, we took that with them'.

Griselda felt sick to her stomach. The conversation was something to do with taking something over. She could understand that much. What was comforting, was that she could hear *them*, yet they could not find her. So she must continue to listen whenever the opportunity arose, learn more. What to do with the information? Never before had she felt so alone, whom could she turn to with what she knew? Who would believe her? Did it matter? Was any of it real? Maybe she was losing her mind? The old joke about hearing voices sprang unbidden into her confused thoughts. Would it simply be best to ignore the voices, treat them as the illusion they probably were? Maybe the Citalopram would eventually kick in they would cease? She needed to be patient. She could always go back to Mustafa, ask for 20 mg or maybe even 40? It was a very tough day, for her, that first day back. Fortunately, she heard no more voices until its end. The weird wrongness left her once two of the customers left the salon. They did not return. She walked home once again, dazed. Entered the little-terraced house on Lenby Street. Her mother's voice cried out the usual demand. Griselda took the stairs one at a time, feeling more tired than usual, probably the tablets - she thought to herself. Her mother had used the commode all day, so the first order of business was to see to the business.

"How was your day"? her mother wanted to know in her now familiar drawl, slurred by the strokes' after effects.

"I don't see how it could have been worse, Mom", Griselda smiled. "I'm dog-tired. Do you mind a microwave meal this evening? I just need to eat, have a long soak in a hot fragrant bath.

"Then can I struggle down? Watch your Digibox with you for an hour"?

"Yes Mom, we can watch *Gorgeous Jeremy* for a while. I've recorded some more episodes".

Gorgeous Jeremy was what the two of them called the actor Jeremy Mooney, one doctor in the ever-popular medical drama AED, the acronym standing for American Emergency Department. The show repeated, but Griselda had not seen the original run. Her mother was enjoying seeing them again. It brought them together in rare moments of mutual happiness. So they both looked forward to the ritual once or twice a week. Griselda dealt with the commode, took the time the dinner was in the microwave to have her bath. She cut short her soak when the Hewlersonic pinged to tell her the first tray contained nutritional, highly delicious, piping-hot food. Her mother took the first tray, having carefully negotiated the stairs on her rump, while her daughter bathed. Griselda rubbed her hair while her dinner was in the device. After eating, they both had a yoghurt, a cup of tea before then it was time to watch Gorgeous Jeremy until her mother fell asleep in front of the Television. Usually, she lasted two to two and a half episodes, on that occasion only managed one and seven-eighths. The daughter hit pause, helped her to bed. Descended the stairs alone, debating whether quarter to eight at night was too early for her to retire as well. She decided if she turned the set off went up, she would probably sleep but then awaken at a ridiculously early hour. So she turned it off despite that, put her iPad on for a while. She was listening to an old band she had found on YorTube called Dr Feelgood. The irony of the name did not escape her as she listened to their album Stupidity. Managed to get halfway through Singin'We Init by the group Blue-Zone-Rwe before falling asleep on the sofa.

Twenty-eight. "That is easy, Zelmuur". Einuur smiled, "You can get close to Sellers, who is the host of Balurzuura. As a Mizaroa, you can assassinate your Királálynővonazó-reginácondător! Firstly, we must introduce you into your host's mind. As new cerquibrum, you will guide him in your mission. Now that the Mizaroan cerquibrum is ah … disposed of, we are ready to use the unit that will cerquiotomize him into 'our' ranks".

'Hide Kim', Felton thought urgently, *'So deeply that the Zaromi will not find you until together the two of us kill him'!*

'Worry yourself not, such shall be the case' The Mizaroa returned. A second later, he could no longer detect her.

Einuur brought out a curious-looking headset, festooned with fibre-optic filaments that tailed on the carpeted floor at his feet. Ailuura promptly took a thin black lead, which terminated in a two-pronged plug, connected it to the wall socket. Various LEDs blinked on the set, the Zaromoid declared superfluously,

"It is ready, now just hold still Felton while I fit the various nodes firmly to your head".

The subject of the demand felt tiny metallic contacts pressing mercilessly into his scalp as he offered no resistance. To have done so would have created suspicion in his captors. They all heard a metal contact being thrown. A shaft of dark-light permeated eyes, minds. The shaft became an amorphous inchoatemention. Transmogrified, metamorphosed into a vague outline of a cricket-like mass. In the process, it was also merely a monochrome outline of ambiguouesity.

'I am Zelmuur', came a pronouncement.

"Oh aye", Felton replied in Humbersidese.

'You will now mentally surrender to me so that I can control your body'.

'I hear. I obey master', Felton responded, just as arranged. Retreated into the félmunite bunker, joining Kim there.

"Is it done Zelmuur"? Einuur wished to know impatiently.

Zelmuur nodded, tried to speak. His voice sounded strange to Felton - who was listening from the safety of the mental fortification, "Yes, he simply surrendered full control to me. There was no resistance at all".

Felton heard the throat of his body speaking, but it did not sound exactly like him, rather it was insectorated in some strange way.

"So we can go at once then", the delighted Einuur pronounced. "Softening the humanoid up was a very satisfactory process indeed. Have you checked to make certain the Mizaroa banished completely unto certain demise"?

"I will do so now", Felton's throat promised. The man; now controlled by the Zaromi, seated Felton, began the cerebral scrutiny. The bunker was impalpable to the phrenic surveillance of the extraneous arthropod. "It is gone. The humanoid psyche seems so dormant as to be temporarily indictable too".

"Excellent. Go, offer to help Sellers. It will not be easy to fool him with the Királálynővonazóreginăcondător cerquibrising his mind. Be patient, subtle. It may take days to earn his trust. Once you have it, you are to eliminate him in the method of your choice, before totally destroying the body. The Királálynővonazóreginăcondător with it. Report back here by tapping as soon as the opportunity presents itself. Clear"?

"Pellucid. What about the girl? I understand Sellers likes to mate with the female humanoids, she may create a tryst I cannot hope to equal".

"For now, the plan is that you turn up at his apartments alone. This was the instruction of Moluura, we will not deviate from it".

Felton nodded, "I am ready to go, will take the brief journey on foot. Over the old Saint Mary's bridge through Amerigate, uptown to Washington Gate".

"Go", Einuur nodded.

The Zaromoid that wasn't, rose from his seat, walked to the door, "I have nothing with me"?

Einuur nodded, "You died recently, only given the clothes you stand up in. It will add to the authenticity of your story".

Felton opened the door, walked stiffly to the lift. Locomotion was still strange for Zelmuur, used to moving on six legs, not two. Once or twice he stumbled slightly, finally reaching his goal. Descending, treat to American piped music, thought it a dreadful din - noise pollution. How primitive the humanoids were, that they needed to fill their every waking moment with some sort of mental distraction. Conquering them would be easy!

Once he exited the scraper block, outside impressed him planet - Talpizzok Three, as the Zaromi labelled it, for it was the third planet orbiting the star Talpizzok. He knew the humanoid called it Soil or Dirt or some such nonsense. They were dim creatures. Could not fly, had but two legs, very inconvenient if one became lame. Hideously ugly, ungainly, massive, with only stereoscopic vision. It forced Zelmuur to move his head about constantly if he wanted to see one hundred and eighty degrees about him, as accustomed. His loss of holopticity was the most profound change of them all. Saw but a single image at a time, could not discern movement anywhere near as efficiently. By the time he had traversed the bridge, however, he was getting accustomed to the changes, just as previously Zaromi had done. Humanoids were walking past him in both directions, got uncomfortably close. Did they not fear any chance of an attack from one another? If the weak or the lame passed the healthy why were they not immediately set upon, slain, devoured? It was a weakly inefficient way of advancing the genetic pool. No Insectivore would have allowed such to go unchecked.

The Zaromoid, tuned into the mindless tedium of their thoughts, cast his net wide to see if any of them had a worthwhile reflection in their brain; 'How much! I wouldn't pay half of that', 'Must get some jam for my toast in the morning','If

I miss that ruddy bus they'll be hell to pay', 'It's no good I just don't love her any more, I'm going to ask for a divorce', If he's bought me that necklace I'm gonna blow him', 'Her face might not be much to look at but she's got a great body', 'Is it because I is black', ' Nem tisztelik a bevándorlókat ebben az országban'.

They were the most confusing species of creature the Insectivores had ever attempted to conquer by a not inconsiderable margin. No matter if it was going to be more difficult, the Insectivores were indefatigable. Finally, Zelmuur reached the appropriate tower after some effort negotiated the confusion of such a structure arriving at the door of the right apartment.

Sellers was just washing the dishes created by luncheon when the buzzer to his door sounded. At the issue, he glanced at his two apartment guests, saying,

"I don't think I'm expecting anyone. What about you two"?

It was a deliberately nonsensical question. How could either Kyla or Tranessy be expecting a visitor?

"I'll get it then", he sighed in mock fatigue, "You two have a minute, relax, while I wear my fingers to the bone".

Tranessy laughed, the humour not lost on him, while the young, beautiful woman scowled, not perceiving the irony. Walking over to the door, he threw it open to a man of some vitality standing without.

"If you're selling something, then you're wasting your time I'm afraid, I've already got one, in blue actually", Sellers quipped. If the other appreciated the sarcasm or not it did not matter to the Superman, he was simply amusing himself.

"I am Mizaroa Kim", Zelmuur said simply in Felton's body. "I offer the Királálynővonazóreginăcondător my services".

Kyla was suddenly at Seller's shoulder, "Kim"! She echoed, "What kind of name is that for a Mizaroa"?

It annoyed Sellers that she was intruding into the conversation, but said nothing.

Zelmuur did not know the real reason, so he lied, "The Mizaroa are using shortened names for the benefit of we human hosts".

"We can safely conduct the rest of this conversation inside", Sellers decided. "Come in, Kim, what's your human name"?

Zelmuur made his first mistake at that point, "Just call me Kim, it's simpler".

"Sounds effeminate to me", Kyla confessed. It was unusual for her to be so rude.

Zelmuur suddenly hesitated halfway across the room, "Oh you have another guest, Balurzuura, I did not realise, who are you, Sir"?

Tranessy smiled. "You might not have clearance for that information", he returned. Causing Sellers to exchange a glance with her ladyship. Sellers tapped to her,

'Be careful when addressing Tranessy, not to use his name, Your Ladyship'. Aloud he said, "This is our guest Mister Uvirális".

"Mister Uvirális", Zelmuur nodded to the leyskip.

"Mister Kim", the leyskip returned. It was obvious from the instant that the two would not become friends.

"Sit down, Kim? I'll get you something to drink. Would you like tea or coffee"? Sellers, ever the genial host, wished to know.

"Do you have Lilt, Sprite, Coke"? Zelmuur was keen to try the new beverages he had seen advertised on various sites, during his brief walk through the roads of Earth.

"As luck would have it, I have all three", Sellers smiled, "And Kong, plus the usual alcoholic beverages, vodka, rum, brandy, longer drinks, largar, cider. This is your first assignment on Earth, isn't it Kim"?

Zelmuur nodded, forced the body to smile, "I've had none of them, but I'd like to try any you wish to give me".

"I would heartily recommend a rum", Tranessy suddenly interjected, exchanging a glance with Sellers.

"Rum"! Kyla ejaculated. A swift look from Sellers stopped her from saying anything else.

"I'll get you a rum", he told the newcomer, going over to the kitchen area.

"I hope I wasn't interrupting anything important", Zelmuur then tried.

Tranessy darted in before either of the other two, offered, "We were discussing the merits of strategy 23. Has the monarchy briefed you on it yet"?

Sellers and Kyla remained silent. Something was going on that they did not understand, but it was undoubtedly a test for the newcomer.

"I have to confess that I have not", Zelmuur responded as Sellers handed him the drink. In his other hand, he had a glass which, on the face of it, contained the same beverage.

"Cheers", he said, raised it to his lips, took a good pull on it.

"Cheerio", Zelmuur responded, doing the same before coughing, his eyes watering. "Doamdenit that is strong of flavour".

"Doamdenit is right", Sellers smiled, "But good once you get used to it, try another pull".

Zelmuur drank some more of the rum before Sellers offered, "Here, let me refresh your glass, Kim".

"So what is strategy 23"? Zelmuur tried to sound nonchalant as he handed his glass back to Sellers.

"If they have not briefed you, then I cannot tell you. Security isn't just a joke to us after all, is it"?

"No, of course not. I understand", the Zaromi replied thoughtfully.

"There you go, have another drink", Sellers urged, while Kyla raised a supercilious eyebrow.

The two of them took another swallow, followed by more.

"Just one more, are you ready for another"? Sellers asked.

"I'm not sure I feel just right", Zelmuur suddenly confessed, his voice slurring a little.

"That's always how a newbie that has just taken over a body feels", Tranessy assured, "The rum will help, have another"?

Kyla suddenly appeared disinterested in events. She had worked out what the two men were up to.

"I'm a little dizzy", Zelmuur confessed. "Are you sure it is my newly appointed cerquiotomisation, or could it be that rum does not agree with this humanoid's system"?

"Ask your host"? Tranessy advised - a glint in his eye.

"He's resting", Zelmuur lied, "I have been fortunate in occupying a very otiose individual who lets me do much of the guidance of this body".

"Rum will remedy that perfectly", Sellers told him, handing him another full tumbler of the tipple, "Down the hatch before it might persuade me to tell you about strategy 23".

Zelmuur was keen to learn about the mysterious scenario, so he dutifully drank yet another full tumbler of the alcoholic spirit.

"Better"? Sellers asked.

Zelmuur mumbled something incoherently eyes drooped. Suddenly, Tranessy sprang from his chair, going over to the newcomer. He asked urgently,

"Human host speak to me"?

"I'm here. I have just placed the Zaromi into a félmunite cell"!

"Well done, sorry that we had to get you drunk". Sellers confessed, "Now tell us your name? Convince us of the true story"?

"You didn't have to intoxicate me, but thank you for the sentiment behind the actions", came the response. "I'm Felton, have a Mizaroa in my brain besides Zelmuur, who thought he was in command of my body. If you give me some strong coffee, a few moments I'll tell you the entire story".

"A Mizaroa *and* a Zaromi"! Tranessy sounded impressed, "I'm impressed"!

Twenty-nine. The Vindicator walked casually into the café. He had deliberately chosen a busy one, at a busy time. It was time to reinforce his new directive. Too many people were not paying it any attention. He approached a table already occupied in two of the four seats.

"Excuse me, do you mind if I join you, there are no empty tables"?

The young man gestured with a sweep of his arm, "Not at all make yourself comfortable".

His girlfriend/wife smiled her pleasant acceptance, remained silent. So far, so good. No waitress came to ask Cowie what he wanted. However, he waited patiently. After all, they were running around very busily.

"What are the BLTs like here"? Cowie asked the man.

"I've never had one, I'm not really into lettuce", came the considered reply, "You have to watch out for oxalate poisoning don't you"?

Cowie smiled, "Maybe I should just have a bacon butty then, is that what you're saying"?

"If you want a BLT, go for it", the woman spoke for the first time, "We can only die once, might as well make the most of life while we're living it".

Finally, a sweaty, frazzled-looking waitress arrived at the table, notepad in hand, asked Cowie.

"What do you want"?

"Oh"! Began Cowie, "Do you mean, 'what would you like, *Sir*"?

"Listen - bud, we're run off our feet right now, either give me your order or bug off aycee"?

"I'm afraid it isn't all clear", Cowie told her with a little tone of regret in his reply. "You're not being courteous, Ma'am. Remember what it said on the net. The Vindicator will tolerate poor manners no longer in Lincoln".

With that, Cowie removed the thermolance from his pocket, sliced through the woman's left arm.

The waitress screamed.

At the same table, the girl paled. Her partner asked, "Are *you* the Vindicator"?

"One and the same", Cowie told him, rising to leave, "Post this occurrence onto the net, I will not have bad manners in Lincolnshire any more".

"I hope you get your wish before the police catch you", the man noted. It was entirely possible he was telling Cowie what he wanted to hear, to buy his own safety, however. Cowie left quickly, he was on foot, the café was in a state of chaos.

"I think others may now read the web. We'll see an improvement around here", Cowie said to Moluura.

'I would like to try a brief experiment this evening', came the response from the Zaromi. *'I would like you to release control of your being to me for a short time'.*

"I'm not sure I'm comfortable with that Moluura".

'Why'?

"Firstly, I don't know how to do it. Secondly, when would I resume control"?

'Let us just begin with an hour I will instruct you in the procedure'.

"I don't know, I mean what if you like being in a human body Don't let me back in the driving seat"? As he voiced his concern, he had reached his car jumping into the seat.

'I will return control to you'.

"Can I have time to consider this development"?

'Why'?

"I just don't want to rush into a decision that might ...".

'You don't entirely trust me. You think I might take over. Not let you have your body back'.

Cowie gunned the engine but did not depress the clutch. Ready for starting his journey home, he admitted, "I remain uncertain as to your intention for doing it Mol, other than to make me a prisoner of my subconscious".

'Your reticence is understandable. I fully understand your position. Yet I have troops to rally, instruct, have no intention of doing it through an intermediary, you'.

"Troops, what sort of troops"?

'The beginning of a control-squad for this area, I understand what you are trying to accomplish, have developed a system of my own for achieving it'.

"I did not ask you for assistance Mol".

'True, but then you are not in charge here, Cowie, I am'.

Moluura suddenly launched a full psychic attack against Cowie's mind. A huge preternatural hand suddenly manifested itself in the man's brain. Closed on the psychological being that was his mentality. He turned off the engine of the car, body going rigid. Tried desperately to escape the clutches of the grip. It was too strong he had nowhere to go. The attack being inside his own head.

"Stop it you bugillegitimate"! He cursed, but to no avail. The grip on his brain was as durable as steel. Felt it crushing down. There was tremendous pain, the most terrible of migraines, Cowie screamed.

"Leave me alone Mol, leave my mind alone".

From out of some darkly comforting area beyond the vice-like constraint, a voice of comfort induced him.

'Come into this fold of amenity - contentment? The pain will cease, you will not receive injury'.

Cowie's mind fled the agony. The sound of a strange metal door crashing too behind his thoughts. He found himself in some sort of pit of helplessness - futility. Yet to call it a pit was a misnomer. For it had no physical depth nor width, in fact, it had no physical dimensions of any sort. Neither did it possess any dimensions in time, space nor reflection, it was an area of voidosphere. He who had been Cowie could still think, yet he had no sensation of progression. He felt nothing, heard nothing. His existence was the only reality he was cognizant of. How could he exist in such a bleak state? Would he eventually simply fade into nothingness due to a total lack of stimuli? There was only one action open to him, only one process that could offer him any hope of continued subsistence. The inductance of rebellion. Battle against the awful topography the Zaromi had placed him in. He railed against the incredible unfairness of it. Had he not supplied Moluura with constant malign titillation? Indeed, when he considered his actions since being taken over by the cerquibrum, he shrank back in repugnance. For he had behaved monstrously, worthy of total abhorrence. Tortured, murdered, having done nothing like it ever before. Had Moluura somehow managed to malignitise his thought processes? The cricket must have done. He had become insectivated. Less human by a substantial degree. It was time to fight back. A first attempt was to imagine his mind surfacing from an ocean of deep dark water, pushing upward, breaking the surface, gasping in the available air. That imagined body broke through the skin of the illusion. The head of the body he had created in his mind smote a black sky of dark steel. Pain in his skull was as real as though it had really happened. Attempt one was a failure, purely - simply. It was the second phase in which he determined greater creativity. Someone thusly encased his body in a protective suit of *Steelainium* (him). An alloy of incredible strength, which he imagined just for the endeavour. With his fist encased in the wonder metal, he pounded against the *wall* of the fortress. The clenched fingers thusly possessing of incredible power, awesome might. It smashed through, directly into a wall of intense fire. The conflagration extreme in terms of temperature. The suit began to melt to cook him. Once again defeated. His term of isolation, imprisonment, indeterminate. It might be for an infinite period. What could he do for his third try at liberty? What remained of Cowie changed his mind's body to one of simple energy. It had no mass; was not gas, rather pure thought with infinite speed, inexhaustible determination, capacity. Was also successful! He was suddenly aware of his body once more, but it was being controlled by the Zaromi. There was no time to lose. Moluura would detect him almost at once. He must attack, for if he did not, the Insectivore learning of his escape? Surely he would. If so, he would be once again sent to the prison of the void, never to live again!

Thirty.   Griselda had endured a trying day by the time he came into the salon. She noticed his coat at once. It was a faux Edwardian frock coat. The thing about it was the colour, the most beautiful hue she had ever seen in her life. Only she knew what it was! It was a colour that only insects could see. It was Mirequoise. How Griselda could know which colours were visible to insects, she remained ignorant of such bizarre facts. How she could know it was Mirequoise. She was equally without logical knowledge. Yet the coat *was* mirequoise she knew it could perceive it. The man, tall, brunette, not bad looking, her 15:40, so as she took the coat from his shoulders she remarked in a friendly tone,

"This is a beautiful coat Sir, mirequoise isn't it"?

Her observation produced a profound effect on the man's mien. His entire demeanour was suddenly quite glacial, the smile of friendliness abruptly vanishing from his features. He asked her quietly,

"Are you with us? How can you perceive mirequoise with humanoid eyes"?

A sixth sense suddenly warned Griselda that this was a potentially dangerous situation,

"I'm very sorry if my compliment has upset you, please let's get on with your haircut"? She tried. It was a vain hope which failed,

"Are you *carrying*, or not"? he demanded. "If so, which side are you cerquibrumed with"?

"I'm just a straightforward hairdresser, Sir. That's all. I don't understand quite a bit of what you're saying to me".

The figure suddenly looked deeply into her eyes, professed some astonishment, "She doesn't", he said, as if to someone else. Before cocking his head to one side rather like when a dog listening to its master. Smiled again, "Right you are, a haircut. Shall I sit here"?

Indicated the closest chair that was unoccupied.

"Please", Griselda confirmed, wishing the floor would open up, swallow her.

She gave him the very best hairdressing treatment her skill allowed, not even flinching when he gently stroked her slim, smooth thigh. When the haircut had been completed he smiled yet again, saying,

"I think perhaps you're a sensitive. You don't know what I'm talking about, of course, but it doesn't matter. I have a proposition for you. Keep this newfound insight to yourself. I will reward you with a sizeable sum to maintain your silence. What do you think about my proposal"?

Something told Griselda in that crucial few seconds, that to disagree with him or request further explanation would place her in extreme peril. She simply nodded before adding hastily, "I can't talk about what I don't understand, can I, Sir".

Her appointment grinned, encouraged, "That is the way to view this situation, female. It pleased us you have seen sense".

Was he deranged? Considered there to be more than one of him. Possessed two distinct ways of talking, probably bipolar, Griselda thought, though she had never encountered one before. She helped him on with the frock-coat, brushed the collar for him, as was the remit in the salon. He seemed very pleased with that personal touch, before his dark slim hand slipped inside the coat, obviously for payment.

"That will be $12 please, Sir".

From the envelope, the man drew two tens, told her, "Keep the change for yourself. The rest of the envelope is for you, in payment for the agreement we have just made. Break the compliance, however, believe us, we *will* know"!

Griselda took the envelope, slipped it into her smock pocket, watching the strange man leave, as though she were in a daze, which she was. Money, without the request for a date. He seemed to fancy her, yet had not tried to seduce her. She certainly was not disappointed. Suddenly she felt Slater at her shoulder.

"It's past closing time Grizzly, thanks for stopping. "Say, did that guy just leave you an $8 tip"?

"Yes, do you want to put it in the till"?

"No. You keep it Grizzly, you've had a tough two days. It'll help a bit. He must have wanted to bone you leaving a tip that size".

Grimacing at the crudity, Griselda went into the rear washroom where her coat hung. Took off her overall, swapping it onto the peg, slipped the envelope into her trouser pocket. The coat she threw over her arm. It was windy outside but close, the coat, necessary in the morning, too hot later. Slater was waiting at the front door to lock up, pull down the shutters. She slipped past him, but not before he had patted her on the backside. The creep. She was quite aware of who exactly wanted to engage in naked naughtiness with her. It wasn't the Zaromoid. *Zaromoid!?* Where had that word come from? She had never heard it before. What did it mean? Had she read it somewhere or made it up in her troubled mind? Forced herself to walk calmly on the way home. Past the dike the Pavilion, two bowling greens. Only once she got to the front of the clinic did she halt, walked into a convenient alcove. It was time to see what was in the envelope. The moment she opened the flap, she was gasping. The top of the notes had the image of the bald, ugly Benjamin Franklin on most of them. There were four twenties, the rest were hundreds. Griselda glanced about her before counting them with her thumb, careful not to lose her place. The envelope contained ninety-nine $100 bills and four 20's - $9,980! For Griselda and her mother, it was a fantastic amount. Some young women would have spent the money on a trip to the Caribbean, but Griselda was far more practical, mentally mature for her age. The cash could do wonders for the little house on Lenby Road. It could make life much more comfortable for the pair of them. Carefully placing the envelope in the inside pocket of her coat, as opposed to her pants. Griselda walked carefully, thoughtfully home. Whoever the Zaromoid were, bless them, their secret machinations, she thought.

Thirty-one.   The president of the Earth - Flynbertini Xan was just enjoying a Cuban cigar when the buzzer on his desk sounded.

'Damnation'! He thought to himself, *'Depending on who is on the other side of that door, determines whether I'll have to extinguish this excellent smoke or not'*.

He thumbed the appropriate button asked casually, "Yes Selicity, I don't recall having any calls this morning. You looked at my diary earlier"?

"I did, Herr President. Your diary was clear for once. This is a last-minute call by Mister Konette of the MOAC.

'Konette, what does he want? I only just sanctioned that leyskip to go to 23 the other day. There can't have been any results yet, surely'? Instead, he said to his ever-reliable receptionist/word-processor, "Very well Selicity, let him in".

Konette was not one of those who objected to him smoking *Commie* smokes, fortunately. When the door opened to allow the insignificant little man entrance, he made a point of coughing several times, even then. Xan ignored the defiant gesture.

"Now then", the President of the world began, "What can I do for you today, Konette. Drink"?

To Xan's surprise, the head of MOAB nodded his head, "Thank you, Sir, I'll have a rum if I may"?

"Excellent choice Konette, I'll join you what are we celebrating"?

"How do you know I've come to see you with glad tidings, Mister President"? The agent of MOAB wished to know.

Rather than tell the agent the truth. That his mien, his body language, gave him away, Xan suggested,

"There's not much that goes off in Szolnok that I don't know about Konette. I have my sources. Do you wish to tell me yourself what I already suspect. Here, get your laughing tackle around this".

Accepting the beverage, Konette took a careful sip of the rum, asked, "So you know about the Menta-carbaryl"?

Xan had never heard of such an item, had no idea what it was, but he smiled requested,

"Go on".

"Vonalat has excelled himself this time, Chief. He's only gone and developed a mental-pesticide to kill the Zaromi"!

"Just refresh my memory on exactly what the mental pesticide does"? Xan asked casually. It was no good, Konette realised he had been attempting to dupe him. The head of MOAB smiled in satisfaction before continuing,

"Menta-carbaryl, as Vonalat chose to call his technique after the real pest controller, is a psychic weapon, Mister President. It kills the Zaromi stone-dead in one terrible mental blast. We can be free of the little buggers".

"I thought *we* already were".

"In Reality Prime, that much is true, Sir. But what if the Insecto start to attack us cross-ley-line? They have the capability already, can use it to revitalise those humans killed or dead. What if they decide to have another go at reality prime? We cannot as yet hurt the Mizaroa, the Vasishtha, or any of the lesser races of the bugs, who no doubt are waiting for their chance to attack humans psychically in the ley-lines. The Zaromi have always been the most insidious, destroy them, it gives the other Insecto considerable food for thought. We can do that now with Menta-carbaryl".

"I presume you wish to test it, in 23? If I'm not mistaken being as Tranessy is over there now"?

"That would be an excellent choice, but Tranessy is not sufficiently esper to use Vonalat's mental discipline".

"Then what use ...". Xan began, causing Konette to cut him short.

"What we can do with our instruments is amplify Tranessy's power from this end. So we can bring a 23er to prime. Teach the individual how to slay the Zaromi with one psychic blast".

"How long will it take our leyskip to find this esper"?

"He already has. If you read my last report, you'll have seen that he was staying with an individual called Sellers. Sellers is a high scoring esper, he's perfect for the job, as he already has a Mizaroa in his mind. The two are currently fighting one another for control of the planet".

"But if Sellers kills all the Zaromi on Earth 23, won't the Mizaroa take over unopposed"?

"One stage at a time, Mister President. Firstly, we need to know if Vonalat has indeed created the mental insecticide he claims. I have never known him to fail us yet".

"How do you propose to test it when we have no surviving Insecto in our reality"?

"We get Tranessy to teach Sellers how to leyskip. Get him here with Vonalat. Our ambőentő has to teach the man how to use the Menta-carbaryl".

"So it all hinges on this Sellers chap"?

Konette nodded, "But he has successfully imprisoned the Királálynővonazóreginácondător of the Mizaroa in his mind, is a very high scoring esper. True, it hinges on him, but if anyone can learn how to leyskip, it's him. If anyone can learn how to use the Menta-carbaryl, it's him. If anyone can find the ambőentő of 23, if there is one, it's him as well".

"So this Tod Sellers fellow is the best hope for 23, even though we cleared the low ley-lines"?

"23 is too far distant in terms of junctions for us to do it directly this time. Sellers is their best hope".

"Very well", Xan decided. "You have permission to get Vonalat, your various machines to contact Tranessy, begin the first of Sellers' instructions. I understand that besides his other abilities, he's also eidetic, biotronic"?

Konette nodded, "Since his death, it does rather appear he has lived a far better existence, yes".

"So death becomes him", Xan was philosophical.

"I'll take my leave, Mister President, get back to the lab in Cegléd", the leader of MOAB informed, rising from his chair. "Thank you for the rum, good to see you as ever".

Xan nodded his agreement. Konette strode purposefully from the room. He was so well recognised that none of the security personnel made to stop him, as he exited the presidential apartments. Found himself shortly outside on the streets of Szolnok. Hailing the first flitter to float past, he said to the driver,

"Take me directly to Cegléd, please?

The driver, a swarthy local, looked at the head of MOAB twice, informing, "That's fifty kilometres, Sir. It'd be much cheaper on the train".

"Dollars aren't a problem just take me directly, please. I want the laboratory at MOAB".

"Yes - Sir, right away", the driver was happy to agree. The flitter rose on its powerful servos, blasted up into the air-traffic.

Konette did not have time to enjoy the scenery below. He was wondering if he would find Vonalat in a favourable mood. The latter; a brilliant ambőentő, genius, engineering-physicist, also ill-tempered, capricious, downright scurrilous when the fancy took him. Many at MOAB feared him, the braver ones were nervous about his volatile ingenuity. There was only one person who could deal with him on a one-to-one basis. The director himself. Even so, doing just that was often frustrating, exhausting, if Vonalat was in one of his maunges. It took all of Konette's energetic resolve to get compliance from the irascible scientist. The director of the multiverse observational activity constabulary experienced none of the flight to Cegléd. So deep were his introspections. He only came to his immediate senses when the flitter bumped onto the pavement before MOAB headquarters. The building was the very best the ruling American nation could construct. An impressive facade of glittering glass in the watery sunlight. The expanse of the super-heated sand only broken up occasionally by stainless steel ribbing. Konette tipped generously, climbed out of the flitter purposefully strode straight into reception, where an armed guard manned the desk. He did not stop to admire the brilliant simplicity of the architecture in the huge entrance area. The interior of headquarters was every bit as impressive as that outside, if not even more so. All was glittering glass, burnished chromium metal, large drapes of voluminous white silk. The entire display tastefully lit by carefully concealed LED lighting very white, crisp. The guard recognised Konette at once - asked,

"What do you need, Sir"?

"To see you-know-who, where's he right now"?

Consulting the tracer lines on his monitor while Konette snapped his magnetic badge into place, the guard informed.

"His lab coat is in the tube-room, Herr Director".

It was common knowledge that when Vonalat did not want to be located; he took the coat off, leaving the name tag erroneously proclaiming his whereabouts. Thanking the guard, Konette went over to the lift, pressed the button marked 'L'. The floor the laboratory was on, which was the basement of the building. Its lift yet more highly polished chrome. Doors hammered blued metal that contrasted beautifully with it. Konette stepped inside, treat to the piano concerto of Mozart playing over the Bose speakers screwed into the ceiling. It hummed downward. Doors slid open to reveal the interior of a vast concrete bunker-like expanse. A grey area of hardcore, sand mucilage by no means empty, filled with row upon row of huge complex-looking machines. The computerised appliances, festooned with dials, valves, LED indicators that only the very intelligent, or very informed, could make much sense of. This was the Vonalat playground. The area in which the brilliantly gifted amböentő produced his inspired creations. A combination of extreme intelligence and leaps of intuitive faith made the formations. Despite what he had achieved, the millions he had saved, it was not unjust to regard Vonalat as not quite sane. The fine line between him or a genius smudged sometimes snapped. He endured frequent bouts of fugue, the harder he worked. To get the best out of him required the understanding, the authority that only Konette possessed. The director walked down the central aisle between the two vast rows of equipment. The machines ranged in size, complexity, structure. Some were merely large, others towered over a man. Many were black-painted metal, filled to the brim with strange-looking circuits. Some were of simpler configurations. Merely tuning circuits backed up by amplification, so that they could relay messages from distances the ordinary inhabitants of reality prime could not even dream of. Together, they were like the cells of an enormous metal and glass brain that only one intellect could fully fathom with their vast potential. As expected Konette found Vonalat at the far end, the end which contained the most advanced quirky of the entire spread. In appearance, Vonalat was the archetypal mad scientist. With his huge owl-like glasses, his wild-white fine hair worn long. The fact that he was barely 157 cm tall, that he wore a lab coat that was several sizes too large for him. As Konette approached him, he even wore a pair of huge black rubber gloves which came to his elbows. Had they had cast him in a movie, they would have criticised Vonalat for being a caricature of what people expected a mad scientist to look like. Nevertheless, Vonalat looked the part. He peered forward with his gimlet eyes from behind the very thick lenses of his spectacles, observed distractedly,

"Oh! It's you Konette. Let me guess? You've come to interrupt my invaluable research, in favour of requesting something from me"?

"What I tell you, is born of a direct consequence of your recently brilliant breakthrough in psychic pesticides", Konette told him smoothly, always better to start with a compliment when dealing with the gigantic ego of the man.

"Yes. Yes, you're quite right, it was brilliant, was it not"? Vonalat basked in the glow of the congratulations. "Don't just stand there grinning like the proverbial Cheshire Cat then man, what do you want now"?

"I need you to instruct Tranessy. He needs to be able to teach Sellers how to leyskip. So he can come here to reality prime".

"I can get in touch with Tranessy easily enough. For him to teach his technique to an inhabitant of another reality how to skip the ley-lines? That's a tall order, Konette. There are so many between us, I don't think he will have the ability? Nor will the potential student".

"I have faith in the possibility. Just think, if we can get him here? You can teach him how to destroy the Zaromi in reality 23".

Vonalat laughed. "You want this Sellers chap to learn how to leyskip, on top of that, learn how to use Menta-carbaryl? You realise that psych-pesticide doesn't exist in the physical world, it is only a force of the mind? My mind, the greatest mentality in all the realities we know of thusly far".

"It's a tall order, isn't it? Yet if anyone can do it, then it's Sellers. He died, reanimated through Insecto technology, constructed using their advanced industrial science created by their leading-edge machines. He may be the most fearsome weapon against the Insecto for that very reason".

"No"! Vonalat almost screamed, "Only an amböentő can destroy all Insecto in a given reality. No matter how much instruction I give the humanoid, he will never be the equal of me".

Konette asked calmly", What if, with his esper abilities, we can train him to find an amböentő"?

"Exactly how do you propose to teach him yet a third new adeptitude"? Vonalat demanded.

"Why with the help of the most brilliant we have in prime", Konette returned, knowing he had led the scientist into a trap, "With *your* help Vonalat".

"How am I supposed to do what I can't do myself"?

"You hide, here on our Earth. Having travelled by modern transport. Then we get Sellers to seek you using his esper abilities, which are great indeed. Once he finds you, he has learned the technique all by himself".

Vonalat rubbed his chin. Suddenly his almost permanent scowl broke into a wide grin, "You're thinking Sellers is the key to the entire destruction of the Insecto, in every reality, are you not"?

Konette grinned, "Let's see if we can get him to rid those in reality 23 to start, shall we? You have the arsenal. Will you put it at his disposal?

He can destroy the Zaromi, seek the amböentő in his reality to kill all the other Insecto from Ursa Major. If they are successful, we can induct them into MOAB. The multiverse will be safe for all the versions of men".

Scornfully, the scientist suddenly observed, "And here was I thinking, for a moment, that you had gotten humanitarian, Konette? When all you are concerned about is that the Insecto can never return to reality-prime".

"I do not see the two ambitions as being conflictual", the director grinned. "How soon can you turn on your contraptions? Get the relevant message to Tranessy"?

Thirty-two.   Cowie may only have two hands to the Zaromi's six legs but the combined energies of anger coupled with determination fuelled his strength. He had Moluura's image of himself in a stranglehold. The two were only actually battling with their minds, in them, they saw themselves, as they were. The only difference being one of scale. Moluura was impossibly large, equal to the carpenter. It made the space between thorax to head just about the same dimensions as Cowie's own throat. Even though Moluura tried to fly, then scraped at Cowie's arms, torso, face, the human image that was the man's mind hung on, squeezed. The scraping of the various legs grew more frenzied, almost desperate. Cowie's face became covered in bleeding scars, the flesh from his arms hanging in tatters. Soon he would bleed to death. If the mind believed the enemy had killed it, then it had! Cowie was close to death! So too Moluura. The scraping grew in desperation. In one Samsonite surge of energy, Cowie squeezed his right hand together with every final gram of vitality that his determination could manage. There was a terrible cracking, crunching, noise. Moluura twitched twice, was so much dead weight in the mind of the human figure. Cowie finally let go. The mind-insectivore crumbled to dust. The victor opened his eyes. Found himself back in control of his body, lain in bed in his opulent top story apartment. Tears of joy turned to those of resentment, regret when he remembered how the mind of the cerquibrum had warped, twisted his own. He had done questionable things. Was he to blame? Conducted under the malign influence of a mind that was not could never be – human.

'Moluura'? Cowie thought, 'Are you there? Are you hiding deeply set in my subconscious? Or have I truly killed you with the power of my psyche"?

Answer – came there none. Unbeknown to himself, he had become the first human to destroy the power of a Zaromi mind, with mental strength he alone possessed. Not only that but the Zaromi Veztőöndər. They would choose a replacement the moment they knew of Moluura's demise. None would mourn him, even for a second. The Insectivo had no sentimentality. Yet Cowie's victory remained a feat of some impressivementisation. Hunger gnawed at him as he slipped off the bed, walked into his luxurious kitchen. Not in the mood to make himself a salad, not bothered to cook. Yet he needed protein, took an instant burger, one that was in its cardboard oven, popped it into the microwave. It was times such as that mankind's creation of instant food seemed divinely sent. Cowie devoured the burger, washed it down with a full glass of full-fat coke, might as well go the whole hog. Seated himself on his opulent sofa, wondered what his next course of action should be. It did not take him long to conclude. For he had experienced first-hand the infamy of the Zaromi. So now, free of their wickedly inhumane influence, he must divert all his energies, resources, into stopping them from taking over more of mankind. Where to start? How did one seek an invisible enemy? Realising he need do nothing, he grinned. Once the tapping discontinued from Moluura, one of his minions would determine the reason for the cessation. What would Cowie do then? In the mood for no more killing. Maybe there was someone he could get in touch with? A team of freedom fighters somewhere, already devoted to opposing the Insectivo. He tried to remember all he had learned while the Veztőöndər shared his mind, a single name jumped unbidden into remembrance – Sellers. Opening his laptop, his fingers danced across the pad. It was easy to find the location of the man. Yorkshire, the third world, according to supreme Python. In the town of Doncaster. Snatching up his wallet, keys, a jacket, he had a purpose once again.

Thirty-three. **"Are you alright,** Uvirális", Sellers asked, "You've suddenly lost all your colour"!

The leyskip, seated on the sofa, glass in hand. Carefully, Kyla took it from him, lest he spilt any of its contents. Felton was still with them, hence the amusing use of the alias. They knew he had subjugated the Zaromi where he could do no harm. Tranessy suddenly told the three of them,

"I'm getting a transmission from Reality Prime. From Vonalat, probably not originated from him".

"Transmission", her Ladyship asked, glancing at Felton.

"Just a verbal communication, but one which I'm not sure I can comply with".

"An instruction then", Sellers concluded, "Difficult orders by the sound of it. Give him his drink back, your Ladyship".

Once the beverage was with Tranessy, he took a pull before informing them.

"It seems my task is to teach you, my discipline, Sellers".

"Traverse the ley-lines of the multiverse"?! Sellers was incredulous. "Even if I had the talent, which is not a given, to what end? It's here I want to defeat the Zaromi".

"It's here they need destroying", Felton added with conviction.

"It seems", Tranessy explained, "That back at RPrime, Vonalat has developed a mental insecticide to achieve just that. He wants to teach Sellers how to use such mental discipline".

"Why can't *you* go back to learn it"? Felton asked, "After all, you already know how to leyskip. It would therefore be quicker".

"Sellers is to learn other disciplines whilst in RPrime".

"Such as"? The subject of discussion desired to know.

"They did not give me the detail, but if you want to destroy the Zaromi here in 23, then you are to learn how to leyskip from me".

"Even you can't do it without the machines", Sellers objected.

"They will set a date and time when the machines activate. They will pull you to RPrime. Your mind must be ready for the experience, Sellers".

"Just the two of us"?

"I'm afraid so. You must leave her Ladyship, our bipolar friend here, behind".

"I was thinking of Mrs Meggins from the Pie Shop", Sellers said earnestly, "I've left her behind too often just lately and she's not happy with me. She increases my moralé too, I could carry her"?

"Mister Sellers", Kyla began, "I'll look after pussy, she'll not want for company".

Felton grinned at the offer, thinking, *'Just like he's looked after yours, no doubt'!*

"No", Sellers was obdurate, "I'm not going on yet another absence without my beloved mascot, that my friends - is my final decision".

Tranessy, a lover of animals himself, sympathised, smiled. "Then you'll have to learn the discipline. Smuggle her into your jacket. We'll lie to Vonalat about your weight. It might just work Sellers. Though very capricious, I understand Vonalat loves domestic felines too".

"It's settled then", Sellers was triumphant, "Megwinda comes with us"!

"The trouble is, although I know how to leyskip", Tranessy confessed. "I've no idea how to instruct someone else in the mental discipline. I don't even quite know how I do it myself"?

"You don't know how you do it"! Kyla sounded exasperated. "I don't see how even you manage it then".

"Might I suggest, that for Tranessy it's instinctual", Felton offered, "Rather like how pigeons find their way home or fish return each year to spawning grounds".

"Sellers is no fish", Kyla reasoned with some feeling, before thinking to herself, *'He's pretty good at spawning though'!*

"If I can connect our minds, then perhaps I can find such instinctual bent, replicate it in my mind", Sellers mused.

"I thought you said Balurzuura was in a deep dark place", Tranessy pointed out, "whilst I have no cerquibrum at all".

"Yes", Sellers agreed. "I wasn't suggesting using the insectivore or Insecto as you call them".

"You mean *you* can link on a mental level with me"?

"I can give it a shot. Never done it before, Old Man. Who knows"?

"I don't have a working alternative, so where do you want me"?

"I think we should retire to the guest room, lay side by side in the darkness, see if I can do what I would like to try".

"Oo-er", Felton could not resist, "Sounds a bit rude".

"Act your age, Sir", her Ladyship cautioned with such vigorous dignity that the men laughed at *her* - rather than anything else. Handing the protesting Mrs Meggins from the Pie Shop to Kyla, where she nestled appreciatively between the soft mounds of her ample bosom, Sellers and Tranessy left the three of them going into the guest bedroom. They lay side-by-side as Sellers told the lights to switch off. He tried to imagine that from his head came the fingers of a psychic hand, just as he had succeeded with before. A finger of the hand drifted upward, across, downward toward the Leyskip's head. Encompassing blue fingers grasped Tranessy's head, such were their size. With sudden ease, they both shrank whilst passing through the skull at the same instant. An extension of Sellers' esper enhanced mind was inside the convolutions of the Leyskip's brain. Diligently, with immense care, Sellers explored the various folds of the mind he had invaded. For his part, Tranessy continued to lie still. Was he even aware that Sellers was in his mind? The Superman of nyloplanyon muscles, duridium steel skeleton, Insectolike mind and brain found the area of Tranessy's that was responsible for hearing. He progressed carefully through emotion, speech, taste, reasoning, when almost ready to despair, found what he sought - instinct. Fortunately, he had not then discovered memory, so there was no invasion of that most precious to the leyskiper. Sellers imagined a huge red button, an expansive green arrow. The button, a mental representation of record, the arrow - play. Pressed the two simultaneously, Sellers could assimilate the instinct necessary to traverse the ley-lines of the multiverse. In a state of excited anticipation, Sellers did so, felt something beyond words to describe flow from Tranessy's mind into his. Not thoughts, recollections, nor anything that any forebrain thought process could observe. It existed in a more primitive state, was rugged, uncultivated, primordial. Strangely, Tranessy was slightly less advanced than the others in the quartet, for him to do what he could. Seller rose from the bed, asked the lights to come up,

"That's it, I have it", it pleased him to inform.

"I didn't feel a thing. Didn't even know you were tapping, that's incredible".

"In the morning, I'll get Megwinda. We can get off".

"Whoa Hoss, it's not quite as easy as that", Tranessy laughed. "You may have the instinct when Vonalat activated the mentalamps, may even follow me, but you're not prepared for the psychological effects of traversing the ley-lines".

"Emotional effects"?

Tranessy nodded. "Unprepared, the journey might just tip you into insanity".

"It didn't, in your case. You must have made the first skip"?

"Another prepared me who, sadly, is no longer with us. I had a mentor of a decade before I skipped the first time".

"What about Megwinda? She'll not go mad will she"?

"Actually, she will be fine", Tranessy admitted. "In our experiments with mice, we found that taking animals through, with their more rudimentary thought processes, proved fine.

"All right then. You can support my body while I esper into my cat's mind".

Tranessy was beyond astonished, "If you can do it, then it's a novel way to avoid insanity, congratulations".

"I can do it", Sellers returned confidently. "I've always wondered exactly what Mrs Meggins from the Pie Shop truly thought of me".

Tranessy chuckled, before asking, "Have you never thought of shortening her name to Megs or some such. It's a rather ungainly handle".

"I considered it - briefly didn't think she'd subscribe to it for a second", Sellers told him seriously.

"If you intend to shelter in her mind, we can go to RPrime once I have arranged it with Vonalat. Will tomorrow morning be a suitable time, say nine"?

Thinking of his last night with her Ladyship for a while. How she would doubtless give him something to remember her by, Sellers smiled. Agreed nine was admirable.

"I don't feel any change", Sellers objected, "Do you? Should I maybe stay in my head for the trip after all"?

Tranessy shook his head, holding his arms straight out at his sides, "No, it's beginning, get into the cat's mind now"!

The superhuman felt a strange tingling around the perimeter of his body. He began imagining a stream of sparkling dashes spilling from the top of his head, falling into Mrs Meggins from the Pie Shop's tiny skull. The stream continued while Tranessy took hold of his husk. Into the mind of his little moggy, he fled.

It strangely distorted all that he perceived when inside Mrs Meggins from the Pie Shop's mind. As though his thoughts had gone mushy. He was aware of what was happening still. Yet felt sedated. Examined his senses.

Unsurprisingly, they were feline. The manhybrocat could hear in any of thirty-seven different directions. Their vision was only monochromatic at a distance, strangely blurred closer to. Movement, enhanced, exaggerated, their ability to track it heightened. They were hot, the creature's coat making it so. For fun, they moved their shared tail. Tried to purr, failed. Something fantastic occurred. An indescribably callous, inhumane mind touched that which had once been the man's.

'What you'?

It was Mrs Meggins from the Pie Shop. Mentally able to communicate with Sellers in their shared mind!

'It's me Megwinda, Tod, Master'.

'Servant'?

The cat was correct. Sellers supplied food, shelter, unconditional love, healthcare, whilst Megwinda responded with little better than mild disdain.

'Yes, Servant. I'm in your mind for the duration of this strange journey. We can converse. Is there anything you would like once we get home? Any changes you would like to make your existence more comfortable'?

'Fish'.

'More fish'?

'Fish'.

'Anything else? Would you like a new basket, a new collar? Would you like to sit on my lap more often, have your own bed'?

'Fish'.

Megwinda's mind was not up to human standards. All he could expect realistically. Beyond them, the journey was beginning. Sellers wanted to watch it through the cat's eyes, he told her,

'I love you Mrs Meggins from the Pie Shop. We can chance to converse another time - all right'?

'Fish, yes. No fish, no'.

Through her eyes, the fantastic mind of the manhybrocat saw the apartment twist. Convoluted, dribbled into puddles that were myriad, stridently grotesque. Pulled their shared vision, a cat-aclysm of cat-astrophe. A scene unsettling - strangely compelling. The apartment suddenly disappeared they hovered over the town. Sellers suffered from basiphobia fortunately the feline part of the dualmind did not. Thusly was the little trial conquered. When the ground suddenly rose to meet them at fantastical speed, their hackles rose all claws coming out. The ground gnarled into a twisting contortion of concrete, tarmacadam, sky. Overhead, as material as everything else as something suddenly sucked them into a terrible epicentre. In his mind, his alone, Sellers would have found the experience terrifying indeed. Through the swirling conglomerate, the trio was suddenly in a vast expanse, floating above a massive motorway. One with myriad lanes stretching off in either direction, infinitely. From such strands of reality, the occasional junction split away above the lanes, disappearing from the event horizon. What they witnessed was the ley-lines of the multiverse. indescribably Tranessy had pulled them into the void beyond. They were at the edge of time, the golden void, the escutcheon of all that was, that was not. Should they not suffocate? It was not their bodies that did the skipping, but their minds. Once their intellect reached its destination, RPrime, Vonalat's fantastic machine brought everything together. Dragged flesh to the same location as consciousness, reasoning, lucidity. Tranessy pointed down to one lane, suddenly dived, as one might go into a pool of water. Indicated the manhybrocat did the same. Megwinda leapt rather than dived, Sellers, little more than an incredulous spectator. Down they plummeted at incredible speed, which would have killed them all had they impacted into the ley-line in biological form. Their cognisance tore through the roof of a gigantic building. Came to land on an expanse of concrete between vast rows of huge, ominous-looking machines. The manhybrocat heard Tranessy say,

"Our destination, you can get back into your head now". It was as though he screamed out the words in the most piercing of voices, hurting feline ears.

'Time for me to leave you dear moggy'.

'A disconcerting experience. Not one I would never want to do again though'.

'You've suddenly become far more eloquent. What's happened"?

It'd seem that proximity to your mind has contaminated mine. I'll be fine. Go, don't forget one thing"?

"What's that'?

'Let's just say I prefer tuna'.

Reversing the process learned in the apartment, Sellers exited Mrs Meggins from the Pie Shop, but as he did, he thought he heard the last pitiful cry of,

'Fish'!

Sellers blinked, straightened himself, Tranessy noted,

"Incredible. You made the journey with your mind in the cat's head. Did it work? Are you all right"?

"I feel fine. An awesome experience, traversing the ley-lines", Sellers assured.

"The mind of the cat", an unfamiliar voice issued from behind Sellers who turned to perceive the figure of the archetype mad scientist. "What was it like,"?

"Initially cold, cruel, demanding", Sellers replied, holding out his elbow, "It's a pleasure - an honour to meet you Herr Vonalat".

"Yes," Vonalat returned, not taking the gesture of greeting, friendship. "Of course it is".

"Ha ha ha how arrogant"! Sellers laughed as Tranessy grimaced, wondering what the scientist's reaction to that would be.

Vonalat grinned, rejoinder-ed, "I don't like your girl's hair".

Sellers returned almost at once, "I'm not surprised, it's only jealousy because yours is migrating for the winter of your life".

Vonalat seemed to enjoy the squabble, "I don't like your beard".

"I don't like your brow-ridge".

The scientist suddenly burst into delighted laughter, "Well done Sellers. You know, I get heartily sick of all the sycophants tiptoeing around me. It's simply ages since I've enjoyed a good old wrangle".

"So are you going to bump or not then you miserable old útonálló"?

"Ha ha ha ha. You speak the local language too", Vonalat bumped the huge elbow of the Adonis. "I'm intrigued to know your entire experience sharing your mind with this delightful creature? May I"?

Sellers handed Mrs Meggins from the Pie Shop over. She immediately purred, rubbing up against the wizened old man. While the traveller explained how their mental melding had vastly improved the feline's intellect. Vonalat found the narrative fascinating, predicting,

"This little cat will play a much larger part in the multiverse than you currently suspect, Sellers. How many languages have you mastered by the by"?

Sellers informed the scientist, "I speak seventeen languages at present Vonalat, but what I'd like to learn to do, is use Menta-carbaryl".

"And it will be my pleasure to teach you that technique", Vonalat beamed.

Thirty-four. Michael Cowie found Doncaster to be overwhelming. It was very urban, noisy, stank after his residence in the countryside. The smell was the worst, the smog of the internal combustion engine. How the Yanks liked their great big gas-guzzling automobiles. Finding a parking spot close to the address, he walked between the skyscrapers. It was not immediately obvious to him, but after two streets, he noticed he seemed to walk parallel to a young couple on the other side of the road. Cowie felt for the Windicator, Revolver, point357 Magnum. It securely nestling in the holder at his left side. The shoulder holster kept it in place nicely. Some sixth sense informed him that the young couple meant trouble even before he recognised the man. They had met briefly, once when Cowie had been more Moluura than himself. He had issued the man a directive to put into motion a series of stratagem designed to result in Seller's death. His allegiance had shifted. He could not let the man reach his quarry. What was curious was that he seemed to intend to make the assassination attempt himself. Which was a detraction from the original plan, where-by a Mizaroan was captured, brainwashed into doing the job for them. That must have failed: Einuur (Cowie suddenly remembered the Zaromi's name) was taking matters into his own hands. Cowie could not let that happen. Nor would he. Neither strong nor brave, he must do what had the best chance of success. Which was to attack without warning -swiftly, mercilessly, soon. Drawing the revolver, he pointed it toward the couple, squeezed the trigger. The sound was far louder than he had expected. The recoil sent the revolver upward. Cowie re-positioned the weapon. Began systematically emptying the revolver's chamber in the couple's direction. Heard a woman scream, did not slow his firing rate. Never saw the result of his attack, nor the bus that struck him head-on. There had been six bullets fired in all. The first two had gone wide of the target before his aim had improved, greater in accuracy. The third bullet struck Einuur in the upper arm, shattering the bone. At that moment, with his other arm, he had pushed Ailuura behind him, using his own body as a shield to protect her. Thusly, the next three bullets struck the Zaromoid in various parts of his torso, the last one that hit him in the chest rupturing his heart. Ailuura felt the body of her comrade stiffen, fall, as the bus smote their attacker. She had been too shocked to react. Finally, regaining her composure, she walked swiftly from the scene where a crowd was rapidly gathering. One woman attempted to take her by the arm, demanding,

"Aren't you going to stop? Talk to the law"?

"I didn't know either of the men", Ailuura stated quickly, "I've a very important meeting soon. You saw what happened, you tell them. Now kindly let go or I'll be reporting an assault if delayed further".

The ruse was impressively successful. Ailuura continued on the way to Sellers' apartment. What could have happened to Zelmuur? Why had they heard nothing from him? He had failed in his assassination, that much was plain. Einuur had ranted, raged over the lack of communication. Now he was dead. Likely Zelmuur as well, which left her. Was she now queen of the Zaromi? If so, should she also risk her life to attack the Mizaroa? Would it not be better to return to the swarm, take her position as queen, issue directives to others? To risk her life, then on that day when alone, why that would be selfish of her. She must return to the ship, assume her role as the new leader of the Zaromi. Having realised her responsibilities, Ailuura turned on her heels, hurried away in the opposite direction.

When Cowie awoke, he felt like a bus had run him over. This was not an unreasonable state of sensation, for one had. More precisely, hit by one. He found himself in a hospital bed, tubes leading out of his arms, securely strapped to it so he could not rise. That would have been problematic, had it been all, but both his legs were in plaster too? Next to one of his hands was a buzzer, he depressed it, to summon a nurse. When she arrived at the private room Cowie alone occupied, an American styled policeman accompanied her.

"Now you're back in the land of the living, I'm going to need a statement from you", the policeman began, "See what he wants nurse then call my colleague? You'll find him over at the coke machine".

The nurse did not look especially pleased to be taking orders from the policeman, but she simply nodded, went about her duties of making Cowie as comfortable as possible before going to look for the absent policeman.

"I'm patrolman Trent", he began, as he pulled a chair up to the side of the bed, "Ah, here's my partner, Esk. We're going to take your statement, Sir. Before we do, we must inform you that anything you say is being recorded, could be used in evidence against you in a court of law at a later date".

"That's just standard procedure, Sir", Esk added in a friendly manner, I'm sure you'd prefer to help us with our inquiries? It always goes more smoothly if you give us your full cooperation".

"I'm more than willing to supply you with an eyewitness account of what happened, while it's still fresh in my mind", Cowie told them.

The two exchanged a momentarily puzzled glance before Trent, who had pressed record on the digital recorder, asked,

"What do you mean exactly by eyewitness account, Sir"?

"I was there. Saw what happened from beginning to end. It was me who wrestled the gun from the assailant, just before backing into the bus. Have you got him in custody yet officers"?

The duo was immediately out of their depth. Other onlookers had mentioned a shooting. A dead victim. They had described a man who fit the man in the bed's general profile.

"Firstly, Sir can we have your full name"? Trent went back to basics.

"I'm the Michael Cowie who is on the driving license. You've no doubt already perused it, Officers".

"And you still live at the same address"?

Cowie nodded, "And I won't be visiting Doncaster again soon if this is what the place is like, shootings in broad daylight? Why it's getting like America"!

"So do we take it you maintain you were not the assailant, Mister Cowie"?

Cowie laughed, "Me, Officers? I've no idea what you're talking about. I didn't know the poor man who got shot. Apparently, this is a very important clue by the by. The shooter was the woman's husband, the victim, her lover. Serves him right for being so immoral, but murder's a bit much, don't you think? How is the poor woman, by the way? Not that we should feel sorry for her really, should we - the dirty cow"?

"Mister Cowie", Trent began slowly, "We have two eyewitnesses who describe the shooter. The description matches you, Sir".

"Now I come to think about it, he was sort of the same height and build, the guy who shot the lover. I heard him cry, 'Screw my wife, will you? You both deserve to die for what you've done to me'. Then he opened fire. Now that I concentrate he was around the same age too. Though he was unshaven whilst I have a tightly trimmed beard".

The policemen thanked Cowie before going to report to their station. Cowie had not planned the confusion it had come to him as he had waited for the nurse. He remembered a radio report he had heard in the past stating that eyewitnesses were notoriously unreliable after a sudden crime. Unobservant, soon forgetful. Try as they might, the police could not connect Cowie to the dead man. Once it got to court, if the Crown prosecuted, Cowie would buy himself the finest solicitor in the land. Sticking to his nonstory. He doubted they would get a conviction. The broken legs were a terrible blow. He could not now warn Sellers what was going to happen. It was infuriating.

Thirty-five.   **"First you must** rest. We'll begin your instruction tomorrow". Vonalat decided. "I'll get someone to escort you to the finest hotel in the city".

"If you do, make it a pretty girl? After looking at your ugly face I could do with resting my superb vision a little", Sellers jibed, to Tranessy's amazement the mad-scientist seemed to find the insult funny. Maybe that was where everyone else had been going wrong with Vonalat, given him *too much* respect. He perhaps had thought he was being fawned over, not appreciating it.

Vonalat gestured to an assistant in a lab coat, who till that time had been admirably in the background. The man was instantly at his side.

"Fetch Cenise, tell her I've a diplomatic duty for her", Vonalat instructed his aid, who promptly scurried away to do as directed.

"Cenise"? Sellers asked. His libido had been insatiable since his death. Probably hyped to greater capacity, just like every other aspect of his top-notch physique.

Vonalat beamed, "Forget it, Super-boy, she's married to one of the greatest electrical engineers on the planet. You'll not have heard of Obrahom, back in that backward filth hovel you call home - 23".

"Is this planet much cleaner"? Sellers asked as he stroked his cat. Absently, the scientist tickled Mrs Meggins from the Pie Shop under the chin. She responded by purring softly. It surprised Sellers at how familiar the old goat could be with his discerning moggy. Normally she did not take to strangers, they came no stranger than Vonalat.

"Of course. This Earth is a verdant paradise filled with every species of animal that nature created".

"Yes alright, even dodo's carrier pigeons, buffalo, black rhino, Siberian tiger".

To Seller's amazement, Vonalat nodded, "The dinosaurs are extinct. It was too late for them. Good job I suppose. The creatures *you* mention all thrive here. Do you know what the population of this planet is"?

"Seven billion", the newest leyskiper guessed.

"Eight hundred, seventy-five million".

Sellers gasped, "Close to one billion! What happened in this world's history to reduce it so much"?

"The SC of 1875".

"What's that when it's all at home"? Sellers wanted to know in typical Yorkshire fashion.

"The Superstition Council of 1875 comprised all the major powers of Earth at that time. They met to decide the future of the world, it's best resolutions to serve that remit subsequently put into place".

"But why Superstition Council"? Sellers wished to know.

Vonalat raised an eyebrow, "Why because the decision was easy. Superstition was the principal cause of many of the world's problems at that time, especially in the third world".

"What great strides toward this heavenly state did they make"?

"The execution of the pope, dissolution of all other major superstitions. Their figureheads, who were consistently robbing the masses blind, encouraging them to continue the beginning of the population explosion. Even back then we had discovered the existence of the multiverse - mathematically, we couldn't access any of the other layers, traverse the ley-lines. Yet we had trans-ley-line viewing devices. In every reality, superstition caused most of the world's problems. Reality Prime killed all the gods. The result - heaven on Earth, just as the world should be. There was resistance to it at first, naturally. Holy wars, the superstitional had enjoyed a comfortable ride for centuries, we, the humanists won, the result, our current world".

"You see no difference between superstition and religion"?

"One is born of the other. Organised into corrupt ways of milking the ignorant. Ah, here's Cenise".

Sellers gazed at the approaching figure with interest. An attractive young woman, very slim, wearing a long, flowing dress of swirling cheesecloth. She wore her blonde-straight hair cut into a fashionable page-boy bob which accentuated her long aquiline nose, large reflective eyes. Eyes made up in sky shadow while the slender lips were bright pink. Sellers felt an immediate attraction to her. One, unexplainable concerning the woman's level of attractiveness. Strangely, he felt there was an indefinable quality about the woman, something more than he could quite grasp. She stopped short of him to speak to Vonalat, saw him, her eyes opened wide, a huge smile creased her glamorous features,

"Don Sellers, what are you doing in the lab? I never saw you come in. I'm a massive fan. I never miss a race. You're very good".

Vonalat burst into delighted laughter, while Tranessy came to Sellers' rescue.

"In our reality, you're a Formula 9 racing driver, Sellers. They prepared me for your appearance. Vonalat did not brief Cenise here before your arrival".

The woman immediately coloured a fine shade of pink, asked politely,

"What's happening Herr Vonalat".

"Don't be so polite to him", Sellers advised, "He's just played a practical joke on the two of us, the wily old goat".

Cenise glanced from the scientist to the driver (in her mind) saw both finding the situation amusing. Finally, Vonalat explained,

"This is not Don Sellers, My Dear. Rather, *Tod* Sellers from reality 23. I would like you to escort him to the Kőröstetétlen Kiváló. See that he's given the best rooms available, please? Will you do that for me, Cenise".

Recovering her composure somewhat, the attractive young woman nodded. Noticed Mrs Meggins from the Pie Shop for the first time,

"Oh! Aren't you cute"? She asked the cat. "Is this your animal, Herr Sellers"?

"Yes, something of a celebrity since she traversed the ley-lines with me".

"You brought her with you? You must be inordinately attached to the little darling".

"I love her more than any pig", Sellers said in a humorous voice. He was a huge Blackadder fan. Did not care if he was the only one who understood the reference, found it amusing.

"Ah, I'm sure you do", the girl returned, which made Sellers smile even more.

"Am I at liberty to take my leave of you then, oh wise, wondrous scientist"? Sellers asked Vonalat. To which, the old man cawed,

"Get out of here. Be back at nine tomorrow for the first of your instructions.

Sellers turned to Cenise, "Right then Asszony Cenise, I'm all yours".

"That would be Frau Cenise, Herr Sellers. Though we are in the continent's region you would think of as Hungary, in this reality, it's German territory".

"I see. Looks like I've much to learn, not to worry I'm a quick study. Will my room at the hotel have the net"?

"Do you mean the Worldweb"?

"I think I do yes, another difference, the nomen".

They got in the lift, Sellers breathed deeply. The scent of the woman was intoxicating. She was very observant, missed nothing.

"It's called *Verführung,* Herr Sellers $127 for a 25 mil spray".

"It's worth every cent", Sellers observed candidly, "I do indeed feel enticed".

Changing the subject, she asked him, "Do you think you'll meet Don Sellers while you're here? It's allowed before you ask me that, it happened once a few years ago".

"How did that go then"?

"The individual concerned was Vonalat, the two of them did a great deal of work together, MOAC was born as a result".

"Two Vonalats. Phew, one's quite enough".

Cenise laughed - a delightful sound. The doors opened directly onto street level. Cenise ordered a taxi. When it came it amazed the superman. It touched down on the pavement before the building. He saw it land through the huge glass facade.

"It can fly"?!

"Of course, can't your taxis"?

"We're still using automobiles driven by the internal combustion engine".

"Ew! Filthy things, how do you breathe"?

"We manage, come on then come fly with me".

They climbed into the taxiflyer which lifted into the air, taking them to Kőröstetétlen Kiváló. As the crow flew, it was not far. The journey ended shortly, but it had given Sellers an aerial view of Hungary. What he saw amazed him. Under the Americ-Germanic pact, they had transformed the landscape into a scene looking rather like a huge central town of America. The reason, simple, with a tiny population, such as RPrime possessed, Man could avoid any extreme. The population no longer lived on fault lines in the tectonic plates. Freezing, sweltering hot regions. Making vast swathes of land in the Middle East, Japanese Islands, Africa, empty of people. Thusly those who prospered on the Earth lived in the temperate zones where the climate was most agreeable. To cope with this understandable concentration of population, humanity had gone upward. The skyscraper was the ruling architecture of the world. The Kőröstetétlen Kiváló was the best hotel in the city, leaving Sellers stunned. A mighty structure clawing into the skyline like some bizarre beast of steel, thermocrete, glass. The taxi dropped them off right at the doors, which hissed open on servos as they approached. Inside, it devoted the entire ground floor to reception. The climate control kept the interior a steady 18 degrees throughout the year, independent of the weather outside. At the centre of a vast expanse of grey tiles was an area of huge ferns, other plants that were bathed in mist twice daily by hidden jets just above the soil-line but hidden by the stone surrounding of the display. Cenise led the way to the desk, which was at the far end, farthest from the lifts. A young man who raised his eyebrows at both Sellers and Mrs Meggins from the Pie Shop greeted her.

"I'm sorry, Herr Sellers, but you cannot ...". he began, Cenise cut him off.

"Vonalat sent him here. He's to have the penthouse the cat too. I suggest you get her a litter tray, little bed to sleep in".

"Oh, I see", the man looked chagrined, "Of course my apologies, let me get you the swipe card, Herr Sellers, room 2021".

He handed the card over with admirable efficiency. Cenise pressed her thumb to a plate on the desk, obviously paying for it with MOAC funds authorised by the scientist. She turned to Sellers,

"I trust someone will be along shortly to take you to your room. You'll need some clothes while you're here, so here is some old-fashioned folding money".

She passed Sellers a confusing collection of dollars, marks, forint, explaining, "They will accept all currencies in the shops. You need nothing else, you'll find the suite will supply all toiletries, linen".

"You're leaving me alone in a big city that I don't know"?

"I have other work to do, Herr Sellers. Other responsibilities you'll be fine you're a big boy. I'll pick you up tomorrow morning at eight-forty-five".

"This evening", Sellers gave her what he had quickly learned was his most winning smile, "Would you have dinner with me, at the place of your choosing, please"?

She looked at him with those fabulously intelligent eyes, noted, "I'm married".

"Does that mean you don't eat then? Dinner is dinner Frau Cenise, pure and simple".

"Could I bring Obrahom"?

"Certainly. Any other friends, acquaintances, it would honour me to meet them".

She smiled, "A project currently obsesses my husband. A scientific one he's working on to the exclusion of all else. My friends will probably have already made alternative plans".

"But you've not, you're available"?

She tried to look at him sternly. Failed, agreed, "I'll be in the restaurant here, at nineteen hundred hours, you'll be ready"?

"I'll be ready".

The penthouse suite was massive, very impressive indeed. All glass, chromed metal. The Primeans (as Sellers thought of the people of that reality) liked pure uncluttered lines, it seemed. Once he had satisfied his curiosity, given Mrs Meggins from the Pie Shop some Finom Macska food (already delivered, along with litter, house, doughnut-bed). He left the feline to settle in.

Going in search of a shopping arcade to buy some clothes. Looked out of place in boho as the Primean men all wore white shirts, black ties, slacks in the same sable absence of colour. When inquiring at the desk it was to discover that the shopping arcade was *inside* the hotel on the fourteenth floor. Back to the lift, the afternoon spent purchasing white underwear, black socks, three white shirts, two pairs of black slacks, a tie. He also bought a pair of black sandals with only a few holes cut into them for air movement, a sort of sandal/shoe hybrid which he found very comfortable due to their huge spongy soles. Loaded down with *returnable* paper carrier bags, on which he had paid a refundable deposit when he took them back, he got back to the twentieth floor with no accidents or mishaps.

"Right Megwinda", he said to the moggy, stripping off his boho shirt, huge loons, "Time for a nice hot soak in that brilliant oyster-shaped bath".

He ran the water as hot as he could stand it, slipped into the fragrant bubbles. Noting as he did so that the towels were black and white, not teal. How long ago, it seemed to him, since he had first discovered the towels in his apartment had changed colour. It seemed like he had experienced more since his death, than everything he had stumbled through in all the years before. Letting the water lull him almost to sleep, he heard a faint cry deep in his mind.

'I am still here Sellers, you cannot do this to me'!

"Balurzuura"! Sellers mumbled. "I'd almost forgotten you. You cannot get out, or attempt to take over again, you know that".

'Then go back to Flamborough, have me removed from this mind-prison you have me in. I will see to it they do not punish you for your crimes'.

"I prefer to keep you where I know you are", Sellers smiled to himself. "Now stop thinking, leave me to enjoy my soak. I'm sorry to inform you, that you are nothing but a deposed Királálynővonazóreginăcondător".

Mrs Meggins from the Pie Shop perched suddenly on the side of the bath, purring loudly. Filled with curiosity. If she slipped it would be just like the last time. A creature looking like some sort of aquatic-rat would scramble out of the water as quickly as possible whilst taking a good third with it, depositing it onto the bathroom floor.

"Now Megwinda", Sellers said gently, "You know you're not as agile nor dainty as you think you are, get down. I'll give you a belly-rub once I'm out".

'And with a bit of luck it won't be the only belly-rub I administer this evening', he added in his mind lasciviously.

In his previous existence, Sellers had been a highly moral person, thinking of all women as ladies until it transpired otherwise. The only trouble with that admirable behaviour, one got scant *action*. They transformed him into an Adonis. Everyone knew the ancient Greeks wore no standard trolleys. He became nothing more than a male slag. That Cenise was a married woman concerned him not in the slightest. If this Obrahom could not keep her satisfied then it was his fault if his Mrs strayed a little. In any event, Sellers could be discreet, so if he never found out, so much the better. It never even entered Seller's mind that Cenise would not *put out*.

Thirty-six,   Obrahom was one of the world's leading electrical engineers. In a world where superstition was void since the end of the nineteenth century, science had flourished unmolested at an alarming rate. The Earth of RPrime was approximately 1,000 years more advanced scientifically than any of its counterparts. Obrahom was at the leading edge of such research, development, as the MOAC possessed. He spent many hours in his laboratory. Too many hours, far too many. It made him aware one day that his lovely wife might find his work ethic a trifle tedious. Although she had known what he did when they had met, for she too was an employee of the constabulary. Time passed, the period of *rose-tinted glasses* had come/gone, Obrahom was still in his laboratory while Cenise was spending greater leisure time left to her own devices. The research engineer may not have been the most attentive or affectionate of husbands, but he was not stupid, far from it. When a certain period had passed, he decided it might be time to monitor his loving spouse's activities. The listening device he had slipped subcutaneously under her skin one night was a marvel of technology. It could transmit crystal clear audio to any point in the world by satellite upload. The spray had anaesthetized her skin, the slit glued back into place so expertly that not even the faintest trace of a scar was visible the following morning. Obrahom could have taken a very different route. Could have reduced his time in the laboratory, spent more with his lovely companion. Or he could have divorced her as they were growing apart. He was not that sort of man. He believed the vows she had made to him at their wedding service. She had known how driven he was in his work from the offset; he considered Cenise - his. She must put up with seeing him infrequently, she must not dally with anyone else. For five months, the audio transmissions revealed absolutely nothing for him to worry about. As an attractive young woman, she received her fair share of flirtation, but she let none of them lead to dalliance, so all was well. After all, what man does not want others to find their wives attractive? It only confirmed what they felt initially. It is then up to their spouse to deter patiently, he who pursues her. When Obrahom heard others make complimentary comments to Cenise, he was pleased. Even more so when she deflected them with consummate ease. Then along came Sellers. Obrahom heard their first meeting. remained perfectly unconcerned until the end of it. She agreed to have dinner with the handsome young man and did not arrange for anyone to chaperon her. For the engineer, that was crossing a line that he believed she should not have. Concerned, he fast-forwarded the digital recording to the next time Cenise broke her silence. His wife was clearly in the bath because he could hear the water moving occasionally, but she had her earphone in it suddenly quietly buzzed.

Cenise - "Hello".

Fean - "It's me. How are you girlfriend? What are'ya up to? I can call over if Obe is in his lab, as usual.

Cenise - "You've just caught me getting ready to go out".

Fean - "Unusual, anyone I know ha ha ha".

Cenise - "Sort of, you know exactly what he looks like".

Fean - "I was joking. Are you going out with a man? Who is it if you are"?

Cenise - "Don Sellers, the formula 9 racing driver".

Fean - "Ha ha ha ha you wish. Who is it, someone from work, one of your female colleagues"?

Cenise - "Keep it to yourself, but I'm having dinner with Don Sellers".

Lengthy silence ...

Fean – "You're not ... are you"?

Cenise – He's asked me to dinner. As he doesn't know anyone in Kőröstététlen. So I said yes, dinner is just dinner, right? Do you think I should tell Obrahom"?

Fean - "Are you out of your mind? If you're not winding me up, you have a dinner date with Don Sellers, the last person on the planet you should tell is your husband".

Cenise - "It's only dinner, Fean".

Fean - "All clear, so look at it this way. Obrahom somehow meets Jennifer Pfeiffer. He asks her out to dinner, she accepts. How would you feel about that"?

Cenise - "It's not the same thing at all, is it? I mean, Jennifer Pfeiffer is so damned hot. Obrahom *is a man*".

Fean - "Don Sellers is so damned hot - you're a woman. A woman with needs. Needs that poor old Obrahom isn't fulfilling (he winced at this revelation)".

Cenise - "I'll be a good girl".

Fean - "With Don Sellers! I wouldn't be"!

Cenise - "I have to go now Fean, there's someone on the other line I want to get ready".

Fean - "Aycee, don't forget to put a diaphragm, some SP cream in your handbag".

Cenise - "Fean! You're incorrigible".

Fean – "Better safe than sorry".

Cenise "Goodbye MYA".

There was no further recording for quite a long time. The device found the next transmissions that involved conversation. Despite his misgivings, Obrahom could not turn the recorder off.

Sellers - "There you are Frau Cenise, I was thinking you were going to stand me up".

Cenise - "I nearly did. I have a reputation to uphold".

Sellers - "Dinner is just dinner, Frau Cenise".

Cenise "You can call me just Cenise while we're dining".

Sellers - "All right, Just Cenise, what would you like to drink"?

Cenise - "A Pálinka, please no ice. It's just - Cenise.".

Sellers – Two Pálinkas please, the menu"?

Voice presumably waiter – "Certainly Herr".

Sellers - "Tell me about this world of yours? MOAC, your role in it all"?

Obrahom fast-forwarded through the next seventy minutes.

Cenise – "Tod (Tod!), thank you for a delightful meal. I'm sure you'll make an excellent student of Vonalat"

Sellers - "You're going? Leaving me - the evening is still young. Too early for me to retire".

Cenise - "Dinner is over that's what I agreed to".

Sellers - "It's only 20:25".

Cenise - "It's been pleasant. You look much better in a proper shirt and tie, but I have to be going".

Sellers "Do you have another appointment? Is your husband expected home"?

You pushy base-born, can't you take no for an answer'? Obrahom thought.

Cenise - "I never expect my husband home".

Sellers - "Then he's a fool".

Cenise - "That's unfair Tod, you know nothing about him".

Sellers - "I know he doesn't pay you enough attention. Forget I said that, what do you say we move on from here, is there a casino in Kőröstetétlen"?

Cenise - "You want to go gambling"?

Sellers - "I want to play cards until the Casino throws me out with my winnings. I've an eidetic memory, will win in a card game simply because I'll know what is in the pack after a while. Tell you what, we'll both play. Whatever we win, we split fifty-fifty".

Cenise - "Just for an hour Don (Don)! Then I'm going home".

Sellers - "You can leave whenever you want. I'll get one of the flying taxis to take you".

Cenise - "All right, we'll go to the Szerencsés Ember just for an hour.

Obrahom was not interested in gambling. Fast forwarded the recording an hour, but his wife was still in the Casino. Did not sound like she had any intention of going home.

Cenise - "I can't believe they let you play as long as you did. I mean to say - HUF50,000"!

Sellers - "It's HUF52,827 making your share HUF26,413.5".

Cenise - "But I lost".

Sellers – "We had a deal, remember? Let's get another drink".

Cenise - "I think I've had enough".

Sellers - "All right, I'll get us a taxi".

Cenise - "Us"?

Sellers - "We can have a nightcap at the luxury suite. You've not seen it yet have you"?

Cenise - "I have to confess I am curious. What are the drapes like, the bed-linen- the towels, what toiletries did you get gratis"?

Sellers - "Come, see, then after one more drink I'll get you a taxi, I promise".

Cenise - "I've already drunk just enough to agree".

Obrahom ground his teeth in incompetent fury. After all, it was a recording. The events on it, he could do nothing about. Should he even continue listening? Would it not be better to wipe the recording not do any more?

No! He had to know if Cenise was faithful to him. He was a Hungarian from a proud family if she had … he needed to know, fast-forwarded thirty minutes.

Cenise – (voice slurred) "Just one more Pálinka, before you can get me that taxi, Don".

(After the sound of fluid being poured) Sellers – There you go, a small-large one".

Cenise - "Ha ha ha ha, you've got a quirky sense of humour do you know that"?

Sellers – (voice very low and muffled) "What else have I got"?

Cenise – Naughty nibbling teeth. Get off my neck if you please. An impressive body …

(The sound of kissing)

Obrahom clenched his fists so hard his nails cut into his palms

Cenise - "That was very naughty of you, Herr Sellers. I should ring the police or something"

Sellers - "Why the police? Do you think I might lose my self-control? Rape you"?

Cenise - "Try anything like that, I'll scream".

(the sound of rustling cloth, other noises the fitful Obrahom could not recognise)

Cenise – (In a deliberately soft whisper) "Help! Police"

(sounds of movement, possibly one being carried as only one set of footprints were heard)

Cenise - "Pretty bedspread".

Sellers - "Pretty girl spread on it"

Cenise - "I'm not spread, I'm being good"

Sellers - "We'll soon fix that".

(Soft rustling sounds of fabric, probably clothing being removed, followed by the sound of quiet groaning from a woman's throat).

Obrahom snapped the recording off paced around the lab in incompetent fury. They had cuckolded him. Despite himself, he had to listen to the end, a sort of fascinated, sick voyeur.

(the sounds of bed-springs rocking rhythmically, before)

Cenise - "Ó, jézus vagyok, jövök a kislány, olyan nehéz leszek" (roughly translated) Oh Jesus, I'm coming babe, I'm coming so hard)

(not long after that)

Sellers - "Cenise, you sweet, sweet thing, oh yes, yes, just the ticket".

(sounds of soft gasping then)

Cenise - "I'll get cleaned up. Is all this yours"?

Sellers - "Hope so, unless you've got a secret to tell me"

(Soft sound of running water, padding of small feet on the carpet, followed by bed creaking again)

Cenise - "I don't suppose you want to cuddle now you've gotten what you wanted"?

Sellers - "Give over, come here".

Cenise - "You're a surprise Sellers".

Sellers - "Call me Don One".

Obrahom could not torture himself *further*. *His* wife had not just had sex with another man in a moment of weakness she had made love to him, not even feeling regret after the unfaithfulness. She had *betrayed* him. He poured himself a large Pálinka, seating himself carefully in his favourite armchair (his lab was expansive) considered his options. There was a separation while Cenise considered the error of her ways. Would she regret her indiscretion? Would she even stop seeing the filthy base-born? No, a separation might only make him look weak. He was many things, not that. Then there was a divorce. Divorce meant she would theoretically get half of everything; the laboratory, summer house in Taşucu (a small holiday hideaway in Turkey). Obrahom loved that house, would not give it up. Maybe Cenise would settle for their municipal property in Kőröstetétlen? He knew she loved Taşucu as much as he, though, would not let him get away with it. Divorce would not be acceptable to him either. What other alternatives were there? Obrahom could hire some *gentlemen* of a certain profession to have Sellers beaten to a bloody pulp. That might send Cenise into his injured arms, the gentlemen might end up apprehended, *spill the beans*, place him in difficulties? The result would cost him his grant for research, leaving him with nothing enjoyable. He could confront Cenise - forgive her, take her back. No! He realised at that moment that he truly hated the deceitful hussy. She must pay for her despicable misconduct. How? His work was close to completion, bordering on the conclusion of a fantastic result. The Duplikátor would soon be finished. The device that could copy matter, designed to create an endless supply of goods, to feed the world. It could duplicate anything; food, drugs, medical supplies, household objects, foodstuffs. All from the micro-pile that drove it. It could even duplicate living tissue. In theory, it could duplicate people!! Obrahom afforded himself a demonic smile. He could finish the Duplikátor. With it, the perfect crime, the murder of his fallacious wife!

Thirty-seven. Obrahom felt exhausted. Could not remember the last time he had enjoyed a good night's sleep. Worked like a man possessed, which, he was. The Duplikátor had almost sucked the life right out of him. It had demanded everything he was capable of giving. It was like a splendid beast devouring his strength a day at a time. All that he could he had given, keeping just enough in reserve to continue once he had snatched a power nap in his favourite chair. Completed, his genius told him it was time to test it. If the experiments proved successful, he would take the ultimate risk! Firstly, the exhaustive tests. He picked up his computer mouse placed it in booth Működő. Went to the keyboard, activated the Duplikátor - pressing *enter*. A humming noise indicated the device required some of the energy stored in the micro-pile to perform its incredibly complex duty. When it ceased, the console informed him the process was complete. Nervously, he approached booth B-hang. Slid open the tall door, glanced inside. There was the mouse. Obrahom returned to booth Működő. The mouse remained where he had left it.

"Success"! he cried. The Duplikátor had created a perfect three-dimensional copy of the mouse. He picked both up, took them to his desk. They were identical in every way. In fact, after handling them, he was uncertain which was the original. Over the next two hours, Obrahom duplicated perfect copies of; an old coin that his father had left him, his bong, his stash, finally one of his Guinea Pigs! The latter being the most important. For he then needed to be the most patient, which proved an almost insurmountable problem for him. It was imperative to determine the rodent was unharmed by the process. The duplicate he monitored also, less concerned. It only needed to live 24 hours. As events transpired, the duplicate showed no signs of ill health the following day, neither did the original. It was time to bite the bullet. Commence the nefarious plan. One which would provide the perfect crime, the murder of his deceitful, immoral wife. Setting the Duplikátor to timer-activation, Obrahom climbed into booth Működő. Heard the micro-pile energising despite the pounding of the blood rushing through his ears. It terrified him. Sweat ran down his fevered features, but his plan depended upon the success of that procedure. All was abruptly quiet. Obrahom climbed shakily to his feet. He had thought to provide the booth with a chair for that particular process. As he emerged from Működő, he saw a man doing the same from B-hang. The two turned as one, they said shakily,

"Koof! It worked, I've duplicated a man"!

Both noted quickly, "I'm the original. You're the duplicate".

"Which booth have you just emerged from"? Obrahom asked the other.

"Koof"! Cursed the other," I'm a simulacrum! This is terrifying, for I feel real, have all my memories, or are they *your memories! If* I know everything you know, am a perfect duplicate in every way which of us has the soul of Obrahom"?

"Don't start with that stupid superstition", Obrahom chided, "I created you for a purpose, to kill my wife".

"That cheating harlot! I hate her, I could kill her myself, I hate with mania".

"You will have that pleasure, while I build us a perfect alibi", Obrahom promised.

"You mean to be somewhere public at the time of her execution? So that the law cannot possibly find you guilty of her demise. Why not let me build the alibi while you kill her yourself"?

Obrahom thought for a second before observing, "It doesn't matter which of us does the deed, does it? Which is at the Thursday card school with the boys".

"I'll go to the card school".

"What if you fall ill whilst there? Fade out altogether"?

"My experiment would never fail in that way. I've run exhaustive tests on the Duplikátor before climbing into it. You think I'd risk my life if it wasn't perfectly safe. We'll be fine".

Obrahom sighed, "I know you're going to find it hard not to think of yourself as Obrahom, but I'm the original. To make the point more succinctly, I'm going to call you Edrahem".

"Why can't *I* call *you* Edrahem"?

"Because I was in booth Működő, Edrahem. As much as you feel you are me, you are a simulacrum as you said earlier. I think you should have the pleasure of killing that cheating whore".

"Only because you know how much *you'd* enjoy putting her down".

"I will not slip up at the card-school, you might".

"Because you know Darius scratches an eyebrow when he has a killer hand, or because Xerxes suddenly develops a nervous cough. One not generated by the phleege"?

"Do you think you may get caught performing the necessary"?

"It's a possibility I've considered. Preparation is the key".

"I know. Want a drink? This is getting a little frustrating".

"Let's have that drink, discuss your role in this". Edrahem returned. The situation was not proving as easy as the original thought it would. He poured two generous slugs, handed one to his replicant,

"Let's clear up the situation", he began. "We're both me. Have the same ambitions, identical desires. The chief one, to kill that cheating whore who betrayed us in the worst way a woman can with a man, intimately".

"You'll get no argument from me on that score", Edrahem agreed readily. "So why don't you give yourself the satisfaction of doing the job? "I've explained why. If it goes wrong, one of us gets arrested - dies in the gas chamber. I'm right in that assumption, aren't I"?

There was no way that Edrahem could win an argument with himself.

"I created you, at great personal risk to myself, I might add".

"Yet I don't want to be the one to be executed. I enjoy living. Just as much as you. By the by, you will not kill me when this is all over, either. If you try, I'll be forced to kill you. You're now stuck with me - Frankenstein".

"I suggest we either play a hand of cards to decide who takes the risk of doing the murder or just cut them if you prefer".

"An admirable suggestion which I was just about to make".

"I've thought of an even more entertaining notion", Obrahom then told his simulacrum, "If you think you know me so well, I suggest I put something small in my hand, put them both behind my back you choose which the item is in. Guess correctly, you go to the card school to create our alibi. Guess incorrectly, you do the murder".

"I love it"! Came the eager response.

Obrahom picked up a simple washer from the desk of his lab. Placed his hands behind his back, to swap the washer from one hand to the other. Brought both fists around to his front, presented them to the doppelgänger.

"Guess correctly. You can go to the card school", he reiterated. "Guess wrongly, you do the murder".

Edrahem looked down at the two fists. "I'm right-handed", he noted aloud. "And would therefore naturally want to place the washer in my right hand, which from *my* viewpoint is my left. You know that though, knowing it, you would put the washer in your left hand … Yet I know you would know that I would know. Therefore, I suspect you would put the coin in your right hand thinking it less obvious".

Obrahom sighed, "Just choose a hand, Edrahem".

"Don't rush me", came the barked reply, "I think you would know the right was less obvious, and therefore choose the obvious thinking I would not go for it. So I choose the obvious, knowing you would double bluff me. The washer's in your right hand"!

Thirty-Eight. Cenise climbed carefully from the *bed of shame*, racked by pangs of incredible guilt. She had allowed herself to drink more alcohol than she should, subsequently seduced by a man's external appearance. She could have no genuine feelings for the traveller from another place in time and space. The action had been vicarious, unworthy of her. True, her climax had been easily the best she had ever experienced, but for that fleeting moment, she would endure months of mental anguish, self-persecution. The adulteress dressed carefully, hoping not to wake him. His senses, highly tuned, detected her absence from the bed. Rolling over, opened his eyes at the sound of her rustling clothing.

"Good morning, were you going to sneak off without so much as a goodbye, or maybe adieu-for-now"?

"It must be farewell Sellers. I'll only see you again in an official capacity. My behaviour has been unworthy of my husband, his standing in the scientific community. I feel ashamed, for him, for myself".

"So no chance of one for the road then"? He chuckled.

"I find your humour entirely inappropriate", she said coldly. Went over to the door with a flounce-faction, hoping her dignity, though tattered, still existed in some small part. Sellers said no more, simply rolled over to go back to sleep. They expected him at MOAC later that morning, but shame on him if he did not make it. Hopefully, Cenise would not run into him while he was taking instructions from Vonalat. She let the door slide soundlessly closed on its servos. Left the hotel quickly, hoping no one would see her. Without the slightest inkling, that her husband was monitoring her every step on the hidden digital transmitter. Sellers suddenly remembered that he was having the first lesson with the brilliant scientist in another hour's time. His internal clock was freakishly accurate since augmentation, strengthening. The minute he arose, Mrs Meggins from the Pie Shop made it eminently plain that she then required her breakfast. Sellers fed her firstly, before doing anything else at all, he went to perform his ablutions. Careful with the patchouli, as it could easily stain a white shirt for he had dressed like a local. Arrived at the mightily impressive MOAC headquarters on time to the minute.

"Are you bringing the cat every day Sellers"? The scientist asked him as he presented himself in the lab. The superman had nestled Mrs Meggins from the Pie Shop in the crook of his untiring arm, purring softly, almost asleep.

"She's part of the Exploration Party", Sellers told him, "I could hardly leave her alone in an unfamiliar hotel room, could I? What if the maid let her escape"?

"You talk almost as though the creature had personality".

"While you're being sardonic because you know she has".

"Very well! Enough of the greetings in the form of banal banter. Let's begin your introduction to psych-pesticide. Working in conjunction with ACID, I developed the Zaromi killing mental agent Menta-carbaryl".

"Working with the use of lysergic acid diethylamide"?

Vonalat smiled, "No, my Dear Sellers, the Anglican Constabulary for Insecto-activity Department. In Prime all the great minds are English".

"It's very similar in 23" Sellers nodded, "With your permission, I'd like to try tapping, an attempt to link our minds".

"You can do that? Call the process tapping, for mind linking"?

"And mind-reading, only the thoughts, memories or disciplines the subject wishes to reveal".

"Prime. Sellers, I didn't know your talents were so dilatant". It impressed Vonalat, "It could save a great deal of time, proceed my dear fellow"?

"Please - take a seat then"? Sellers requested. "Close your eyes? Try to empty your mind of all extraneous thoughts other than that you wish me to know".

Sellers seated himself quickly opposite the scientist, closed his own eyes. Began a mind projection trial and error had informed him was effective over the past few weeks. He imagined a giant syringe hovering over Vonalat's cranium, into the chamber of this bizarre receptacle he poured his mentality, cornflower of hue. Once loaded the syringe containing the mind of Sellers carefully entered the brain of Vonalat by injection just under the ear. The super-leyskiper was thusly inside Vonalat's brain. Journeyed through the medial temporal lobe (the inner part of the temporal lobe, near the divide between the left and right hemispheres) he knew to be involved in declarative, episodic memory. Deep inside the medial temporal lobe, he roamed through the region of Vonalat's brain where his limbic system lay, the area which included; the hippocampus, his amygdala, cingulate gyrus, thalamus, hypothalamus, epithalamus, mammillary body. There nestled particular relevance to the processing of memory. Vonalat's hippocampus was essential for his memory function, particularly the transference from short to long-term memory, control of his spatial memory, behaviour. The hippocampus, where his brain could grow new neurons, although such ability was being impaired by stress-related glucocorticoids. The amygdala also performed a primary role in the processing, the memory of emotional reactions, social, sexual behaviour. After roaming Sellers found the marvellous bundle of ganglia he sought, soaked up the information with his super-brain. Within minutes, he knew how to create Menta-carbaryl!

He backed out of Vonalat's mind, informed him verbally, "I have it Vonalat, I can kill all the Zaromi in my home-reality".

"That's not possible"! The wild-eyed scientist countered, "It took me months of mental discipline to produce the formula that would work in my imagination. You could not have it and use it, in such a short period, no other man could".

"I could show you the formula you imagine in your mind's eye if you doubt me. Write it on a sheet of paper".

"Even with the formula, you would not have the mental discipline to use it in your mind".

"I learned the technique just now, from your brain".

"All right! All right, show me the formula - then"? Vonalat demanded.

Sellers put Mrs Meggins from the Pie Shop down on one of the laboratory desks, taking up a Nelson-pencil, sketched the formula that up till that instant had only existed in Vonalat's mind.

Thiamethoxam (250 g ha-1), imidacloprid (700 g ha-1), *M. anisopliae(M. a.)* (3 × 1012conidia ha-1), A1 (3 × 1012*M*conidia ha-1+ 65 g ha-1of thiamethoxam), + rioxthathozam (555 g ha-1) 2x 1012M +A2 (3 × 1012*M. a.*conidia ha-1+ 125 g ha-1of thiamethoxam), A3 (3 × 1012*M*conidia ha-1+ 187.5 g ha-1of thiamethoxam), A4 (3 × 1012 *M.*conidia ha-1+ 175 g ha-1of imidacloprid), A5 (3 × 1012*M.*conidia ha-1+ 350 g ha-of imidacloprid), and A6 (3 × 1012*M. a.*conidia ha-1+ 525 g ha-1of imidacloprid).

The analyst in Vonalat looked down at what Sellers had written in incredulity.

"How could you know this? You are not a chemist, not even a lab technician.? You drew this out of my brain, Sellers. It's incredible. How long will you remember it, the necessary mental-technique for employing it"?

"Indefinitely, my dear Examiner".

Suddenly Vonalat's smile changed from one of consternation to enigmatic, he informed,

"So you have the formula to kill the Zaromi. You have the Királálynővonazóreginăcondător of the Mizaroa imprisoned in your head, but the collocation for detecting the ambőentő is more intuitive than simply a learned technique".

"I think my esper abilities will aid me with that particular cerebral control", Sellers offered.

"I wouldn't bet against it", Vonalat smiled, deeply impressed.

Thirty-nine.   The professor walked through the brightly lit streets of neon-bathed Kőröstetétlen. It had recently showered just long enough to make the asphalt sparkle with moisture, the multi-coloured illumination reflected up to the pedestrian. He casually strolled down Jászkarajen út then around the roundabout to Kocséri út where the MOAC centre resided. In his Edwardian frock-coat pocket was a standard needle-gun available in any reputable retailers. The phase three darts he also had, outlawed. One and two, were for general use, even though two - was deadly. What made three so taboo was the insidious nature of their toxins. Those whose skin they penetrated by the stylus of a level three dart were not *lucky* enough to die instantly! Rather, the target thought sometimes erroneously that they had survived being shot, only for thirty minutes to pass, the pain to start. A Machiavellian ache that soon turned into agony throughout the entire body. The time it lasted determined by the fitness, endurance of the individual concerned. Strong, fit targets could writhe around for a full ten minutes before either heart failure or collapse of the lungs resulted in suffocation. The lucky ones were those who died quicker. Another aspect of the learned man could have used level one darts, that killed in little over a single second, but he wanted Cenise to suffer, so he had told the professor of their decision, the original or copy had approved, as it was exactly what he had done. The latter slowly walked brazenly into the wife's place of employment. He did not fear detection, for he was a frequent visitor there. None would challenge him. Only later, when an eyewitness placed him at the scene of the crime, could he roll out his alibi, prove that the witness must have gotten their dates mixed up. For there would be nobody once Cenise had died. The furnace in the building's basement would take care of that. Even bones, teeth would burn to ash. Once the approximate time and date of Cenise' absence were reported by MOAC, when she failed to report for work the next day, there would not be a body. No way of connecting her 'husband'[!] to the disappearance. The *both of him* would have a cast-iron alibi. Another aspect of the learned man walked toward the Kőröstetétlen Szálloda Ragyogó. The Hotel Brilliant, in the city. He was enjoying the anticipation of the coming evening. On the one hand, he always had a pleasant evening's camaraderie with his friends at the card school. On the other, he knew that when he got back home, his other aspect of the same person would have murdered his slut of a wife. He would also win some money like as not. He usually won. Darius always scratched an eyebrow when he had a killer hand. Xerxes suddenly developed a nervous cough. Only the Romanian, Vasile, could sometimes fool another aspect of the learned man, even then perhaps a third of the time. That the other three lost, did not even seem to concern them. They were all successful businessmen, played really for the social aspect of the Thursday gathering, rather than out of any financial consideration. They enjoyed one another's company, had some drinks, smoked a few too many lichcigs from Mars. Went home happy. On that occasion, another aspect of the learned man knew he would not be the exception to that rule! The room they booked was always the same, second-floor, third room, door 23. Inside, the other three had already arrived, were waiting for him. They had taken their seating around a circular green baize topped table, each had a glass full of various spirits. From the glowing end of Vasile's lichcig, a wavy line of blue-grey smoke drifted upward, to create a cloud over them all.

"Aah the late-comer", Darius noted, "We were just discussing stakes Obrahom. Vasile wants to up the base bet by ten HUF what do you vote"?

"I vote to leave it alone", came the engineer's thoughtful response, "If it costs any of us too many forints, it will take the fun and sociable aspect out of our Thursday evenings".

"One for, three against", Darius stated with a certain degree of satisfaction, "Sorry Vasile, but the majority have rejected your proposal".

"Fair enough", the Romanian did not sound especially displeased, "I just thought it might make things a bit spicier, that's all".

"We're ready to begin then once Obrahom gets himself a drink, takes his seat".

Another aspect of the learned man poured himself a vodka and Orang-U-Can added ice and then lit a 1in2, the cigarette that was 66% Snufz to 33% tobacco and illegal in most of the countries of Earth and Mars. On Venus, it had never taken off at all, to the relief of the Makers-Guild family. For they were the manufacturer of the equally narcotic principal competitor, the Dreadnought. 33% tobacco, 12% Snufz, 55% special ingredient, the constituents of which were known only to the Makers-Guild family. Taking a long drag on his 1in2 and an equally satisfactory pull on his drink, the latest member of the card school to arrive took his seat, waited while they dealt the cards.

"Damnation", he blurted, "My watch has stopped, who has the precise time"?

"We all do except you", Vasile smiled, "As we have digital watches, why do you bother with that antique wind-up Obé"?

"I've told you before", another aspect of the learned man explained as he pretended to wind his KGB officer's wristwatch from Sebastopol, "One day this is going to be a particularly sought-after collector's item".

"Yes", Darius laughed, "In about another hundred years".

Having established the time precisely, another aspect of the learned man devoted his attention to the game. It was all proving too easy to establish 'his' alibi. Not only that, but as was usually the case, 'he' cleaned Xerxes out, won handsomely from Darius and Vasile. Just as all four of them were completely *sozzled*, flagging, he said to the other three,

"I don't believe it. The ruddy thing has stopped again. What time is it now, Gentlemen"?

"Quarter too - you need a new timepiece", Vasile laughed, "I'd throw that. Buy yourself a new one with some of your winnings".

Once again another aspect of the learned man had established the exact time. All he had to do then was pull together his pile of notes on the table, thank his friends, go see how his mirror image had done. The professor found Cenise in her office. Only one person had seen him enter the building. Good, only one erroneous eyewitness account to disprove by the alibi, that made things easier. Cenise looked up from her laptop, exclaimed,

"Obé, what are you doing here"?

"Do I not have the right to visit my wife in our place of work"? The other aspect of the learned man asked mildly, pleased she did not realise he was but fifty percent of a pair of conniving, originals.

"Of course", Cenise returned with what he perceived to be slight guilt, "I just wouldn't have expected you on a Thursday evening. It's your card school night, isn't it"?

"It's 'my' card school night, as you know only too well. That's why I came to see if you were here", an aspect of the professorial study said with innuendo, "I was wondering if you were at work or in bed with your fancy-man between your salacious thighs"?

Cenise tried to pass off his words with a chuckle. Her reply, "Hilarious, you know how dedicated I am to my work".

"I do", The professor admitted with personal irony. *He knew* that, but then he let her know exactly what he knew! "That's why it surprised me when you let Sellers screw you after one illicit meeting, **like the slutty tramp you are**"!

Cenise' eyes opened very wide as did her mouth, no doubt to emit some pathetic denial. The words froze on her lips when she saw the needle-gun that had flashed in the professor's fist. She managed not so much as a squeak of protest before he fired the pneumatic weapon that discharged the dart at velocity. It struck Cenise in her rather gracefully swan-like neck. A slim hand went up to her throat, while her features registered a combination of pain, surprise, terror. For a few moments, she waited to black out. Erroneously presuming the dart had been a level two. As the seconds drifted by, nothing happened she looked even more afraid.

"What have you done, Obé"? She asked, pulling the dart free, glancing down at it. The colour-coded end, yellow, proceeded to cause abject dread to rise in her breast. Yellow was level three! (One, steel coloured or lacking any colour, level two was black).

"Atyácska! No. You could not be so cruel"!

"I could say the same about you, who allowed yourself to be *intimate* with another man. Is that not the ultimate betrayal, Cenise"?

"I guess so", she admitted, tears beginning to run down her handsome features. Such would have melted his resolve if he had not already shot her with the deadly toxin Emlélegzik 3. "You're right, my behaviour is inexcusable. Naturally, I did not expect you to levy such a high price. Do you feel nothing for me at all"?

"We still love you".

"Load a level two dart quickly, then? Make an end to me before the pain starts. Do that for me, please, Obé? You are Obé"?

"I cannot", he admitted. "We did not bring plan to bring any other levels with me".

"So you intended I should suffer? Who is in this infamous act with you, Obé? Will you kill Don too"?

"Why, do you care for him"?

"Ironically, no. I care about the Insecto threat in 23. I also think you'd not find him so easy to dispatch. Despite everything, I still care about you".

The first wave of pain took her breath away, she gasped, "You'll stay with me ... till the end".

He could do nothing other than nod mutely.

Another aspect of the learned man asked, "I presume that part was not so easy to endure? - I found in that next twenty minutes, that I did not like us quite so much for coming up with such a cruel plan. - The body? - Went into the furnace. There's nothing left of it. - Witnesses? - Buntz was on duty at the desk when one of us entered the building. By the time that aspect left, even reception looked closed. The building locked from the inside. So he saw us enter, but not leave.- Time? - 19:05. - Excellent we got the card school to tell us the time at 19:03. Stayed with them until 22:45. We're in the clear. We could not have been in the MOAC centre between those hours. Buntz log will show Cenise leaving. - She suffered terribly, you know - She betrayed her husband. She should not have let him into her pants".

Forty. **"I'll get it**, Your Ladyship", Felton offered as he strolled to the door. His eye went to the spy-lens. It informed him of nothing, other than the man standing without was unknown to him. A handsome young man, not especially tall, rather lean, dressed in dishevelled clothes with what looked like bloodstains that someone had attempted to launder out.

"Do you know him", Felton asked Kyla when she had eased him to one side to have a look for herself. He was conscious of the fact that one of her plump breasts was pressing against his arm.

"No, but he doesn't look like he possesses the mass to trouble me. I can take him if things get awkward. Let's see what he wants"?

Obligingly, Felton opened the door. The newcomer afforded them a friendly smile, before asking, "Mister Sellers"?

"Mister Sellers is not available at the present moment. What is the nature of your business, Sir"?

"Never mind that", Kyla went immediately to the point, "What do you want with him? Who are you"?

"Michael Cowie, once possessed by the Zaromi, Moluura", the newcomer admitted candidly, directly.

"Moluura"! Felton gasped, "The Veztőöndər! What do you mean *once possessed*"?

"You'd better come inside", her Ladyship decided. "Then make your explanation very brief, authentic".

Twenty minutes later, while Cowie sipped NATO-style tea, he concluded,

"Once the pots came off, the police had nothing with which to hold me. I determined to join the resistance to the Zaromi. What better way than by offering my services to the Királálynővonazóreginăcondător of their declared enemy? I guess you are harbouring the Woţialideruliavezetőeleségekirá-lálynővonazóreginăcondător Vezetőéţia, that you're the Lady Kyla Coleman of Heartbridge".

"Was, her Ladyship", Kyla admitted. There seemed no sense in denying it. "The title is merely a courteous one now, Cowie. How is it you know so much about us"?

"The Zaromi. Informed, organised, I suspect they will win the battle for Earth".

"Yet you join us"? Felton wondered.

"I killed Moluura, snapped the little base-born's neck, in my minds-eye of course. He's dead. They've a new Veztőöndər, a female called Ailuura. I guess the Woţialideruliavezetőelesége-királálynővonazóreginăcondător Vezetőéţia will have already informed you"?

"Tőéţia, as I call her, is suppressed by a drug from RPrime that Tranessy left us, as are Kim and Zelmuur in Felton".

"Tranessy"?

Felton urged, "Careful your Ladyship, this was the leader of the Zaromi"!

Cowie responded, "I fully understand your caution. Were the roles reversed, I may very well feel the same. Perhaps it'd be better to wait for the Királálynővonazóreginăcondător's return".

"Sellers is the Királálynővonazóreginăcondător", Kyla saw no reason not to tell him that much, "Like you, he overcame his Insectivorous puppet-master".

"We might be better off with none of them", Cowie noted.

"But it was different for us", Felton told him, "We owe the Mizaroa our lives".

"With strings attached. They only ultimately offered a novel form of slavery. Would take over their human host's bodies given the strength".

"You're right", Kyla agreed. "We need to rid ourselves of all of them".

Cowie offered, "Which might take two things, time, money. I've plenty of both, can help, I'd like to join you. I live in Lincolnshire, not far away, so if you need me I'll give you my email all right"?

"That's a sensible offer gratefully accepted", Felton reasoned. "We're waiting for Sellers to return, to see what he will have in his mental arsenal to combat this invasion".

Cowie rose from his seat on the sofa. "I think it's time for me to take my leave. I'll await your message if it turns out you need me".

"If we don't", Felton began, "What'll you do with yourself"?

"I loved working with wood. I'm not dependent upon financial drive. Can do exactly what I want. I believe I'd like to start work on a line of bespoke furniture for the home".

"Good luck with that. Thank you for dropping by. Mind how you go".

The new acquaintances parted. It seemed much hinged upon how Sellers would return to reality 23. When?

Forty-one.   Solan Buntz had secretly admired Cenise greatly for some considerable time. Indeed, he could not remember a time during his tenure for MOAC that he had not engaged in secret fantasies about her. So when announced three days after her disappearance that she could be found nowhere, he requested an interview with the lofty Konette. It had not been a straightforward decision for Buntz. He was a lowly security guard, Konette the director of the entire organisation. Yet he felt he had to tell someone what he knew. There was no better way of offering his information, than by going directly to the very top. Outside the director's office, he wondered if he was doing the right thing? The decorative Selicity suddenly informed him that Konette would see him. He entered the fabulous office of glistening glass, equally lustrous chrome-plating, filled with awe for everything he saw. The figure of the director was the only thing in the room that did not impress him greatly. At least, he was well mannered,

"Come in Solan", the head-man requested breaking the ice by using the security guard's former name. Most did not use the outdated system, but Solan Buntz was a very mature man for his age, preferred to keep to use both occasionally.

"Would you like a drink? Tea, coffee, something stronger, or maybe just water"?

"May I have a cup of tea with one sugar please, Sir"? Buntz replied.

Konette threw a switch on his desktop, relayed the request to his secretary. The security guard reflected that another glimpse of Selicity's superb legs would not be something he would fail to enjoy, either.

"I understand you wish to impart some information to me that may throw some light onto the sudden inexplicable disappearance of one of our employees, Mz Cenise"? Konette came straight to the point, a busy man who liked to cut-to-the-quick in situations of that sort.

"That's right, Sir", Buntz agreed as the door opened. Selicity handed him a waxed-paper cup full of piping hot beverage. He watched her legs retreat out of the office. Konette noticed the behaviour but merely gave a tight smile.

"What is your information then, Solan"?

"Just this, Sir. On the night that anyone last saw Mz Cenise, I was on duty at the desk doing the noon till midnight watch. Everyone had gone home by 18:00 except for her. I believed she and I were the only two people left in the building. Then at 19:10 or thereabouts, who should show up but Professor Obrahom, the wonderful lady's husband".

Konette looked at his PC monitor for several moments before noting, "The professor has been working in his off-site lab for the last eight months on some sort of material duplication project, funded by us. He could only have come here for one reason, to visit his wife".

Buntz nodded, "I didn't stop him, as he has clearance. I'm not even certain he saw me at all, we didn't speak".

"When did he leave"?

"I never saw him leave. So it must have been during a comfort break or on handover. When I went to check the front doors someone had thrown them open according to the board, left them locked, so the building was still secure, Sir".

"Don't worry about that", Konette assured, "You're not in trouble Buntz, but I'm calling the Rendőrség asking for the detective who's overseeing the case for us. I want you to give him or her a statement. I'm certain Obrahom will already have been helping them with their initial inquiries, but this puts a rather different complexion on things. Go back outside, I'll buzz you in - once the officer arrives".

His mind in turmoil, Buntz did as directed.

"Can I get you anything Buntz"? Selicity asked him then, "Maybe a magazine or pad to read"?

"I'm fine thanks", he muttered mechanically, but thirty minutes later was just about to change his mind when a strikingly tall, dark female strode into the reception area, asked the secretary,

"Is he inside"?

Selicity nodded, "Go right in, Detective, he's expecting you".

Once the door closed behind her Buntz asked, "Do you know her"?

Detektív éDesajak is the young woman who has been making inquiries about the missing Cenise", came the reply.

There was a tense ten-minute wait before the boss instructed Buntz to go back into Konette's office.

"Aah Solan", he began, "this is Detektív éDesajak. She's the officer I reported Cenise' disappearance to initially now assigned the case. She has a few questions for you. Sit yourself down, have a chair over there.

Buntz sat, faced the quite attractive young woman. She smiled frostily, asked him,

"I want you to consider your answers before you give me them, Herr Buntz. Cast your mind back to last Thursday, tell me whom you saw enter this building. The time, as precisely as you can"?

"I saw Obrahom, the missing lady's husband, enter this building just after 19:00".

"Never saw him leave"?

"No. I know he did because he'd thrown the security lock from the outside later. Thinking about it, he probably had his wife with him. No search for her on the premises turned her up so ...".

"Herr Buntz, are you certain the man was Obrahom"?

"Yes, I know him very well as an employee of MOAC. I'm not sure I understand what you're driving at Detektív"?

"I'm trying to make certain the man you saw was Obrahom, not someone who resembled him".

"It *was* Obrahom"!

She nodded patiently, asked, "As to the time, you say it was after 19:00, how certain are you of that"?

"It was about five or ten minutes after 19:00. I know roughly because the chime in reception rings on the hour, the board might be slightly out but only a few minutes. I'd heard it ring seven times, just a short while before Obrahom came in".

"Chime, desk"? éDesajak echoed. Konette came to Buntz' rescue,

"We decided on it, as opposed to a bell or buzzer, to signal the changing of the hour so workers know where they are. The desk counts footfall through the main door".

"It couldn't have been *out* on Thursday? Out as in inaccurate"?

"It's radio-regulated by Greenwich's atomic clock, the Hewlett-Packard model, Detektív, it chimes on the hour accurate to a billionth of a second".

"Then we have a dilemma", éDesajak declared. "Being as at 19:03 Obrahom was a couple of hundred metres across town playing cards with three reliable witnesses. There, from 19:03 to 22:45. What time did you notice Cenise had supposedly left, Herr Buntz"?

"Supposedly left Detektív? We've searched this building most thoroughly. Cenise is not here", Konette cut in.

éDesajak smiled thinly, informed both, "Since I met you earlier yesterday, Herr Director, you gave my forensic detail full access to this building. They have, as you say, raked the place. Thoroughly including water tanks on the roof, the expanse above the floors, the lift wells, the boiler room where the firm keeps the furnace. One thing of extreme interest they found was this"!

Rummaging in her jacket, she threw a green zip-top sealed evidence bag onto Konette's desk, saying as she did so,

"Cenise never left the building Gentlemen, what parts of her that did not go up the chimney is still under the grate of the furnace. Obrahom could not have committed the crime, for he was not in the building while the supposed homicide was taking place. By your admittance, you were, Herr Buntz".

Buntz looked at the item in the bag in confused dismay. The incisor of a human, female.

"I wouldn't harm a hair of Cenise' head", he heard himself saying. It was like some incredible nightmare. One he was suddenly right in the centre of.

"Find a motive, Detektív. If you intend to arrest Solan", Konette pointed out.

"We're working on it, Herr Director. I don't think Buntz, the killer. Why construct an elaborate story to try covering his crime, thusly drawing attention to himself, if he was? One thing is certain, someone killed her maybe earlier that day, threw her body in the furnace. The man you saw, Buntz, wasn't Obrahom".

Konette looked at the security guard, who confessed, "I know it doesn't look good to maintain my story. I'm telling the truth. I'll take any test you want to prove it".

"Mistaken identity is very common in eyewitness cases", éDesajak replied tiredly, "I know you're convinced Buntz. Right now, we have no intention of testing you. Don't leave Kőröstetétlen for now while we continue our inquiries".

She rose to leave. Konette showed her to the door. When he returned brow furrowed in consternation, he told Buntz,

"You're no regular eyewitness Buntz. If you say you saw Obrahom, I, for one, believe you. Yet how could the man be in two places at the same instant"?

Buntz rose, "I've two weeks leave owing Sir. I'd like to take them right away. Make a few enquiries into our Herr professor - myself"?

Konette grinned, "Permission granted Solan. Good luck".

Buntz left the MOAC headquarters only after visiting the precinct. Buying himself an enormous selection of; snacks plus meals in containers that only needed opening, drinks, some still fruit, some carbonated, like Orang-U-Can. Ready for, what was described in the suitable vernacular as a *stakeout*. He intended to park his groundauto outside Obrahom's residence, record the man's comings, goings. *Knew* what he had seen. It had been Obrahom who had been in the MOAC headquarters that night. Certainly the case. It pointed to the fact that he could have killed his wife thrown her body into the building's furnace. There were better ways to spend a vacation, but if he brought a murderer to justice, a certain satisfaction in that. Cenise had been a lovely, vibrant young woman of considerable attraction. Buntz had succumbed to her innocent charms (so he thought of her). The ground-auto was a Csepel Autógyár, the sort that littered every street in the city would not raise attention or suspicion. It was a forest green sedan. Most of them were. They did not note Csepel Autógyár for offering a great deal of choice. For two days Buntz remained outside the house of the professor. Drove home, had a quick shower, returned. Just as he was suspecting the man was a recluse, he tripped down the steps leading to his front door. Walked down the pavement. The instant he was out of sight, Buntz climbed out of the sedan, crossed the street toward the house. What better time to have a look around than while the professor was absent. Even so, he might have a maid? Buntz went to the door, rang the bell. Not inordinately surprised to hear someone coming to open it. As it yawed wider, he gasped in utterly shocked astonishment. Standing before him was either Professor Obrahom or the most amazing double anyone had ever enjoyed!

"Buntz - is it"? The professorial figure recognised him. "What are you doing here? What can I do for you"?

"I've been cleaning out Cenise' desk, Professor. Wondered if you'd be wanting any of her personal effects", he lied. The story, already prepared for just such an eventuality. Lest the help had challenged him. There, though, was the professor. Yet Buntz had just seen him leave but a few moments earlier. Of course, it explained the alibi. How had he found such a perfect body double?

"Are any of them of intrinsic value"? The professor asked him.

"I suppose they may have some sentimental value, to you", Buntz suggested somewhat sardonically.

The professor did not look entirely comfortable with the conversation, in the security man's opinion.

"I doubt she would have left anything precious in the office", he mused. "Keep anything you like or need, dispose of the rest, Buntz".

'Just like you disposed of your wife, you base-born', Buntz thought but merely nodded, "I won't trouble you any further then, Sir". He said aloud, turned to leave. The professor curtly closed the door. Thoughtfully, Buntz returned to the sedan.

After a moment's reflection, decided upon a stratagem. Continued to wait. After an hour or thereabouts, he saw the *professor* returning shopping bags in each hand. He jumped out of the car, intercepted the man before he could reach his front door.

"Buntz isn't it? What are you doing at this neck of the woods? I thought you lived over to the east"?

The man looked like the professor, sounded like him. How could such an identical individual exist?

With a feeling of déjà vu, Buntz gave him the exact excuse as before, waited to see what *th*at figure would say.

"I'm too upset to think about things like that right now Buntz", Professor Obrahom mark I or II replied, "Can you box them up? Store them for me? I'll look at them at a future time when my mind's clearer".

"Of course, Professor. Totally understandable under the circumstances. I miss her too, you know. I was a big admirer of your wife she was a wonderful woman. Remember that surprise party she threw for you for your thirtieth birthday"?

"You're confused Buntz, that wasn't Cenise and I. I had no party for my thirtieth. In fact, I was in New Munich when I turned thirty. Now, if there's nothing else, you must excuse me? I have arrangements to make, you understand"?

"Yes, sorry to have troubled you, Sir".

The figure before him was the professor. He had not fallen into Buntz' trap, so the man in the house must be the double.

Buntz let him go, observing that the gait was the one the professor used, the slight lean to his right.

As he climbed back into the sedan, a nefarious thought struck him. Once he had identified who the double was, he - Buntz could commit the perfect murder! For who would miss a man who was not missing? The only trouble was - who had killed Cenise? The double or the man he impersonated? He knew a way to find out. It was daring, even more attractive for that reason. Driving to the local weapons shop through a scorching hot day in June, the sun beat down on his head as he walked from the car. Birds chirped, proclaimed their joy at the sunshine, but in Buntz' heart, it was dark as pitch. A young woman was behind the counter of the shop. He made a quick purchase. Left hoping she would not remember him, even though it probably mattered neither way. Drove quickly back to the professor's house, once again went to the door, rung the bell. A man who was the image of Professor Obrahom answered. His features registered annoyance at the security man's second appearance that day.

"Buntz, what is it now, Man"?

Buntz drew his needle gun without a word, shot the figure in the throat. The dart was level two. As expected, the figure crumpled, fell at Buntz' feet. Who quickly folded the body into the hall, closed, then locked the door behind him. He heard a voice cry out,

"Who was it this time? How can I work with these constant annoying interruptions"? From around a doorway, a man who was the image of Professor Obrahom appeared, his mouth falling open in surprise mixed with trepidation as Buntz calmly shot him as well.

"The situation is like this", Buntz began, to the identical figures duct-taped to two hardback chairs. "One of you is Professor Obrahom of MOAC, the other is a body double. One went to the professor's card school last Thursday, while the other murdered Cenise, threw her body into the building's furnace".

A man, the image of Professor Obrahom, asked, "What's your intention, Buntz? Would a vast sum of money deter you from your planned course of action"?

"No, it would not", Buntz replied in no uncertain tone, plainly believed.

"So what do you want then"? The image of Professor Obrahom asked the security man, "Justice"?

"No, vengeance for Cenise. I admired her greatly. Whatever your motive for killing her, I think you were momentarily insane, or perhaps totally".

"Vengeance? In what form"? One of those who looked like the professor asked.

"I intend to execute the murderer myself. Knowing the survivor will not tell the law. To do so would cause the survivor plus myself going to prison for a very long time".

"You'd go to the gas chamber", one of the identical figures noted. "For murder".

"I don't think so", another of the identical figures contradicted his mirror image, "With good legal representation, he'd probably get justifiable homicide, or homicide whilst under a temporary state of diminished responsibility".

'The academic who looked exactly like professor Obrahom blurted in some haste, "I'm Obrahom, Buntz. He's the killer. Give him a level one, let's get it over with".

The other academic responded sharply, "You liar! You know full well you did it, while I went to the card school, to give you an alibi".

"Stop this. It'll get us nowhere", Buntz demanded. "I can't trust either of you to tell me the truth. That much is evident. You'll both lie to save your hides. It may cause me to kill the wrong man. What I want to know is where did the double, whomever he may be, get such skilled surgery to make him so totally identical"?

The duo remained silent. Slowly Buntz decided, "One of you is the murderer, the other, a willing agent of collusion. In that way, you're both as guilty as the other".

"But you can't kill us both whilst being certain to get away with it, Buntz. The police will have you as a chief suspect, even if you dispose of both our bodies. So *kill him*. Release me"?

"No, Buntz! That would be a grave error. Kill *him*, release me"!

It would go around. Buntz was losing patience. He decided already having loaded the third dart into his needle gun, the dart that was a level one, he fired the device.

He had decided.

(Was it the right choice? How had he chosen? What would you have done Dear Reader)

Forty-two.   On the third day, Sellers was exasperatedly tired. Confessed to the amböentő-scientist,

"It's no good Prof, there's only one way I'll ever be able to detect another amböentő, that's if you let me scan your mind from top to bottom, inside, out".

Vonalat shook his head, "My mind's private. There are areas of my brain I don't want tapping by you or anyone else for that matter. Every one of us has darkly private thoughts, inner demons that we'd not wish anyone else to know about. What you suggest is tantamount to mind-rape"!

"Then I can't detect an amböentő", Sellers concluded. "Even with eidetic memory, I'd need to read the mind of one, to seek another".

"You've made remarkable progress", Vonalat observed. "I think you're ready to return to 23".

"I could go in. Steer clear of any areas you wished private, I just want to find the part of your brain ...".

"No"! The genius scientist was firm. "I don't want any other to understand me so precisely. If the roles were reversed would you agree to it.? Don't you have some thoughts, no matter how deeply buried in your id that you want none to know about"?

Sellers shrugged, "I guess there is the odd ...".

"You see! We've all certain desires or notions that we're not proud of.

You can leyskip, you'll be able to slay the Zaromi in your home reality. Or at least the one you now reside in. Your search for an amböentő must take a different course. Our association is ending Sellers, I wish you good luck".

The scientist even scratched Mrs Meggins from the Pie Shop behind her ear affectionately. She purred appreciatively. The cat who, no matter how the realities changed, was the constant in Sellers life.

"I'll go make my farewells to some agents I've met whilst here before Tranessy and I skip back home". Sellers decided.

He spent a busy hour doing precisely that, before changing into his more familiarly comfortable boho clothes. He reflected on how it was strange the way Buntz had reacted when he had said farewell to him.

"I will not shake your hand, thank you very much, Mister Sellers. I have certain suspicions regarding you".

"Suspicions? Sellers felt confused, "Want to tell me what they are, Buntz"?

"I have no evidence to accuse you of anything, Mister Sellers. I don't think you're the knight in shining armour that the others around here seem to believe. Go home, good luck, goodbye".

Sellers had not thought it worth pressing. Clearly, the security guard had made his mind up about something which he did not have time to pursue. Soon to be homeward bound, looking forward to seeing her Ladyship, even Nicole again. Seeing quite a lot of them, in fact. Once more he presented himself to the scientific genius. Tranessy, was to remain surprisingly in his company. They both shook his hand with enthusiasm, the latter advised.

"Now you've done it once, my friend you won't find it difficult to summon the same state of mind to skip the ley-lines. Especially with the machinery in here boosting you on your way. Good luck with the Zaromi I hope you locate an amböentő".

Vonalat nodded, "My mechanisms are operating to acceptable parameters Sellers, look after Megwinda, she'll be missed around here".

Sellers emptied his mind of all extraneous thoughts. Took the bony little cat up into his arms. With that, the humming of the machines grew fainter as the laboratory at MOAC Headquarters shimmered, dissolved into invisibility. If Sellers had expected the return trip to be the same as the outward journey, he would have been wrong. This was a pushing experience rather than a pulling one. For a few moments, he almost experienced apprehension. He could feel the power of the mechanisms of RPrime hurtling him down the highway of the multiverse. Or should that be up against the highway? Such frames of reference were obsolete. Traversing several dimensions at once rendered them inapplicable. A weaving strand of lilac roadway passed beneath him at incredible velocity. Mrs Meggins from the Pie Shop suddenly mewled pathetically.

"I know Megwinda, you feel it too, but don't worry we're going home".

In this assumption, Sellers was wrong! Had miscalculated the junction he was seeking. For it was somewhat subfusc, consequently, he overshot it. Not that he knew that whilst it happened but by the system that those in prime used, Sellers was heading for reality 26! He tried to discern details in the constantly shifting motorway of ley-lines rapidly passing beneath his feet when he had guesstimated the right one, put on mental brakes lowered the flaps. The result, abrupt cessation of movement, crash landing. Thanks to the genius calculations of the great Vonalat, Sellers landed in his flat. Or rather the flat of the Sellers, who possibly lived in reality 26. Coming in at a 45-degree angle, he went sprawling onto the lounge floor; the carpet cushioning some impact of the fall. Mrs Meggins from the Pie Shop went screeching sideways, but like the cat she was, landed on all fours.

"Sorry Megwinda", Sellers apologized at once, "Come here, Baby"?

The cat reluctantly allowed him to stroke her, tickle one of her ears, before going in search of Purina. For the first time, Sellers glanced about him. Damn Her Ladyship. While he had been absent she had changed much of the décor? What did she think she was doing? He immediately exited the apartment, rode down in the lift. Needed to see what time of day it was. The apartment - devoid of windows. Had the crazy mare covered them over, something was amiss. Sellers walked out onto the street, gasping in astonishment. None of the skyscrapers had any windows! It filled the entire skyline with concrete, steel, the facades of the buildings, blank. They reminded Sellers of monolithic bunkers, rather than places for people to work, sleep, live. He knew then that he was not in the correct reality. Until he learned some point of reference, there was no progress to further skipping. Which way would he go? How far? There were very few street-lights in the reality he now found himself. The city was darkly foreboding. The stars in the night sky chiaroscuro with their unrivalled brilliance. At least the constellations were familiar. In that bizarrely sinister place, the stars were the first bit of comfort to him. What to do? The time-clock within him informed it was morning. He could not sleep the darkness away. Where was everyone, anyway? Was he the only inhabitant of the town? Doncaster had never looked so ... alien! Sellers so isolated. For the time being, he reasoned the apartment was probably as safe as anywhere else. Reluctantly, he returned to it. At least, Mrs Meggins from the Pies Shop made herself at home. Sellers wandered around for several minutes looking at the differences, with no enthusiasm. There was no intention of staying in this bizarre reality for longer than was necessary. Just as he wondered what to do next, a knock at his door. Slowly he went to see who it was, looked through the spy-hole. To his utter astonishment, Cenise was on the other side of it. He threw the door open, said gratefully,

"Hi". The young woman blinked with her large, attractive eyes, "Hello, are you ... who are you if you don't mind me asking"?

"Please come inside, I get the impression the hall might not be safe".

"Get the impression, surely you know it's not".

She stepped inside, but still did not relax once the door closed.

Sellers guessed, "We've not met before, have we? You're Cenise".

The young woman shook her head, "My name's Griselda". Her hair had changed to brunette. Otherwise, she was easily recognisable as another version of the woman he had *known*. "You're right, we haven't. Please answer me, are you the one I'm looking for"?

"Sellers conceded, "Sellers. What do you want with me ...er, Griselda"?

"I sense you're not an Anthophilamorph. Your mind, still your own".

"My mind *is* mine, but I've no idea what an Anthophilamorph is? Is it a person with an Anthophila mind sharing their own? Can I get you something to drink? Sit down, please? We have much to discuss".

As she seated herself, he admired the slimness of her legs. She noted, "You don't know what an Anthophilamorph is? Great Scott, where have you been these past few months, Sellers"?

"First things first, Miss Griselda, let me get you a drink you look like you could use one".

"I'm starving, you wouldn't give me something to eat, would you"?

Sellers smiled as assuredly as he could. How like Cenise she looked. The girl he had seduced in *RPrime*, who had disappeared shortly afterwards. He wondered where she had gone.

"Let me have a look in the freezer, see what I've got? While I prepare something, what can I get you to drink"?

"Anything with a kick in it. I need one. If you've something Italian, I'd like it. Thank you for being so kind, accommodating".

Sellers made a reconnoitre of his kitchen nuked a lasagna. Poured two gin and tonics (doubles), handed one to the girl.

She asked after taking a generous pull at her beverage, "How come you don't seem to know what's happening in England, Sellers"?

He gave her a summarized history of his past couple of weeks. Once he had finished, she looked shocked, bemused,

"Are you Sellers? I mean the right one. Crikey, this is confusingly cockamamie".

"I agree, however, it's also the truth I swear to you. Tell me what's happening in this ley-line of the multiverse"?

"The Anthophila came to Yorkshire. They offered to heal the sick, bring the recently deceased back to life. At first, it was great. Then they took over the minds of those they shared, turned everyone into Anthophilamorph. Men, women, children who no longer had control over their bodies. Bee-like creatures in human form. There aren't many people left who don't have an Anthophila controlling them. They all do the whim of '**She All Must Obey**".

"**She All Must Obey**"?

"The queen of the alien insects, the one they all serve, worship like some goddess. Which, in many ways, she virtually is".

"How did you escape their clutches"? Sellers asked as the microwave pinged to tell them the lasagna was ready. "Come, sit to the table, save a bit for Mrs Meggins from the Pie Shop. She loves cheese".

"You've got a companion in here, another free of the Anthophila"?

"Yes, you could say that. Megwinda is my cat".

"Oh! I don't like cats, it can keep away from me".

Sellers felt disappointed. This Cenise, whilst being physically identical to Cenise, was not like her at all.

"So Griselda, how did you evade the Anthophila, the Anthophilamorph"?

"Do you know what an amböentő is"?

"I do indeed. When I get back to my version of the multiverse, I need to find one. Does one exist - in this reality"?

The girl nodded as she shoved pasta into her mouth. Once she had chewed, swallowed, she informed him,

"I should say I do, I'm one"!

"How did you hear about me"? He asked, momentarily stunned.

"I didn't. I sensed you. Somewhere in this reality, the proper you is free of the Anthophila too".

Sellers smiled, "The proper Sellers"?

"Sorry, you know what I mean, though. The Sellers who belongs in this junction-thing, or whatever you call it".

"It certainly throws up an interesting conundrum. What if the Sellers of this reality returns to find me here? What will two versions of myself meeting mean to me? Or maybe you sensed my arrival? I being the one, the only Sellers of this layer of the multiverse"?

"Oh cripes, no idea", Griselda was plainly out of her depth. For all Sellers knew, she didn't believe half of his story. Thought his experiences in the weird reality had affected the balance of his mind.

"That's not your problem, is it"? He observed, hoping to take the jeopardy out of her situation, "Why do you wish to team up with me, Griselda, when you're an ambӧentő"?

"I'm uncertain what you mean", the girl finished her meal, put her cutlery down with considered movements.

"You don't know what your powers of ambӧentő enable you to do"?

She shook her head. "Not all of them. I know I can sense whether people are people, or taken over. It helped me find you. Never having met another like me, how would I know all my capabilities"?

"How do you even know the term"?

"Oh, when things started getting tough, the EBS put out a message that the President was looking for one. They described some things an ambӧentő could do. By the time I realised I was one, things had gotten very much worse, so I went into hiding. A final message issued that anyone who was still free of the bee-things was to seek you out. Here I am".

"What's the EBS"?

"English Broadcasting System of course, just how different is your ley-thing if you don't know that ha ha ha".

"And England has a president"?

"The President of America and all its 62 states overseas, some of them are as far-flung as ...".

"I get the general picture, Griselda. Thank you. The question we need to ask ourselves is why the President wanted people free of the Anthophila to report to me. How did he even know of my existence"?

"That's easy you're the resistance Lídersupremo. You're quite famous".

"Famous in a world filled with Insecpuppets, a leader with no troops, marvellous".

"Maybe the proper you is off somewhere leading the resistance"?

"The proper me, great"!

"I didn't mean it like that. You know what I meant, I meant Sellers, why don't we give you a different name to save confusion"?

"I'm not confused. Although talking to you I think I'm getting there. You call me what you want while I try to think of some sort of strategy".

"Alright let's see what do you look like ... you don't look like a Kevin or a Lee ...".

"You don't look like a clever bitch. Appearances can be deceptive", he grinned. "Can we do the thinking in our head, amböentő, do you think"?

Griselda pursed her lips, fell silent. Her eyes looked even larger as she did so.

"It seems to me", Sellers mused after a few seconds, "That I have to find, stop, permanently '**She All Must Obey** . Do the Anthophila seem to display a hive mentality"?

"Yeah Mark, they do, like bees, you know".

"Mark"?

"Don't you think you look like a Mark"?

Sellers smiled at the innuendo that was generated by that question. Needed to keep Griselda on the point, so nodded, (even though he didn't) asked her,

"Could you, with your abilities, take me to the Queen of the Anthophila"?

Griselda's eyes widened at the notion, they filled with apprehension - understandably so,

"Won't she just kill us? Or the Anthophilamorph who guards her"?

"It might present certain dangers. I'll do my utmost to protect you. If this is the apartment of Sellers, there should be a weapon of some sort left around this place".

"What sort of weapon"?

"Let's go look"?

"It'll have to be something impressive, or I'm out".

"Could you use your power of amböentő to slay all the Anthophila mentally"?

Griselda thought about that for a second, answered honestly, "No. I don't think I could".

"Why not"?

"To kill so many reasoning beings? I couldn't do it. I mean I couldn't kill a nest of bees, so why could I kill all the Anthophila"?

"The Anthophila've enslaved the human race. Or at the very least, the state of England, bees from Earth wouldn't".

"They might if they grew clever enough. I just couldn't use my mind to kill so many thinking creatures, even if I knew how, Mark. Which I don't".

"You wouldn't even give it a shot"?

"Let's search for a weapon, shall we"?

So much for that. An amböentő that hadn't the stomach for mass killing. For all Sellers knew, that was the way it was meant to be. Maybe mankind had seen the end of his days? At least in one layer of the multiverse?

"All right, let's do that", Sellers agreed.

It didn't take long for the girl to find what they were looking for. She came back to him, still in the bathroom, with an AK47 in her hands.

"Would this do? I found it in the wardrobe, just propped in a corner".

"Is there ammunition with it"?

"Sure come see".

A few moments later Sellers was balancing the gas-operated, 7.62×39mm assault rifle, developed in the Soviet Union by Mikhail Kalashnikov in his hands. All he had to do was view an Utube video on how to use it for him to be totally familiar with all its workings. That was if in that crazy ley-line there was still an operating www. There was. Even after decades, the AK47, its variants remained the most popular, widely used assault rifles in the world because of their substantial reliability under harsh conditions, low production costs compared to contemporary western weapons, availability in virtually every geographic region, ease of use. To fire, the operator inserted a loaded magazine, pulled back, released the charging handle, pulled the trigger. In semi-automatic, the firearm fired only once, requiring the trigger to be released, re-depressed for the next shot. In fully automatic, the rifle continued to fire cycling fresh rounds into the chamber until the magazine became exhausted or pressure released from the trigger. Sellers intended to pump quite a few rounds into **She All Must Obey**. First, though, he had to find her.

"I now possess the ability to protect you, Griselda. Will you lead me to the queen of the Anthophila"?

"Some of the Anthophilamorph will probably have guns too".

"I won't lie to you. I'd be more than a little surprised if they didn't. I ask you this, though, Griselda. Do you want to live in a world filled with Anthophilamorph, where you are the only normal person"?

"There's the resistance"?

"Can they hold out forever? How many do you think there is, while the Anthophilamorph might very well now number in their millions. If they don't, if there's a place in England where they haven't yet reached we need to kill the queen of the Anthophila before they spread any further, don't you agree"?

"I guess. It seems unlikely they've reached the Far East yet though".

The Far East? Sellers would normally have asked why the girl had mentioned the Orient. He was not in the mood for an economic geography of R26 at that moment. If he found it hateful later on, he could always skip again until he reached a reality pleasurable to his sensibilities. He, therefore, returned.

"And you guess right, so let's concentrate. Let your mind wander, let it float out of your body, seek the most powerful mind you can detect. If you give me her precise location, I will even go alone, finish this".

"No", the girl seemed to make a decision that made her suddenly resolute. "I couldn't let you go alone when this isn't even your England. I'll come with you even though I'm scared".

"Good girl. I promise to keep you safe. So, are you going to try find the queen? The queen of the Anthophila"?

"Come and lay on the bed with me"? She asked, "No funny business. At least not until I find her, anyway".

It appeared in two layers of the multiverse a powerful attraction existed between the two of them. Sellers ignored it for the moment. His current quest claimed paramount importance in his mind. With no one to ask other than the naive girl, he had no chance of finding out what R26 was like to him. He did not even know it *was* 26. So the two of them lay side by side, closed their eyes. Sellers sent out a finely threaded tapping to see what was going on in Griselda's mind. Discover himself locked out! He could not tapp the amböentő. Her mind was a total mystery to him. That fact impressed him immensely. Even though Griselda was jejune, instinctive, her mind might still be superior to his own. He lay perfectly still, silent, waiting. Momentarily impotent. Wondering how long it would take for Griselda to sift through all the mental data she might encounter. Find the most complex of the vast hive-mind - that was the Anthophila. Suddenly she sighed, rose onto an elbow, declared,

"I think I'm too het-up, need to do something to relax me".

"What about a bath? A good soak always relaxes me"? It was more of a question than a statement. Everyone had their personal preferences.

"I'll try that then", she declared, climbed off the bed. Sellers lay listening, heard the water run, the rustling of clothing, her stepping in. It went quiet, while she must be soaking. Made him jump with a start when she suddenly called out to him.

"Mark, come do my back"?

The inference was obvious. With a sigh, he rose, entered the bathroom. Griselda, seated, held out the sponge, an enigmatic smile on her pretty features. She gazed at him keenly.

"You only look into my eyes. Have you seen me undressed before"?

"It was a different you, but yes I have".

He took the sponge, began to softly cleanse her back,

"That's nice", she murmured, her head dropping toward the water. "What was she like? The other me"?

"She looked just like you. Different in her outlook, her circumstance".

"You were lovers"?

"We slept together once. A very pleasurable experience".

After a pause, she declared candidly, "I'm jealous of her. Will you bathe, join me on the bed? I'm not loose, you understand. It's just that there is now none out there as would be for me. It'll help me relax ... afterwards".

"In the interests of Yorkshire's future it would be rude to refuse, would it not"? He quipped.

"You'll make love to me in the interests of the future of the county, no other reason"?

"You're a very attractive girl I'm a full-bloodied man. I find you eminently desirable". Yet he found he was lying. Griselda was not Cenise, biology had its fervour, however.

She climbed out, towelled herself dry. As she did so, demanded with a certain relish,

"Take your clothes off, Mister".

Totally without self-consciousness Sellers tugged off his clothes. Griselda's eyes grew even wider, if that were possible?

"And when I say, Mister ... I mean Mister", she declared.

Sellers bathed with an economy of movement flannelled most of the water from his magnificent physique, towelled off the residue of the moisture. It was too warm in the bathroom to clean it then. It would have caused him to perspire. When he did, he wanted it to be for a very different reason. He strode into the room, glided onto the bed. Griselda raised her face to his, kissed him with passionate hunger. Their tongues plunged, quested, entwined. He broke free, traced a series of kisses from her mouth, down her neck, onto a high pert breast. The nipple hardened beneath his nibbling attention. She moaned in satisfaction, her fingers going through his long blond hair. Slowly, she eased his head lower. He performed the Venus Butterfly upon her with diligent skill. She responded with her first ecstatic climax even before he had entered her. When he rose, their mouths met once more. He slid easily into her wetness. The pleasure of giving to her then became mutual as she felt a ripple of smaller orgasms. He emptied himself into her with a groan of fulfilment. She jumped from the bed as he withdrew. Hurried to the bathroom to clean herself up. Sellers remained supine, nearly completely spent. On her return, he felt himself rise to the occasion once more when she took him into her mouth. It was not long before his second release; she did him the extreme compliment of swallowing what he had given her. Griselda lay down beside him, declaring,

"Now I can relax, see what I can find"!

"Glad to have been of help", he mused with a certain degree of disparagement.

"You were just the ticket", she murmured, already falling asleep. "Satisfactory, Mark, more than assuasive".

Sellers fell asleep. Sex always made him hebetudinous.

When he awoke several hours later, it was to discover that he was alone in the bed. Rose, pulled back the sheet to allow the bed to air. The bathroom was nagging him. When cleaned thoroughly to his personal standard, he sauntered back into the lounge dressed only in trolleys. Griselda, seated at the breakfast bar, had a mouth full of cereal.

"Any luck"? He wanted to know. She took a while to chew, swallow, causing him to quip,

"You're not supposed to put so much food in your mouth, that it becomes difficult to breathe or see out".

"Hilarious".

"Well"?

"Not yet, maybe we should get it on again, see if I can stay awake afterwards this time".

Sellers assumed a look of hurt, complained,

"I'm not just a piece of meat, you know, Griselda. I'm a person too. Stop treating me like a sexual plaything".

"Ha ha ha ha, very funny, you loved it you liar".

"Seriously, for a minute, we have to make some progress. Who knows how many more the Anthophila have created every minute we tarry".

"I doubt many, Mark. Let's go take a look on the street, it's about 09:00".

"I'll get some breakfast. Get dressed. We can do a reconnoitre if you like. Have you fed Mrs Meggins from the Pie Shop"?

"The damned moggy? No way am I going near it".

"She's been my constant companion through several adventures to date, is a bona fide member of this team, must have all her requirements met".

"You're crackers do you know that"?

"Maybe, but if you want my help, Megwinda wants something, you give it to her, understood"?

Griselda offered him a mock salute barked, "Yes Sir, Sergeant Major, Sir". It was funny. Sellers opened a sachet of Felix, squeezed it into Mrs Meggins from the Pie Shop's dish. The darling little cat descended on it, gobbled it down with purring gusto. Once the leyskip had seen to himself the two humans descended in the lift to the ground floor. Out onto a brilliantly lit - empty street. Sellers had the AK47 over his shoulder on the provided strap. The reflected heat from the pavement must have been around 32 degrees. It prompted Griselda to observe,

"You can't blame the Anthophila for the global warming".

"Who do you blame"? He was curious.

"The fossil fuel burning Chinese". With Griselda, what one saw was what one got. She did not bother with diplomacy.

"What say we walk? Try sensing the presence of the leader of the aliens"? Sellers suggested.

She nodded. "Have that machine gun ready? Just in case we run into any of the *workers*, the Anthophilamorph".

Sellers abruptly swayed, stumbled, held himself up with an outstretched hand on one building fascia. He must have looked ill because Griselda asked,

"What's up, Superman? I didn't take that much out of you last night, did I"?

Sellers hardly heard her. Balurzuura was crying from inside his mental cell.

'Sellers, let me out. I can help you. I'll find the queen Anthophila. Let me be of assistance"?

"Seriously Mark, you look to be on the skids. What's wrong? Got a bellyache or something"? Griselda sounded genuinely concerned.

"I'm getting an offer of assistance from the Királálynővonazóreginăcondător of the Mizaroa. Currently in a Félmunite cell within my mind, one composed of Phostiron".

"What're you talking about"? Griselda asked, not unreasonably.

Sellers took the time to explain carefully when done, she replied,

"I knew I could sense something strange about you Mark, but I put it down to you not being from Earth".

He did not bother to correct her with a more concise distinction.

"I'm surprised you couldn't detect him - despite that", he observed.

"I'm new to this", she complained. "Give me time to work my way into it".

"Time is a luxury we can't afford", Sellers pointed out. "Please concentrate or I may have to accept the dubious aid of the Királálynővonazóreginăcondător".

"Ruddy stupid title if you ask me", she murmured in response, but then closed her eyes for some moments. When she opened them again, she declared candidly,

"I've bugger-all, Mark, you'll have to let the dragonfly out the box".

"Hope I've the power to put him back in when it suits me"?

"Hey, we've nothing else".

"Alright then", Sellers said for the benefit of the girl who was listening., "Balurzuura, I'll give you a chance to help us, with one condition. You agree on peace between the Mizaroa, the humanoids, as you call us. You can live in the minds you already share in my reality, but you can't take over their bodies. If you agree to the armistice, I'll cease seeking ways to destroy you all, the war will end".

'There is no war, Sellers. We are a peaceful race. What do you mean by **your** *reality'?*

"You don't know how much more I know than the last time we spoke Balu. I've been in contact with Vonalat, in RPrime where the Mizaroa had attempted to do what the Zaromi is now undertaking in reality 23. Which reminds me, which layer of the multiverse is this - by the same reckoning"?

'Before I tell you anything or agree to any terms, I want a promise from you', Balurzuura replied, *'Your solemn word that you will not harm me nor my race on your world'.*

"You have my solemn word that I will never break an armistice if you also do the same".

'That is acceptable, Sellers of the humanoids. I sense the queen of the Anthophila over to the north of this city. The city that resides in Yorkshire'.

It seemed Balurzuura knew nothing of the lay-lines. Content to exist in one layer, as were almost all creatures.

"She's over to the north end of town", Sellers told Griselda. "Near the temple".

"Temple"? Sellers echoed, always very sceptical of any sort of organized superstition. Griselda nodded,

"The new one the Chinese Confucianists built a few years ago. A modern place of worship constructed of mainly stainless steel boarding, concrete. You can see the hip-and-gable roof style, also known as the Xieshan roof, over there, look"!

A great erection clawed its way into the skyline like the talons of some huge mineral beast.

"It's the New Temple of Confucian Philosophy of Politics", she told him, "Open to any Buddhist too".

"Of course, to fill seats", Sellers was deeply atheistic. His gods were nature, the sun, animals, the simple wonder of life. He believed in only real things observation or science could prove the existence of.

"Let's go meet '**She All Must Obey**"?

The two of them walked carefully down what Sellers regarded as Hall Gate, which had become Yang Shan Jiēdào onto a High Jiēdào, completely devoid of shops or structures he found familiar. They were about to enter Fàguó Mén when four figures emerged from a doorway at the base of one ziggurat. The quartet was all dressed in bright yellow onesies with black helmets on their heads. Instantly they reminded Sellers of bees, even before Griselda warned superfluously.

"Anthophilamorph"!

"Are they dangerous to us"? Sellers demanded.

"It's a recruitment patrol, so yes", Griselda's voice shook with trepidation, confirming her fear.

The four of them carried night-sticks, but Sellers could not see any firearms.

"Are the night-sticks all the weaponry they possess"? he asked as the two of them drew to a halt.

"Yes, but they can be pretty devastating I've had friends who..."

Sellers was not listening. He handed the AK47 to her,

"Only fire if they beat me, otherwise don't put your finger on the trigger. I don't want to catch a slug in the back and in the street", he instructed. The Kalashnikov looked huge in the girl's slim hands.

"Let us pass? I won't hurt you", Sellers told the advancing quartet confidently.

"You are *rogue*", declared one of them. The one with chevrons on his shoulders.

"That may be true, but let us pass and I won't have to kick me some Anthophilamorph ass", Sellers warned in rather colourful vernacular. As they went to draw their sticks, the Superman rushed forward. His fist connected with the closest of the four's jaw. There was a tremendous crunching noise as the already unconscious body of the Anthophilamorph crashed into the other three. Before they could regain their balance, Sellers kicked out at a second. The crunching noise told him he had broken his leg. The drone fell to the floor. Sellers snatched the night-stick from him as he was going down. During the brief, appallingly violent clash, the Anthophilamorph had remained unsettlingly silent.

"Give it up now"? Sellers advised. "You're clearly outmatched for speed, strength, resolve. There can be only one outcome unless you let me pass".

"You are *rogue*". The pseudo-sergeant repeated as though that was his only thoughtful motivation.

Griselda cried out with unsuspected passion, "They're just drones, Mark, finish'm".

Sellers moved at a speed barely perceptible to human vision. Grasped the arm of the sergeant, using him as a weapon. He whirled him around so that he crashed into the last of them. The two smote one another with a bone-jarring impact, knocked insensible. A second or two later, all four lay at Sellers' feet.

"Wow"! Griselda gasped. "You're like Sylvester Tom Van Damme, only much taller, blonder. I'm so turned on right now".

"So not like him at all then", Sellers grinned.

"What I meant was you're a hard-ass".

"Come on, we're wasting time, while we chin-wag the reality is being turned into a Zaromoid State".

Turning down Bākè sī tè mén, they were lucky enough not to encounter any more patrols. As they entered the street, renamed Shèng ko˘ ngzi˘ guān, they ran into a score of them.

"Give me the gun", Sellers demanded.

As Griselda complied she urged,

"Remember, they were human once".

"Right now they're in my way", Sellers returned grimly. A sudden shot rang out. The patrol drones had better weaponry than those previously, it seemed.

"Get in that recess? Don't come out until I tell you", Sellers barked, switched the AK47 onto fully automatic. As Griselda stumbled into the safety of cover. She heard the cacophony of the machine gun Sellers used. A spraying-action, emptying a full magazine into the drones. Vapour was rising out of the hot barrel as she peeped around the edge. In front of the temple, lay bodies, inert, probably dead. She shuddered, knew it necessary to sacrifice them to free so many, many more. Sellers was sweating, the weather decidedly hot that day of June 29th 2018 - probably around 24 degrees. There was not a single cloud in the sky. The sky was a lush blue. In sharp contrast, the street in front of the dual-carriageway stained freshly with crimson gore.

"Come on", Sellers urged, "Let's get out of the heat, "At least the heat of the sun, anyway".

Inside the templetic repository, there might be more drones, better equipped to stop him. He took two automatic side-arms from the fallen, quickly instructed Griselda in their use. Tucked a further two into his belt. They would have weighed an ordinary man down with the AK47's magazines in addition, but Sellers was far from that. Inside the unarmed doors they strode, the coolness, quietude, dimness, preferable. The bizarre duo walked over to their right. The aisle was before them. Rows after row of seats stretched to their either side. Not simple benches, modern, comfortable seating. Sellers wondered to which god the Anthophila preyed? Or perhaps they used the cathedral as a site for indoctrination, as was the way with pseudo-superstition. Right at the end was no altar, rather a huge winged-backed chair of amber coloured studded leather. He looked keenly at the figure reclining in it. At such a distance could not discern the features.

"Is that '**She All Must Obey**'"? He asked Griselda.

The girl nodded almost reverently, "I think it must be. Where is everyone? Her guards"?

"Who cares, let's do what we came here to", Sellers stated simply. Strode between the first row of seats. The sound of a klaxon was instantly deafening. Doors opened from vestibules, drones spilling out, armed with pistols. Griselda ducked down beneath some seats while Sellers fell to one knee. He began firing the Kalashnikov on fully automatic once more. The volume of the furore was deafening, made doubly loud by the ambience of the worship place. Live indeed, only when the brouhaha lessened did Griselda dare raise her head above the pews to see what had occurred. She could not know it. Sellers, with his speedy reflex, 100% accuracy for aiming, had not missed with a single round. It had reduced the drones to three, those, sensible enough to dive for cover, hope to pick Sellers off by becoming snipers. They only had automatic guns, while Sellers had the accuracy of an automatic rifle. After four minutes of sporadic fire, Sellers picked off the last of the resistance. Without so much as a word, launched himself down the aisle, only to be brought up stock-still before '**She All Must Obey**'.

"Nicole"!

Nicole, whom he had loved through more than one incarnation. Whom he had accepted in several guises. This - the hardest to accept. For in the chair, a twisted, disabled body, beneath the face he knew so well. In one bizarre way, the queen of the Anthophila had done her a favour by taking over such a crippled form. In another, it was scornfully cruel to make her the object of almost religious adoration. She spoke,

"Sellers! I thought you dead"?

"Maybe the Sellers you knew in this layer of reality was killed, Nicole. I'm not he, I'm 23".

Before the grodious conversation could be continued, a shot rang out. Sellers whirled around half a second after it had echoed through the temple. The vapour rising from one of Griselda's automatic barrels told him what had happened even before she explained,

"One of them wasn't dead, he was about to shoot you in the back".

"Thanks", he said swiftly. Returned to face forward. Nicole, too disabled to have moved.

"You will kill an entire species if you kill me", she told him. "For I'm the queen of the super-hive. All depend upon me for direction, purpose, meaning. Without me they will die pining for me, they will simply lose the will to live".

Sellers returned resignedly, "When you have to shoot, you shoot, you don't talk".

The bullet shattered her skull. Blew it to bloody fragments. Neither the Anthophila nor the subjugated quiddity of Nicole could have survived it. Sellers turned away, strode past the girl who had executed the **She All Must Obey** for him. To save him from having to do it himself. By the time she caught up with him, it was to join him. Seated on some overlarge wall coping stones, that formed the perimeter of the pseudo-holy place, he asked her,

"Got a cigarette by any chance"?

"Only med-cigs".

"What by Gehenna are they"? She pulled the Chinese style pack from her pocket.

"They're safe, they've removed all the carcinogens from then".

"Are they still tobacco"?

"Certainmoi, they're like med-coffee, med-beer, just like the real thing, but not harmful".

"Speak to me in bastardised French ever again, I'll kill you", his humour as pitch as to suit the current mood. "Have you a lighter"?

She reached over, thumbed the med-cig into a conflagration.

The two smoked in silence. When smoked, Sellers decided, "Right then, Balurzuura, time to go back to headquarters. You are going to help rebuild society here. Mrs Meggins from the Pie Shop might be able to help you"!

Forty-three. **Mrs Meggins from** the Pie Shop nestled into Sellers embrace and began to purr loudly.

"I still don't like cats much", Griselda smiled, "But I hate bees".

Sellers laughed, "You might have to get used to Megwinda, Babe. Before everything gets back to normal here". They had passed people on the way back to the flat. Wandering about looking dazed, but free.

"I guess it's goodbye then", Griselda noted, their farewell kiss was lengthy, passionate.

"She asked him. "You know where to find *me* if you want to give me one from time to time".

Sellers laughed, "I just might do that ambōentő. What's the village called now"?

"Wānqūlì ˇ .

Sellers surprised himself by letting the girl go. There again, she had made the ultimatum, Mrs Meggins from the Pie Shop had won out. It was a miserable afternoon, with only the diminutive feline for company, but then he could always anticipate the return of Her Ladyship, even if such hope was to fail him. he retired early, Into bedding covered in Chinese symbols. Closed his eyes tumbled straight into the bizarre dream.. A sudden, almost imperceptible wrongness seemed to twist the back of his head just above the neck. It was rather like the feeling one gets when experiencing travel sickness. As with that, Sellers felt nausea grip his vitals, he made the mistake of opening his eyes. There was a riot of confusion before him, overlaid with a rather sickly film of mustard colour that was illogically repugnant to him. Travelled enough, sensible enough to know that nothing would make a great deal of sense when in a realm of non-space a sort of joint between two ley-lines. He was effectively in the opposite of vacuum with his mind, what would the opposing state be? Anti-vacuum – density of rarefaction, void of vacuity. Could sensible thought even exist in such a medium? Or even a medial of asininity. A figure slowly walked through the mass of dementia. A composite. The torso was human, the head, that of a salamander, while the legs were the rough stumps of a rhinoceros.

"You must be a leyskiper", the figure observed from out of his wide, amphibious slit of a mouth. The head was black/yellow, covered in a film of mucus. "I am Lord Embryology, have you come to visit the Chamber of Forfeitura Animata. What name do you go by Miss"?

"Mister", Sellers corrected with a grim smile, "Don't mind me but I'm just passing through, Your Lordship".

"Oh but I do mind"! Embroilogy snarled with a very sudden change of mien, "I mind a very great deal Frau, a great deal indeed".

"Well mind then", Sellers could see no sensible alternative, "Mind all you want".

"What is your name Señorita", Lord Embroilogy demanded then. "I want your name for I am making a list, yes a list. You will go on it nothing is more certain".

"In that case", Sellers thought about it, beginning to get the gist of the creature who tested him, "My name is Lord Embroilogy".

You dare probation me, Kisasszony. I the Lord of carousal. For such a slight I will penalise you, yes. You must pay the forfeit, or you will be detained here forever".

Sellers closed his eyes, tried to cut out the upsetting illogicality of what was happening, found himself trapped in sleep from which he could not wake!

"What sort of forfeit Lord of Misrule"?

"You shall give to me, the cat in your jacket. Then I will let you proceed on your way", came the demand.

"What do you want with Mrs Meggins from the Pie Shop"?

"What I want, or do not want with the moggy is beside the point Domnişoară. The fact is I have set my heart on her and shall have her, yes I shall have her".

Once again Sellers tried to extricate himself from the hysteria of his delirium. Was this incubus or, delusion? He had no way of discerning one from the other when all was a neurosis.

"No matter where I am or who opposes me I shall never hand over Megwinda to another, Lord Embroilogy. If you want her you must first kill me".

"None die in the Chamber of Forfeitura Animata, my dear young Sumuvaty. There again none live either. I will give you a chance to redeem yourself if you wish it"?

"Name your chance".

"If you answer my riddle truly I will let you free, but answer erroneously, you stay here for one second longer than forever".

"Ask your riddle Prince of Fools".

"Very well, two eminent scientists claim that Lord Embroilogy was their brother, but I claimed I had no brother, which of us was not telling the truth"?

Sellers took but a second to think about it and then replied, "None of you was not telling the truth, because none of you was lying. The eminent scientists were your sisters".

Lord Embroilogy looked crestfallen that his conundrum had been answered so correctly, quickly, his head began to morph. Melted onto a dribbling body. Out of the sleeves of his frock-coat he ran, melted, thawed. As Sellers looked on in grim surprise, the Lord of the Chamber of Forfeitura Animata trickled away like so much heated wax, with a jolting bump Sellers found himself on the highway of the multiverse. It took him a couple of moments to re-orientate himself, then he began to send his mind down the vast cosmic highway in the opposite direction from which he had come. Reality whatever was vermilion. He found the junction of repetition which was maroon. Continued on his way as velocitously as his mind could project itself. Past the junction of uniformity, which was fuchsia. Reality junction's shone out like hideous beacons of pusillanimous non-light. Without spectrum, devoid of hue, rather a chroma of impossibility. He fled down the forbidding junction that he did not want to allow his mind to return to. Fell onto the floor in a graceless, uncoordinated heap. Thankfully without damage. Had it been a dream or had he made a mental connection with another facet of himself? Was one of the Sellers trying to get back home without Vonalat's help? Shaking his head to clear it of the fuddle he went for his first shower of the day. Glorious weather remained. July 1^{st,} the temperature 26 degrees in England, marvellous. It didn't suit everyone.

'Can I trust you to keep your word to me, Királálynő-vonazóregináccondător? to share my brain? With no further attempts at subjugation'?

'You possess the ability to kill all Zaromi. That is my bond' Balurzuura admitted. *You have the solemn word of the Királálynővonazóreginăcondător that the Mizaroa will learn to live alongside the humanoid, Sellers'.*

Seller relayed this promise to his moggy, being the only audience he had since Griselda's departure. Thusly the creatures similar to Earth dragonfly settled for a peaceful coexistence with Men. Sellers dressed with an economy of movement, cleaned, dried, polished the bathroom in his customary fashion. As he left it the delightful aroma of cooking food greeted his nostrils,

"Griselda. You did not protest for long, you the cook".

"If Mrs Meggins from the Pie Shop turns her nose up, then I'm off again. I did my best to stay away", the cool brunette beauty complained, with a smile.

"And your best was deplorable".

She had created a delicious cooked breakfast. The food lay heavy in the stomach however, afterwards, Sellers decided to try a power-nap his internal clock shot to hell, the incubus having only made him feel even more tired. He opened his eyes an indeterminate time afterwards to find Griselda beside him. Wearing nothing but knickers together with a lascivious smile,

"I thought you might fancy a mid-afternooner before you do your thing", she suggested throatily"

"Might as well", he returned with a grin, "After all it would be rude to refuse". The knickers came off shortly thereafter. Three-quarters of an hour later Sellers raised himself up onto an elbow, declared,

"Right I'm ready to start helping rebuilding this world".

Griselda was not having such a bad day. Her inexplicable spasms had been far less frequent recently she had begun to hope they would eventually terminate altogether. She and her mother had never been so content. The older woman had fallen completely in love with Mrs Meggins from the Pie Shop. Looked after her while Sellers did his rebuilding, Griselda at work. Sometimes when customers came into the salon, those that set her teeth on edge and her pulse racing, she could remember the feeling of disquietude; almost. That day had not been like it, hardly anyone that came into the hairdressers emanated residual *waves*. Was it that some people had not the wit nor way withal to discover their newfound freedom? Then *he* came into the salon. There was instantly several things about him that set him apart from any other customer she had ever seen before. He was a most beautiful man. 196 cm if he was a centimetre, over a hundred kilograms, but without a gram of useless fat. He was broad, muscular, had golden brown skin, long flowing hair the colour of bright sunlight. Bearded, emanated magnetism with his smile. Griselda seemed as entranced by him as every other female in the salon. Yet she was the only one who shared his bed,

"Sellers 11:20 for a shampoo, slight trim, beard trim".

"Can you turn around then please Sir and put your neck in the rest".

He afforded her a smile that was for her and her alone, she basked in its radiance. As she turned the spray on to wet his wondrous mane, a wave came over her as powerful as any she had ever felt. Yet this one was different in its feeling. It contained no menace whatsoever, rather, a feeling of assurance, desire, amour. Whatever the others had unwittingly broadcast to her, this man, this beautifully magnificent creature, was unique. Regathering her composure she began to run her slim fingers through his thickly healthy hair, letting the water soak it. When she shampooed it she asked him,

"You just want the very end taking off do you? The beard tidying ever so"?

"Please". He remained tacit while his head was supine. She squeezed his hair as he stroked her thigh. The other girls broke into a muted chatter. They were ignorant of the childish deception the lovers were perpetrating.

"That's it go back to the chair please, Sir".

His movements had the grace of a cat, the power of an elephant, he was almost something other than human. As she began to brush his hair ready to trim off just the broken ends, promote growth, he asked her in a voice just loud enough for everyone to hear,

"I wonder if when you've *done me* in here, Love, if you'd come back to my place so that I could *do you*"?".

Seemingly doing her best not to look too startled, to keep the natural shake of timorousness from herself, she asked him in an equally indiscreet whisper,

"You mean for free, I never do anything for free"?

"Name your price, Hot Stuff, I'll pay it".

"Let me find out what break I'm on from the boss, once I've cut your hair I'll meet you, then rock your world".

The two of them left the beautique laughing at the effect their deception had caused. Much later in the day, Griselda grew reflective.

"Insects! In people's brains, if it hadn't happened I wouldn't have believed it"?

"Alien creatures that resemble our Earth's insects", he corrected. "You can develop the ability to discern their presence. As an ambӧentő, you are still very valuable to the human race Griselda. You can learn to recognise the thought patterns of the Mizaroa. Be the first to detect any incursion by future invasive attempts from their rival Insecto".

Griselda objected, "I'd rather be normal".

Sellers laughed, "You're not abnormal Griselda, but gifted, one in millions possess your ability, view it as a very very special gift, for indeed that's what it is".

"What am I going to do? How can I carry on being a hairstylist when I have this .... this ".

"You have no need to worry about your future Griselda. It's mapped out for you if you want it to be. You a devoted lover who has a friend who is a millionaire. I located Cowie last night, still living on the upper mezzanine of his fabulous skyscraper in Lincolnshire. He told me for freeing him of his slavery to the enemy I could name my price. I won't be greedy".

"We'll continue to live in Doncaster"?

He nodded, "I'll be a frequent visitor to Cowie's, we'll need to be vigilant that the other Insectivore do not attempt to inveigle themselves into the minds of people on Earth. That's where you come in. Come and meet the others at Cowie's where we are having something of a small get-together on Friday? You can take your time at deciding what you want to do, no pressure to make a decision in any direction".

Griselda smiled for the first time since Sellers had begun to tell her what was happening,

"You cannot be fairer, Tod. I'll come to the party".

Forty-five. **"Michael, I want** you to meet the amböentő, Griselda", Sellers said to the former leader of human resistance to the Mizaroa on Earth. The two smiled appreciatively at one another, just two from the very special guest-list that Cowie had arranged.

"I've heard a lot about you", the Carpenter-millionaire said to the hairdresser. "Come, let me get you a cocktail you can tell me about your experiences"?

Sellers let them drift away, glanced over to the doorway of the penthouse where two young women were just entering. Kyla, emancipated former bee-drone, Lady of Heartbridge, rushed across the room to be the one to bid them enter.

"I'm very pleased you could both find a window of opportunity in your diaries", Kyla was saying to the bemused young ladies, "I know how busy you both keep". There was a certain amount of irony in her tone. Lady Jennifer Cove of Kentmere observed a trifle nonplussed,

"You seem to have the advantage of us Mz, have we met before? I'm sure I'd remember"? The almost surreal beauty of the gorgeous brunette before them disarmed her.

"I never forget a face", Madison Reed of Illinois added. "And I certainly haven't seen you before".

"Not as I am now, no", Kyla was revelling in the other's confusion, "but we know one another quite well. I'm Kyla Coleman. There was an automobile accident, I suffered heinous injuries. There was extensive reconstructive surgery. This is how the Mizaroa re-modelled me before the Anthophila enslaved me.

"Oh yeah", Madison's tone made the affirmative sound like a negative as was the way in Americanese.

"I could tell you some secrets that happened when we were in school together if you want me to qualify my identity, but you'll only then believe me if you really want to". Kyla smiled sweetly.

The Lady of Kentmere took her by the arms gazed into her features,

"Those dragonflies do fantastic work, truly fantastic"! She gasped. "There's no evidence of scar tissue in even the slightest of degrees. You must give me the name of the surgeon. I presume he now resides in the head of a Harley Street surgeon"?

"But Jennifer", Kyla chuckled throatily, "You don't need any work doing, you're way too young to even be thinking of considering it".

Sellers approached the trio with strangely conflicting emotions warring in his bosom. Even though he then lived with Griselda, reality 26 had robbed him of the incomparable Kyla. "These must be your glamorous school-friends, Your Ladyship. Let me guess, you are Madison from Illinois".

He took the American's hand, pressed it to his fine lips. She simpered, noted loudly enough for all of them to hear,

"I don't care who you are or claim to be, my dear. You simply must introduce me to this divine figure of a man at once. Do you hear"?

"I'm Sellers", he smiled, quite used to the reaction by then, "But I'm afraid I must disappoint you Madison, the young lady talking to Cowie, she and I are, how shall I put it, very close".

"Then I'm crushed", Madison reclaimed her composure with admirable swiftness, "But I wonder why you call Kyla, Her Ladyship, yet only introduce yourself by surname, Sir"?

"Because he's English, Madison", Jennifer explained, offered Sellers her hand, "I'm her Ladyship too, Mister Sellers".

"It's very agreeable to meet you both, Ladies. Now I must circulate. You can get drinks in the middle lounge, I'm sure. Cowie decided not to get staff in for this rather intimate get-together".

He strolled away, reasoning that the party would have been complete if Tranessy had managed to make the event, even known about it. Felton and Ottershaw were engaged in deep conversation at the far side of the room several other local guests looked totally out of place in the expansive penthouse suite. He wondered how Konette would have appraised the state of the resistance to the Anthophilous threat in 23? He certainly doubted he would have approved of the alliance with the Mizaroa. A shame neither aspect of the duo could not have travelled to see them all. He had met them the once, proving ultimately to be the very last time? He needed another drink, becoming morose. Felton and Ottershaw look like they had bonded for life. Goodness knew what they were talking about so animatedly? He strolled over to an attractive young woman who struck him as intriguing.

"Hello, if we don't know one another, we should".

"I know you quite well by reputation, Sellers", she returned.

"You have the advantage of me"?

"I'm Alice Mawson, former leader of the Anthophilamorph for a short while - until the Menta-carbaryl slay them all".

Sellers' eyebrows rose high on his forehead, interest heightened by Alice's past.

"The Menta-carbaryl only serves to *mop-up* the few stragglers in actuality", he explained. It was the death of their queen which devastated their number before that, heralded their defeat".

As Sellers shook her hand Alice admitted, "I'm not sure why I even got an invitation"?

"Friends old and new as the invite said", Sellers returned smoothly. "Just between us, Michael wanted a house-warming, but he didn't know very many people. Always been something of a loner. I offered to loan him a few friends of my own. You'll like him. He's a very amiable chap. The gathering will warm up once the drink flows a little more copiously. What are you drinking Alice"?

"I always drink G and T's", the young woman admitted pleasantly enough. "I'm not one for wines or beers. Tod, are you still taking your photographs "?

"You know about them? Have you been cramming up on me"?

"You know what they say about friends and enemies", Alice laughed. Her laugh was a very attractive one. "Don't worry though, the enemy's gone for now".

"I'm into investing in commodities", Sellers smiled vaguely. "I've a backer who values my intuition, but I'll never totally stop taking photographs".

With that, his mind went suddenly back to a perched position on the cliffs around Flamborough. How his death had been the beginning of the most fantastic adventure of his life.

Epilogue. **Sellers and Griselda** stayed together for the rest of their lives, which were long and very, very happy. With Cowie's financial backing, Griselda opened a salon in Lincoln. It was stunningly successful. She and Sellers married after a long engagement, had three sons, all of whom were later members of *Earthwatch*, a secret society that made certain the Insectivores of Mizar A never again threatened the peoples of the world. Balurzuura kept his word to Sellers. The alliance between humanity and Mizaroa lasted for centuries. They did not live forever. Felton and Ottershaw maintained their friendship until the doctor died some years later aged 88. Jennifer Cove married into *old-money,* becoming fabulously rich as a result. Her husband of some twenty years senior, died of a heart attack whilst performing his husbandly duties one fateful evening. She retired to Italy, emailed Kyla for many years thereafter. Madison Ivy went to Harley Street, there to seek the same level of pulchritude as her friend. After twenty-five such operations that never satisfied her in the slightest, she succumbed to heart failure whilst on the operating table, never regained consciousness.

Tranessy leyskiped from RPrime in search of new allies. With the help of Alice Mawson, continued to fight the Insecto for many years to come. Their other coadjutor, one - Mrs Meggins from the Pie Shop, was to lead them in her ensuing adventures. Her graceful nature by which - she undertook all in her four-legged stride. She became known as, *'That Cosmic Moggy'!*

Contact the author at:
jarquix@yahoo.com

Printed in Great Britain
by Amazon